Amy Tolnitch

A Lost Touch of Magic

D0003749

Jewel Imprint: Amethyst
Medallion Press, Inc.
Printed in USA

(continued)

OUTSTANDING!

"A LOST TOUCH OF BLISS is a rare treasure. Being a paranormal romance set in 1196, this engaging tale is one I truly loved and hated to see end. Reminiscent of Jude Deveraux's early historicals, Ms. Tolnitch's writing will have you wanting to read more. For readers that enjoy a truly wonderful tale of finding love when it seems all is lost, then you need to add A LOST TOUCH OF BLISS to your 'to buy' list!"

—*K. Ahlers, Independent Reviewer*

"Fans of historical and those of otherworldly will appreciate this second chance at love in which the present (that is twelfth century present) and the deceased share so much in common."

—*H. Klausner, Independent Reviewer*

"Ms. Tolnitch writes with much passion and wit as you read A LOST TOUCH OF BLISS and highly entertains the reader with her debut novel! This is truly an author to keep your eye on in the coming years as she delivers a heart stirring story told with a passion that weaves a web around the reader and leaves you wanting more. Run to grab A LOST TOUCH OF BLISS and be carried away with a tender romance that delivers all the right touches and hits you on every level."

—*Love Romances*

A LOST TOUCH OF PARADISE:

"Fans of Fairy Tales, Historical, and Paranormal Romances will find a new author to add to their shopping lists . . .

With a blend of fairy tale, medieval, and highland romance, Amy Tolnitch was able to reach out and grab this reader from the opening scene; a witch burning. Brilliant characterization, stunning descriptive ability and a truly romantic hero; A LOST TOUCH OF PARADISE has it all."

A LOST TOUCH OF INNOCENCE:

"Readers will enjoy this well-written tale."

—*Jani Brooks, Romance Reviews Today*

"A LOSS TOUCH OF INNOCENCE is a marvelous fairy tale romance that all who want that perfect ending will love. Amy Tolnitch has crafted a lovely story with interesting and believable characters. Her writing flows easily and I thoroughly enjoyed the ride. Although the third book in this series, I was able to read this as a stand-alone story without any difficulty. Of course now I have to add A LOSS TOUCH OF BLISS and A LOSS TOUCH OF PARADISE to my must have book list."

—*Lori Sears, The Romance Reader's Connection*

"The sequel to A LOST TOUCH OF BLISS is an entertaining medieval paranormal romance starring an interesting lead male with two intelligences battling to control his body and the innocent woman who completes the demonic triangle. Piers is a fascinating protagonist as he literally battles with an inner demon for control of his body and soul. Although Giselle adapts to life out of the abbey too easily, she risks her soul to help the man she loves win the war against the malevolent Fin Man. Sub-genre fans will enjoy Amy Tolnitch's latest Veuxfort thriller in which hearts and souls are on the line."

—*Harriet Klausner*

"A LOST TOUCH OF INNOCENCE is a truly unique tale with lovers with paranormal skills. It is such a tightly woven tale that it is hard to put down. Readers will enjoy the dynamic changes of primary characters and the antics of the secondary characters. This is a must read."

—*Morgan, Novelspot*

"A LOST TOUCH OF INNOCENCE reads like a dulcet, [an] emotionally intoxicating song dedicated to innocence, redemption, and the endless possibilities when love and destiny are on your side."

—*Romance Junkies*

"A LOST TOUCH OF INNOCENCE is the best historical book I've ever read in a really long time! Amy Tolnitch transports readers into another world and is quickly going to become a must have on readers' autobuy lists."

—*Rosie Bindra, Fresh Fiction*

"A LOST TOUCH OF INNOCENCE has an intriguing and unique plot . . . This tale of paranormal romance will delight lovers of historical fiction."

—*Amelia, Joyfully Reviewed*

DEDICATION:

For Styrling, the best child in the
universe. I love you more!

Published 2008 by Medallion Press, Inc.

The MEDALLION PRESS LOGO
is a registered trademark of Medallion Press, Inc.

Copyright © 2008 by Amy Tolnitch
Cover Illustration by Adam Mock

Typeset in Adobe Garamond Pro
Printed in the United States of America

ISBN:9781934755518

10 9 8 7 6 5 4 3 2 1
First Edition

ACKNOWLEDGEMENTS:

Many thanks to my family and agent for their continued support. My daughter deserves credit for helping me come up with a lot of the ideas in this book, as she has done with the prior books in the Lost Touch series. As always, Mary Lennox's sage advice keeps me on track. I also owe a thanks to Elizabeth Ader, my relentlessly determined trainer, and Sky, my horse, for teaching me so much about horses and riding. Finally, thanks to the team at Medallion Press for doing such a great job!

Prologue

Most people believe, if they still do at all, that there was only one place like Atlantis. Only one utopian paradise filled with untold wealth, peace, and wonders we can scarcely envision. Rings of sparkling, clear water surrounding a central mountain from which the benevolent ruler governed. Columns of gold flanking grand promenades paved with pure white marble. A place blessed by the gods.

But they are wrong. There were, and are, other such places. The hidden lands of the Tuatha de Danann. The idyllic beauty of the Druid Otherworld. And realms such as Paroseea.

Places where life should be perfection.

However, just as in Atlantis, there are always serpents hidden in the lush beauty of paradise, ones seeking more than their due, seeking power. Paroseea was fortunate enough to stop the betrayer in its midst, and avoid devastation. For centuries, the kingdom of Paroseea has remained well hidden from human eyes, veiled where no one would ever suspect, yet closer than anyone could have imagined.

Until now.

Chapter One

Northumberland, 1213

Cai's warning growl came an instant before Padruig MacCoinneach found himself gazing at his sister Brona. The only problem with her sudden appearance was that Brona was dead.

"Padruig," she said softly, her gossamer form gaining substance.

He stared at her, his gut clenched in shock, his heart tight with the beloved sight of her. *So, it has come to this*, he thought. "Brona, you have good cause to haunt me, I ken, but I would prefer to be left alone."

Her pale lips quirked in a familiar smile that brought back the pang of memory. "I've not come to haunt you, Padruig."

He looked down into his cup, wondering just how much wine he'd drunk this eve.

"I am no delirium brought on by drink," she rebuked.

"I must be going mad at last. Mayhap I should be thankful for it."

3

"Nay." With a tinkle of laughter, she drifted closer and settled on a stool. "You are not mad."

Cai growled again, and crouched down as if to leap upon her.

"Down, wolf," Brona said.

Cai dropped to the floor, but didn't take his gaze from her.

"You must return, Padruig. At once."

"Return?"

"To Castle MacCoinneach."

He barked out a bitter laugh. "You jest. There is naught for me there. This," he said, gesturing around his snug home, "is where I belong now."

She gazed around his dwelling, taking in the living area where she perched, the tapestry spread upon the floor, the simple trunks and pegs along the wall next to stone steps, the other tapestries hung on stone walls to keep out the chill air. "You have made yourself a comfortable refuge here."

"It suits me," he said, knowing the words for a lie, but also knowing there was no other place for him anymore.

"Och, Padruig, how can you bear to be so alone?"

The damn fire must be smoking overmuch, he thought, blinking away a touch of wetness from his eyes. "I have missed you, Brona. As for the rest, I am content here."

"I shall always be with you, Padruig," she said in a low tone that skittered over his skin and lifted the fine hairs on his arms.

"*You*, of all people, should well understand why I cannot return." Sorrow and regret swirled in his mind, ripening into the pain and shame he lived with each day.

"Nay, you are wrong." Her eyes suddenly flooded with color, the vivid blue startling in her wispy face. She traced a finger down the scar bisecting his cheek, leaving a strange coolness along his marred skin. "You are like a wounded animal seeking its den, hiding away. 'Tis not the way of the Laird of the MacCoinneachs."

"I am not the laird," he told her, hating the sympathy in her eyes, sympathy he did not deserve.

"Freya needs you. The clan needs you."

He frowned. "You are mistaken."

"Nay!" she shouted, rising in a swirl of red and gold. "*You* are the one who is mistaken. You must return. Grigor is laird, Padruig."

"Grigor? What of Alasdair?"

"Ousted by Grigor and his followers."

Grigor as laird? Padruig found that hard to believe. The man had been at best a barely adequate guardsman.

"'Tis worse than that. Grigor intends to marry Freya to Angus Ransolm. The entire clan suffers under his rule. *Your* clan, Padruig."

"Angus Ransolm?" Padruig felt the blood drain from his face and fisted a hand. "Why in sweet heaven would Grigor marry Freya to such a mon? He is naught but a foul brute."

"Aye. But I tell you true."

Padruig slammed his cup down and stood. He did not want to face any of this, did not want to face what he had done, did not want to ever face his clan again, but Brona's expression was unrelenting. "What of Mother?"

"She is of no aid," Brona said slowly, her form beginning to melt away.

"Brona, do not ask this of me. I cannot—"

"You *cannot* fail Freya, Padruig," she said, and disappeared.

He picked up the cup and hurled it against the wall. Do not fail Freya, she'd said. She didn't need to add, "As you failed me." That knowledge was ever with him, ever a cold, heavy weight upon his heart.

Dear God, how could he allow his sister Freya to be wed to the likes of Angus Ransolm? The lass was no more than fifteen years of age. Angus was at least two score, and each of those years had been spent in selfish depravity. Padruig had been a guest at Ransolm Castle once when his father considered an alliance with the Ransolm clan. As the day drew on, Angus had emptied his cup time and time again. Eventually, he ended up roughly taking a servant girl in full view of everyone in the hall, sending her off with a none too tender slap when he finished. By the reactions of those in the hall, but for Padruig, his father, and their men, such an occurrence was far from uncommon.

Padruig grimaced, seeing the man's expression of satisfaction, his casual attitude that using a servant such was no more than his due. When Padruig's father had inquired about Angus's wife, the man had dismissively announced that she was dead. Thinking back, Padruig remembered his father muttering that Angus had a habit of losing wives.

Brona was right, though how she knew was something he did not wish to ponder.

There was no choice for it. He would have to go home.

Aimili de Grantham smiled in her sleep, and let out a soft sigh of contentment. Her dream swirled in her mind, the same wondrous dream she'd had time and time again. Striding across the thick, emerald-green grass, he came for her, sunlight gleaming over her very own golden man, his blue eyes tender and fierce all at once. She flung herself into his strong arms, and he laughed, twirling her in the air, before sliding her down his body, his beautiful mouth lowering to hers . . .

"Wake up!" a voice intruded, followed by a rough shake of her shoulders.

She fought the command, twisting away from the hand. Unfortunately, her shift in position put her nose in close proximity to a newly deposited pile of horse dung.

"Ye cannae sleep in the stable, as if you were no more

7

than a stable hand," the voice said, which Aimili now recognized as her younger sister, Morainn's.

"Morainn, I am exhausted. Leave me be."

Morainn sniffed. "I am no surprised, given your morn with that devil horse. But you have a perfectly fine bed."

Aimili slowly blinked her eyes open, more than a wee bit disgruntled with her sister for interrupting her sleep, and more importantly, her dream. "I like being close to Mist."

Her sister gave a louder sniff. "Who nearly dumped a pile of dung atop your head. By the saints, Aimili, one would think you cared more for this horse than anything or anyone else."

The horse in question bent down her velvety, gray head and snuffled Aimili's hair. Aimili stroked Mist's soft nose and rose to her feet, choosing to ignore her sister's unusually perceptive comment.

"Asides," Morainn said with a sidelong glance at Aimili, "Father sent me to fetch you."

Aimili groaned.

"Ye cannae think he would not hear of this morn's deed." Morainn shook her head and sidled out of the stall. "I cannae understand why you take such risks. No one can ride that beast."

"I can," Aimili protested, pushing away the memory of landing in the dirt more than once earlier that day.

"Oh?" Morainn lifted one perfectly arched brow.

"As you did earlier?"

Ignore her taunt. Ye shall succeed, a gentle voice murmured in Aimili's mind. She turned and put her face against Mist's neck. *Aye, I will,* she answered silently. When she turned back to her sister, she squared her shoulders. "It will take time to earn Loki's trust." She spat in the straw. "Angus Ransolm abused him terribly."

Morainn simply shrugged. "Father is waiting."

Reluctantly, Aimili gave Mist a last pat and followed her sister across the busy bailey. They had almost reached the entrance to the great hall when she felt a tug on her arm.

"My lady," Gunnr, one of the stable lads, said on a rushed breath. "Were you wanting us to leave Loki out in the pen? He's runnin' awful fierce."

She smiled down at the boy. "Let him run. I shall return anon to bring him back in."

Gunnr's thin face drew into a frown. "Are you sure, my lady? I can bring the beast in."

"I shall do it. He must become accustomed to me. Asides," she said, ruffling Gunnr's mop of red hair, "he needs to run." She turned away and walked into the great hall, suppressing another groan to find not only her father awaiting her, but also her eldest brother, Wautier, who gave her a smug look.

"Aimili!" her father's voice boomed across the cavernous hall. Servants scurried about, setting up tables for the midday meal. Well used to hearing the Laird of the de Grantham clan chastising his daughter, they went about their duties, though one of the younger maids gave Aimili a quick glance of compassion.

"Greetings, Father," she said.

He frowned and leaned over to pluck a long piece of straw from her hair. "Lass, what were you thinking?"

Wautier snickered behind her father.

Aimili gratefully accepted a cup of wine from a passing servant and took a sip. She gazed around the great hall, looking over the smoke-blackened timbers, the wall hangings depicting one battle after another, and the impressive array of blades on the wall behind the dais. Above the weapons, a wide banner hung, embroidered with the motto of Clan de Grantham. "Dare all," she read aloud, fastening her stare on her father, whose frown deepened.

"'Tis a war cry for the men of the clan, no an instruction to a young lass." Her father shook his head, his shaggy, dark hair swinging back and forth. "What am I to do with you? How will I ever find a mon willing to wed such a reckless lass?"

As her father launched into his familiar discourse cataloging Aimili's unacceptable behaviors, in sharp contrast to perfect Morainn, Aimili stopped listening, instead taking her mind back to the dream.

And to the man who begat it.

Padruig MacCoinneach, once Laird of the Mac-Coinneach clan, now but another story carved from the harsh mountains of the Highlands, floating in the mist over the lochs. Almost too comely to be a flesh-and-blood man. Kind and gentle to a young girl whose careless stubbornness led her to injury. All the things that she'd never found in any other man.

"Lass, are you heeding me?" her father barked, breaking into her yearning thoughts.

"As always, father," she said, giving him a wide-eyed look.

He snorted, but then smiled. "Go on with ye now. I'll expect you at dinner."

Grateful that today's lecture was over, Aimili hastened away toward the rear of the hall.

"And be careful with that animal!" her father called after her.

How I hate this ugly bastard, Freya MacCoinneach thought, glaring at her thankfully several times removed cousin, Grigor. She stood in the laird's solar, the fading sunlight cloaking the chamber in ribbons of gold. A sliver of sun caught the gleam of Grigor's ring. The ring of the laird.

She fisted her hand in the skirts of her woolen bliaut. Grigor didn't even look like a laird, she thought in disgust. His thin, angular face matched his lean form, his small eyes a colorless gray. "Nay," she said, proud beyond measure that her voice did not shake.

Grigor glared back at her and casually took a sip of wine. "Aye. I have spoken with Angus and it is decided." He gave her a sly smile. "He is most anxious to gain a young bride, particularly one of your undeniable beauty."

Bile teased the back of Freya's throat. She knew she was beautiful, of course. Everyone at Castle MacCoinneach had told her so repeatedly, just as they had pampered and indulged her all of her fifteen years.

Until today. She lifted her chin and took a step forward. "I shall never marry the likes of Angus Ransolm. He is old, filthy, and"—she gulped—"all have heard the tales of his . . . appetites."

"Rumors," Grigor said, waving a hand. "You should be thankful. Angus is a powerful laird, and the clan is a prosperous one."

Freya glanced back at her mother, Mairi, who hovered in the doorway. How she wished that her mother would fight for her, but there would be no aid there, despite the burn of anger Freya saw in her mother's gaze. Life and the loss of Brona had left her mother a broken shell of herself, beaten and bitter. Freya turned her attention back to Grigor, whose gaze ran over her in a very uncousinlike manner. "Angus Ransolm is a pig!" she spat.

"'Tis unwise to voice such slurs about your future husband." He sipped more wine. "And master."

"Nay." This time Freya could not help her voice from shaking. "How much did he offer you?"

"Tis no concern of yours. The bargain was well met."

Freya was seized by the nearly uncontrollable urge to throw Grigor's cup of wine in his face. How could he do this? As she stared at him, she realized how. He cared for nothing and no one but himself and the power he'd seized. It made no difference to him at all that he would sacrifice her to a depraved old man, who would likely kill her with his enthusiastic abuse.

Another figure appeared in the doorway, and a fragment of hope unfurled in Freya's chest.

Alasdair, her brother Padruig's former advisor and the man who *should* be laird, stepped into the solar, his expression grim. "Grigor, mayhap you should reconsider this match. Freya is young and beautiful." He gave her a glance of support. "She can do much better than Angus Ransolm."

Grigor leapt to his feet and slammed down his cup. "I need no advice from you, old man."

"I will not do it," Freya shouted. "I have heard the stories myself." She shivered. "The man is foul and cruel. I will not wed him. Ye cannae do this to me."

The blow came so quickly that she had no time to duck. Stumbling backward, she would have fallen if Alasdair had not caught her in his arms. Her face burned and she stared at Grigor in disbelief.

But for a spark of satisfaction in his gaze, his expression remained calm. "You will wed Angus Ransolm by All Hallows' Eve."

Despite her fear, Freya could only shake her head. The horror of what he demanded was too much to bear.

"Rauf!" Grigor shouted.

Rauf, a beefy guard, lumbered into the solar, his thick lips flattened into a mocking smile. Grigor nodded toward Freya. "See her to her chamber and lock her in."

From outside the solar, Freya heard a soft moan.

Grigor's lips curled back into a chilling smile. "Do not gainsay me in this, Freya. I am your laird and I have made my decision. You shall abide by it."

"Or?" she whispered.

"Or," he leaned closer, "I shall do whatever is necessary to persuade you." He chuckled. "Mayhap Angus would like to visit his future bride before the blessed event."

Terror gripped Freya's belly and she nearly spilled the contents of her stomach upon Grigor's fine tunic. "You would allow him to . . ." She could not say it, the idea was so repellent.

"Grigor, nay," Alasdair said. "Ye cannot treat the lass so. She is the daughter of the laird."

Grigor's gaze flashed anger. "The *former* laird, whose only son left in disgrace."

"Duncan would never approve of this. Nor would Padruig."

"Well, Duncan is naught but bones and ashes, and

your dear Padruig is not here, so what they may or may not approve of is of no matter."

"Grigor—"

"Cease!" Grigor barked. "Rauf, take her from my sight. And you, Alasdair, would be wise to remember that 'tis only by my sufferance that you remain here at all."

Rauf half-pulled, half-dragged Freya from the solar. Within a few minutes, she found herself thrust into her chamber, the sounds of a bar being mounted on the door confirmation of the horrific fact that Grigor did, indeed, intend to sentence her to life with Angus Ransolm.

The only boon was that most likely that life would not be long, she thought, hysteria creeping into her mind.

She buried her face in her hands and wept. Oh, *Padruig, how I wish you were here*, she silently chanted.

Aimili woke in her bed, terror lodged tightly in her throat. She scanned her chamber, the glowing embers of a fire leaving most of it in deep shadow. Slowly, she took a deep breath and let it out, focusing her senses.

Naught but the rumbling snore of her hound, Bobo, sounded in the room. She clasped the bedcovers in her hands and stared into the dying fire as if it could give her answers.

Chills rippled down her back that had nothing to do

with the coolness of the chamber. She tried to remember her dream, tried to draw out the details, but instead could only barely grasp a feeling.

It was a feeling of evil. Covetous, angry evil.

And it was coming into her life.

No, Aimili, she told herself. *It was only a dream. A silly dream, no doubt brought on by your stuffing your mouth with one too many of Cook's apple fritters.*

She yawned and stretched, telling herself to stop being foolish. The de Grantham holdings were secure and peaceful for the most part. Nearly hidden in the heavy forests around Loch Fynnen, they lived a fairly isolated and protected existence. And though her father could be harsh at times, the people held great loyalty to him.

For a moment, an image of Wautier's face sprang into her mind, but she pushed it away. Wautier was arrogant and disapproving, but she could never suspect him of harboring the kind of evil she'd felt in her dream.

An unsettling tendril of it clung to her even now.

She gathered up a blanket and slid to the floor, huddling close to Bobo so that she could put her head on his furry belly. He let out a sigh, but didn't shift away from her.

Snuggling close, Aimili absorbed the dog's warmth and told herself to forget the strange dream. *You are as adept at sensing danger as you are at communicating with animals,* her inner voice reminded her. No, Aimili told herself. *It was simply a bad dream. Evil has no place here.*

Yawning again, she closed her eyes. But as she drifted into sleep, a fragment from her dream would not fade. Like an insidious vine, it wound around her mind, dark and slithering just beneath her consciousness.

She clutched Bobo tighter.

Sebilla, Queen of the fey kingdom of Paroseea, gaped at Artur in disbelief. He knelt before her on the cool, white, marble floor of her palace, his head bowed. The pink rays of the afternoon sun glinted off his silver hair. "How . . . how could this have happened?" she whispered, dread coiling its cold tendrils through her body. "How?" she asked again when Artur did not answer.

"I am no sure, my queen."

"You are no sure?" She fisted her hands in rage, forcing herself not to expend her anger on Artur simply for delivering the news. "Caradoc is . . . was one of our finest warriors."

"When Caradoc did not return, some of us took the risk of journeying to the surface." His throat worked. "We found his body in the loch."

"Curse that whoreson, Vardon!"

One of her attendants rushed to Sebilla's side, her pale pink silk gown fluttering around her like butterfly wings. Sebilla waved her away. "Leave us." She jumped from her gilded throne and paced across the floor, her soft slippers barely making a sound. "I do not understand this, any more than I understand how Vardon escaped. The cavern of sorrows held him for hundreds of years!"

If possible, Artur looked even more miserable.

The choking beginning of a sob caught in Sebilla's throat. Caradoc had been more than a fine warrior. He had been her friend. She shoved back her grief and replaced it with angry determination. "He shall have a funeral of honor. I will preside over it myself."

"As your majesty wishes."

"Oh, for the goddess's sake, Artur, stand up," she snapped. "You've no need to stay on your knees. I am hardly likely to punish you for this . . . this latest travesty."

Slowly, Artur stood.

She studied him for a critical moment. His clear blue gaze met hers, his jaw set into grim lines. Artur had long been in charge of the men ensuring that Vardon never left his barren prison. She knew Artur took it as his personal failure that Vardon escaped and, as yet, could not be retrieved. "Have you *no* idea how he escaped?" Though she'd asked the same question again and again, she couldn't help asking once more.

Artur shook his head, but Sebilla caught the flush of red on his cheeks and paused. "Tell me," she ordered.

"'Tis only my suspicion, a theory," he stuttered.

"Surely, you know how bad this is? You know the kind of man who is now free."

"Aye, my queen."

"Then, tell me what you suspect."

"One of the young guards spoke with Vardon often." He frowned. "You know how manipulative Vardon can be, how . . . charming. I believe that over time, Vardon became able to direct the guard, and to learn his thoughts somehow. Vardon discovered the spell to lower the shields imprisoning him for the instant he needed to escape."

"How would a simple guard know such things?"

"My queen, I do not fault him or . . ."

Sebilla's lips tightened. "Or whom?"

Artur flexed his jaw. "Vanasia."

"Arailt's daughter?"

"Aye. She and the guard, Ulf, have long been involved. I do not believe Arailt even knows, but I happened to come upon them once."

"Vanasia works in the archives."

"Just so."

"Fools!" Sebilla snapped. Though a part of her wanted to summon the lovers to her at once for punishment, she realized that Artur was right. Vardon had outwitted them all.

"At least we know where he is now. Castle Mac-Coinneach." Artur shook his head, his puzzlement evident. "I dinnae understand why he remains so close."

Blindly, Sebilla reached out for the arm of her throne to steady herself. No, Artur would not know why Vardon would seek out the MacCoinneach clan, but Sebilla did. Revenge.

Artur stared at her, his face hard and tight. "We await your instructions, my queen."

"I . . . I must consult with my advisors. We will conceive of a plan to return that creature to where he belongs."

Unfortunately, despite her confident tone, Sebilla had no idea how to accomplish such a feat. Simply put, her people did not leave the kingdom of Paroseea. Such a thing was strictly forbidden, except in the direst of circumstances. Their safety, their way of life, depended upon remaining a secret, one that had survived so long that those in the mortal world thought lands such as Paroseea no more than fabled legends.

She rushed from her receiving chamber in search of Lucan, her chief advisor. Shock, anger, and confusion swirled in her mind, the emotions leaving a trail of golden sparks in her wake. Vardon had been imprisoned so long Sebilla had nearly forgotten him, believed the threat to their peaceful existence within Paroseea vanquished.

The cavern of sorrows had been designed specifically to hold its lone occupant. Sealed with powerful magic, the cavern should not have been subject to breach, nor should Vardon have been able to so completely manipulate two innocents.

No, there was only one way he managed to escape.

The same way he'd been able to so easily vanquish Caradoc.

He'd become even more powerful.

And far more dangerous. A creature such as Vardon would be nothing short of lethal to the MacCoinneach clan.

A sennight after leaving the refuge he'd discovered over a year ago, Padruig began to see the familiar landscape of the Highlands near Castle MacCoinneach. He drew to a halt at the top of a fell overlooking a dense growth of pine and rowan trees. The silver thread of a small stream wound though the land before the woods. Beyond the next fell lay a wide vale that gradually led to another forested area where Castle MacCoinneach waited for him.

He drew in a deep breath of the fresh air, his senses glutting on the smells and sights of his beloved Highlands. Maybe it was his imagination, but the very air seemed cleaner, sharper, the scent richer, deeper than in England.

Padruig guided his mount down to the stream, with Cai loping alongside. As they neared the water, Cai suddenly stopped and let out a low growl. Immediately wary, Padruig drew his sword and slowed, his gaze scanning the area ahead.

From the trees, a man emerged. The ragged condition of his clothing told Padruig he'd been traveling for some time. Padruig squinted, trying to make out whether the man posed a threat, at the same time flicking his glance around to see if he was alone.

"Cai, easy," he murmured as he rode closer.

The man's face remained partially shaded, as if he waited for Padruig to grow near. Suddenly, the man let out a whoop and ran straight toward Padruig. Bringing his sword up, Padruig prepared to charge the running figure, as Cai readied himself to lunge.

Before he could spur his horse forward, to Padruig's utter amazement, he heard his name being called.

"Padruig! By the saints, man, I cannae believe it."

Padruig's jaw dropped as he found himself staring into the eyes of his old friend and clansman, Magnus. "Hold, Cai," he ordered, lowering his sword.

Magnus came barreling to a stop, a wide grin on his tan face. His blond hair had grown long, and he looked as if he hadn't had a bath in months. His bright green eyes were so welcoming that Padruig had to return his smile. "I thought you long dead, my friend," Magnus said.

Padruig jumped off his horse and slapped Magnus on the shoulder. "I probably should have been."

Magnus gestured to Cai, who stood patiently, studying Magnus through intent round eyes. "A new companion?"

"Aye. One of the best."

"I cannae believe you've come back, thank the saints. I thought never to see your ugly face again."

Padruig snorted. "We cannot all be as pretty as a young lass."

"What brings you back?"

"You would not believe me if I told you."

Magnus's mouth quirked in a smile. "I just might. Come. If your friend there does not object, I've drink and some food."

Padruig took his horse's reins and let him drink from the stream, before tying him close to Magnus's horses and taking a seat before a small fire. Magnus handed him a skin and Padruig took a long drink.

He opened his eyes wide and coughed as heat shot through his body. "What is this?"

"Nectar of the gods, by way of Balcharn Abbey." Magnus's eyes twinkled. "I traded the good monks a fine chalice for it."

Padruig took another sip. "'Twas worth it." He eyed Magnus. "A trader, are you now?"

"Aye. I cannae bear to remain long at Castle Mac-Coinneach with Grigor in charge." He spat onto the ground, then lifted a knowing gaze to Padruig. "Are you back, then, Laird?"

Laird. A title he once wore with pride and lost through arrogance. Padruig gritted his teeth and nodded. "I am."

Magnus eyed him closely. "Twill not be easy to take MacCoinneach. Grigor has many loyal to him. Particularly after . . ." He fell silent and looked away.

Padruig's throat burned with something other than the potent drink. "After my terrible lack of judgment caused my sister's death and the death of many of our clansmen."

"Och, well, I have long suspected we do not know the whole of that story, Padruig. But, aye, to be sure, there are those in the clan who will not easily trust you. Others will, though."

Padruig chewed on a piece of dried beef, thinking as he had this sennight past of how best to approach Castle MacCoinneach.

"Ye must challenge Grigor. I shall aid you as I can, but 'twould be better to have a few more men at our backs."

"Grigor will die before he gives up his position."

Magnus raised a brow. "How do you ken?"

"You will think me a lackwit." Padruig frowned at Magnus, who said nothing. "'Tis Brona," he finally said.

"Brona? But . . . but, Laird, she is dead."

"Just so."

Magnus's mouth flapped open then shut so many times that Padruig was tempted to laugh. "A . . . ghost?" Magnus's gaze shot around the clearing where they sat as if he expected the trees to be harboring Brona's spirit.

"She is no here at the moment."

"Give me that flask."

Padruig handed it over and Magnus took a long slug. "You say your sister has visited you?"

"Aye. She is verra insistent that I return to Castle MacCoinneach."

"Well." Magnus took another drink. "Well, then."

"But I agree that 'twould be foolish to do so alone. I thought to seek out the Laird of the de Granthams for aid. He has long been an ally of our clan and was a boon companion to my father."

"Aye, 'tis a fine idea."

Padruig sucked in a breath, knowing that he was about to take one more step toward a destiny he'd once foresworn. "Will you accompany me?"

Magnus slowly smiled. "Aye, Laird, I shall indeed."

Chapter Two

Freya heard the scratch of the bar at her door being lifted, and her heart lurched in panic. *Dear Lord, save me*, she silently prayed. *Please let it not be Angus Ransolm.* She knew he could not have arrived so soon, but the prospect was so terrifying her thoughts were without reason. As the door edged open, she held her breath, slumping with relief when she saw it was only Huwe, one of the newer guards, carrying a cloth-wrapped bundle and a flagon.

"My lady," he said. "How do you fare?"

Tears stung the backs of her eyes at his unexpected kindness. "Have you heard?"

"Aye. All at Castle MacCoinneach have heard that you are to wed with Angus Ransolm." He sat the bundle and flagon on the window seat. "I brought you food and drink."

"I am not hungry." In truth, she was starving, but her belly was in such knots that she couldn't bear to eat.

"Starving yourself will not change things, lass."

"At least my death will arrive sooner," she snapped and rose. "I cannot believe this is happening to me. I hate Grigor!"

"He has made an interesting choice of husband, no doubt."

"Interesting?" Freya realized she was shrieking, but couldn't stop herself. "'Tis not interesting; 'tis vile. Angus Ransolm is an old, foul man who is legendary for his cruelty." The last came out a sob, and tears spilled down her cheeks.

"Och, lass, have some wine."

"I do not deserve this," she said. "Look at me, Huwe." She threw out her hands. "I deserve a young man, someone strong and kind who will cherish me, not that . . . that filthy whoreson. Father always promised me that I would have a say in who I would marry. He promised!"

"Your father is dead."

"I well know that, Huwe," she said with a sniff. "If Grigor were any kind of man, he would honor my father's memory by keeping his promise."

"'Tis a shame your brother is not here."

"Why would you say that? Are you not loyal to Grigor?"

Huwe shrugged. "For the moment."

Freya widened her eyes in the kind of pleading expression that had always gotten her whatever she wanted. "Padruig is not here. There is no one to aid me."

He met her gaze, then shook his head. "I cannot change Grigor's mind."

"But he trusts you. He relies on you."

"Aye, but I tell you in this his mind is made up. You shall wed Angus Ransolm. Unless . . ."

"Unless what?"

"Well, it might be different if Padruig returned. Do you know where he is?"

"Nay." Freya let out a long sigh. "'Tis as if he vanished. We have had no word from him in more than a year."

"Och, weel, then you must accustom yourself to the idea of wedding the Ransolm laird."

"Oh, God, I cannot do it," she wailed. "I have done nothing to earn such a fate."

Huwe patted her on the shoulder. "I must go. Drink some wine."

"There isn't enough wine in all of the Highlands to make this any more bearable."

Huwe's only response was the sound of the door closing and the bar sliding into place.

Freya's hand shook as she poured a cup of wine. For a moment, she'd thought, hoped that perhaps Huwe would aid her, but she could see in his eyes that he would not go against Grigor. She couldn't really blame him for it. Grigor would just respond by killing him.

In despair, she looked around at the stone walls of her chamber. Long ago, her father had told her stories about secret passages within Castle MacCoinneach. When she was younger, she had spent days and days searching her chamber for such.

How I wish I had found one, she thought. *I would take my chances out in the woods rather than face being bound to the likes of Angus Ransolm.* The very thought made her stomach clench, and she took a long drink of wine.

There was no hope for it. Her life would be over soon. She would never willingly submit to Angus, and when she refused him, he would kill her.

"Damned beast," Aimili muttered as she dragged herself toward the hall. Loki absolutely refused to listen to her, refused to communicate with her at all, and persisted in launching her into the air over and over again.

She could swear he was laughing at her.

Her whole body consisted of one large ache. Dusty and bedraggled, she plunged into the hall, intent on finding a cup of cool ale.

In her rush, she headed straight for the kitchen.

And slammed into a body.

The force of it pitched Aimili backward onto her already sore behind. "Oh!" she cried, and glared up at the person who'd stopped her progress. She felt as if she'd just run into a stone wall.

The man stared down at her from what seemed a great height. His silvery blue eyes were wary, as if he sought to determine what had just run into him. Lines of whitish scars etched a pattern into his rugged features. He took a step back, frowning slightly.

Those eyes, she thought. *I know those eyes.* An unsettling tremor shivered down her spine.

"Forgive my sister, Padruig," Wautier said with a glance of disdain. "She has no doubt come from the stables."

Aimili's mouth dropped open. This huge, grave man was her Padruig? She awkwardly scrambled to her feet, and brushed ineffectively at her boy's garments. "Padruig? Of the MacCoinneach clan?" she sputtered out.

He nodded, and before Aimili could smile in welcome, turned his back on her and walked away with Wautier, dismissing her as if she were no more than an annoying child.

Out of the corner of her eye, she caught her father's disapproving frown.

"Morainn, perhaps you could assist your sister in"— her father frowned—"attiring herself more appropriately in light of our guests."

Aimili felt the blood rush to her face as her sister took her arm and pulled. With a sniff, Morainn said, "We shall stop in the kitchen for water first."

Though Aimili opened her mouth to speak, her

words stuck fast. Padruig, here after all this time? How could it be? And why? As Morainn tugged her from the hall, Aimili could not take her eyes from him, though he spared her not a glance.

One thing became very clear. This man bore no resemblance whatsoever to the Padruig MacCoinneach of her dreams.

Morainn was quiet while she helped Aimili clean the dust from her face and hands, an unusual event, for which Aimili was thankful. Her head spun with the discovery of Padruig MacCoinneach himself at de Grantham Castle, and her belly clenched with the sight of the man he had become. There was no kindness or gentleness about him now, only serious reserve. And he had dismissed her presence as if they'd never shared . . . Well, Aimili had to admit, they truly had not shared all that much, although it had meant everything to her.

"Aimili, quit dawdling," Morainn said. "I want to get back to the hall."

Aimili scrubbed a last bit of dirt from her cheek. "Why is Padruig here?"

"I do not know." Morainn frowned. "I do not like the looks of him." She made a face. "All those horrible scars."

Aimili had not found them all that horrible, but she didn't refute her sister. "I wonder where he has been all this time," she said as she drew on a deep green bliaut.

"No doubt hiding in shame at how he thrust his clan into a bloody feud."

"Padruig did not kill Brona or Malcolm."

"He may as well have. He didnae believe his own sister, God rest her soul. It was his duty to protect her and instead he favored a man who murdered her."

"'Twas a terrible tragedy," Aimili said. "But—"

"Hurry. The only way we shall find out what he wants is to be."

But they learned nothing during the long course of supper in the hall. Aimili sat between Morainn and their brother Colyn and tried to keep from staring at Padruig, who engaged in low-voiced conversations with her father and another man he had apparently brought with him.

She had hoped that the sight of her in her fine green bliaut with her hair carefully braided might cause him to look at her differently, might bring a gleam of recognition to his beautiful eyes. There was nothing. Either he didn't remember her at all or didn't care enough to consider her presence.

Still, she stared, hiding her gaze behind her cup of wine and forcing herself to eat bites of the fine supper Cook had prepared. *Padruig looks like a warrior of old*, she decided. Battle-scarred, with a heavy weariness about him. His mouth never curved in a smile, and his gaze was intense.

Still, he drew her, touched emotions so deep within her that it seemed they belonged only to him. She realized with a sinking heart that they had lain dormant for years awaiting his return.

"We shall continue this discussion in my solar," her father suddenly said and rose, cradling his cup of wine. Padruig, his companion, and her two brothers also rose.

Aimili knew she would learn nothing this night. The uncomfortable feeling of being shut out washed over her. *You are being foolish*, she chided herself. *Even if you have long thought of Padruig as yours, clearly he is not. Nor is he the man you once knew.*

She gazed at him and, to her surprise, he finally looked at her. Really looked at her. For an instant, something flashed in his eyes, and his expression softened.

Then he turned and followed her father.

Aimili simply stared after them. He did remember, she thought. He did remember.

Padruig followed Laird de Grantham and his sons and strove to quell the disquiet that coiled in his gut. The laird was up to something, he would swear it. Padruig and Magnus had been welcomed, yet the laird had yet to give any indication of how he viewed Padruig's request for aid. Padruig set his jaw. If the laird refused, he would find another way. Somehow.

On his journey back to the Highlands, he had come to some realizations. He could not stand by idly and watch Freya being wed to a man such as Angus Ransolm. His responsibility to stop such a horror went beyond his love for his sister. Though he had banished himself and foresworn his position as laird of the clan, the fact that he was laird was bred into his very bones. Along with that position came duty to the clan, a duty that called to him now even though he doubted he was up to the challenge.

Above all, he had a duty to protect the innocent. He had failed once, but he swore he would never do so again.

For a moment, his thoughts went back to the girl who'd sat so silently at the high table. Clearly, she thought she was being circumspect, but he'd caught her staring at him time and time again through her big, dark eyes. No doubt shocked and repulsed by his scarred appearance.

He remembered her from a lifetime ago. It was on one of his father's visits to the de Grantham holdings. Padruig had accompanied him, but quickly found himself with little to do as his father and the Laird of the de Granthams talked. He'd wandered onto the training field and found a young girl attempting to take on two older boys with some ridiculous excuse for a sword. She'd ended up flat on her back, with her arm splayed out at an odd angle, but still she taunted the boys.

Even though she was down, they would have struck her again had he not intervened.

From her earlier dash into the hall, it was clear the child had lost nothing of her recklessness. Her appearance, though, had changed mightily, he thought, stamping down the sharp swell of awakening in his nether regions, appalled at his body's reaction.

Smooth, unmarred skin; pink lips; even white teeth; clear brown eyes slightly tilted up at the corners. Childlike, he reminded himself. Long legs, the gentle flare of hips, a hint of round breasts. A woman, the man inside him declared.

Forcing his thoughts to the matter at hand, he walked into the solar and leaned against the wall.

The laird eyed him steadily. "You ask a great deal of us, Padruig."

"I ken. The situation at Castle MacCoinneach demands immediate action, and I do not have time to secretly gather those loyal to me into an army."

"Twould no doubt gain Grigor's notice if suddenly a good part of his clansmen went missing," Wautier observed.

"That, as well."

"The question is whether there are still clansmen loyal to you," the laird said, a question in his gaze.

Magnus stepped forward. "There are many, Laird."

"How do you know?"

"I am one of them. When I am not traveling, I live within the castle walls. 'Tis true, Grigor has a loyal following, but many of the clan are unhappy with his rule."

"Enough to fight against him?"

"Aye. And the lass is a favorite of the clan."

"We must either find a secret way in or draw Grigor out," the laird said. "I cannot leave my own holdings unprotected, and I have not the men to mount a siege and protect my own at the same time."

"There are ways into the castle that few know of," Padruig said, recalling the many hidden passages his father had shown him.

"Or we could invite Grigor on a hunt with us," Colyn suggested. "Ambush him."

Though to use stealth and betrayal went against Padruig's code, he had to admit the idea had merit. "'Twould allow me to face Grigor directly without risking too many others."

"Aye."

"It may work," Magnus agreed. "Stores at Castle MacCoinneach have been lean for some time. The prospect of fresh meat should bring Grigor outside the safety of the castle walls. But he will not be alone."

"Would he trust you?" Padruig asked the laird.

The laird shrugged. "He has no reason not to. I have not involved myself in matters of your clan. I do this out of my fond memories of your father."

His message was clear. Padruig had yet to prove himself worth the trouble. "I thank you."

The laird slowly smiled. "You have not heard my

condition yet."

So, here it is, Padruig thought.

"In exchange for my aid, you shall wed my daughter, Aimili."

Padruig's mouth dropped open as the girl's face shot into his mental vision. "She is but a bairn."

"Nay. She is of an age to marry."

"Nay. I cannot." He clenched his jaw, determined not to shout out his anger over the laird's request.

"Once you have reclaimed your place as laird, you shall marry her."

Padruig's thoughts flashed back to the girl at supper, and his anger deepened. The very idea was beyond ridiculous. *She is far too young, far too innocent for one such as me*, he thought. *Far too tempting*, his inner voice mocked, to his shame. "I have no need of a wife."

"You will eventually. If you succeed."

"Laird, I mean no disrespect to your daughter, but I have man's work to do. 'Twill be some time afore I can even consider taking a bride." *And when I do, it will be a full-formed woman who can tolerate my sorry visage, give me sons, and otherwise leave me be*, he thought.

"I am in need of a match for Aimili."

"Surely you can find a man more suited to a young girl."

The laird let out a sigh. "Aimili follows her own path. Ofttimes, 'tis not one most ladies would trod."

Wautier laughed. "Dinnae coat the matter with

honey, Father. Aimili is a willful termagant, who spends nearly all of her time either in the stables with the horses or in the woods doing only God knows what."

"She has a good heart," the laird countered. "And she is skilled with the horses."

Padruig could scarcely take in the fact that the child's father and brother were arguing her merits to him, let alone that they actually expected him to wed her. "Laird, I cannot agree to this." In truth, the very thought sickened him. A young lass deserved someone young in heart and spirit, not a man scarred both without and within by the past. Memories shifted through his mind. The glint of a dagger in firelight, the burn in his face as the blade struck true, the rage in the eyes of the MacVegan clansman. The broken body of his sister, Brona, barely over the threshold between child and woman. No, he could not wed a tender lass.

"Then you shall not have the aid of the de Granthams," the laird said. "Think on this, Padruig. With us, you have a good chance of regaining Castle Mac-Coinneach. Of saving your sister from a truly horrible union. Without . . ." He shrugged. "'Twill be much harder. Agree and you gain a pretty young bride to warm your bed."

Wautier and Colyn started to laugh, but the laird quelled them with a look.

Padruig could not imagine bedding the girl. Could he? An image flashed into his mind of Aimili lying atop a bed of thick furs, all soft and silken skin, her dark eyes gleaming up at him. No, he told himself.

His mind whirled in search of options, but he knew the laird's words to be true. An alliance with the de Granthams was his best chance. Damn it to hell. Marriage. "I shall think on this, Laird. In truth, I have grave reservations about the matter."

"'Tis a good offer. Do not think that I do not place worth upon my daughter." The steely look in the laird's eyes confirmed his claim.

The question remained—why offer her to Padruig? Was the girl so lacking that he was desperate enough to appeal to the outlaw laird of another clan? "By your leave, Laird, I shall retire to think upon the matter."

"Do so. I expect your answer in the morn."

Having come to the realization that the only way she would be permitted out of her chamber was to pretend acquiescence, Freya managed to swallow her bile long enough to do so. As a result, she sat in the great hall for supper, picking at chunks of beef in a mustard sauce and trying very hard to avoid glaring at the smug bastard who presided over supper as if he were the king himself.

As usual, her mother took her meal in her chamber,

leaving Freya at the high table with Grigor, Rauf, and, thankfully, her "cousin" Efrika, and Alasdair, both of whom sat down and sent her identical expressions of sympathy.

She sipped wine and gazed out over the full hall. Many members of the clan caught her eye, their own gazes filled with a combination of sympathy and anger. *Why are none of them brave enough to crush Grigor like the insect he is?* she silently lamented. *It isn't fair. Where is my champion?*

"Do not frown so, Freya," Grigor said, his voice oozing superiority. He snapped his fingers, and the poor serving girl who hovered behind him filled his cup. "You do not wish to mar that beautiful face with unsightly wrinkles. 'Twill lower your worth."

Beside him, Rauf chuckled, and Freya gripped her cup tight.

"I am pleased that you finally saw the reason in my decision," Grigor continued.

"You gave me no choice."

He lifted a brow and fixed his gaze on her breasts. "You are naught but an overly coddled young wench. 'Tis fortunate for you that I am here to make decisions for you."

For a moment, anger surged through Freya with such force that she started to rise. Efrika grabbed her arm and held her in place. "Do not aggravate him," she whispered.

Freya gritted her teeth. "Any woman likes to feel she has a choice."

"The illusion of choice, mayhap. You shall be well settled, and that is what matters."

Efrika clung to Freya's arm tighter. "As you say," Freya managed to spit out.

"I have heard from your future husband. He is most anxious for the wedding to take place. Indeed, he shall be here within the fortnight."

"That seems rather rushed, Grigor," Efrika said, her voice mild. "Surely Angus can wait a few months. Allow Freya to become accustomed to the idea."

Grigor snorted. "Time to cause me more trouble. Nay, Angus is eager to claim her and that is what shall occur."

Freya couldn't keep the flush of distaste from her face, and Grigor smiled. "Aye, Angus wants to breed a few bairns off her before he grows too old to do so."

Dear Lord, preserve me, Freya silently prayed. She averted her gaze from Grigor and took a deep drink of wine. Perhaps she would spend the rest of her days so saturated with drink that she would forget the pampered life she'd once led, with people who cared about her.

A loud gasp broke into her morose thoughts. She turned to find Grigor, whose face had turned pale as snow. He clutched his belly and moaned.

"Laird, what is it?" Rauf demanded as he gripped Grigor's shoulders to keep him from toppling from his seat.

"Pain," Grigor rasped.

Rauf backhanded the serving girl across the face. "What did you give him?"

The girl's face paled, but for the vivid red of her cheek. "Naught but what I was given by the butler, I swear it."

Grigor panted heavily, his face creased in pain. "Get me to my chamber," he ordered. "And find out who is responsible."

"Probably just a piece of soured meat," Efrika commented.

Rauf narrowed his eyes and glared at her. "Then why is he the only one to fall ill?"

Efrika shrugged. "Foul humors, no doubt."

Grigor lurched to his feet. "Fetch me a healer." He glanced at Efrika. "Not that fraud, but a real one." As he stumbled from the hall, he let out a loud groan.

Efrika took Freya's hand under the table. "Well, that should keep him busy for a time," she whispered.

Freya's gaze widened. "You . . . what did you—?"

"Shush. I am merely buying us some time to figure a way out of this."

"I fear the only way is for Padruig to return."

"Mayhap. Do not give up, child. And above all, try your best to avoid being confined to your chamber. If we are to find you a way to escape, you must be free to do it."

"Aye." Freya quirked a smile. "My thanks, Efrika.

'Tis a fine thing to see that pig brought to his knees."

"My thought exactly, dearling."

Queen Sebilla sat at a table topped with gold-flecked white marble. The soft splashing sound of a nearby fountain, and the sweet scent of the gardenias she tended filled the air.

Such frustration gripped her that she could barely speak.

"He must be captured and contained," she announced. "As soon as possible."

Lucan, her closest friend and advisor, nodded. "We all agree, my queen. The question is, how?"

"He will expose us all if he is not stopped," Arailt added. "Someone will discover that he is not of the human world."

"We know why he is at Castle MacCoinneach," Niall said.

"Aye," Sebilla agreed. "He seeks revenge for the aid the Laird of the MacCoinneachs granted us long ago."

"Why not just destroy the clan, then?" Cinnait wondered. "By now, he possesses the power."

"Because the laird is not there," Sebilla told her. "Not the true laird, the descendant of Aelfric."

"And because he no doubt wishes to play with them before destroying the clan."

"Aye, Vardon has ever been fond of his games."

"What shall we do, your majesty?"

For the first time in her life, Sebilla railed inside at the burden of her position, resented the fact that ultimately it fell upon her to safeguard their world. "We must study the old books. If there is an answer, it must lie in what our ancestors did long ago. Arailt, you are the one most familiar with our archives." She had decided not to tell him of his daughter's unwitting involvement in Vardon's escape. Arailt would be beyond mortified. She would, however, speak to the girl herself when time allowed.

"Aye, my queen. I shall commence my study at once." He rose and with a bow left her presence.

Sebilla drummed her fingers on the smooth surface of the table. "I may have to tend to this matter myself."

She'd expected immediate protests from her other advisors, but none came. Each gazed at her with a somber expression.

"You may," Lucan said. "As much as I do not like the idea. You are the most powerful of all of us."

"With the possible exception of Vardon."

Lucan's face darkened. "I shall not believe that."

Sebilla smiled gently. "Thank you for your confidence, my friend."

"Let us pray that Arailt discovers something in the archives and it will not come to that," Niall said.

Sebilla's smile faded. "I fear prayers shall not suffice this time." She rose. "I wish to be alone. You may go about your duties."

After her advisors left, Sebilla went to her private chambers. Her retreat was usually a place of calm, comprised of spacious rooms draped in light shades of sea foam and turquoise. Her rooms opened to a terrace overlooking a clear blue pool. Pink and white flowers cascaded from stone arches above.

Today, she felt as if she had no refuge. After lighting a brazier set on the terrace, she retrieved a wide copper bowl and a box filled with various plants, herbs, and other sacred objects. She poured clear water from the pool into the bowl, and set it over the fire, then added pinches from her cache. Borage, fennel, fumitory, pennyroyal, rosemary, and mugwort. Lastly, a sprinkle of amber fragments.

The water began to simmer and swirl, changing colors as it did. Blues and golds melted into greens, finally leaving the center clear. Sebilla sat cross-legged on a cushion, closed her eyes, and stretched her arms to her sides.

"Mother Goddess, aid me," she said. "Show me what I must do."

She opened her eyes and peered into the bowl. Slowly, an image took shape. A girl; no, a young woman. She stared at Sebilla through dark, deep eyes, auburn hair curling around her lovely face. Clad in a dark green tunic and braies, she stood in a forest clearing, mist swirling around her legs. In the background, Sebilla saw the faint shape of a horse tethered to a tree and something else, another animal. A deer perhaps? No, Sebilla realized as the image cleared a tiny bit. A wolf. The girl's hand rested atop its head.

The image disappeared.

Puzzled and disappointed, Sebilla sat back. What could it mean? Could the girl be meant to help her?

Beset by confusion, Sebilla drew off her robes and dove into the water. She floated among the flower petals and stared up at the lavender sky, mulling over the image she'd seen. There had been something about the girl, something different.

Could she somehow be the key to vanquishing Vardon?

Sebilla clung to that hope and let her body relax, buoyed by the soft, warm water. For the span of a few moments, she let herself believe that they would succeed in regaining control of Vardon.

Before he did something that would bring angry outsiders to the portals of Paroseea. Before he killed more innocents in his quest for power.

For if Sebilla knew naught else, she knew Vardon would not stop with simple revenge. He had always lusted for more. Hundreds of years in a cell barren of all but basic needs would have honed that lust to something fearsome.

Chapter Three

H is calloused hand caressed her neck, then slid over her shoulder and down her arm, his touch leaving tingles of awareness in its wake. Enfolding her in a warm embrace, his low, rumbling voice whispered words of love, of desire, of things that inflamed her senses. She turned in his arms and traced the lines of his face, her fingertips learning him, claiming him as hers.

When he kissed her, she opened her mouth, greedily tasting him, sinking into the magic of his lips. It was madness; it was glorious; it was all of that and more. Yet not enough.

When his big hands cradled her bottom and pressed her close, she whimpered, feeling him through the fabric of their clothes, hard with his own need. She shivered, her mind imagining, anticipating what was to come. What had always been inevitable, meant to be.

"Yes," she whispered.

In an instant, they clung together, skin to skin. As he lowered her to the floor, she opened her eyes wide, not wish-

ing to miss a moment. Finally, to become one with him, to know him completely.

He smiled softly and smoothed a hand over her belly, his fingers probing lower, touching her, preparing her . . .

Aimili woke up shaking and panting, her sheets twisted around her body. It took a moment to realize she was in her own bed. Alone.

With a groan, she flopped her head back on the pillow and closed her eyes. The dream swirled through her mind, and she bit her lip in embarrassment. Never had she dreamed of him so vividly, so intimately.

By the saints, she was truly pathetic. Padruig barely noticed her existence at all.

Determined to go about her duties, she got out of bed, washed from a bowl of cool water left by the maid, and dressed in her usual attire—Colyn's old, cast-off clothing and sturdy boots. She bound her hair into a plait and headed straight for the stables, skirting the great hall.

She pushed questions about what her father and Padruig had discussed last eve from her mind, and focused on drawing in the soothing scent of horseflesh and hay. First, she stopped to visit Mist, who was contentedly munching on hay in her stall.

What ails you, lass?
Naught of importance.
Mist snorted in response.
Aimili felt her face relax, only then realizing that

since she'd awakened, she'd been gripped tight with tension. That wouldn't do for the task she had ahead of her this morn.

She continued down the walkway and stopped in front of Loki's stall. He gave her what could only be termed a baleful look. "Good morning, boy," she murmured.

Gunnr peeked out of a nearby stall. "Are you goin' to try to ride 'im again, my lady?"

"Aye. Today, I am going to ride him." She led Loki out of his stall and began brushing him. He truly was a magnificent, powerful animal. Ember black, with an arched neck, he stared at her from large almond-shaped eyes that seemed to hold a wealth of knowledge, none of which he'd seen fit to share with her as of yet.

Within a few minutes, she had Loki saddled, and led him out to the ring. By the time she was ready to mount, she had gained an audience of Gunnr; the stable master, Thomas; and two of the other grooms.

They each gazed at her as if she'd lost her wits.

"Watch it when he tries to put his head down," Thomas advised.

Aimili nodded, though she already knew that was Loki's signal that he was about to try to buck her off. She patted Loki on his withers. *We are going to have a nice ride today. No bucking, rearing, or bolting off.*

Not surprisingly, he didn't answer her, but just flicked his ears.

Aimili swung herself into the saddle. She gave Loki

a gentle squeeze and he began walking.

"He looks calmer today," Gunnr called out.

"Aye," Aimili agreed. Though she had a firm grip on the reins, she let her hands move with the swing of Loki's head. *Nice and easy, Loki.*

He blew air out of his nostrils and walked faster.

Aimili slowly eased him into a trot. She grinned as she passed Gunnr, but jolted when she saw that Padruig had joined the group. He stared at her so intently, she felt a flush burn up her cheeks. Images of her dream resurfaced in her mind, and her face heated further.

In an instant, Loki sensed her distraction and gleefully took advantage. Before she could gather herself to respond, his powerful muscles tightened, and he reared straight up. Grimly, Aimili hung on as Loki came down with an angry neigh, erupted with a huge buck, and tore across the ring as if a pack of wolves were chasing him.

"Keep his head up," Thomas yelled.

Damned beast, Aimili thought as she hauled on the reins and leaned back. *Contrary animal.* They tore around the circular ring, Loki bucking over and over again despite Aimili's best efforts.

Damn you, I said nice and easy.

Why?

She yanked the inside rein back to her hip, forcing Loki to turn. *Because that is what you need to do. That is what every horse needs to do if they wish a nice place in my stables.*

Loki slowed a bit, and Aimili let out a breath.

Only to suck it back in when he spun sideways, dropped partway to the ground, and came up sharply, lifting all four feet off the ground. Aimili sailed through the air once more.

She landed in a heap in the dirt, trying to catch her breath and silently cursing Loki.

Out of the corner of her eye, she saw Padruig running into the ring. He tried to catch Loki's reins, but the horse shied away from him.

"He is no too fond of men just yet," Aimili croaked as she levered herself to a sitting position.

Padruig scowled at her. "Why?"

Aimili struggled to her feet, realizing that her head ached, and her stomach roiled with nausea. "Angus Ransolm."

Padruig's scowl deepened. "What do you mean?"

"Do you see the scars on him?" she asked, pointing at Loki's flanks. "Those are thanks to Laird Ransolm."

Something dark and lethal flickered in Padruig's eyes. "I am no surprised," he finally said.

"Do you need aid, my lady?" Thomas offered.

"Nay," Aimili said automatically, though she was beginning to think she might indeed. She forced her aching body forward and took Loki's reins, who was quiet now that no one was on his back. Padruig brushed her aside and removed Loki's saddle and bridle, draping both over the railing.

"Sit down afore you fall down," he told her.

His tone grated. "I am fine," she insisted.

He gave her a narrow look. "Then, you are lucky." As Loki loped away, Padruig crossed his arms and studied her. "What were you thinking to ride such an animal?"

Not you, too, Aimili thought, and lifted her chin. "I ride the horses all the time. 'Tis what I do."

"My lady, are you sure—" Thomas began.

"I am fine," she assured him. She limped out of the ring, Padruig following close behind. She could feel the heat of his stare burning a hole in her back.

"You lack the age and strength to take on a beast like that."

Aimili whirled around and immediately regretted it. Her head pounded anew. "I am seventeen years of age."

"As I said."

"Do not concern yourself with me, Laird. I am sure you have far more weighty matters on your mind."

He muttered something under his breath, and fixed her with a steady look. "It seems I must concern myself with you."

Aimili froze. "What . . . what do you mean?"

There was no mistaking the dismay in Padruig's expression. "I have need of your father's aid to regain Castle MacCoinneach."

"What has that to do with me?"

"You are the price."

"What?" She winced at the shrieking sound of her voice.

"Aye."

"But, I—"

He held up a hand. "Neither of us has a choice. I need your father's men, and he will not commit them unless I agree to marry you."

Aimili's jaw dropped. "Marry?" she whispered. How could her father do this to her? At the same time, a thrill of excitement wound through her. She had imagined wedding Padruig MacCoinneach countless times, had envisioned her heart light with love, safe in the knowledge that he was wholly hers.

His next words crushed her excitement flat. "I shall be honest with you. I have no wish for a bride, much less an innocent child, but I need your father's men."

Her throat burned at the realization that she was naught but an unwanted burden, clearly a woman—no, a child he would never willingly select. She gazed into his eyes, flat with resignation, and something sacred, something carefully tended and guarded, shriveled inside her like an apple left too long in the sun to rot. "You . . . you are not the man I remember."

His jaw tightened. "No, I am not."

"I cannot marry you."

His gaze narrowed. "You must."

"Nay." Despite the pain ringing through her head, she stalked off, torn between shouting out her anger at her father's casual disposal of her and dissolving into tears at the death of a dream.

Aimili stormed into her father's solar without knocking. All the way from the stables, she'd cursed her father; Padruig, the patronizing pig she'd once idolized; and most of all, the fact that absolutely no one could accept her as she was.

Her father glanced up from his worktable and immediately stiffened. "Aimili—"

"I shall not marry that man!" she shouted. "How could you . . . barter me off like some poorly performing cow?"

"'Tis for your own good that I do this."

"A lie," she spat. "'Tis to rid yourself of responsibility for me."

Her father sighed long and hard. "You have ever been outspoken."

"I am no meek miss to sit on a stool doing embroidery all day and leave the path of my life to others."

"I knew Padruig's sire well, as you ken. The de Granthams have long been allies of the MacCoinneachs."

She crossed her arms and glared at him.

"You need to marry. 'Tis the way of things. And Padruig is willing to take you."

Hurt and shame burned through her gut. "Because you give him no option."

"Be that as it may, the marriage shall take place. You shall gain a strong husband and a home of your own to manage."

"I do not want to manage anything but my horses."

"What shall you do, Aimili? Stay here? One day soon, Wautier shall wed and bring his bride here. She shall expect to establish her role as chatelaine. I have already had a number of inquiries about your sister. I've no doubt she shall be taken care of soon, as well."

Aimili fought back the sting of tears. "I dinnae care who is in charge, Father. You know I do not concern myself with the running of the castle."

"I have found a good man to take you, Aimili, and that is what you shall do."

"He does not want me, Father. He made that quite clear."

Her father waved a hand. "'Tis simply the suddenness of it. He shall become accustomed to the idea, as will you."

"Nay. You are wrong."

"You shall marry him, Aimili. As soon as he regains Castle MacCoinneach you shall be wed."

"I have always been an embarrassment to you, haven't I, Father? Not like Morainn."

"Aimili, you have your own special qualities about you. 'Tis simply different."

She smiled sadly. "You do not even hear what I am saying. He. Does. Not. Want. Me."

"I will see you settled, child."

With his last word, she let out her breath in a hiss

and rushed from the solar. Child. Just a child. The words rang over and over in her mind until she could barely see, barely think. As she entered the bailey, she broke into a run. Within moments, she was on her way into the forest.

Padruig stood watching the black stallion run back and forth inside the paddock and felt an odd empathy with Loki. When Padruig leaned on the rail, Loki stopped and eyed him. "We are both trapped, boy," Padruig murmured.

The horse snorted and turned its rump toward Padruig.

Magnus strolled out of the stables and halted next to Padruig. "That went well."

"By the saints, Magnus, what else can I do?" Padruig gritted his teeth. "If naught else, the sight of what that whoreson Ransolm did to his own horse would decide me. I cannot let Freya go into his hands."

"The lass is comely."

"She is a child. A child who remembers a Padruig of a lifetime ago."

"Are you sure that Padruig does not exist still?"

"Nay. That man died on the same field as Brona."

Padruig shook his head. "It does not matter. It cannot. I shall do what needs to be done to protect my sister. Aimili shall not go for want."

Magnus raised a brow. "What if the lass desires more of you?"

A bitter laugh escaped his lips before Padruig could rein it in. "Look at me, Magnus. Why would she? She'll be glad to be left alone with her horses, I have no doubt."

A boy raced out of the stables and nearly collided with the two men. "My lord," he said over a breath. "The laird bid me to find you."

Padruig frowned at the boy, wondering what new conditions the laird had thought up now. "I have already spoken to the laird this morn." And faced his smug acceptance of Padruig's reluctant agreement remained clear in his mind.

"The laird does no wish to have speech with you, my lord. He bids you fetch back Lady Aimili."

"What? From where?"

"One of the guards spied her leaving the castle, my lord. No doubt heading for the woods," he added, pointing his finger.

"By herself?"

"Aye."

Padruig briefly closed his eyes. Not a full day into their "betrothal" and already the lass stirred up trouble.

Magnus grinned. "Do you wish me to accompany

you, Laird?"

"Nay. 'Tis best I take this matter in hand by myself."
He turned away. Foolish wench, he thought. All matter of dangers lurked in the forest for a young girl alone.
He'd seen more than one man return from the hunt with
grievous wounds. And that was just from the animals,
not whatever human danger lurked in the dense trees.

Padruig retrieved Cai from the kennel where the laird
had insisted he be confined. Once Cai got Aimili's scent,
they set off. As Padruig walked out of the castle gate,
his gaze drifted over the countryside. The land rolled in
fells and vales, carpeted with lush green grass. Beyond
the castle lay Loch Fynnen, its still waters gleaming in
the morning sun. A low mist still hung over the water.
For an instant, Padruig thought he saw movement in the
mist, but when he shook his head it was gone.

He smiled. *No more than a few days back in the
Highlands and you've started to see things that don't exist*,
he chided himself.

Cai ran back and forth over the ground, searching for
Aimili's scent as he and Padruig headed into the forest.
Big, thick trees heavy with leaves filtered the sunlight
onto them and muffled sounds. Abruptly, Cai halted
and gave a soft woof. He took off through the trees and
Padruig followed, deeper and deeper into the wood, the
air growing cooler as they continued.

What was the girl doing? Padruig wondered. She'd
not struck him as one to be out gathering whatever

plants healers oftentimes needed, but appeared singularly devoted to the horses. Could she be meeting a lover? *No*, he thought. *The girl is far too young.*

Isn't she?

Why the thought was more disturbing than it ought to be was a matter he refused to contemplate.

Cai stopped and sniffed the air. Padruig stepped forward and spied a small clearing. He halted, puzzled. Aimili was indeed there, sitting on an overturned log, the gleam of sunlight picking up the reddish gold glints in her hair. Clad in her dark green tunic and braies, she looked as if she were a part of the forest itself.

There was a stillness about the scene, a serenity he was oddly reluctant to disturb.

The strangest thing was that next to the girl sat a dark gray wolf. From the way the girl's face turned to the wolf's, it actually appeared as if they were conversing. Nay, Padruig told himself, shaking his head. That was impossible.

But he could hear the soft murmur of her voice, though not well enough to make out the words. Well, he'd been known to talk to Cai often. Not that Cai ever answered.

The wolf laid its head on Aimili's leg and gazed up at her, almost as if it . . . *No. It is my imagination*, Padruig assured himself.

He reached out a hand to halt Cai, but it was too late. With a yip, the wolf bounded into the clearing. Aimili's companion immediately leapt up, bared its teeth, and stepped in front of Aimili with a low growl.

Cai dropped to the ground and put his ears back.

"Aimili," Padruig called as he stepped into the clearing.

For an instant, surprise and guilt flashed across her face. She put her hand on her guardian's nape and stood. "What do you do here?"

"Your father sent me to fetch you. What are you doing out here alone in the woods? With a wolf, no less."

As they talked, Padruig noticed Cai crawling slowly but steadily toward the other wolf, who silently watched him.

"'Tis none of your business."

Padruig gritted his teeth. "The forest is no place for a lone young girl."

She shot him a smug look. "I am safe here."

Padruig's gaze caught on the two wolves. Cai was lying on his back, his tongue lolling out and the other wolf, which Padruig realized was female, crouched over him. *By the saints, my wolf has turned into a lovesick fool*, Padruig thought crossly. *What next?*

"Aimili," he began, summoning up his patience. "I am to be your husband. Seeing to your safety is part of my duty."

"Duty," she sneered. "I want none of your duty. Nor do I need it." She waved a hand around her. "As you see, there is no threat here."

"What of . . ." He pointed to the female wolf, now nuzzling Cai's muzzle with hers.

"She is no threat to me."

Padruig stared consideringly at the two wolves. Cai was the only one of his species that Padruig had known to accept a human, and Padruig still wasn't quite sure why Cai did. He turned his attention to Aimili, whose gaze could only be termed mocking.

"Come," he told her.

She crossed her arms, reminding him of a petulant child. "I am no ready to return."

"Are you always this obstinate?" he muttered.

"When I have cause to be."

"I hope such behavior will not be frequent once we wed."

He was pretty sure she hissed at that. "I shall not wed you. I told you that."

Padruig saw the anger in her gaze and knew the cause. By the saints, what a tangle this was. "I know I am not the kind of man a young lass dreams of marrying. I am sorry for that, but there is naught I can do. I will never have a pretty face."

Her expression softened a bit.

"You were right earlier. I have changed. When we met, I was a green lad. Now, well, suffice to say I am not. I am sorry if I bruised your tender emotions, but I do not wish you to harbor any false expectations of this marriage."

"False expectations?"

"Aye. I will do what I must to ensure the safety of

my sister and my clan."

"And I am simply the price you must pay."

Padruig opened his mouth to correct her, but the truth was, she was absolutely correct. Marrying her was a price he was loathe to pay, a kind of penance. Of all the women he might have wed, he could think of no one less suitable than a young, beautiful lass with a body made to tempt a saint. As the thought entered his head, he shrank from it. Where had that come from? "You shall be treated well, lass, that I vow."

"And if I refuse?"

For a moment, he felt sympathy for her, then stamped it down. He could not afford such gentle emotions, not now. "You cannot. You know this."

Such a bleak look appeared in her gaze that he instinctively took a step forward.

"I shall return to the castle with you," she said softly.

He opened his mouth to speak, intending to reassure her, but in the end simply nodded. There really wasn't anything to say. He needed the laird's aid and the laird needed a husband for his wayward daughter. They would both just have to accept things and go on.

Still, when he turned and retraced his steps, all the way back to the castle he felt the waves of her dismay rolling through what remained of his heart.

The next day, Padruig sent Magnus ahead to Castle MacCoinneach, trusting him to gather those who remained loyal to Padruig and ready them for his arrival. He had considered Colyn's idea of luring Grigor from the castle, but eventually discarded it. It simply was not his way. Asides, he hoped to remove Grigor short of causing the man's death.

Before he left, Magnus had clapped a heavy hand on Padruig's shoulder and given him an earnest look. "All will be well," he'd said. "Trust in the clan."

"'Tis not my trust that is in question," he'd told Magnus. He had thought over his plan many times in the past hand of days. The first step was to enter the castle without detection by the guards. That, he could do, thanks to his knowledge of Castle MacCoinneach's labyrinth of passages. The second step was ensuring he had enough men at his back to avoid being immediately cut down by those loyal to Grigor. Though Padruig knew himself to be a skilled swordsman, no man could prevail against overwhelming numbers for long.

The real key to his claim, however, was the reaction of the clan. Would they accept his return, assent to his leadership again, or stand behind Grigor? Magnus had assured him that most would not support Grigor, but Padruig did not share his confidence. Many had lost husbands, sons, and brothers in the battle against Clan MacVegan. He imagined some still did when they had the misfortune to run across a MacVegan clansman vengeful over Padruig slaying Symund.

Would his clan acknowledge him as laird? And if not, what then?

He could not force them. Ultimately, they must choose to accept him or nay.

Either way, he would save Freya from becoming the beaten broodmare of Angus Ransolm or die trying.

He could not fail his remaining sister.

Vardon was well used to biding his time. Had he not learned to do so, he would undoubtedly have long ago descended into the very madness his enemies accused him of.

Fools, all of them. Hiding from a world they could easily rule.

Even Paroseea itself was soft. All anyone talked about was how beautiful it was. Lavender skies, for the goddess's sake. A pink sun of all things. Flowers everywhere. Roads paved with white marble. Mosaic walkways. Temples devoted to scholarly study. And those damned dolphins, who some past weak excuse of a ruler had allowed his wife to make the symbol of Paroseea. The young men weren't even required to learn how to wield a sword anymore.

Anger rose up in him, and burned his gut. How he hated the self-righteous rulers of Paroseea, smug in their exalted positions, the so-called high families of Paroseea. Daring to pass sentence on him.

They were the ones with the purest bloodlines, blessed with the best of everything: the most powers of magic, the most wealth, the greatest respect of the people. Not ones like him. Or at least that's the way it was supposed to be.

But he had proved them wrong. He who didn't even know the identity of his sire found that he possessed more raw power than many of those highly placed pretenders.

They would not accept it, of course, declared him unnatural, deemed his acts wicked and venal.

How he hated all of them. Oh, he would see to them in time.

But first things first. A shame he could not exact revenge upon Aelfric MacCoinneach, the bastard who had helped to bring about Vardon's temporary downfall, but the whoreson had long crumbled to dust.

His descendants, however, lived on. The shallow chit, Freya, would be easy to dispose of. She thought of nothing but herself and the marital fate that awaited her. He might even let her live long enough to experience the attentions of Angus Ransolm. She was a comely lass, though, he thought, allowing himself a small smile. Perhaps instead he would enjoy her first.

Three hundred years was a long time to go without a woman, after all.

He strode across the hall, nodding greetings to passing servants. Grigor had not yet been able to leave his chamber, still beset by the malady that had struck him down at supper. Briefly, Vardon wondered if Freya had a hand in that, but dismissed it. He doubted the wench had the knowledge or ability to do more than add a bit of honey to wine. Now, her cousin was another matter.

He chuckled to himself. If Efrika had found a way to leave Grigor heaving his guts out, good for her. The man was possessed of limited intelligence and prone to random acts of cruelty. Vardon had no use for a man bound by such limitations.

No, the one he wanted was Padruig MacCoinneach. The poor man, losing his sister, his own visage scarred so no woman of any beauty would consider him, exiled from his clan. It was all so richly satisfying.

His death would be the final delicious pleasure.

Aimili awoke to the sound of her door opening. She blinked and sat up, pressing a hand to her head, which still throbbed with a dull ache.

A cup was thrust into her hand. "Drink this," Morainn said.

"What is it?" Aimili peered into the cup.

"Wine, with a few herbs to aid your headache. Chamomile."

"My thanks." Aimili gingerly sipped the wine as Morainn lowered herself to the side of the bed.

For some odd reason, Aimili nearly burst into tears at the expression of sympathy on her sister's face. After Padruig had "explained" things to her, she'd spent the rest of the day hiding in her chamber, the reality of her situation pounding through her mind. Her father had seen a way to get rid of her and taken it. Her intended husband had made it clear that he wanted no part of her, only agreeing to take her out of dire necessity.

"Oh, Aimili, I am so sorry. I cannot believe that Father would do this." Morainn patted her shoulder. "Padruig is out on the training field now, wielding his sword like no one I've ever seen."

Aimili couldn't think of a thing to say to that. She drank more wine, breathing a little easier as her headache began to abate.

"Whatever shall you do?"

"What can I do? Father has made it abundantly clear that he will not change his mind."

"Has he spoken to you?"

"Aye." Aimili couldn't help but grimace. "Only to

inform me that he does not want to take me to wife, but will do so to gain Father's aid."

Morainn put a hand on her shoulder. "'Tis not quite what you dreamed of, is it?"

Embarrassment burned through her as Aimili realized her girlish fantasy of Padruig was not a secret. "Nay."

"Perhaps in time, I mean . . . Oh, I do not know what I mean." Morainn stood and walked over to gaze out of the window slit, her hands fluttering in the fabric of her gown.

Aimili finished her wine and forced herself to stand. "As long as he leaves me to my horses, I shall endure it." Somehow, she added silently, knowing the lie for what it was.

Morainn turned and cocked her head. "I would imagine even Padruig MacCoinneach will wish a wife to spend her time attending to his home."

"Well, he isnae going to get one." Aimili drew on an old tunic. "He made a bargain and he shall have to accept what he's granted." Inside, her belly clenched in fear. Surely, he would not object to her work with the horses. The image of his frowning face watching her being tossed off Loki spilled into her mind, and she gritted her teeth. "Help me dress."

"Mayhap you should don a gown."

"Nay. 'Tis best the Laird of the MacCoinneachs understand that I am not the kind of woman to adorn his castle and see to his mending."

Morainn quirked a smile as she plaited Aimili's hair. "Do you wish me to accompany you?"

Aimili looked at her sister, appearing as always the beautiful, refined lady of the castle, and shook her head. "'Twill only remind him of my lack." She yanked on her boots and left her chamber.

As Aimili walked out of the tower, she gazed across the bailey and spied Padruig at once. He was engaged in sword-play with her brother Wautier, and even from a distance, Aimili could see Wautier was providing little challenge.

She walked slowly over the trodden earth, cautioning herself to be calm and pleasant, no matter how the man aggravated her. As she neared the men, Wautier spotted her. An instant of relief flashed on his face.

"Your bride approaches, Laird," he said, putting down his sword. The sarcasm in his voice made Aimili wish she'd waited long enough for Padruig to beat him into the ground.

"My lady," Padruig said, his voice cool. "How may I serve you?"

"I wish speech with you."

He sheathed his sword and nodded, before casting a glance at Wautier. "We shall finish this anon."

Her brother's face tightened, but he merely said, "Aye. I look forward to it."

Aimili suppressed a smile at his reluctant tone.

Padruig's gaze raked her from head to toe. "I assume you are on your way to the stables."

"Aye."

He fell into step beside her. "Not to ride Loki, I trust?"

"No." She paused a moment, then said, "Mayhap on the morrow."

He said nothing, for which Aimili was grateful, though she suspected he merely delayed telling her he forbade it. They stopped at a large ring holding a pair of mares. Aimili watched the two play, kicking out their legs and leaping about the grass.

"I want to—"

"I want to—"

"About our marriage," Padruig began.

"To which I have not agreed."

"Castle MacCoinneach is a fine keep, Aimili. I vow I will see that you are well fed and clothed, with a comfortable place to sleep."

Her heart sunk a little farther in her chest. He could have been describing a favorite hound. "What of my horses?"

He waited to respond for so long that Aimili was tempted to smack him on the shoulder. Not that he would feel it. In the years since she'd seen him, Padruig had grown into a big man seemingly formed of slabs of granite muscle. "You may have access to the stables. And your horses. As to Loki, well, we shall see." He gazed down at her. "It is not my intention to make you miserable, Aimili."

"I know little of running a household. Nor do I have much interest. I have always devoted my time to the horses."

"I have said you may have your horses."

"What . . . what of our marriage?" She could barely get the words out.

"What of it? We shall be wed."

And that is all, she thought. "You care nothing for me. You barely remember me."

"That is not unusual. You know that. You shall be mistress of your own home. I have said I shall see you fairly treated."

Aimili averted her gaze, blinking back the sting of tears, disgusted at her weakness. She felt as if she stood on the edge of a road leading down into her future, one cold year upon another, ever awaiting some scrap of affection from her husband, ever without. "I wanted more," she said softly. "I wanted a husband to love me." *I wanted you*, she silently cried.

Again, he said nothing until she turned and looked up at him. His eyes were completely empty. "I cannae give you that, lass. I am sorry."

"So am I." She walked away.

Chapter Four

F reya snipped off a piece of henbane, wishing she could put enough in Grigor's ale to make his illness of the permanent kind. Unfortunately, he was recovering from whatever Efrika had given him, and his temper was worse than ever. He'd become convinced that someone or someones were out to kill him. If only she were so fortunate.

She brushed a finger lightly over her bruised cheek, yesterday's evidence of Grigor's anger over what he deemed her shameful lack of gratitude. No matter how hard she tried, she simply could not act grateful for being sold to a monster. Nine days she had left. Nine short days before Angus Ransolm arrived and her life ended.

How had this come to pass? It seemed only a moment ago that she'd had everything—beauty, wealth, a doting family. She gazed down at her faded, blue bliaut and grimaced. Now, thanks to Grigor's selfishness, she did not have even a decent gown to wear.

"Freya?"

She turned with a cry. "Magnus! You are back." Smiling, she took in the beloved sight of him, his green eyes flashing, his beautiful face returning her smile.

As he drew closer, his easy grin faded, and he frowned at her. "By the saints, what has happened to you?"

"Grigor." She looked down, embarrassed to have him see her in such a state. "He . . ." Her voice broke on a sob. "He is forcing me to marry Angus Ransolm."

Magnus gently lifted her chin. After glancing around them, he bent close and said, "Maybe not."

Freya caught her breath, afraid to let herself hope. "Will you aid me?"

"Always."

"I must flee." A sob gathered in her throat at the fearful prospect of going out on her own to an uncertain future. "Soon, afore Grigor realizes my acceptance of the marriage is feigned and locks me back up."

"Flee? Nay." He took her hands and Freya's heart beat a little faster. She knew Magnus looked upon her as a little sister, but she had never felt that way, not even when she was very young.

"I have no choice," she said, fighting back the sting of tears.

"Nay." He glanced around the garden, empty but for the two of them. "Ye must not breathe a word of what I am about to tell you."

"What is it, Magnus?" Hope flared in her chest, and she squeezed his hands.

"Padruig returns."

She swayed and would have fallen but for Magnus's strong grip. "Padruig? Where?"

He put a finger against her lips. "Not so loud. Grigor must not discover this until we are ready."

Her eyes filled with tears that spilled out down her cheeks. "Is he here?"

"Not yet. He gathers allies, as I do here."

"Magnus, I have only nine days before Angus arrives."

"Be patient. 'Tis to save you that Padruig returns."

"But . . . how did he know of my fate?"

A slow grin filled Magnus's face. "Och, weel that is a tale."

Out of the corner of her eye, Freya spotted Huwe approach, and pulled her hands free. "I am so glad to see you before I leave for the Castle Ransolm," she said brightly.

Magnus blinked, then shifted to look at Huwe. "'Tis fortunate that I decided to return to Castle Mac-Coinneach when I did. I shall be sure to give you a special bride's gift afore you depart."

"Magnus. Lady Freya," Huwe said, nodding. "The laird bid me to escort Lady Freya in to dinner. He wishes to be assured that the lady is keeping up her health."

Freya's mouth turned down. "Like a cow being fattened for slaughter."

Huwe said nothing, but looked pointedly at the purplish mark on Freya's cheek.

"Come, my lady," Magnus said, taking her arm.

Though Freya had no interest in food and even less in sharing a table with Grigor, she forced herself to walk to the hall and yet another opportunity to hone her play-acting skills. If she did have to flee, perhaps she could make her way as part of a traveling troupe, she thought.

Hurry, Padruig, she silently prayed. *Hurry.*

A sennight after Padruig MacCoinneach's invasion of her life, Aimili walked across the bailey and realized that she might have a way out of a cold, heartbreaking marriage. After all, she'd made no promises, set no conditions.

Her father had made a strategic error in not wedding her to Padruig before joining with him to retake Castle MacCoinneach. After Padruig realized his goal, there was no reason for him to press her into marriage. Indeed, he would probably cheer with relief at hearing her refusal.

Ignoring the pain in her heart at the prospect, Aimili told herself to stop being foolish. Her memory of Padruig did not match the man anymore. Maybe it never had, was never more than a product of her lonely fantasies.

His honor will demand he marry you, her inner voice said. *He cannot walk away from his agreement with your father, no matter how much he may wish to.*

And what of you? her voice continued. *What shall you do? Work with my horses*, she told herself. *As I have always done.*

Determinedly, she made her way to the stables.

And nearly ran into the subject of her thoughts.

"Aimili," he said.

She stopped short, ignoring the jump of her heart at the sound of him saying her name. Pitiful girl, she chided herself, keeping her face blank. "Aye?"

Padruig crossed his arms and looked down at her. His leather gambeson emphasized the breadth of his chest, and he stood with legs slightly spread, legs about the size of tree trunks. His hair was tied back with a scrap of leather, and he smelled of leather and sweat, clearly having come from the training field.

Aimili tried to tell herself that none of it was appealing at all.

"On the morrow, we go to regain Castle MacCoinneach."

A vision of bloody blades, shouts of attack, and fallen bodies flitted through her mind. "Have you enough men?"

"Aye. We shall prevail, doubt not."

She opened her mouth to urge Padruig to take care, but before she could utter the words, he said, "*You* shall remain here, of course."

"I am well skilled with a blade," she instinctively protested, though in truth she had no desire to go with the men.

"You are a wee lass. Lasses do not go to battle." He frowned at her. "I shall send for you when I have retaken the castle."

"You need not hurry," she muttered, looking away.

When he said nothing, she slowly shifted her gaze back to his. Silvery blue eyes stared back at her in obvious frustration. "I made an agreement with your father. We shall wed as soon as the castle is mine once more."

"Why hasten?" She waved a hand, trying to appear indifferent. "Surely, you will have much to do for your people at Castle MacCoinneach. You need not take the time to wed right away."

His lips tightened. "Your father made it very clear that he expects us to wed at once."

"Mayhap he fears you will change your mind."

"I will not."

Aimili gathered her courage and said, "You do not want me to wife, Padruig. You've made no secret of it." Squeezing the words past the boulder in her throat, she continued, "Why not consider Morainn. She is everything a mon could want, and only a year younger than I."

"Aimili," Padruig said slowly, uncrossing his arms. "Your father bade me take you in exchange for his aid. You and you only. 'Tis our agreement and 'tis what shall come to pass."

"But I—"

He held up a hand. "Best pack what belongings you

wish to bring with you to Castle MacCoinneach. I do no intend to tarry in ousting Grigor."

Aimili gritted her teeth. "I imagine it will take me some time to do so."

A flicker of a smile crossed his lips and his gaze moved down to take in her old tunic and braies. "Aye, I can see that you are verra devoted to your wardrobe."

"Fine gowns have little place in the stables."

He lifted a brow. "Just so." He turned away, then paused. "If you wish a woman to accompany you, feel free to make the arrangement. I dinnae ken what I shall find at Castle MacCoinneach."

"Perhaps you will find something to offer my father in repayment for his aid."

"His price is you. He has made his wishes verra clear."

"What of my wishes?" she asked, aware of the bitterness in her voice.

"What would you have me say? I have told you that you will be cared for, that you may continue with your horses. You must accept what will come to pass and put aside your romantic fantasies."

If you only knew, Aimili thought. The irony of it all bubbled up in her belly as she stared at Padruig's set face. "I wish you luck, then," she finally managed to say.

He nodded and trudged away, one hand resting on the pommel of his sword, his back rigid, his stride purposeful. No, it would not take him long to defeat

Grigor and retake his place as laird, Aimili thought. Every movement of his body, every word he uttered, every look in his eyes bespoke grim resoluteness.

She let out a breath and walked into the stable, trying but utterly failing to stave off an increasing wave of emptiness. She slumped to the dirt floor and leaned against a stall.

This depressing attitude of yours is really becoming quite tiresome. I mean, it isn't as if the man mistreats his horse. How bad can it be?

"What?" she said aloud and sat up. Over the top of his stall door, Loki gazed down at her.

He let out a snort that could only be construed as disgust. *I thought you a courageous lass, no a weakling who caves at the first sign of plans going awry.*

"I—" Spying Gunnr poking his head out of a stall down the walkway, Aimili broke off her reply.

"My lady? Can I do aught for you?"

"Nay. I was just . . . talking to myself."

Laughter echoed in her ears.

I am brave. I get on your sorry back, don't I?

That is not brave. 'Tis reckless. But I am no talking about horses.

You do not understand. He does not want me, not as a woman.

Then 'tis your job to change his mind. Loki snorted again. *How is he to realize you are a woman when you dress and act like a young lad? You need to soften.*

Aimili just stared at the horse in disbelief. Dear Lord, it had come to this. She was receiving advice from the most recalcitrant beast she had ever encountered. *Soften? What blather are you spouting?*

Do you realize how many times I have had naught to do but observe you humans and your mating rituals? 'Tis a ridiculously elaborate process you put yourselves through.

Aimili smothered a giggle. *Well, not all of us simply come into season, and position ourselves for the first man to trot by.*

'Tis far simpler.

I fear I do not know how to be soft.

Hmm. I shall think on this.

Why would you wish to aid me? You've done your best to grind me into the dirt.

Apparently having had enough of the conversation, Loki turned his ample rump toward the stall door and began munching on some hay.

"Soften," Aimili muttered as she rose. Sounded like a block of butter. What utter nonsense.

Sebilla stood over Caradoc's grave and fisted her hands. They had laid him to rest in a tranquil grove, filled with lush green grass, old rowan trees, and bright wildflowers. The soft sounds of a harp drifted on the fragrant air, the traditional tune of a final farewell causing Sebilla's eyes to tear and her chest to tighten in grief.

Damn Vardon to everlasting hell.

Beside her stood Lucan, ever faithful, as well as the rest of her council. Caradoc's brother, D'Ary, stood across from them, as still as stone. His features looked as if they'd been hacked from cold marble, and his amber gaze was flinty. He was all that remained of Caradoc's family. The brothers had been close, though so dissimilar to make one wonder if they truly had a shared parentage. While Caradoc was a fine warrior, he was also a man with a ready smile and a playful bent. D'Ary had always been more of a rocky atoll, his home somewhere beyond the main city, his time spent patrolling the perimeters of Paroseea alone. Even at Caradoc's funeral, he came as if he were in battle, his tall form arrayed with blades. He stood apart, no one brave or foolish enough to go near him.

He transferred his gaze to Sebilla and looked directly at her, his stare absent of any sign of respect for her position as his queen. Sebilla lifted her chin and held his gaze, though the knowledge that she had sent Caradoc to his death churned through her.

"'Tis done, my queen," Lucan murmured. "There is naught more we can do for him."

Sebilla nodded, breaking her gaze away from D'Ary. She placed a spray of snowy white gardenias across the mounded grave site and stepped back.

As she turned to walk away, she saw a guard rush up to Artur and whisper something. Artur's expression turned confused.

Grateful to have something other than the pain of Caradoc's death to focus on, Sebilla approached them. "Is something amiss, Artur?"

He bowed low before lifting his gaze to hers. "I am no sure, my queen. It seems that there has been much activity at Castle MacCoinneach. Not Vardon," he said quickly. "The former laird of the clan has returned."

Sebilla gripped a fold of her skirt. "Padruig Mac-Coinneach returns?"

"Aye."

And now it would start, Sebilla thought with an inward shudder of dread.

Vardon's true revenge.

"Queen Sebilla?"

She blinked, realizing that Artur stared at her. "'Tis no doubt what Vardon has been waiting for. Padruig is the descendant of Aelfric, once the laird of the Mac-Coinneachs. Aelfric is the one who aided us in defeating Vardon."

Artur's eyes widened.

"Aye. Vengeance is no doubt foremost in Vardon's mind." She frowned. "Would that we had someone—"

"I will go to Castle MacCoinneach," a rough voice said.

Sebilla knew it was D'Ary before she turned. "Nay.

'Tis too dangerous."

The coldness in his gaze told her the danger would not sway him. "Vardon shall not know I am of Paroseea."

"He is powerful, D'Ary. More powerful than we knew."

D'Ary's lips flared. "I can conceal my true blood. He will see me as no more than a new arrival. A simple man."

Arrogant, Sebilla thought. The question was whether his arrogance was justified. "He will sense the use of your power. He will know that one of us is there."

"Nay. He will not."

D'Ary sounded so certain that Sebilla caught back her order for him not to go. She studied him, and he cocked a brow. She realized that she might have underestimated D'Ary, misjudged the extent of his magic. "You are certain."

"Aye."

"Very well. Go then. You shall report directly to me what goes there as soon as possible."

"As my queen desires."

Somehow, the words were correct, but D'Ary managed to convey another meaning altogether. Lucan made a noise under his breath and stepped forward, but Sebilla put her hand on his arm. "Be careful," she admonished D'Ary. "Your brother—"

"Was no a match for the likes of Vardon."

"And you think you are?" Lucan asked, his tone just short of a sneer.

"Well, we shall see, won't we?" With a final nod to Sebilla, D'Ary turned and strode away.

"Insolent," Lucan muttered. "He is likely going to his death."

Sebilla sighed, thinking how easily men butted heads over who was tougher, who was more powerful. Thank the gods, a woman had long ruled Paroseea. Men were far too interested in preserving their patch of turf, real or perceived.

Though D'Ary surprised her. She stared after him. She'd rarely given him much thought, rarely seen him at all. Indeed, she realized she knew very little of him.

"Perhaps," she finally said, answering Lucan. "But, perhaps not."

Vardon watched from the shadows of the great hall, a smile rising inside him though his face revealed nothing of his feelings. The fallen laird has returned, he thought, studying Padruig MacCoinneach as he stood in the center of the hall accepting oaths of loyalty from the blind sheep of the clan overjoyed to have their laird returned to them.

How it disgusted him.

Not surprisingly, Padruig had easily retaken the castle.

Since Grigor's mysterious illness, his behavior had grown increasingly bizarre, alienating many of those once allied with him. The attack by Padruig and men from Clan de Grantham could scarcely even be called a battle, really more of a skirmish, over quickly with little bloodshed.

A shame, that.

Truly, the best part of the whole affair was the expression of shock and betrayal upon poor, pathetic Grigor's face when he realized that most of his men, including Vardon, had no intention of casting away their own futures by standing with Grigor. A single blow by Padruig had sent the man to his knees, and within less time than it took Vardon to ensure he appeared as if he welcomed Padruig's return, Grigor was dragged off to the gatehouse.

As he watched, Freya fluttered across the hall and threw herself into her brother's arms. Vardon barely repressed a sneer. The silly wench was fortunate she was a beauty as she surely possessed about as much intelligence as the butterfly she reminded him of. Mayhap less, in fact.

Jankyn, a guard Vardon occasionally played of game of dice with, pressed a cup of ale into his hand. "A fine day, is it not?" he asked with a wide grin.

"Och, that it is."

"Good to see the true laird back again."

Vardon looked around the hall, studying the faces of the gathered clan.

"Grigor was naught but a pig," Jankyn spat.

Vardon laughed and took a deep draught of ale. "True enough. I wonder what will happen to the fair Freya now."

Jankyn cocked a brow and grinned. "She's a comely lass."

"To be sure."

"Too good for the likes of us."

Too good? Vardon wanted to shout. *She should be on her knees before me, overcome with the privilege of attending to anything I desire. Anything,* he thought, eyeing her sparkling green eyes, the swell of her young body beneath her gown. Reining in the urge to smile at the thought of what things he might enjoy having the wench perform, he nodded agreement.

In his mind, he envisioned Freya stripped of her concealing garments, her hair a silken swath of red, her firm young breasts smooth and ripe, her lips parted in fear and knowledge that she had no choice but to do his bidding.

"Well, I'm off to find a lass willing to join me in a cup of celebration," Jankyn said with a wink.

Vardon didn't bother to answer as the guard lumbered off. He couldn't fathom sinking so low as to take on the servant wenches known to be available to pleasure a man. No, he deserved better.

As he watched Padruig twirl Freya in the air, her twinkling laugh drifting across the hall, he allowed himself to smile. Aye, he deserved better.

"Where is Mother?" Padruig asked his sister.

"Oh, in her chamber, no doubt," Freya responded airily. "She is forever closing herself off in there."

Efrika put a hand on his shoulder. "'Tis a fine thing to have you back, my boy." She hugged him close and said in a low tone, "Your mother, God bless her, has never been the same since Brona's death. Like a wraith she is, drifting about the castle, seldom speaking to anyone." With a quick glance at Freya, she continued, "Mairi did not even speak up when Grigor betrothed Freya to that horrid Angus Ransolm."

Freya's face paled. "Padruig, I cannot marry that beast! Please do not force me to wed him. I shall die!"

"Dinnae fash yourself. I shall send a message right away to Ransolm."

"He will want his coin returned," Efrika advised.

"Coin?"

"Aye," Freya spat. "Grigor sold me like a prize broodmare."

"I shall find it," Padruig assured her, for the first time thankful he hadn't taken Grigor's life. "Magnus," he called out.

Magnus turned from discussion with Alasdair.

"Aye, Laird?"

"See to it that food and drink are prepared for the de Granthams. I shall return anon."

Magnus nodded and set off toward the kitchens.

"Who has been seeing to the castle?" Padruig asked Freya and Efrika.

Efrika sniffed and gestured toward a woman standing at the edge of the hall. She met Padruig's gaze, then averted her eyes as if it pained her to look upon him. Padruig clenched his jaw and narrowed his eyes. "Who is she? I do not recognize the woman."

"Grigor's whore," Freya chirped.

"Her name is Ciara," Efrika added. "Despite her . . . relationship with Grigor, she has at least ensured that there was something on the table for mealtimes. Naught much else. Oh, 'tis so good you are here, Padruig."

"Has it been so terrible under Grigor's rule?"

"I have not had a new gown since he named himself laird," Freya complained.

Padruig knew that in Freya's world, that was dire, indeed. He turned questioning eyes to Efrika, who slowly nodded. "You shall find out soon enough. Our stores are low." She kicked at a mat of filthy rushes. "The servants have grown lazy as Grigor was more interested in drinking and whoring than anything else."

"When I wed, my wife shall see to things." Though he sounded confident, inside he wondered if that would, indeed, be the case. He would have to find a way to pry

Aimili from the stables to accomplish such a feat.

"Wife?" Freya's eyes widened.

"I am to wed Aimili de Grantham."

Freya blinked.

"Ah, so that is how you were able to gain the de Grantham's aid," Efrika commented.

"Just so." Padruig glanced over at the de Granthams, happily swilling ale in celebration of their easy victory. He tried to push the image of Aimili from his mind, but failed. What was he to do with the child? "Please attend to our guests. I am going to see Mother." He left the hall and slowly made his way across the bailey to a large, square tower along a nearby wall. Near the top of the curving, stone steps a corridor opened up and Padruig soon found himself standing outside a heavy wooden door.

He pounded against the wood. "Mother?"

There was no answer.

He pounded again. "Mother, 'tis Padruig!" he shouted.

When his only response was silence, he pushed on the door. It swung open to reveal a spacious solar dimly lit by a glint of afternoon sunlight.

His mother sat on a wide window seat, gazing out over the placid waters of Loch Moradeea. As his boots clunked over the old plank floor, she turned.

Padruig halted, shocked at her faded appearance. Once, his mother had been a lovely, vibrant woman, with a gentle smile and a light in her green eyes. No more. Her once brown hair held streaks of silver, her body had grown thin, and there was no welcome in her gaze.

"How dare you return?" she whispered.

He'd known this would be the hardest part of his homecoming, though until this moment he realized he'd hoped time had mellowed his mother's anger. "The clan needed me," he stated. "Freya needed me."

"Needed you?" Her lips curved in a mockery of a smile. "To cause more bloodshed, make more enemies?"

Padruig gritted his teeth. "Brona—"

His mother leapt up, her hands fisted. "How dare you utter her name? She was all that was good and you, you killed her!"

"I did not kill Brona."

"As well as."

The hell of it was he agreed with her. Still . . . he'd hoped for something, some indication that she was at least pleased her only son still lived. Gazing at her hard face, he knew there would be nothing but the same anger and bitterness that had helped send him from Castle MacCoinneach. He forced himself to unclench his jaw. "I am pleased to see you are well, Mother," he said.

She turned away.

How had this happened? Aimili wondered. She sat at a table on the dais within the great hall of Castle Mac-Coinneach, clad in a bliaut fashioned of dark green silk with soft slippers on her feet, her hair carefully brushed to fall in long tendrils around her face and down her back.

Was it only this morn she'd arrived at Castle Mac-Coinneach?

Dear Lord, she was wed to Padruig MacCoinneach, Laird of the Clan MacCoinneach. She was not sure if she should laugh or scream. Either would reveal the hysteria swirling inside her.

Her husband sat by her side on the dais, but he might as well have been sitting a world away. She thought of the innumerable times she'd fantasized about being with Padruig MacCoinneach, had envisioned him running to her across the thick grass with a loving smile and sweeping her into his strong arms. Inside, she cringed in embarrassment and regret. Be careful what you wish for, she thought, glancing at Padruig's forbidding countenance.

The only one obviously pleased with the events of the day was her father. He sat farther down the table, his conversation with a man Aimili didn't recognize punctuated with loud guffaws and calls for more drink. The fact that he was clearly happy to be rid of her only added to the ache in her belly.

"You look beautiful," Morainn said in an overly bright voice.

Aimili looked at her sister and barely managed a wan smile. She'd heard some of the whispers from the Mac-Coinneach clan folk comparing her to Morainn. "What a pity the laird did not get the comely one," was the most common. "Thank you," she said. It wasn't Morainn's fault that she was so lovely. Aimili sipped some wine and looked past Morainn to where Padruig's sister gazed at her in obvious curiosity. Aimili attempted a smile, but the girl looked away.

Beyond uncomfortable, Aimili shifted in her chair and looked out over the great hall. It was an impressive place, perhaps twice the size of the de Granthams' hall, with thick stone pillars extending up to the high timbered ceiling. Oddly, the walls were bare of decoration but for an old wall hanging so faded that Aimili couldn't make out the details. The long table at which she sat was covered with a white cloth, and they drank from silver goblets, but the fare was plain, particularly for a wedding feast. Clearly the clan had not prospered in Padruig's absence.

She was far too miserable to eat in any case. "How long must I sit here?" Aimili murmured to Morainn.

Morainn flushed. "Until, well, you know, until your husband is ready . . ."

Panic surged through Aimili and she barely managed to get her cup to her mouth without spilling wine all over the table. When she spied the glimmer of sympathy in Morainn's eyes, she nearly burst into tears.

What a travesty this all was. It barely felt real, the ceremony passing in a solemn blur, this evening interminable.

"I have had enough." Aimili lifted her chin and turned to Padruig. "My lord, I am tired."

He slowly turned as if he had just remembered her presence. Flat, silvery eyes gazed into hers. "You are free to retire."

Aimili made herself breathe past the crushing force in her chest. "And you?"

His face hardened. "There are matters I must speak on to my men yet this eve. Take your rest, my lady."

In other words, she should not await her husband. Part of her was relieved, but the other part, the tender core of her that wanted a real marriage, wanted the Padruig of her dreams and memories, was hurt and offended. She frowned at him, but became aware of the stares focused upon them. No, this was not the place to vent her feelings. Clenching her jaw, Aimili nodded and stood.

The next moments passed in a blur of motion. From the corner of her eye, she caught a glimpse of a woman swiftly approaching the dais. Her features were twisted in anger, her fists clenched.

As she neared Padruig, her gaze lit with purpose.

Aimili saw the dagger in the woman's hand and

drew her own. "Nay," she shouted, leaping to intercept the woman.

The woman shrieked and tried to stab Aimili, but Aimili jumped away in time.

"Die, you whoreson!" the woman shouted, her lips drawn back. She leapt forward to strike as Padruig jumped from his seat. Aimili grabbed the woman's wrist and at the same time thrust her own dagger upward.

For a suspended moment, Aimili stared into the woman's surprised gaze. Blood flowed from her chest, spilling over Aimili's hand. While people rushed around them, the woman slowly slid to the floor, her eyes dimming.

Strong fingers grasped her shoulders and yanked her around. Padruig's eyes glittered with anger. "What were you thinking?" he bellowed, looking between her and the woman on the floor.

Aimili wiped her hand on her bliaut. "About saving your life."

His lips were drawn so tightly they were white. "I can take care of myself. You could have been killed!"

"You are welcome, my lord," she hissed, abruptly aware that silence cloaked the hall. Every eye was on her, most filled with shock. So much for pretending to be the typical lady of the castle, Aimili thought.

"You . . ." Padruig shook his head as if he couldn't figure out what to say. "I knew Ciara might attempt something. I have been keeping a close eye on her."

"Apparently not close enough." She glanced down

at the woman's bloody form, and fought back the urge to crumple onto the floor. Aye, she was skilled with her blade, but in truth she had never had to use it to kill another human being. By the saints, she would not reveal any weakness to this grim, accusatory, ungrateful cur masquerading as her husband.

Padruig shook his head again. "Do you think you can manage to find our chamber without getting into more trouble?"

Aimili felt Morainn's hand on her shoulder. "By your leave, my lord, I shall see to my sister," she said.

"Please do."

"You—" Aimili began, but stopped when Morainn squeezed her shoulder. "Not now," her sister whispered.

Aimili realized that her legs were trembling. "My dagger."

Padruig rolled his eyes as if he were in pain. "I shall retrieve it."

Aimili let Morainn lead her away. "Ungrateful pig," she murmured to her sister.

Morainn let out a small giggle. "Not what everyone expected from the new lady of Clan MacCoinneach."

"They should be pleased I had enough sense to act."

As they passed a trio of servants huddled together, Morainn said, "One of you lead us to the laird's chamber. And we need warm water and an ewer of wine brought."

Two of the women scuttled off, the other nodding.

"This way, my lady," she said, addressing Morainn. Aimili was so overwhelmed with shock and hurt that she didn't even care that the servant showed such disrespect to her new mistress.

"Do you ken who that woman was?" Aimili asked as they crossed the bailey.

"Grigor's leman, I think."

"She would have killed Padruig."

"Do you really think so?"

Aimili let out a breath. "Was I supposed to wait to see?"

"Nay." Morainn patted her arm as they entered a spacious chamber, dismissing the servant with a wave of thanks. "Ye did the right thing, but Padruig, well . . . he is a mon."

"Sometimes I wonder if there is a warm-blooded man inside of him at all." She slumped onto the window seat, sorely tempted to give in to a bout of feeling sorry for herself.

"'Tis a fine chamber," Morainn commented.

Aimili fought off her malaise and looked at her surroundings. Morainn was right. The setting sun spilled over a wide plank floor and a big bed draped with deep blue hangings. Several trunks lined the stone walls and two chairs sat in front of a fireplace. A tapestry depicting dolphins splashing in a turquoise sea adorned one wall.

"Mayhap Padruig needs time," Morainn said. "It has only been a short while since he returned to the

Highlands, and even less since he regained his position as laird."

"Perhaps." She waved in two women carrying water and wine.

"Here," Morainn said, sticking the bowl of water next to Aimili and putting her hands in to soak. The water turned pink, and Aimili stared at it, the horror of what she'd done washing over her.

Morainn suddenly let out a shriek and jumped up onto the window seat.

Aimili looked down and spied Cai's furry muzzle peeking out from beneath the bed. She started laughing. "Morainn, be at ease. 'Tis only Cai, Padruig's pet."

"But . . . but that is not a dog."

"Nay." Aimili finished rinsing her hands and dried them on a length of cloth. *It is all right, Cai. Come to me.*

The wolf crawled out from under the bed, stood up, and shook himself before padding over.

Aimili slipped to the floor and stroked his head. *What a handsome boy you are.*

Thank you. Cai sniffed and let out a soft growl. *Are you injured?*

Nay. 'Tis another's blood. Aimili glanced up at Morainn. "Truly, he will not harm you."

Morainn slowly lowered herself to the cushioned seat where Cai rested his shaggy, gray head.

"Morainn?"

"Aye?"

Aimili lifted her gaze. "Do you think there is something wrong with me? Something . . . unlovable?"

"Nay!" Morainn sighed and rested her hand on Aimili's head. "'Tis just that you are different."

"Do you mean because of—"

"Shush." Morainn glanced around them. "'Tis best not to talk about that."

That, of course, being Aimili's ability to communicate with animals. Morainn was the only other person who knew.

"I wish Mother were alive. I dinnae ken how to guide you."

"I wish that, too." Though Aimili's memories of her mother were vague, she remembered how her mother would hold Aimili in her arms and sing to her.

Morainn's face turned pink. "I know naught of the . . . bedding."

Aimili laughed, but it wasn't a sound of mirth. "I dinnae think I need to worry about that."

"What? But . . ." Morainn's voice slowly trailed off. "Oh."

"'Tis just as well."

Morainn shivered. "No doubt."

A sharp knock at the door preceded a woman's entry. She had bright red hair, deep green eyes, and although she was shorter than Morainn and even Aimili, her presence filled the chamber. She beamed a smile in their direction.

Ever the hostess, Morainn rose smoothly to her feet.

"My lady?"

"Call me Efrika, please," the woman said.

"May we aid you?"

Efrika let out a huge sigh. "Not why I'm here. I am Padruig's cousin, God bless the stubborn addlepate."

Aimili bit her lip and shared a glance with Morainn. Cai slinked into the shadows.

Before Aimili could speak, Efrika marched over to the window seat and eyed Aimili from head to toe, tilting her head first this way and then that, as if she were inspecting a particularly dear ell of silk. "How many years have you, child?"

"I am no child," Aimili snapped before she could stop herself.

"Aimili," Morainn said.

"I am seventeen years of age."

"Oh, thank heavens. I had no idea and you, well, surely you know that you appear, well—"

Aimili took pity on her, embarrassed by her earlier outburst. "Younger than my years. Yes, I do know, though I do not like it."

Morainn giggled. "I imagine she realized that, sister."

Efrika sat down and poured herself a cup of wine. "Fine thing you did, ridding us of that dreadful woman. Little better than a whore she was, and consumed with gaining power at Grigor's side."

Aimili blinked, uncertain how to respond. "I, uh, I acted without thinking, my lady."

"Efrika. And 'tis good that you did. Else poor Padruig may well have ended up with a dagger in his back."

"He does not see it that way."

Efrika mumbled something under her breath that sounded very much like the oath the stable master used when he thought Aimili was not about. Shaking her head, Efrika turned to Aimili and patted her leg. "Since your mother isnae with us, and Mairi will be of no use, I thought to help prepare you for tonight."

"Tonight?" For a moment, Aimili had no idea what she meant, but then understanding dawned. "Oh." She reached for a cup and poured herself wine.

"Who is Mairi?" Morainn asked.

Efrika frowned. "Padruig and Freya's mother."

Anxious to avoid discussing the bedding that was not going to happen, Aimili said, "I did not see her at the feast. Is she ill?"

"Och, well, no, not precisely. 'Tis a long story and one for Padruig to tell you, but Mairi is a bit teched."

Aimili and Morainn exchanged a glance. "Has she always been that way?" Aimili asked.

"Oh, no, only since Brona died. And that is all I shall say about it. Now, dear, you must not fear the bedding. I am sure Padruig will be gentle with you even though he does not look the type."

Aimili blinked.

"Have you any idea what will happen, child?"

"I . . . I have seen animals mate, my lady." Aimili

was so embarrassed she didn't even care that Efrika had called her child.

"Hmm, well, 'tis much the same I suppose. Though," she said with a wink, "if a man is skilled, there is much more pleasure to be had. A satisfactory mating should not be rushed."

"Oh," Aimili managed to say.

"Do not be afraid of Padruig. I know his visage is fearsome, but the man inside is a good one."

"How did he come by the scars?" Morainn asked, her eyes wide. "Was it when the MacVegans—"

Efrika shook her head sharply. "'Tis not my place to say." She peered at Aimili. "Do you have any questions?"

Yes! Aimili wanted to shout. *Why does Padruig not want me? What happened to him? What happened to the man I knew? What am I to do now?* Inside, she cringed in shame, knowing her husband was avoiding their chamber, knowing that the clan was surely talking about the strange fact that Padruig had sent her off alone and yet lingered. "Nay, my lady. I thank you for your concern."

"Well, then, I shall leave you to enjoy the remainder of the evening. On the morrow, we have much to discuss."

"We do?"

"Of course. Now that you are the laird's wife, you will wish to take over the running of the castle no doubt." She sniffed. "Surely, Ciara did little on that score."

"Uh, my lady, Efrika, I really have little interest in such things."

Efrika's eyes widened. "But . . . you are the laird's lady."

"Aimili, perhaps—"

Aimili cut off Morainn with a sharp look before turning to Efrika. She felt as if she were the object of a great jest. The laird's lady. Hardly. "My work with the horses takes all of my time."

"Horses?"

"Aye. I breed and train them. 'Tis what I do."

"Well." Efrika blinked. "Well."

Aimili took pity on her obvious shock. "Padruig is aware of that. No doubt he has someone in mind to manage the castle."

"But . . . but he told Freya and me that you would see to things once you were wed."

"He did?" Anger began a slow simmer in Aimili's belly.

"Aye."

Aimili paced across the room, ignoring Morainn's look pleading her to remain calm. "He assured me that I could continue with my horses!"

"Well, perhaps he meant when you had time away from your duties as chatelaine," Efrika suggested with a bright smile.

"I will *not* spend my days counting bedsheets and making sure the cook does not use too much saffron," Aimili snapped. She started for the door, intending to confront Padruig, but Efrika's soft voice stopped her.

"Pray, do not begin your marriage in anger. Surely, you must discuss matters with Padruig but . . . 'twould be more fruitful methinks if you awaited him in bed."

Anger surged in her blood. "I am no whore, to bargain my body for the laird's favor."

Though Morainn's face blanched in shock, Efrika simply gazed at Aimili. "'Tis part of a marriage."

Aimili gritted her teeth. "Your cousin has made it very, very clear that he does not want me that way."

"Nay," Efrika gasped. "You must be mistaken."

It was all Aimili could do not to burst into tears.

"Oh, my dear, you are simply overset with the day's events." Efrika patted her shoulder. "Have a cup of wine and rest by the fire. Everything will work out, you shall see."

As Efrika sailed out, Aimili's shoulders slumped. "Damn him," she muttered.

The sympathy in Morainn's eyes made Aimili feel worse. "I am going to sleep," she announced. "This day . . ." She couldn't even think how to express how she felt. Within the span of mere hours, she'd wed the one man she'd long fantasized of, only to find a man who treated her with cool indifference. On top of that, she'd finished the evening by stabbing a would-be murderer to death, not that her husband offered up a bit of gratitude.

Morainn covered a yawn with her hand. "I am weary, too." She gave Aimili a tight hug. "It will be all right."

Aimili watched Morainn leave and sat on the

window seat staring at the partially open doorway. Would Padruig come? Part of her hoped he would and part dreaded it.

Finally, she stripped down to her chemise and crawled into the big, empty bed alone.

Chapter Five

Padruig walked into his chamber, weighted down with a bone-deep weariness that arose not from lack of sleep, but from the myriad of challenges he faced. Though he had yet to meet with the seneschal, Efrika and Alasdair both had told him they lacked the stores to survive the year. In addition, it was apparent that some of the clan viewed him with, at best, wary suspicion.

Neither of those problems posed as great a challenge as the one in this room, he thought. He had delayed as long as possible until too many curious gazes drove him from the hall.

A single candle burned atop a small table, and the remnants of a fire yet sparked in the hearth. He sank onto one of the chairs and stared toward the bed, which was near hidden in shadows. He could just make out a small form, and could hear the soft, even breathing of slumber. Cai lay at the bottom of the bed. He lifted his head at Padruig's entry, then settled back down with a grunt.

Padruig let out a sigh and poured himself a cup of

wine from the flagon he'd brought with him. What in the saints was he to do with his new bride?

Not a single idea occurred to him. At times, Aimili seemed like the child she appeared, impulsive and guileless. At other times, she seemed as old as time, steeped in mysteries no man could solve. Either way, he lacked the slightest notion of how to deal with her.

And she'd killed to save him. He could still scarcely wrap his mind around it, though her feat was the talk of the hall long after she'd retired.

A warrior wife for the laird, one clansman had called her.

A wife he would never touch. He stretched out his legs and leaned his head against the hard back of the chair. His wedding night was not exactly the one he might once have envisioned. But the man who'd once blithely tumbled a comely woman as often as possible was gone. The man who'd once thought that when he did marry, it would be to a beautiful lass with generous curves and the desire to satisfy him found that he didn't deserve such a blessing.

What could he do? The deed was done. Freya was safe.

Somehow he would work out the rest. As long as Aimili had her horses, she would be content. And he, well, he would keep busy doing what needed to be done to take care of the clan. That would have to be enough.

He stared at the flickering flame and gradually realized that he wasn't alone. "Brona," he said, as his sister's spirit settled into the opposite chair.

"'Tis good to see you back where you belong, Padruig."

"Aye. You should be happy. I came back as you asked, and Freya is safe from Angus Ransolm." As long as I can find his coin, he thought.

"You have done well, as I knew you would."

Brona looked almost solid. If Padruig let his gaze go unfocused, he could nearly pretend she sat across from him in the flesh. "You can be at peace now."

A soft smile lit her ethereal lips. "Not just yet."

"What? I defeated Grigor. Freya is safe. I will see to the good of the clan somehow."

"Ah, Padruig, 'tis not so simple." She tilted her head toward the bed. "Why do you sit here alone when you have a new bride in your bed?"

"A bride who is an innocent child." He snorted. "My penance."

"You still punish yourself."

"As well I should." He leaned forward. "I can still remember that day as if it were today. My arrogant refusal to heed your warning that all was not right with Symund yielded disaster."

"Mayhap there is more to it than that."

He frowned. "Brona, I was there. I know Symund killed you and Malcolm both. Many more of our people died that day because I was too filled with my own sense of superiority to see Symund for who he was."

"Och, Padruig, think about that day. 'Tis not all what it seems." She gave him a sad look and began to dim.

"Brona, wait! What do you mean?"

She faded into nothing.

What could she mean? he wondered. As much as he hated thinking back to that fateful day, he forced his mind back. It had been late afternoon when Brona's maid had sought him out, told him that her mistress had snuck out of the castle earlier to be alone with Malcolm and had not returned. Padruig had been furious with Brona. He'd forbidden her to be with Malcolm, and had told her that he intended to accept Symund's suit. Not only had he stupidly believed Symund the better man, but he'd thought that the marriage would cement an alliance with the Clan MacVegan.

He'd found Symund standing over Brona's bloody body, a dagger in his hand. What happened after that remained a blur of anguish and fighting. He knew he'd slain Symund at once and when the troop of MacVegans arrived, many more.

The one thing that had always bothered him was why the MacVegans had appeared just then. However, Symund had been a favorite of the laird's, so perhaps his absence had been noted much as Brona's had.

Padruig shook his head, the memories swirling too quickly to catch hold of. He'd been lucky to survive, though at the time he'd not seen it that way. Idly, he traced a scar on his cheek.

Though he'd forgotten many things about that day, he could never forget the look on his mother's face when they'd brought Brona's body home. That day, whatever love she'd held for Padruig turned to hate.

And he knew he'd earned every bit of it.

Aimili's eyes flashed open. Her heart raced, her skin tingled, and the feeling that something frightening and malevolent lurked nearby choked her. Where was she? She forced herself to take a deep breath.

Gradually, she remembered that she lay in a strange bed, in a strange chamber, with a wolf lightly snoring from the bottom of the bed. Some weak glimmers of early light drifted through the latched window shutters, but Aimili could tell it was not even full dawn yet. She rose on one arm and scanned the chamber, finding Padruig half-covered by a blanket and lying on the floor in front of the now dead fire.

For a moment, her breath hitched with suspicion. Could the feelings she sensed be from him? No, she thought, she could not believe that.

Still, she stared at him, more stunned than she'd thought she'd be at the fact that not only had he not wished to consummate the marriage, but he could not even bear to share a bed. Her heart splintered even as she admonished herself for being a fool.

In slumber, Padruig looked different, softer, the dim light blurring the scars on his face. She could almost envision him opening his eyes, and smiling at her the way she'd imagined so many times.

A young girl's dream, spun of naught but moonbeams and stardust. Truth was, she was alone but for her horses, and likely ever would be.

She glanced at the shutters, tempted to sneak out to the stables, but realized it was too early for a new bride to be seen leaving her wedding bed. The clan already had much to talk about their new lady, she thought, a twinge of resentment winding through her at the memory of Padruig's reaction to her defending him.

She flopped back onto the pillow and stared at the beamed ceiling overhead.

How had she ended up thus? True, she'd never been the biddable lass that Morainn was, but was that enough to deserve a life bereft of warmth and affection but from animal friends? Apparently it was.

How she yearned for it to be different. No one knew, not even Morainn, how Aimili longed for a babe. No one would believe it, considering such a desire far too "womanly" for one such as Aimili. Before she could catch herself, a tear leaked from her eye and trickled down her cheek. She'd always believed that even if no one else understood her, even if no one else truly loved her, it would be all right if she had a child. One perfect child whom she could lavish affection on, and who would return such affection and love.

That was not going to happen now. Padruig's position on the floor made it abundantly clear that her heart's desire was as much a chimera as her girlish dreams of her husband.

She turned her face into the pillow and silently wept.

Sebilla walked slowly along the wide marble road, soaking up the quiet of early morning. The pink sun was no more than a pale shimmer in the sky, and the air was fresh and warm. From the sides of the pathway rose bright gold columns carved with the symbol of Paroseea, a dolphin within a swirling Celtic pattern. Between the columns, at widely spaced intervals, colorful mosaics paved the way to broad homes made of pale-colored stone.

As she continued on, she caught the faint tang of the sea and decided to watch the sun rise over the water. A well-trodden path led to the pink beach, a mild breeze blowing the slight scent of salt to her nose. With a sigh, she settled onto a flat rock and simply watched the sky lighten.

Offshore, a dolphin suddenly leapt from the water, its blue skin melding with the water. Sebilla laughed as the dolphin let out a happy screech and splashed down.

How peaceful it is, she thought. *How beautiful.*

How threatened. She shivered, contemplating what would happen if Vardon exposed them. The humans of the world would look upon Paroseea as possessing treasures to be plundered, people to be hated and feared. Of course, they could defeat attackers, but at what cost?

"Queen Sebilla?" a voice asked.

For a moment, Sebilla didn't acknowledge Arailt's voice. From his tone, he was not interrupting her with good news. Reluctantly, she shifted her gaze from the blue dolphins cavorting in the water and turned to Arailt. "Yes? Have you found anything to aid us?"

Arailt shook his head. "Not yet, my lady, but I am still looking. I thought to engage my daughter Vanasia's aid if that is acceptable to you. She is quite familiar with the archives."

She started to tell Arailt just how familiar his daughter was, but held back. Vanasia was distraught enough over her unwitting involvement in Vardon's escape. Her father's embarrassment would only unnecessarily worsen the matter. "That is fine, Arailt. It is imperative that we find a way to harness Vardon and return him where he belongs."

"Or vanquish him completely."

"Kill him, you mean."

"Aye."

Sebilla sighed. "I fear that may end up being the only solution open to us."

"We will find a way, my queen."

"I hope so."

"May I escort you to the palace?" Arailt stood a little straighter, and puffed out his flat chest. Though he was neither a tall nor particularly robust man, over his many years of life Arailt had developed a regalness about him, an appearance that fit his character and scholarly ways.

"No thank you, friend. I think I shall enjoy the tranquility of the morn a while longer."

Arailt bowed and shuffled off.

Sebilla turned back to gaze over the water, but found her ability to simply enjoy the sight and smell of her beloved land was gone in the light of Vardon's threat. She rose and made her way back to the marble pathway and on to her palace, grateful that it was still so early she met no one on her way. Everyone knew Vardon had escaped, and everyone knew he was a threat, though few knew the particulars.

As she walked into her rooms, she wondered how D'Ary fared. She sent up a prayer to the mother goddess that his ability to conceal his true self was as good as he apparently believed it to be.

The waiting, the not knowing, was driving her mad with frustration. She knew if there was an answer in the archives, Arailt would find it, but it was terrible to wait while she had no idea what Vardon was up to, particularly now that the true laird had returned.

Once more, she set out her scrying bowl, this time adding a scattering of moonstone fragments to the water.

As she waited for the water to heat and clear, she sat on her marble terrace and closed her eyes, focusing on breathing in the fragrant scent of gardenia blossoms, opening her ears to the sounds of birdsong and the gentle gurgle of the water, willing her spirit to calm.

When she opened her eyes, the water in the bowl appeared clear and endlessly deep.

"Goddess, aid me," she whispered. "Aid me."

Slowly, a picture took form beneath the water. Sebilla sucked in a breath as she saw the same woman she'd glimpsed before. Now, she was no longer in the forest, but in a large stone chamber. As the image sharpened, Sebilla realized several things.

The chamber lay within Castle MacCoinneach, yet close to Paroseea itself.

The woman fairly glowed with the power of the fey.

She was the laird's new bride.

Sebilla felt as if she'd fallen into the depths of the water, taken far from her palace terrace. She didn't fight the feeling, but embraced it, searching for answers. *Who is she?* Sebilla silently asked. *Who is she?*

Aimili MacCoinneach is part of the key, an other-worldly voice answered. *Give her the dagger.*

Sebilla jerked back, stunned at the last direction. Give a *human* the precious dagger of Artemis? A fey human, she reminded herself. But still . . . every part of her screamed in protest. She could not possibly let such a powerful object leave Paroseea, leave *her*.

The goddess has spoken, her inner voice said.

With shaking hands, Sebilla walked into her inner chamber and retrieved the carved, gold box holding the dagger. She sat on her bed and took it into her hand, immediately feeling its surge of power. How could she give such a powerful object to another? And not just another, but a mere girl of the mortal realm.

The dagger had been in possession of the ruler of Paroseea for as long as she could remember, centuries at least. The blade was sharp and straight, the hilt intricately carved with dolphins, their eyes set with stones that changed color in the light. No one knew for certain who had crafted it.

Some said he was a powerful druid who harnessed all the power of nature to rest within the blade. Others believed the gods themselves had created it, gifting it to Paroseea as a mark of favor.

It held magic, that much was certain.

She carefully put the dagger away, knowing she had no choice. If putting the dagger into the hands of the girl called Aimili would help her defeat Vardon, then so be it.

Padruig blinked his eyes open, noting the gray of the

early morning light filtering in around the window shutters. By the saints, his neck felt as stiff as . . . damn, he thought, looking down at the obvious bulge in his braies. He moved his head from side to side, wondering why he felt so uncomfortable.

And then he remembered.

He turned toward the bed and saw Aimili staring back at him. Her presence struck him like a bolt to the chest and for a moment he simply forgot to breathe. Her hair was in wavy disarray around her face, her eyes huge dark wells in her flawless face. In the faint light, he could see the curve of her breasts beneath her thin chemise.

Silence thickened between them as they stared at each other. Padruig swallowed with far more effort than he wished and said, "Good morn." He winced inside at the gruff sound of his voice and the flash of hurt in Aimili's eyes.

No, he said to himself, *this way is for the best*. In time she would accustom herself to her role at Castle Mac-Coinneach.

And what of her role as your wife? his inner voice taunted. He ignored it and rose to his feet, stretching the crick in his back. "Did you sleep well?"

"Aye." She looked away from him, and patted Cai, who let out a contented snuffle.

Padruig felt like a green lad of ten summers. What was he to do? *Get the hell out of the chamber*, he thought, *before she realizes your rod has other ideas*. He rose and quickly splashed some water on his face, intent on doing just that, then abruptly realized that he could not go just yet.

Just be plain with the lass, he told himself. *'Tis best to begin as you intend to go on.* He removed his wedding tunic and carefully hung it on a hook, then drew off his undershirt. At a soft sound from the bed, he forced himself to turn.

Aimili's gaze had grown even wider.

"'Tis not a pretty man you've wed," he said. Along with the jagged scar on his back, he sported several more on his chest and back.

"Those must have hurt."

"Aye. A bit." Like his skin was on fire, but he was not about to admit the same to her. "Cai has taken a liking to you," he said, pointing to the wolf.

"I am usually good with animals."

Padruig cast about for something else to say, but ran out of ideas. "Aimili, 'tis important for the clan to believe they have a strong leader, a leader with a loyal helpmate at his side."

"I would think none would question my loyalty after last eve."

He scowled, having forgotten the incident. "You shall not endanger yourself like that again."

She scowled back at him, and lifted her chin in obvious defiance.

It was all he could do not to launch himself at the

bed, so arousing was the sight.

Say it plainly, he chided himself. "When I say loyal, I also mean . . ." Damn, he could feel a flush steal up his cheeks. "Consummated," he spit out.

"I am no the one who chose to sleep on the floor."

For a moment, he just stared at her. What was she saying? That she would welcome his presence in her bed? Nay, surely not. The lass was innocent. She was too kindhearted to tell him to take his ease elsewhere. That had to be it. "I need the sheet, lass."

"What?"

God in heaven, why was she making this so difficult? "I need to mark the sheet so that none questions the marriage."

With a puzzled look on her face, Aimili slid out of bed and wrapped her arms around her. The air in the chamber had cooled, and, God save him, Padruig could clearly see the points of her nipples against her chemise. He rumpled up the bedcovers, and made a shallow cut on his forearm. Blood dripped onto the sheet, and Cai sprang off as if the whole business was an affront to him.

"There," Padruig said, studying the stain. "'Tis done." He turned to gaze at Aimili and found her watching him in bewilderment.

"Why do you do this?"

"I explained. Everyone will assume I have taken you."

"Taken me."

"Aye. Mated."

"Oh." Aimili's voice was no more than a whisper. "But you did not."

Padruig frowned. "Of course not. I'd not subject such a tender young lass to such."

"I see."

"Now, will you come and break the fast with me, or would you rather rest a while?" He strapped on his sword. "I've duties to see to."

"I think I shall stay in here for a bit. Could you send someone up to tend the fire, and perhaps bring some warm water?"

Padruig snapped his fingers. "Aye, a good thought. I shall have a bath sent up. The clan will understand that you might be in need of such this morn." He smiled at her, relieved beyond measure to put the whole matter of the bedding behind them. He had much more important things to see to, beginning with locating Angus Ransolm's payment for Freya.

"Thank you."

With a final nod, Padruig left.

After he went, Aimili slumped down into a chair, rubbed her arms, and stared unseeing at the closed door. In all of her wildest dreams, she could not have imagined a wedding morn like this. She was freezing, her husband had no interest whatsoever in touching her, and her only sleeping companion was to be a wolf.

Stop feeling sorry for yourself, she told herself sternly.

You've a fine chamber to sleep in, ample food and drink, and soon your horses. If it is not the life you envisioned, then it is up to you to make the best of it.

A short knock preceded the arrival of an army of servants. At the rear came Morainn, a bright and patently false smile on her face. "Good morn," she said in an equally bright voice.

Cai took the opportunity to pad out of the chamber.

"Good morn, sister," Aimili said, eyeing the wooden tub some burly grooms hauled in. Within a few moments, a fire burned, and steam rose from the tub, with soap and drying cloths set on the table before the fire. Another servant bustled in with a flagon and cups, along with a platter holding bread and cheese.

"Is there aught else we can do for your comfort, Mistress?" an older woman asked.

Aimili was so surprised to be addressed so that for a moment she didn't answer. "I . . . no, this is fine. Thank you."

They trooped out but for Morainn, who came to rest a hand on Aimili's shoulder. "How do you fare?"

"Fine."

"Come, let me help you into the bath."

"I can tend myself, Morainn. I am not an invalid." Disgusted, she tossed off her chemise and stepped into the water.

"Here," Morainn said, pressing a cup of wine into her hand.

Aimili caught her eye. "Why are you being so attentive?"

"Well, I . . ." Her voice trailed off, and then she whispered, "Was it terrible?"

"It?"

"You know. He is so fierce. And such a big man." She shivered. "I worried for you."

Aimili took a long sip of wine. She understood Padruig's reason for wanting his clan to believe the marriage had been consummated, but surely she could tell the truth to Morainn. "Nothing happened. I told you, he does not want me that way."

"But, 'tis not natural. He is a man. Why would he not want to lie with you?"

"I dinnae ken, not exactly." She trailed her fingers through the warm water, more disheartened by the moment. "He sees me as a child."

"Well, perhaps 'tis for the best that you are spared his . . . attentions."

"Perhaps."

"As I said, the harvest was poor," the seneschal, Alard, told Padruig for perhaps the sixth or seventh time.

Padruig was fast losing patience with the man, no

matter how fawning and earnest his manner. "Because not enough seed was purchased."

Alard's throat worked. "Aye, Laird."

"'Tis your responsibility."

"Aye, Laird, but Grigor would not provide me with sufficient coin. I did the best I could."

"Not enough." Padruig looked down at the accounting of what stores the castle possessed. The lack of grain was bad enough, but the number of sheep was down by almost half, as well, and the number of cattle so low to be nearly nonexistent. An unknown disease, according to Alard.

The simple fact was that there was not enough to feed the clan through the winter. "Where is this coin?"

"The Lair—uh, Grigor kept it locked in a trunk in his chamber, I believe."

Padruig gave the man a narrow look. Alard had been at Castle MacCoinneach for a long time, but not in as high a position as seneschal. Padruig didn't really know the man, and wasn't sure whether he trusted him or not. "Are you kin to Grigor?"

Alard looked as if he wanted to flee. "Aye, Laird. He is my brother."

"I see."

"Please, Laird, do not paint me with the same brush. 'Tis true our relationship is why I hold my position, but I have truly tried. I have not agreed with Grigor's spending. Ask anyone."

"What did he spend coin on?"

Alard's nose wrinkled. "Trinkets for his whores. Fine garments for himself. Drink."

"You are the seneschal. At least for the moment," Padruig added. "What do you propose we do?"

"I . . . uh, well, we must determine how much coin remains, Laird. I offer to speak to Grigor myself if you wish. Perhaps we could, I could travel to Inverness to purchase additional foodstuffs to see us through until spring."

"We shall both talk to Grigor. After I search his chamber."

"Very good, Laird. I am at your disposal."

"You may leave the accounts."

Alard bowed and began backing out of the room, then suddenly stopped. "Laird, some of the villagers are here to see you."

Though he'd paid little heed to the village on his way to Castle MacCoinneach, Padruig had little doubt that the villagers had fared even more poorly under Grigor's control. "Tell them I will see them in the hall anon."

"Aye, Laird. And if you require aught else—"

Padruig raised his hand. "You may be sure that I shall send for you, Alard." He looked down at the accounts and frowned. Pray God he found enough coin remaining or they were all in peril.

He spent the next three hours listening to a litany of complaints from villagers clearly distraught and beaten down by the strictures and failures of Grigor's rule. He'd restricted their ability to cultivate plots for their own sustenance. Many of their homes were in need of repair. It was the same story over and over. His people needed help desperately.

He vowed to see it done, but the how of it remained a question.

Finally, he sat alone in the solar, sipping a cup of ale and pondering his next move. Of his bride, there'd been no sign. Presumably, she was in the stables, readying things for her precious horses.

When he thought back to waking up in his old chamber with Aimili looking sleep tousled and far too tempting, he cringed inside. He'd handled the situation as best he could, he told himself. When he thought of actually bedding the lass, which was far too often for his peace of mind, the thought of touching all of that youthful innocence seemed so very wrong, so wicked.

And yet, she was his wife. What a damnable state of affairs.

Aimili marched to the stables, determined to seize what she could salvage of her own life. She ignored the curious stares she received along the way, and held her head high. When she entered the dimly lit stables, she found her way blocked by a man she'd never seen before.

He was, of all things, stroking Loki on his head, and the blasted beast actually seemed to be enjoying it.

"Who are you?" she asked.

"I am called D'Ary, my lady," he answered with a smile.

Aimili looked between the man and Loki, growing suspicious. This man did not appear a mere stable hand. He was tall, well muscled, with handsome, sculpted features and warm amber eyes. Despite his plain garments, he held himself as if he were a warrior. And, most surprising of all, Loki apparently liked him. "What do you do here?"

"Anything the stable master requires," he answered with a shrug. "Though I hope to have the chance to aid you in your work. I have heard that you have a rare talent with the horses."

"Have you been here long?"

"Nay."

The stable master, Hugo, saw them and strode down the aisle of the stable with a grin. "Ah, so you have met D'Ary, my lady. Good."

"Aye. He was just explaining to me where he hailed from." Aimili rocked back on her heels and gave D'Ary a smile.

"Far away, my lady. I fear I am a bit of a wanderer."

"Have you experience training horses?"

"Aye."

"Lady Aimili is moving several more horses to Castle MacCoinneach," the stable master told him. "Fine steeds, to hear of it."

"That they are," Aimili assured him. "Twelve mares, three of whom are in foal; three stallions, including Loki here; and five young horses I have in training."

D'Ary gave a low whistle. "'Tis a fair amount of work."

Aimili shrugged. "I am used to it."

"I thought perhaps D'Ary here could be of help to you, my lady," the stable master said. "The beasts respond well to 'im."

"'Twould be my pleasure."

Oddly, Aimili found herself looking to Loki for guidance. *What think you?*

Take the man's aid. He is a good one.

Fine praise, indeed, coming from you.

Just so. Apparently, disinclined to comment further, Loki turned and bent down to snuffle some leftover pieces of hay.

"Very well," she said. "We shall give it a try."

D'Ary gestured toward Loki. "Would you like me to tack him up?"

"Not today. I thought to give him a few days to grow accustomed to his new home. Loki has been a very difficult horse to handle."

"I saw the marks on his flanks."

"Aye." Aimili scowled. "Courtesy of Angus Ransolm. Loki has not recovered from that mistreatment."

Mayhap I just do not wish to be a beast of burden to you humans again.

Hardly that. Most of us highly value our horses. And what else shall you do?

Live free.

That wouldn't last long. You know that. Besides, here you have food and shelter and you are not in danger from any predators. 'Tis not such a bad bargain.

I could use a bit more grain.

Even in her mind, Loki sounded so disgruntled that Aimili had to bite back a smile. She gazed up at D'Ary, who regarded her with a very odd expression. She coughed, and looked down. "Perhaps tomorrow I shall work with Loki, but until my other horses arrive, I've little need for your aid."

"I have enough to keep him busy," Hugo said with a chuckle. "Come, D'Ary."

Aimili watched the men walk away, wondering just whom she'd taken on as her helper. Far away, he'd said, when she'd questioned him of his homeland. And it was almost as if . . . no, she told herself. That was absurd. No one had ever guessed that she could communicate with animals.

She shook her head and walked to Mist's stall, opening the door to give the horse an apple. The horse nuzzled her hand, then contentedly munched the sweet fruit.

"That is my good girl," Aimili said as she brushed Mist's velvety coat. "Today, we are just going for a ride."

Outside of the castle, Aimili thought. Beyond the walls that seemed to bear down upon her with every passing hour. *It will be all right once you are riding across the countryside, she told herself. It is not the first time you've sought solace in the outdoors.*

And based on the events of this morn, it would be far from the last.

Aimili quickly mounted Mist and rode out of the gatehouse with a wave to the guards. Though one looked shocked and started to yell something, Aimili pressed Mist into a canter and left him behind.

She let out a breath, the tension gripping her shoulders for the last day and a half slowly easing away as she rode over thick green grass. Loch Moradeea lay behind her, its deep blue waters shimmering in the sunlight. She rode along the edge of the forest, breathing in the scents of crushed leaves and hints of heather. At the sight of a small herd of red deer, she pulled Mist up just to watch the little family make their way deeper into the trees.

Aimili and Mist meandered along, eventually circling around to head back to the castle. A part of Aimili wished she could simply keep riding, but she knew how impossible that would be. Not that Padruig would come after her, she thought with a grimace.

She patted Mist on the withers. "Thank you, girl."

My pleasure. Do you feel better?

Aye.

They finished the ride in silence. As Aimili neared the castle, her enjoyment of the day slowly gave way to foreboding. With each step closer to the castle, the feeling deepened, clogging her throat and tightening her chest.

You feel it, too, Mist said.

Aimili shivered. Aye.

There is evil here.

I know, but I cannot tell from what or whom it hails.

Nor can I, but I know one thing.

What?

It is growing stronger.

Aye.

Be careful, Aimili. Very careful whom you trust in this place.

I shall.

Which left no one at all, Aimili thought.

At the gatehouse, she saw a guard shout and point to her. When she entered the bailey and dismounted, she found Padruig waiting for her. Behind him stood her father and brothers, each with identical expressions of disappointment in their eyes.

Padruig stood with arms crossed, a terrible scowl on his face and fire in his eyes. "Do not *ever* do that again," he bellowed.

She handed Mist off to a groom. "Do what?"

She hadn't thought it possible, but Padruig's scowl grew harsher. "Go outside the castle walls without guards.

Without telling anyone your destination. Without asking permission!" he finished.

At the last, Aimili's chin came up. "You jest," she snapped. "I am no prisoner to be treated such."

"Nay, you are the wife of the Laird of Clan Mac-Coinneach. Ye are no longer free to play the reckless child."

Child. By the saints, how she *hated* that word. "I will not be caged," she spat. "Not by *anyone.* Not even my"—she paused to sneer—"husband."

He took a step toward her and narrowed his gaze. "You shall do as I say. And that does not include running off without a suitable guard."

Aimili gritted her teeth. "I shall do as I please."

"Nay." Something in Padruig's fierce gaze gave her pause. "You do wish your horses delivered to Castle MacCoinneach, do you not?"

"You bastard," she hissed. "You promised me my horses."

A thin smile crossed his lips. "Not exactly."

Rage ripped through her, stripping her of speech.

"A guard, Aimili, or you shall remain within the castle walls." He leaned toward her. "There is much to do here. Mayhap you could work on your embroidery skills. As you have no doubt noticed, we are in dire need of tapestries for the great hall."

She closed the distance between them, furious beyond reason. "I curse the day I was foolish enough to marry you," she spat.

His expression showed no reaction at all. "That makes two of us," he said softly, then turned and stalked off.

"Lass, ye cannot continue to behave this way," her father said. "You be a lady of your own castle now."

"If that means I have forfeited my freedom, I want no part of it."

"'Tis too late."

Aimili opened her mouth to dispute him, but realized she would do naught but further disappoint her father, who would likely not believe her story of her wedding night anyway.

"We depart." Her father stepped forward and laid a hand on her shoulder. "Try, Aimili."

Try to be someone she wasn't, he meant. Aimili just gazed back at him, until her father sighed and signaled to a waiting groom.

Morainn enfolded Aimili in a big hug, but Aimili didn't feel the warmth. She felt as if she had turned into a cold stone that nothing could reach. "Be well, Aimili," Morainn whispered. "Everything will be all right, you shall see."

Aimili could tell from the tone of her sister's voice that Morainn didn't believe her words any more than Aimili did. "Make sure that Father sends my horses as soon as possible. Then I will be all right."

"I shall." Morainn pulled back and Aimili saw the tears in her eyes.

"Morainn," their father called. "We must be away."

"May God keep you," Morainn said.

"And you, sister."

Aimili stood in the bailey and watched her family ride away. Only Morainn turned back as they crested a rise and lifted a hand in farewell.

Chapter Six

Padruig marched straight to the training ground, wanting nothing but to smash something, anything. For the next hour, he traded blows with Magnus, their swords clanging as they leapt and feinted across the training ground. As time wore on, Padruig felt a strange sort of peace settle over him. No matter the condition of the castle, the ever-perplexing problem of his unruly wife and the eddies of distrust whirling amongst the clan, here at least he knew his value and his place.

Finally, Magnus held up a hand and put his sword down. Sweat ran down his face, and he wiped it away with the sleeve of his tunic. "Enough."

"Tired?"

"Only of serving as an outlet for your frustration with your bride, though you finally provide me with a challenge."

Padruig sheathed his sword with a grunt. "I could have beaten you at any time, as well you know. But you have improved somewhat." He looked around for other possible opponents, but the other men all appeared conveniently busy.

"What now, Laird?"

"I need to search Grigor's chamber. I have sent a messenger to Angus Ransolm, but the man will not accept the loss of Freya without return of his coin."

"Damn Grigor to hell for thinking to condemn sweet Freya to such a man."

Padruig started at the vehemence in Magnus's voice. Could it be that his friend had a care for Freya? No, Padruig told himself. *Freya is but fifteen years of age and Magnus at least a score and five.*

No more than the difference between you and Aimili, his inner voice taunted.

Aye, he thought. *And that is one of the reasons why Aimili shall sleep alone.*

"Would you like aid?" Magnus asked.

"Of course." Padruig started walking toward a large square tower that loomed from the far left corner of the curtain wall. He led the way up winding steps until he and Magnus emerged onto a wide stone landing. An arched doorway led to the interior chamber once possessed by Padruig's father and claimed by Grigor.

Padruig had never cared overmuch for the chamber. It was well protected, true, but at the cost of open air and the views from his own chamber.

Magnus whistled as he walked into the chamber. "Grigor fashioned a comfortable lair for himself."

"Aye, so it would appear. Though the hall has been nearly stripped." Padruig looked around, disgust roiling in his belly. Thick tapestries lined the walls and covered the wooden floor. Heavy, woolen hangings encircled the bed, which was piled high with fur pelts. A variety of trunks and cupboards sat against the walls.

Magnus picked up a bedcover made of pine marten. "Nice," he commented.

Padruig thought of his chilly spot on the floor of his chamber and slung the fur over his shoulder. "Check the trunks," he said. "Surely he hid away the coin somewhere in here."

There were seven in all, six of which were unlocked and held various items of clothing. Padruig and Magnus dug beneath the garments, but found nothing. Padruig took the hilt of his dagger and broke the lock on the last trunk.

"Pray God this is it," he muttered as he opened the lid.

It was empty.

"Filthy whoreson," Magnus swore. "Must have hidden it elsewhere."

"Aye. Which means I am off to talk to Grigor next. We need coin, and not just for Freya's sake."

"I ken. What of the de Granthams? Surely, they would—"

"Nay," Padruig snapped. "I am the laird. 'Tis my responsibility to see to the clan."

"Ye cannae make silk out of naught."

"I will find a way."

"My lady?" a female voice asked.

Aimili turned from brushing Mist and saw a young girl staring at her with round, blue eyes. She wore a simple, undyed woolen bliaut, her light brown hair woven in a single plait. "Aye?"

"The lady Efrika asked me to find you. She wishes to speak with you."

Before she could stop it, Aimili closed her eyes and let out a soft groan of dismay. No doubt to discuss her responsibilities as the laird's wife, she thought, stifling another groan. "Where may I find her?"

"She is in the great hall with Lady Freya."

"Tell her I shall be there anon."

The girl nodded.

"Thank you . . ." Aimili realized she had no idea of the girl's name.

"Kenna," she said with a bright smile.

"Thank you, Kenna." Aimili turned back to brushing Mist, running the soft bristles over her velvety coat until it shone.

Your husband was worried for you.

Aimili snorted. *Worried that I was not here under his thumb. That I was not busy remaking myself into the lady*

136

of the castle.

Surely, he will come to understand that you are special.

Special. I thank you, dear friend, but I fear the true description is "unusual." No one has ever accepted that. Why should Padruig be any different?

I hope that he will be. I want to see you happy.

I am happy as long as I have you and the other horses to work with. That is all I need. All I have ever needed.

When you were a child, true, but now you are a woman grown.

You are the only one who thinks that.

Mist snuffled her shoulder. *I am not sure about that. Sometimes, the way Padruig looks at you is not a man gazing at a child.*

The sun must have been in your eyes. He of all people has made it crystal clear that he thinks me no more than a reckless bairn.

Mmm. Perhaps.

I must go. Efrika awaits, no doubt to try to entangle me in the management of the castle. She gave Mist a last pat, latched her stall, and walked straight into D'Ary.

He caught her by the shoulders, and Aimili felt a strange tingling flow down her arms. She flashed her gaze to his, and stepped back, confused.

For a moment, she thought he knew what she'd felt, but then his gaze lightened. "My lady, I thought to offer my services the next time you wish to ride. It shall be my pleasure and honor to accompany you."

Aimili flushed, realizing that he along with much of the castle no doubt heard Padruig and her father chastise her. "I need no guard, despite what Padruig may say."

"Then think of me as a friend." His voice dropped. "'Twill make it easier for you to venture out."

She considered his offer. As much as it infuriated her to admit it, Padruig had a point. Though it was little more than a pretense, in the clan's eyes she was the laird's wife. Were she to be captured or injured, their honor would demand retribution. "Very well," she grumbled. "Have you any skill with a sword?"

D'Ary smiled. "Aye, a bit. Enough to see to your safety, I think."

"I am not unskilled myself."

His smile widened. "Och, well then, we have naught to fear."

"Thank you, D'Ary."

"As I said, 'tis my honor and pleasure."

She nodded and left the stable. As she walked across the bailey to the hall, she wondered about D'Ary. Had she really felt a tingle when he touched her? Why? He was a very handsome man, but he didn't interest her even if she were not wed. It must have just been something in the air, she decided. Maybe a storm was on the way.

A shout drew her attention, and she paused to watch the falconer carefully transfer a hawk from his wrist to one of the low stone blocks standing outside the mews. The bird was beautiful, its round black eyes shifting back and forth over its surroundings, gleaming with intelligence. Though Aimili rarely hunted, she admired the hawk's physical beauty and ability.

The hawk fixed its gaze on her.

Be at ease, little friend.

The unblinking gaze didn't waver.

"'Tis a shame," a woman's voice said in a hushed tone. "The laird was once a mon any woman would gladly take to bed."

Aimili inched around the mews and spied a group of laundresses pounding out bedsheets.

One of them giggled. "You would know all about that, Beatha."

"Aye, that I would."

The woman speaking was plump, with big breasts swelling above the edge of her bliaut. She let out a hearty laugh. "The laird lay between my thighs on many a wondrous occasion. But now——"

"Those scars," another woman said.

"Aye, but 'tis more." Aimili saw Beatha shiver. "'Tis something dark inside him. Hard. I would be afraid to lie with him now."

"He is wed, Beatha."

Beatha crossed herself. "Och, the poor lass."

"I wager the lady can take care of herself. Did you not see her take down that slut, Ciara?"

"The marriage bed is different. She has no choice but to submit to him, the poor thing. Pray he is not too harsh with her. She is such a spare lass."

Aimili looked down at the front of her tunic and suppressed a sigh. She did not possess the ample breasts of Beatha, no question.

"You would not deny him, Beatha," one of the women scoffed.

"Aye, I would. He frightens me the way he looks so grim. And I saw the sheet. 'Twas soaked with blood."

Aimili almost started forward at that, but held herself back. She would not explain to a laundress clearly seeking attention.

"Beatha, enough. You talk of our laird."

"Hmph."

Before she heard any more, Aimili sidled away, her thoughts more troubled than ever. Despite the woman's exaggeration of the blood, Aimili sensed an element of truth in the rest of her speech.

Whom had she married? Not the tender, golden man of her dreams, that was certain. A man hardened by tragedy, or something more?

Something dark, Beatha had said.

Like in Aimili's dreams.

"Tell me where the coin is and I shall do no more

than banish you," Padruig said to Grigor.

Grigor glared at him and spat onto the dirt floor. "I deserve naught but your thanks."

"Oh?"

"Aye. You abandoned the clan."

"The clan had accepted Alasdair as laird."

"That weak old man?"

"A man of honor and good judgment."

"It was I who kept the clan together, I who kept the castle from being taken by the MacVegans."

"I was not aware that they had attacked," Padruig said dryly, crossing his arms.

"They would have if a strong man was not laird."

"The coin, Grigor."

"Why should I tell you? You've imprisoned me and killed my woman."

"Your whore tried to kill me."

"A shame your lady is quick-witted."

One of the guards threw Grigor up against the stone wall. "Laird, leave him to us. We'll get the answers you seek."

"There are still those in the clan loyal to me," Grigor insisted. "You'll not win their favor by beating their laird."

"I am the only laird."

The guard slipped a dagger into his palm. "I'll be more than happy to shut him up, Laird."

"Hold," Padruig told him. He looked at Grigor.

"Because of your incompetence, the clan's survival is in peril. The storage vaults are not filled, there are too few animals to be slaughtered, and the hall is barren while your chamber is filled with luxuries. I know you received coin from Angus Ransolm. Where is it?"

"I'll tell you." Grigor smiled. "If you can beat me on the field."

Padruig laughed. "If? You are a fool."

The guard shook his head. "Why would the laird bother?"

"To regain some of the respect he lost when he nearly destroyed the clan, then abandoned them like a cowardly dog." Grigor gave Padruig a smug look. "Surely, you know that not all are witless enough to trust in you. You have already betrayed the clan once."

Padruig stared at Grigor, thinking. Selfish whoreson the man may be, but he had a point. Padruig did know that not every member of the clan thought him skilled enough to lead them well.

"When I win, you will tell me where you have hidden the coin. All of it."

"If you win, I shall. And if I win—"

"In that very unlikely event, you will be provided supplies and escorted from our lands without harm."

"Not much of a bargain for me," Grigor said.

"You are not in a position to bargain. 'Tis all I will offer."

"Very well. I accept."

"Aimili, there you are!" Efrika called out as Aimili walked into the great hall,

"Good day, Lady Efrika and Lady Freya," Aimili said as she sat.

"Just Efrika and Freya, dear," Efrika said with a smile.

"Have you been riding?" Freya asked.

"Aye."

Freya wrinkled her nose and smoothed out the pale blue silk of her bliaut. "I do not care much for horses. Such big, dirty things. And you never know when they are going to see something that scares them and forget they have a rider on their back."

"I . . ." Aimili was so confounded she wasn't sure what to say.

"Freya took a bad fall a while back," Efrika told her. "She has been afraid of horses ever since."

"'Tis a shameful thing, I know, but I cannae help it," Freya added.

"I would be happy to teach you how to ride better so that you reduce your chance of falling," Aimili said.

Freya bit her lip. "That is kind of you, but I am not sure."

"'Twould be a fine idea," Efrika said. "You need to overcome this fear if you ever wish to travel anywhere."

"I know."

"Please consider it," Aimili said, thinking that riding would be a good way for her to get to know Padruig's sister. "You can ride Mist. She will not do anything frightening, I promise."

"I shall think on it."

"Good," Efrika said. "Now, Aimili, I know you are still acclimating yourself to your new home, but we are in dire need of your aid. Cook awaits instructions on the meals. You may not realize this, but our stores are low, thanks to Grigor's greed and incompetence. An inventory needs to be made, and—"

"Efrika." Aimili took a sip of wine from a cup deposited by a servant. "I told you I do not have time for such duties."

Both Efrika and Freya just blinked at her.

"But-but you are the laird's wife," Efrika said. "'Tis your responsibility to see to the management of the castle. Even the herb garden is in disarray. People are willing to work, but they need instruction and supervision."

Aimili felt as if an iron collar tightened around her neck. "You do not understand. I am not skilled at those kinds of matters. I have always spent most of my time in the stables or outside the castle walls. Surely there is someone else who can see to things. You?"

"I, well, I suppose . . ." Efrika's voice trailed off. Her

expression of pity was matched by Freya's.

"Your mother died when you were young?" Freya asked.

"Aye, when I was three years of age."

"Ah."

That simple word held such a wealth of sympathy and censure that Aimili stiffened.

"Was there no one to instruct you?"

"I . . ." Aimili vaguely remembered a distant aunt trying to interest her in the workings of the castle, but she could never be bothered. Morainn, on the other hand, had always taken pride in managing the castle affairs so that food remained plentiful and the castle as comfortable as possible. "I had much instruction."

"Oh?" Relief spilled over Efrika's face.

"The stable master taught me much about horses. One of the guardsmen taught me how to wield a blade. Another of the clan taught me of the wonders to be found in the forest."

Freya rolled her eyes. "That is not what Efrika meant."

"The clan will expect you to take up these responsibilities," Efrika said. She looked past Aimili and smiled. "Oh, Padruig, come sit with us."

Aimili fought the urge to jump up and flee. Instead, she forced a polite smile to her face and took a deep draught of wine.

"Did you find Angus Ransolm's coin?" Freya asked,

smoothing her bliaut over and over.

"No yet, but soon. Grigor refuses to divulge his hiding place unless I best him on the field."

Aimili turned to him in surprise. "You are going to fight him? Again?"

"Aye." His gaze was flat with resolve.

"I could give him another of my special drinks instead. He'll be willing to reveal anything to relieve his suffering," Efrika said.

Padruig smiled at her, and Aimili's stomach turned over. The smile transformed him, clearly revealing his affection for Efrika, and sending another spear of pain into Aimili's belly. "While I appreciate your inventiveness, 'tis best I handle this in a man's way."

"When?" Efrika asked.

"At noon."

"But why . . . why would you arm such a man, give him the chance to harm you?" Aimili sputtered.

He briefly glanced at her. "He will no best me."

"Of course not," Efrika said. "Now, Padruig, we were just discussing with your new bride the need for her to take up her duties as the laird's wife."

Aimili clenched her jaw and poured more wine down her throat. *Wife,* she thought. *No more than a sad jest.*

"Alasdair is working on determining the extent of our resources," Padruig told Efrika.

"I ken, but we all know 'tis not enough."

"Which is one of the reasons I must find where Grigor hid the coin. 'Tis my hope that it exceeds what he obtained from Ransolm."

Aimili saw him frown as he looked around the hall. She followed his gaze, noting the dirty rushes on the floor, the blackened hearth, the lack of adornment. "The castle does need a woman to direct the servants, to see that the victuals are improved," Padruig continued.

"'Tis exactly what I explained to Aimili," Efrika said.

"And I explained to Efrika that she does not have time for such. Just as I explained to *you* before we wed," Aimili added, frowning at Padruig.

"But I do not have the same authority as the laird's wife," Efrika said. "And Freya is, uh, well, too young."

Freya sniffed. "'Tis not youth, but a matter of respect."

"Most of your horses have not arrived yet," Padruig said, gazing at Aimili. "Until they do, surely you can make the time to do"—he waved a hand—"whatever women do to make the castle clean and the food palatable."

Padruig, Efrika, and Freya all gazed at Aimili expectantly.

She would have thrown her cup against the wall, but that would only have added to the mess that now she was apparently responsible for seeing cleaned up.

"Well, Aimili?" Padruig prodded.

Why should I? she wanted to ask, but Padruig was right. Her horses had not arrived yet, and it would just be stubborn and mean-spirited not to help. And the state of things in the castle had clearly declined under Ciara's "management." "Until my horses are here I shall try to help."

"Thank you." Padruig rose. "I shall leave you ladies to it." Without another glance in Aimili's direction he strode off.

For the next hours, Aimili, with Efrika and Freya accompanying her, set herself to household management and the kind of tasks she had always avoided. She met with Cook and discussed how she might improve the meals. She toured the storage vaults and checked the amount of various spices on hand. She even inspected the herb garden and gave orders to the gardeners to weed and pick what herbs they could to dry before frost killed the tender plants. By the time she explained, very clearly, to a group of women servants that she wanted all of the rushes from the great hall removed, the floor scrubbed and fresh rushes put down, she had such a pounding headache that she felt sick at her stomach.

Efrika patted her on the shoulder. "'Tis almost noon. You will attend the fight in support of Padruig, of course. Perhaps you should change into something more appropriate for the wife of the laird."

Aimili made herself take a deep breath. "Efrika, I am who I am. Padruig knew the kind of woman he was gaining as a bride. He married me simply because he had no choice. Naught more."

"Many marriages begin that way, but—"

"Enough!"

Efrika's eyes widened at Aimili's harsh tone, and for a moment Aimili regretted hurting the woman. Still, she would not lose herself in this place, not for anyone, least of all a husband who didn't want her and his relatives who refused to accept her. "Asides, I fear I lack any embroidered silk bliauts," Aimili added, in a softer tone.

"I could lend you one of mine," Freya said brightly, clearly undeterred by Aimili's comments. "We are close to the same size. Although I've nothing new," Freya finished with a pout.

Efrika shook her head and closed her eyes. "You still have garments finer than anyone at the castle."

"I appreciate your offer, Freya, but 'tis not necessary."

Efrika bit her lip, but thankfully said nothing.

Freya grinned. "Let us go. I want to watch Padruig pound Grigor into the dirt."

Aimili had focused so much on her "duties" that she'd nearly forgotten Padruig was set to face Grigor. As she followed Efrika and Freya out of the hall, a shiver of foreboding snaked down her spine. She stopped and glanced around her, but all seemed as it should. Still, it felt as if someone watched her.

Of course, there is someone watching you, she chided herself. *You are the new curiosity of Castle MacCoinneach.* She put the matter from her mind and walked out to the training field, where a large group had already gathered.

In their center, Padruig stood, bare-chested, arms crossed, and legs spread. Aimili's gut clenched at the sight. Slabs of muscle defined his chest, his biceps sculpted by countless hours of training. The weak sunlight lightened his tied-back hair to flaxen, and his blue eyes looked darker, focused. With the scars crossing his cheek, he radiated power and brutally forged pride.

He could have been hewn of living marble, remote and alone, though he stood within a crowd of his people. And though he infuriated her and wounded her with his indifference, still he fascinated her.

Grigor strode into the circle, a smug smile of confidence on his lips, his sword catching a flash of sunlight.

Padruig uncrossed his arms and rested one hand atop the pommel of his sword.

The crowd backed up to give the men more room, and Aimili found her vision blocked by a pair of burly guardsmen who were in the process of making a wager on the winner. She tapped one of the guardsmen on the shoulder. When he turned and spotted her, his gaze widened. "You should be in front, my lady," he said.

"Will you aid me?" Normally, she hated to ask for help, but knew she could never push through the crowd on her own.

He nodded and punched his companion in the arm. Between the two of them, they quickly cleared a path for Aimili, and she found herself at the edge of the circle with the two men flanking her.

"Let it begin," Padruig said, unsheathing his sword.

"Aye. The clan shall know when you are defeated who is the rightful laird." Grigor advanced and swung his sword in a killing arc.

Padruig easily dodged the blow.

Grigor growled and swung again, this time missing Padruig completely.

"Is that all you have?" Padruig taunted. "You waste my time."

As the afternoon sun waned, Aimili watched in growing amazement as Padruig wore Grigor down. There really was no contest, she realized as she watched Padruig move. He jumped, he leapt, he lunged like some kind of big, wild cat. She'd seen many men train, and many fight, but she'd never seen anyone like Padruig.

Grigor went down onto one knee and Padruig knocked his shield aside.

Gasping for breath, his face bright red, Grigor glared up at Padruig, who did not appear to be even winded.

"Surrender," Padruig said. "'Tis over."

"You bastard," Grigor spat.

"Do you want to die today?"

Grigor smirked. "Do you want the coin?"

"'Twas our bargain."

"Mayhap now I wish to renegotiate."

"Tell me and live. Refuse and die. I shall find your hiding place soon enough."

"I doubt it."

"Make your choice. I am thirsty."

Grigor's eyes glittered with hatred. "This should have been mine. I should be laird."

"Leave off. Your game is over. You neither deserved the position nor served it well."

"You think you shall do better?" Grigor cracked out a laugh. "You've already proven your judgment flawed. Because of you, we're in a blood feud with the MacVegans."

"I shall not debate the matter with you. Make. Your. Choice."

"In the chapel," Grigor finally said. "Under the shrine to Saint Columba."

"Magnus?" Padruig called.

"Aye, Laird." Magnus turned and walked toward the chapel.

"Ivarr?"

One of the guards next to Aimili stepped forward. "Aye?"

"Leave him a dagger and provide him with supplies for a fortnight. He can take one of the lesser rounceys from the stable. See that he departs MacCoinneach lands tomorrow."

"Tonight?"

"Keep him locked in the gatehouse." With a last contemptuous look, Padruig turned and walked away.

Grigor let out a howl of fury and charged.

Aimili screamed a warning, but it wasn't needed.

Padruig whirled, blocked Grigor's sword, and sank his own deep into Grigor's chest. As Grigor slumped to the ground, satisfaction cloaked Padruig's face, now splattered with Grigor's blood.

He pulled his sword free with a hiss. "Throw the bastard's body into the loch," he ordered the guardsman. "Let the fish have him."

"Aye, Laird." Ivarr and a handful of other men rushed forward to seize Grigor's limp body.

And Padruig's gaze found Aimili. Splashed with blood, sweat matting his hair and streaking his chest, for the first time Aimili felt a shiver of doubt. She should be glad she'd wed such a warrior, but a part of her shrank from the ruthless, predatory gratification she saw in his gaze.

He was pleased that Grigor had invited death. Very pleased.

And it disturbed Aimili down to her very soul.

As he approached, for a wild moment she wondered if he was tempted to tak his blade to her, freeing himself from an unwanted responsibility.

Instead, he sheathed his sword.

"Well met," she managed to say.

"It needed to be done."

"Aye."

"I am off to find a bath."

"Do you . . . need aid?" Aimili swallowed thickly, wondering what had possessed her to make such an offer.

"Nay."

Aimili knew she should be relieved, but instead she felt the all-too-familiar pang of rejection. She watched Padruig stride away to the congratulations of many of his clansmen and thought he would probably find someone like Beatha to help him in the bath. A woman with full breasts and wide hips.

Though a crowd surged around her, Aimili felt apart from them. She wandered back to the stables. Perhaps she could work on Loki.

And try to forget the look in Padruig's eyes when he slew Grigor. Grigor deserved it, she reminded herself. Aside from the many wrongs he'd done to disfavored members of the clan and helpless servants, he'd attacked Padruig after he'd been beaten, attacked when Padruig's back was turned.

She glanced up to find one of the guards watching her.

He nodded. "Quite a skilled swordsman your husband is, my lady."

Not wanting to get into a discussion of Padruig's prowess with weaponry, she murmured, "Aye, that he is." She brushed past the man and entered the stable.

Just as she passed inside, she felt a cold tendril of fear flow through her. It was the same feeling she'd had that morn—the feeling that something was terribly wrong at Castle MacCoinneach, that something or someone lay in wait with menace on his or her mind.

The question was what? Or whom?

Padruig's bloody image flashed through her mind, but she refused to accept it. "I will find out who you are," she said softly. "You cannot hide from me."

In the stillness of the stable, for a moment she thought she heard laughter.

Sebilla was sitting on her terrace, enjoying the early evening light and a goblet of sweet, golden wine, when something erupted from her pool in a great splash that soaked her thin gown. She leapt up with a gasp.

"Damned, unpredictable portal," a man's voice muttered before D'Ary climbed out of the pool onto her terrace.

He stared at her, and Sebilla fought the urge to cross her arms over her body. "Do you have a drying cloth?" he asked, his gaze traveling over her.

"What are you doing here?"

"Following my queen's instructions. Did you not bid me to report to you of the affairs at Castle MacCoinneach?"

"That does not include bursting into my private chambers unannounced."

D'Ary shrugged. "I came as I could."

Sebilla set her goblet down and went in to fetch drying cloths. Once inside, she quickly changed into a dry and much more concealing gown before returning to the terrace.

"Thank you," D'Ary said as he draped a towel around his neck and sat on the marble floor.

"You don't like me very much, do you?" Sebilla asked, immediately unsure why she stooped to voice the question. Or why it mattered.

"You are my queen." D'Ary fetched another goblet from a nearby cupboard and poured himself wine from the flagon.

"That is not an answer."

"I do not like most people," he said, before fixing her with his amber stare. "And I do not know you well enough to like or dislike you."

"You blame me for Caradoc's death. I understand that. I blame myself."

"Nay. Caradoc was a man, a warrior. He made his own choices. I blame Vardon, as should you."

Sebilla held his gaze, discomfited by words of support coming from such an unlikely source. "Have you found him?"

"Nay, but he is there. I can feel his presence, but he cloaks it well. And there are many at the castle."

"The laird? He is well?"

"For the moment. As is his bride."

"Aimili."

D'Ary looked at her in surprise. "Aye, that is her name."

"She is different."

"That she is. Her fey blood is obvious to me. Possibly to Vardon, as well."

Sebilla considered telling him of her vision, but held back. She would see to that matter herself. And she wanted to meet this Aimili MacCoinneach.

"I have attempted to befriend her."

"Why?"

"I like her. And she needs a friend. The laird . . ." D'Ary tossed back a drink of wine. "He cannae see what he has."

"Could it be Vardon's doing?"

"I dinnae think so. The laird is a tough man, but inside he is hiding something. I haven't yet discovered what it is."

"You've not felt any threat?"

"Worried for me, Sebilla?" His gaze warmed.

"I . . ." By the saints, she was blushing, she thought with increasing embarrassment. "I did not give you leave to use my given name."

"That is not an answer."

Sebilla took another drink of wine, hoping to calm her jangling nerves. The men of Paroseea simply did not speak to her this way. Not even Lucan was so familiar. "Of course, I have concern for your welfare. I am your queen."

"I thought perhaps 'twas a bit more than that."

"You are impertinent." Heavens, she sounded like a stiff, snobbish noblewoman.

"I find it makes things more interesting."

Scrambling for a way back to safe ground, Sebilla asked, "What do you plan from here?"

"For now, I am trying to just blend in, learn the clan members. Vardon will do something eventually. I want to be around when he does." His teasing expression hardened.

"You are not to battle him alone."

He just stared at her.

"We have not yet discovered a way to return Vardon to his prison," Sebilla admitted. "But we will."

"I dinnae care if the bastard returns to prison. He should pay for Caradoc."

"Agreed. If need be, I shall see to Vardon myself."

D'Ary cocked a brow. "You?"

Irritation danced along her nerve endings. "There is a reason I am queen of Paroseea, D'Ary. No one's power matches mine."

"I ken you are a powerful woman, but your powers are more of a peaceful sort."

"Not all. Just because I have not had to use the others often, they are still there. I will use everything I have to defeat Vardon."

"As will I."

"Good."

D'Ary tilted his head toward the waning sunlight. "I should be back for supper. 'Tis a good time to observe people."

"Be careful, D'Ary."

He rose and took her hand, pressing a kiss on her palm before she found the sense to pull away. "I intend to." Whistling he walked into the palace.

Sebilla stared after him, then shook her head, sipping wine. What an enigmatic man, she thought. Hard and remote at times, impertinent and flirtatious at others. And far too intriguing to lose to Vardon's evil.

On the morrow, she would find a way to deliver the dagger to Aimili MacCoinneach.

"I am not going to ride you today," Aimili told Loki as he trotted around the grassy ring.

Good.

But tomorrow I will.

Why bother?

Because I think you can be a very fine horse. If you cease throwing tantrums.

Loki snorted and turned to trot the other way. *You probably have not noticed, but my balance is not as it should be.*

I noticed. Aimili watched Loki trot and recalled how bouncy he felt. She'd never been able to stay on long enough to figure out why.

I didn't used to be this way. I can still sire a good horse. What happened?

Angus Ransolm happened. The man can't ride, and whenever he fell off balance, which was most of the time, he hauled on my mouth, kicked me, and if he was in a mood, added the whip. As you've seen.

I don't use a whip. And the only times I've hauled on your mouth have been when you are trying your best to throw me off.

Just give me the mares and leave me alone. 'Tis best.

Oh, no, you'll have to earn that. If you'll trust me, I can help your balance.

Help me canter without feeling I am going to fall over?

Yes. You need to find your feet and get them and your hind end under you.

I don't know what you are talking about.

I will show you. Aimili grinned. This was what she was best at, why the horses she trained were so sought after.

I shall think on it. Loki stopped running and blew out a snort. *What progress have you made with your husband?*

None. Nor am I likely to. He avoids me unless he is criticizing me or asking me to be the "lady of the castle."

So you are just giving up?

What else can I do?

Quit hiding behind your hurt and talk to him. Tell him what you want. Don't let him avoid you. Stop being so polite. It doesn't suit you.

Aimili thought about that. Loki was right. Somehow, between finding Padruig MacCoinneach in her father's castle and wedding the man, she'd let her pain over Padruig's treatment strip her of her spirit.

I believe I shall do just that.

Chapter Seven

That night Aimili did not go to bed. Instead, she curled up on the window seat, clad only in her chemise, and cracked open the shutters to let the cool air help her stay awake. She knew Padruig wouldn't come to the chamber before he thought she would be asleep.

She glared at the thick fur piled on the floor in front of the fire. The moment she'd entered the chamber and seen that, she knew she could wait no longer to confront him.

I am not an ugly woman, she told herself. *My hair is thick and fine, my eyes big and dark, and the rest of my features, if not beautiful are not unattractive. I may not have breasts like Beatha, but my body is toned, not soft and flabby. I have all of my teeth. I bathe every day, if only from a basin.*

I can embroider even though I usually don't have the time for it. And I breed and train good horses, very good horses, the kind to bring in coin.

Well into her litany of attributes, Aimili scarcely heard the door creak open. She snapped her gaze to the doorway and found Padruig in midstep back.

"I didnae think you would still be awake."

"Obviously." Her expression dared him to back out of the chamber.

He was carrying a candle and a flagon of wine, which he set on the table. "Is there aught wrong?" he asked as he sat.

"May I have a cup of wine?"

"Of course." He poured and delivered the cup before returning to his seat.

Aimili took a bracing sip. "Why do you hate me?"

"What?" He blinked. "What are you talking about?"

She ticked off the reasons on her fingers. "You avoid me during the day, you barely speak to me at mealtimes, and you sleep on the floor."

"Aimili, I—"

"You criticize me at every turn, and treat me like a wayward child." By the saints, it felt good to say it out loud. Aimili sipped more wine.

"I do not hate you." Padruig rose and paced across the floor.

"Then, what is it? What is it about me that is so abhorrent to you?"

When his gaze met hers, Aimili forgot to breathe. For a moment, just an instant in time, his eyes flashed silver heat that seared her blood. Then the moment was gone, his expression once more impassive.

"I seem to recall you cursing the day you wed with me," he said.

Aimili flushed. "Words spoken in anger. I am sorry. One of my many flaws, as you have no doubt noted, is that on occasion I can have a bit of a temper."

Was that a quirk of lips she saw?

"As can I, lass. But the fact remains that we are ill suited. 'Tis more my fault than yours."

His words stirred a memory. In one of her father's early attempts to find her a husband, he'd arranged a visit by a distant cousin and his son, Roger. Roger had been handsome and charming, and for a time Aimili let herself consider the possibility of marriage. Unfortunately, the visit had ended with a seemingly heartfelt proclamation by Roger that he could not marry her. It had nothing to do with her, he'd assured her. It was he who was lacking, who just wasn't enough man for a woman like her. Horse dung, she'd thought.

With Roger, she'd simply nodded and let him go. Not this time. "What do you mean?" she asked.

Padruig appeared startled by the question. "Well, we are very different."

"What does that have to do with anything?"

"Everything." He sighed. "I know you are impatient to have your horses here, and I appreciate your taking a hand with the castle. Soon, you will have your horses to occupy your time and all will be well."

"Padruig, this is not about my horses. This is about

my marriage."

"I think it is going fine," he said.

She stared at him, vaguely aware that her mouth was hanging open. "Have you no interest in lying with me?" Part of her could not believe she was brave enough to ask, but the other part didn't care a bit.

He peered at her as if she'd lost her wits. "We discussed this."

"Do you not want sons? Children?" Aimili held her breath waiting for his answer.

"'Tis not possible."

Her eyes widened, and her gaze dropped to his groin. "Did you suffer an injury?" Could that be it? she wondered. Maybe he was unable to perform.

"Nay! That is not what I meant."

"What *did* you mean?"

"I meant that it will not happen because I have enough control not to force myself on you." His voice was low and harsh.

"I am your wife."

"And, as such, to be treated with honor and respect."

"What if I want children?"

"You do not understand what you are asking. You are little more than a child yourself."

Aimili slowly set her cup down, stood, and walked until she stood but a handbreadth away from Padruig. "I am not a child!"

He flinched as if she'd struck him.

She cursed the tears spilling down her face.

"Aimili, I do not mean to cause you pain."

"Then stop treating me like a bairn. Sleep in the bed with me tonight."

He backed away. "That I cannae do, lass."

"Cannot or will not?"

The soft click of the door shutting behind him was his answer.

Aimili picked up her cup and flung it at the door. Why she was surprised at how badly their conversation went she didn't know, but she was. Surprised, disappointed, and unaccountably hurt.

Padruig did not want her. He could scarcely make that fact plainer, even dressed up in talk of "sparing" her. More horse dung.

Now, he most likely thought her brazen, as well. She shuffled over to the bed and sat, gazing into the fire. *I wonder what Loki will make of this*, she thought, then crushed a hand to her mouth to keep from letting out a sob.

If only she could let it go, accept the terms that Padruig offered, be glad that she was wed to a man who let her pursue her passion and demanded little of her. It could be much worse she knew. She was not so isolated growing up that she hadn't heard stories of much more ill-fated unions. She could have ended up with someone like Angus Ransolm, she thought with a shiver of revulsion.

She'd been so strong for so long that she herself had

almost forgotten a young girl's dreams. Almost. Still, there was a part of her hidden deep inside that longed for the things people would expect a woman like Morainn to covet. A husband who adored her, who cherished her differences and her strength, but enfolded her gently in the protective cocoon of his own power. Love. The swell of her belly as her child grew, the soft touch of tiny hands, the gurgle of a first smile.

Her dream seemed so far away now. Images spilled through her mind. The grass green and lush, beneath a clear blue sky. Fragrant flowers in shades of pink and yellow. A man with golden hair and silvery blue eyes reaching for her, laughing as a little girl darted between them, her own mop of flaxen hair shining in the sun.

Time to put away such dreams, Aimili, she told herself, recalling the cool look in Padruig's eyes. *Time to put them away.*

Padruig nearly ran down to the great hall. By the saints, how had he gotten into this mess? His child bride had just boldly asked him to . . . He couldn't get his mind around it, though his body seemed to understand quite well.

When she'd stood, with the fire behind her, he'd

felt as if she'd just leveled him with the blunt edge of a sword. Young she might be, but Aimili's body was far from childlike.

Dear Lord, give me strength, he silently prayed as he neared one of the chairs set up in front of the hearth.

Images bounced around in his head. Full, uptilted breasts just the right size to fill his hands. A narrow waist tapered to hips perfectly flared. Firm thighs leading down to graceful feet.

"Padruig?"

He stopped, abruptly aware that he was fisting and unfisting his hands. "Magnus. Do you have any more of that drink from the monks?"

His friend swept up a flagon from the floor and handed it to Padruig. "Sit, Laird."

For a few minutes, Magnus let him sit in silence, letting the warmth of the drink flow down his throat and warm his belly. "The pine marten you took from Grigor's chamber too hot?" he finally asked, his tone suspiciously innocent.

Padruig slanted him a look.

Magnus just smiled.

"Do you not have a warm bed to find, Magnus?"

"Ah, I imagine the comely Kenna would welcome me, but I find myself oddly disinclined to visit her tonight."

"What of your own quarters?" Padruig knew Magnus had a small stone dwelling near the stables.

He'd seen to its construction himself.

"I have been traveling so long it is sometimes difficult for me to settle back into being in one place."

Padruig had a feeling it was more than that, but he didn't ask. He certainly didn't want Magnus prying into his personal affairs, dismal as they were, though he doubted he would be spared. "Will you be leaving again?"

"Nay. One day I may wish to wander, but now that Grigor is gone there is no urgency." He looked at Padruig. "Asides, I would support you as I can."

"Thank you."

Magnus nodded. "You will have to come to terms with her, you know," he said softly.

"Aye, I ken." Padruig sipped more of the potent drink. "I am no sure how."

"Mayhap you should give this husband role a try."

"She is—"

"Not a child, Padruig, though at times she looks like one. She is a woman of age."

"Well, I know," Padruig answered, gritting his teeth. The insistent pressure in his groin told him that. Loudly.

"The lass is brave, as well. Impressive the way she dispatched Grigor's whore. And anyone who is willing to ride that devil horse of hers does not lack ballocks."

"That beast is a menace." Padruig shot back another drink.

"Aye, but I think your lady will tame him."

His lady, Padruig thought, unable to suppress a tinge of pride. "Mayhap."

"I would wager on it."

Padruig stared into the fire. "Magnus, have you ever seen something so pure, so unsullied, that you feel if you touch it you will irrevocably defile it?"

Magnus was quiet for a time, then said, "Aye."

"Then you understand."

"Nay. The things I have seen like that are *things,* objects, places, not living, breathing people."

"'Tis the same."

"Is it?"

"Aye."

Magnus yawned and stretched. "I believe I shall seek out my bed. You may keep the flagon."

"My thanks."

"Padruig," Magnus said as he stood and put a hand on Padruig's shoulder. "Think well upon the life you are creating for yourself. And for Aimili. There may come a day when you cannot change it."

"I've no wish to," Padruig said, wincing inside at the baldness of the lie.

The next morn, Aimili lingered after mass, wanting to be alone in the chapel. Efrika also hung back, obviously waiting for Aimili, but eventually gave up and left. Aimili kept her head bent, waiting for the chapel to empty.

When the chapel quieted, she let out a breath and gazed up at the ornate, golden cross atop the altar. Though she didn't always agree with the priest, she loved the peaceful feeling of being in a chapel, loved the sense of being in a place where someone, even if you couldn't see him, loved and looked after you.

"He is a murderer, you know," a woman's voice spat.

Aimili whipped her head to the left. An older woman stood there, her hair a mix of gray and brown, her green eyes alight with something that caused Aimili to scoot back. "Who are you talking about?"

The woman's mouth curved into a snarl. "Padruig, of course. Your husband."

"Padruig is not a murderer."

"What do you know? You have been here less than a fortnight."

Though Aimili at times harbored her own doubts about her husband, she could not believe him capable of such a cold-blooded, brutal act as murder. "Padruig is not that kind of man."

"Simple child."

Aimili leapt to her feet. By God, she was beyond tired of being referred to as a child. "Who *are* you?"

"His dam. The one who, to my sorrow, gave Padruig

birth."

"You are called Mairi?" Aimili remembered Efrika's words. *A bit teched*, Efrika had said. Aimili thought it was a great deal more than that.

"Aye. Surely you have heard the story."

"Are you talking about Brona's death?"

"My beautiful child. Padruig killed her."

"My lady, Symund MacVegan killed her," Aimili said gently. "All know of how Padruig came upon him with the dagger in his hand."

"Nay! 'Twas Padruig's fault. All of it. Look at his face. He bears the devil's marks to show all his wicked nature."

"He was injured in battle. Padruig is not the first man to bear a scar."

It was as if Aimili had not spoken. "He refused to let Brona follow her heart. If he had, she would be alive. She would have borne me grandchildren by now. Instead, because of him, I am left with nothing. I curse him." Mairi's gaze was feverish, her bony hands outstretched like claws.

Aimili took another step back. *Dear God, what am I to do?* "What of Freya, your other daughter?"

Mairi blinked. "I lost Brona." Tears dripped down her face. "Because of Padruig, I lost my Brona."

Aimili spied the priest enter a side door, and frantically motioned him over. "Father, the Lady Mairi needs your aid," she said.

Father Thomas put his arm around the sobbing woman and led her to a bench. "Now, Mairi, let us pray together."

"I lost my Brona," she said.

"Aye. Let us pray for her blessed soul."

Aimili ran out of the chapel into the morning air and took a deep, cleansing breath. The woman was mad, clearly. Poor Padruig. Aimili had heard the stories of that horrible day. It was a tragedy, and depending on who told the story, Padruig was at the least, guilty of poor judgment, and at most, solely responsible for his sister's death and the ensuing carnage.

Still, how could a mother hate her own child so? Aimili couldn't imagine that.

Unless there was something she didn't know of that day. Unless there was some truth beyond a madwoman's ravings.

She frowned, considering seeking out Padruig, but inside she cringed. Not after last night's disaster. She'd all but begged Padruig to take her to bed, and he'd fled, his expression telling her just how futile her overture had been.

"Well, Loki, let us see what you have to say now," she muttered to herself, turning for the stables.

Padruig sat in his solar, staring at the pile of coin as if by will alone he could multiply it. Magnus leaned against one wall, his arms crossed, while Alasdair sat on a stool. "'Tis enough to repay Ransolm, but not much more." Padruig slammed a fist down on the table. "Damn Grigor. And damn that useless Alard!"

"Alard is not all to fault, but truth be said, he did not try to control Grigor very hard," Alasdair said.

"You shall immediately take over as my seneschal," Padruig said, drumming his fingers on the table.

The older man straightened his shoulders. "I shall be happy to."

"I have a store of pelts. Some ermine," Magnus said. "And two finely wrought gold necklaces, set with pearls. We could trade them for food in Inverness."

"Damn," Padruig muttered again. He knew Magnus had worked hard to gain a measure of wealth. It was not fair that he sacrifice it all to the clan.

"I will see to the task myself," Magnus said. "I know a merchant or two who owe me a favor."

"'Twill not be enough, Magnus," Padruig said. "And I hate to take all that you have." Unable to remain seated, Padruig stood to pace. Everyone was depending upon him to find a way to see them through the winter, and he felt completely useless for the task. Why had he come back to this?

Freya, his inner voice reminded. *The clan. Home.*

Magnus shrugged. "I am a part of the clan."

Padruig flipped over a silver coin. "We cannot make it alone."

"The de Granthams?" Alasdair questioned.

"Have already done their share. And God knows what the laird would demand of me this time."

Magnus snickered.

"I shall send to Giselle," Padruig announced.

Alasdair's brows rose. "Giselle?"

"Ah, so the laird did not spend his time away without female companionship," Magnus said.

"'Tis not like that."

Both Magnus and Alasdair chuckled.

"'Tis a long story, but I found myself in a position to aid a young woman. At the time, her family offered me a reward, but, of course, I declined."

"So you will claim it now."

"Aye."

"It must have been quite a bit of aid."

"I saved her life." Padruig smiled, thinking of how happy Giselle had been when he left England.

"Who is this woman?"

"She is wed to the younger brother of the Earl of Hawksdown. Giselle and her husband, Piers, reside at Kindlemere Castle."

"A wealthy holding," Magnus remarked.

"Aye. Alasdair, determine exactly how much we need. I want to dispatch a messenger as soon as possible."

"Aye, Laird. I will speak to Alard also."

Padruig rubbed his chin. "Is he worth keeping on as your assistant?"

"I am not sure."

"Give him a sennight."

Alasdair nodded and departed the solar. At the same time, Freya swept in. "Padruig," she said. "A merchant has arrived!" Her eyes sparkled with excitement.

"Ah, great tidings, indeed."

Freya opened her eyes wide and pouted her lips. "Please, say I may buy some cloth. I am in desperate need of new clothing. Desperate!"

Padruig glanced at Magnus, who was gazing at Freya in a way that was definitely not the expression of a big brother. "Weel, we cannae have that, can we?" He slid a coin from the pile. "Purchase enough to fashion yourself a new gown."

"Oh, thank you, Padruig." She rushed over and hugged him tight. Padruig patted her back, and couldn't help but smile despite his concerns over their lack of funds. Freya's exuberance had a way of being contagious.

"Choose something for Aimili, also."

Freya stood back and tilted her head. "Do you wish me to find her so that she may choose?"

"She will most likely choose something more suited to a lad."

"Aye." Freya grinned. "She is not one much for silks I fear, but every woman should have at least one beautiful gown."

"I agree. Choose well. And check with Efrika to see if she requires anything."

"I shall." Freya disappeared in a swish of well-worn wool.

Magnus was smiling, Padruig noted. Smiling like some kind of besotted fool. Had Padruig never noticed, or had Magnus's feelings changed over the time Padruig had been gone? By the saints, Freya was only fifteen.

Many girls have already borne a bairn by fifteen, his inner voice taunted. Freya should be at the least betrothed.

"She shall ruin the man she marries," Padruig commented, "just keeping her in silk and baubles."

"He will not mind."

"Magnus," Padruig began, but halted at the look on his friend's face.

"I know," Magnus said quietly. "Freya can reach much higher than a simple trader."

Brona's face appeared in Padruig's mind. *I love Malcolm*, she'd said, her blue eyes filled with tears. He'd discounted her feelings as a young girl's passing whim. Malcolm had been a simple guardsman, not the kind of man suitable for the laird's sister. Or so he'd told himself.

"Does she know how you feel?" Padruig finally asked.

"I doubt it. Do not worry, Padruig. I would not dishonor your sister."

"I am not worried about that. I but wonder if Freya

returns your affection."

"She thinks of me as another brother. Naught more."

Padruig found it hard to envision Freya having feelings for any man, but knew he was deluding himself that she was still the angelic-looking child who followed him about looking for mischief.

As you delude yourself about your wife? his inner voice mocked.

He pushed the thought aside with disgust. "She is young, Magnus."

Magnus glanced at him with a knowing look. "Not too young."

"First, I need to get rid of any claim Angus Ransolm might think he has."

"You sent a message revoking Grigor's agreement?"

"Aye, but until now I lacked the coin to repay Angus. He wants Freya."

"He cannot have her."

"Nay. 'Tis why I returned, as you know. I shall deal with Angus Ransolm."

"And then?"

Padruig grinned at him. "And then we shall see."

Chapter Eight

This makes no sense at all, Loki said. *What kind of man rejects what is freely offered?*

Humans are more complicated than horses, Aimili told him.

Loki snorted. *Not from what I've observed.*

Aimili combed pieces of straw out of Loki's long, black tail, the familiar rhythm of the work soothing her. *Well, clearly Padruig is.*

Tell me more of this. Were you wearing the same clothes as the lads?

Nay.

What, then?

A simple chemise.

You need to wear something to entice his interest.

Aimili rolled her eyes. *I cannot believe I am receiving advice on my wardrobe from a fractious stallion.*

Ignoring her comment, Loki continued. *Surely there is a woman in the castle with a sense of these things.*

And what am I to say to this woman I do not know?

My husband refuses to treat me as a wife? Please help me transform myself into a woman he shall desire.

That might work.

And the entire castle would be talking about the laird's ignorant and unwanted bride.

What exactly did you say to him?

Aimili busied herself putting the saddle atop Loki's back. By the saints, how she hated to recall the embarrassing scene. *I asked him why he ignored me. And I asked him . . . I asked him to sleep in the bed with me.* Her face burned with remembered humiliation.

Did he?

No. He left. Quickly.

Hmm. Mayhap he is scared of you.

Aimili laughed as she tightened the girth. *Scared? I am half his size, and the man is deadly with a sword.*

Loki sighed. *I am not talking about who can beat whom in a fight.*

Aimili put the reins over Loki's neck and looked him in the eye. *Time to work. I do not want to think about my husband anymore.*

Work? I was thinking of taking a nap.

You can nap later. After you've earned it.

Aimili finished with the bridle and led Loki into the ring. Oscar, one of the stable boys, poked his head out of a stall and walked over to stand outside the ring. "He seems calmer today, my lady. Mayhap he is settling in here."

"He is behaving with you?"

"Aye. He senses I won't hurt 'im."

The boy is right.

"Good," Aimili told Oscar. Between him and D'Ary, she might actually have the help she'd long needed. "Well, let's see how Loki is really feeling today."

Cooperate, she told the horse.

Or what?

Or you will not get the apple I brought. Oh, did I mention I have a mare due to arrive soon who is coming into season?

Food and sex. Maybe you know more about males than you realize.

Aimili grinned and clucked at him. "Walk," she said with a small squeeze of her calves against his barrel.

Loki ambled forward, swaying from side to side.

"Oscar?"

"Aye, my lady."

"Come in here and lead him. I want to close my eyes."

"I shall do it," a man's voice said. D'Ary.

Loki? she asked silently.

For a couple of moments, the horse didn't answer. Aimili slowed him to a stop as D'Ary entered the ring. *I will allow him to lead me, though 'tis not necessary.*

Forgive me if I remain unconvinced. "Thank you, D'Ary," she said aloud.

Loki let out a sigh.

D'Ary took the reins and began walking Loki.

Aimili closed her eyes and let her body simply follow the movement of Loki's.

"Are you looking for something in particular?" D'Ary asked.

Keeping her eyes closed, Aimili said, "Aye. He is not in balance. I am trying to determine why and how best to correct it."

"His walk does not look too bad."

Too bad? Loki muttered.

Aimili squeezed slightly. "He is not using his hind enough. There, better," she said to Loki. She opened her eyes as Loki picked up a trot.

"No. Walk."

Loki slowed.

You have to learn to propel yourself forward by stepping through with your hind end and lifting your shoulders.

That is harder.

I know, but better for you and for a rider.

If horses could groan aloud, Aimili was sure Loki would have done it, but he began trying to step up with his back end instead of dragging himself along with his front.

"That is better," D'Ary commented.

"Aye. I'll take the reins back now."

He looped them back over Loki's head but kept walking alongside Aimili and Loki. Aimili took up the reins and circled Loki to change direction, at the same time urging him to keep working his hind.

After they completed a couple of walks around the ring, Aimili decided to try the trot. "D'Ary, you may wish to move out of the way before I trot."

"Why?"

"Because that's when he goes crazy," Oscar called out.

Not today, Loki told Aimili.

Good.

"Do you want me to ride him, my lady?"

Aimili's instinct was to take offense, but realized D'Ary was not impugning her ability but simply offering to help. "Nay. I have a feeling today shall be a more successful ride."

"As you wish." D'Ary moved back against the rail close to Oscar.

"All right, boy," Aimili said softly as she squeezed Loki's barrel. He shot forward, his head down, bouncing Aimili along as if she were a rock skipping across the loch. "Easy, boy," she said. *Remember, hind, not front.*

She pushed him forward, and at the same time used the reins to try to capture his energy. By the second time they circled the ring, he began to settle down and step through with his hind, but still Aimili bounced.

Aimili circled to go to the right. "Tell me what you see," she called to D'Ary.

"His shoulder dropped at the turn," D'Ary called back.

Harder, Loki said, swishing his tail.

Think of pushing yourself forward from the back, not

pulling forward with your head and front shoulders.

I shall try.

Slowly, Aimili felt the shift and the trot smoothed slightly. She looked down at Loki's front shoulders. "His muscles are uneven," she said to D'Ary as she slowed Loki to a walk and then to a halt near D'Ary and Gunnr. "Much less muscle on the right than on the left."

"And he is stiffer on the right, particularly in the hind." D'Ary walked over and put a hand on Loki's right shoulder, smoothing his hand down, then moving around to do the same on the left shoulder.

Ransolm never could sit straight, Loki said.

He leaned to the left?

Almost always. 'Tis one of the reasons he could never find his balance.

And so you moved under him.

Not that it did any good. The man would just end up flopping around and beating me for his failure.

"The stiffness is most likely from learning to brace against Angus Ransolm's cruel form of riding," Aimili said with a frown. How she hated someone who would mistreat an animal, particularly when it was the man's own fault, not the animal's.

"Perhaps. We need to build up the muscle, though."

"Aye."

D'Ary gave Loki a pat. "You are a good rider, Aimili."

Aimili grinned down at him. "My thanks. 'Tis

something I have always loved to do." As she swung off Loki's back, the horse took a step to the side, and Aimili ended up stumbling into D'Ary's arms.

"Careful," he said.

That same odd tingling feeling spread down her arms, infusing her fingertips with warmth. She caught D'Ary's gaze and for a moment, was sure she saw a flash of recognition. Loki bumped her with his head, and she moved away from D'Ary's touch.

"Where did you say you hailed from?" she asked.

He smiled. "I did not say."

Aimili cocked a brow.

"'Tis a small village far to the north called Parth. You will no have heard of it."

"Parth."

"Aye. A simple place. Too simple for me, I fear."

Aimili did not believe a word of it, but had no way to disprove his claim. Was he fleeing something? Or someone?

"Would you like me to take Loki?" he asked, nodding to the horse who stood patiently.

"Nay. I shall see to it. My other horses are due to arrive on the morrow. See if Hugo needs help preparing their stalls."

Put the mare close to me, Loki said.

You shall have your chance. She patted his neck.

"Very well, my lady," D'Ary said. "And well done today."

"Thank you, D'Ary."

I am definitely ready to nap.

Aimili chuckled as she led Loki back into the stable.

Padruig stood watching his wife follow the new stable hand into the stables and clenched his jaw. He'd heard more than one lass in the castle prattling on about the man, how broad his shoulders were, how beautiful his golden eyes were, and on and on.

And he'd touched Aimili, touched her with a casualness that burned in Padruig's gut no matter how he told himself he didn't care. Did the touch mean D'Ary was already familiar with Aimili?

By the saints, he realized with horror, he was so jealous he could scarcely stand it. It wasn't just the contact, but the way they spoke so easily, the smiles they exchanged. Every conversation *he* had with Aimili seemed to end in discord.

And whose fault is that? his inner voice taunted.

He knew he should be gentler with the lass, but each time he tried he found himself unable to do it. It was as if he stood atop a sharply sloped fell, fearful that if he took the first step, that step would become another and another. Eventually, he would be unable to stop himself from doing the one thing he'd vowed not to—taking his child-wife's innocence.

Unless she had already given it to the pretty new stable hand.

Padruig forced himself to unlock his jaw and take a

deep breath. Do *not act the jealous fool*, he chided himself. *D'Ary is helping her with the horses, naught more.*

Still, he lingered, watching to see Aimili reappear. When she did, he ducked behind the stable, feeling even more foolish but not wishing her to know he spied on her. She ambled across the bailey, and disappeared into the smithy's.

Cease skulking about like a half-wit, Padruig told himself. *You've no time for such nonsense.* He headed for the training field.

Magnus finally found Alasdair deep in conversation with a young man surrounded by grazing sheep. "Good, then," Alasdair said. "I shall discuss matters with Cook myself." He turned and spotted Magnus.

"I had forgotten how much work this is," Alasdair said as he approached.

"Particularly when there is not enough coin."

"True." They began walking back toward the castle walls. "What brings you out here on such a fine day?"

"'Tis the kind of day that bids me set out for warmer climes." A misty drizzle dampened everything, the sky was slate-gray, and the breeze carried the bite of fall with it.

"'Twill just make you soft."

"Alasdair, I have been thinking about the day Brona died."

Alasdair crossed himself. "A dark day for all of us."

"Padruig blames himself, but I am no convinced 'tis that simple."

"Neither am I."

"It haunts him, Alasdair. I fear he will never be free of it unless we discover the truth."

"Many who were there that day died."

"Aye, but there are those who remain. I spoke with Culloch. Though he is old, he still remembers the day well."

"We all do."

"Aye, but he remembers something that strikes me as odd. Did you know that it was Brona's own maid who told Padruig Brona had gone off with Malcolm? And where they had gone."

"Brona's maid?"

"Aye."

"I assumed it was one of the guardsmen who saw them leave."

"As did I. I find it strange that Brona's maid would go against her mistress's wishes. Surely she knew that Brona wanted to be with Malcolm."

"Their feelings for each other were no secret." Alasdair furrowed his brow. "Where is the lass now?"

"Dead. Her body was found by the loch the day after we fought the MacVegans."

"Probably killed by one of them."

"It seemed so at the time, but now I am not sure. 'Tis too convenient."

Alasdair halted. "What are you saying?"

"I am wondering if all of it was just too opportune. Padruig arrived just in time to find Symund standing with a bloody dagger next to Brona's body. Within moments, the MacVegans descended upon us, armed for battle."

"You think someone set it up? But who? And why?"

"I dinnae ken. Brona had no enemies, and Malcolm was well liked by the clan."

"Mayhap it was aimed at the laird."

"Grigor—"

Alasdair snorted. "Lacked the wit to concoct such a scheme."

"The maid's sister still lives in the village. I thought to talk with her."

"Let me know what you find out. If someone intentionally tried to either have Padruig killed or driven from Castle MacCoinneach, they will no be happy at his return."

The same thought had occurred to Magnus. "Nay. They will try again." He frowned. "'Tis a shame that Brona has not shared the truth with Padruig."

"From the grave?" Alasdair laughed.

"Padruig told me that she has appeared to him many times."

Alasdair's smile abruptly disappeared. "Truly?"

Magnus shrugged. "I have not seen her, but Padruig is definite on the matter. 'Tis why he returned."

"Ah." Alasdair shook his head. "Ghosts. Still, it makes sense. I wondered what brought him back."

"Mayhap she does not know who was responsible."

"Or maybe it is as we believed at the time."

"I hope not. Padruig is a fine mon, but he has long stood alone. He continues to do so even though he has a comely young wife."

"To whom he pays little attention."

"Aye." Magnus sighed. "All the more reason for us to find out the truth of that day."

After working with Loki, and making sure the stable was ready for her other horses, Aimili felt as if her throat was filled with dust and grit. She paused on her way across the bailey and looked toward the gatehouse. Though the portcullis was up, guards patrolled the upper battlements, guards who would no doubt notify Padruig if she dared to venture out alone.

A part of her understood Padruig's concern, but she had spent too many years of freedom not to bristle at such restrictions.

Reluctantly, she returned to her chamber, and splashed water on her face. Someone had carefully folded the length of pine marten Padruig used as his covering and placed it on the bottom of the bed. Aimili smoothed a hand over the thick fur. The maid probably thought Aimili and Padruig had sat before the fire upon the fur.

Aimili snorted, recalling the shock in Padruig's gaze at the idea of sharing her bed. She walked over to the window and swung open the shutters. The window opening looked down upon Loch Moradeea. The surface looked cool and blue, with a slight mist dancing across the water.

Come, a voice whispered.

Aimili glanced back into the chamber, but saw no one.

Come, the voice said again. Aimili could not tell if it was male or female, but the soft tone held clear command. She peered down at the loch, and saw the water ripple as if something stirred beneath its depths.

Aimili let out a breath and shook her head. *You are being fanciful*, she told herself, but even as she had the thought, she was moving toward the door. Hot, by the saints, she was hot. A swim in the cool waters of the loch would feel good. She scooped up an extra set of garments and a length of linen and crept out the door.

She hesitated at the top of the steps. How was she to escape the castle walls without a guard noticing? Disguise herself? As who? And how?

The image of a small, wooden door sprang into her

mind. She narrowed her eyes, focusing on the image, willing it to become clear. Of course, she thought. The postern door.

Watching carefully for patrolling guards, she made her way across the bailey, somehow managing to act as if she were simply strolling about the castle. No one paid her any particular heed, just kept attending to their duties. She smiled when she saw the pile of filthy rushes outside the great hall. At least nothing would crunch beneath her slippers tonight as she walked to supper, she thought.

Within a few moments, she slid through the postern, leaving the door slightly ajar to allow her reentry. The door opened onto a steep, rocky slope that led down to the loch. Aimili quickly scampered down the hill where it flattened out next to the water.

She gazed out over the loch, and breathed in the fresh air, heavily laden with the verdant scent of grass, moss, and the plants surrounding the loch. It was a beautiful spot, lush and green, with the water a platter of deep blue. A flock of colorful kingfishers made cheerful squawks as they skimmed the water looking for fish. After stripping down to an undershirt and braies, she ran and jumped in, unable to stifle a yelp as the coolness wrapped around her skin.

She swam a ways from the shore and floated on her back, looking up at the clouds overhead, stretching her arms out to the side. Water lapped against her cheeks, and quiet enveloped her. She closed her eyes and let her body drift for a bit, soaking up the sensation of being cocooned. The water was cool, but not uncomfortably so, and it soothed her. If only she could stay this way forever, floating on a soft pillow, the demands and noises of the world far away.

When she opened her eyes, she blinked in surprise. The mist had thickened into a dense fog that surrounded her in drifting white. It was so thick that she could no longer see the shore. Shoving a twinge of panic aside, Aimili began swimming in the direction she hoped the shore lay, when the mist retreated, exposing a glimmering, pale blue circle of water in front of her.

Before she could finish a prayer for salvation, Aimili watched as a woman emerged from the depths. The woman floated motionlessly in the water, her long silver hair spread out around her, her deep blue eyes fixed on Aimili. Into the air blew the faint scent of some flower Aimili didn't recognize.

The woman wore a white robe embroidered with a strange turquoise pattern, and her skin was pale gold. She was absolutely the most beautiful woman Aimili had ever seen.

Aimili's mouth opened and closed a few times before she managed to ask, "Who are you?"

The woman smiled. "I am Sebilla, Aimili Mac-Coinneach, bride to the Laird of the MacCoinneachs."

"Where did you come from?" Aimili glanced around, looking for a boat, but could see nothing beyond the fog.

For a moment, the woman studied her and Aimili had the clear sense she was deciding whether or not to trust Aimili. "I am of Paroseea," the woman said.

"What? I have never heard of such a place."

Sebilla laughed, a soft tinkling sound. "No, you would not have."

"You talk in riddles, my lady."

"Have the animals always spoken to you?"

Shock rolled through Aimili. How did this woman know her secret?

"I know, just as I know you are special," Sebilla said.

"Special." Aimili twisted her lips. "Odd."

"Perhaps in some eyes. Not in mine."

"Who are you? What do you want with me?" Aimili nervously eyed the fog. Was it even thicker than before?

"As I said, my name is Sebilla. I am . . . Queen of Paroseea."

She is mad, Aimili thought. *There is no kingdom called Paroseea.*

"Oh, there is, indeed."

Aimili frowned. "Stop reading my mind. 'Tis rude."

Sebilla's mouth quirked. "My apologies. Paroseea is my home."

"Where is it?"

"The way is hidden. It is at the same time far away and very close."

"More riddles." Aimili shivered.

"I have seen you in my visions." Sebilla floated closer until tendrils of her silvery hair touched Aimili's arms. Wherever the hair touched her, warmth followed. "You are destined to aid us."

"I . . . I do not understand."

"Nor do I. Not fully. Yet." Sebilla drew a short scabbard from the folds of her robe and lifted it to Aimili. "This is for you."

Aimili stared down at the elaborately engraved silver scabbard, and foreboding cascaded down her spine. "I don't—"

"Take it. And guard it well."

Slowly, Aimili reached out and plucked the blade from Sebilla's hands. Warmth washed through her, spilling down her body and into her cold toes.

"'Tis a powerful weapon, Aimili."

"Why . . ." Aimili swallowed and tried again. "Why do you give such a prize to me?"

"'Tis fate." Sebilla put both her hands on Aimili's shoulders. "There is danger at Castle MacCoinneach. You must take great care. But you know that," she finished with a knowing smile.

"Danger from whom?"

"I do not know his name."

"What do you want from me?"

"When it is time, you shall help us defeat him. 'Tis your destiny."

Aimili blinked and found herself back on the shore, sitting on the grass and holding the silver dagger in its scabbard. If not for the dagger, she would have thought it all a dream, but the metal was very warm and real in her hands.

Water dripped from her lank hair, added to by the onset of a light rain. Though Aimili wasn't cold, she couldn't seem to stop shaking, turning the odd dagger over and over in her hands.

Who was that woman? Queen Sebilla, she'd called herself, as if that explained everything. And Paroseea, what kind of land was that? Why did it sound so much like the name of the loch spread before her?

Danger, Sebilla had said. Now, *that* Aimili believed. She gazed around her through the falling rain. A cool breeze fanned her cheeks, and she could still smell a faint floral scent in the air.

There was something beyond her ken here, she thought. Far beyond. Still trembling, she gathered up her bundle, carefully shielding the dagger.

Her throat tightened as she climbed the slope. How she wished she could confide in Padruig, but she had no doubt he'd deem her mad. He'd already suspected something when he'd come upon her in the woods. No, she could not confide in him. Asides, what would she say? *I snuck out of the castle for a swim and met a woman who simply emerged from the depths of the loch?* He would probably bar her in their chamber for "her own protection."

No, she had no ally here. Her thoughts drifted to D'Ary. There was something different about him, too. She hadn't imagined that tingly feeling at his touch. As she slipped through the postern, she wondered if he knew Queen Sebilla, then derided herself for her stupidity.

With a sigh of relief, she saw that no one was close to the door, and sprinted for her chamber.

Vardon stared across the training field at the laird and fought the urge to sneer his contempt. Padruig fought well for a simple mortal, but from the other men's worshipful looks and comments, one would think they had battled a god.

At the moment, Padruig was laughing at something a young, moonfaced guard said, standing with his sword in one hand and a cup of ale in the other. His very stance shouted arrogance and command.

"Laird," Vardon called out. "I could use a bit of practice. Would you indulge me?"

Padruig turned to him with a grin. "Of course."

Vardon forced himself to return the smile, though

inside hate bloomed for the descendant of the man who'd helped crush him.

Padruig didn't wait, but attacked at once, clearly intending to put Vardon on the defensive. Vardon easily blocked his blow and advanced. His blade landed against Padruig's shield with a loud thwack.

"Well done," Padruig said, dodging to the left and coming at Vardon again.

As if you are worthy to judge my abilities, Vardon scorned silently. He jumped toward Padruig and swung his sword once more.

Back and forth across the field they went, trading blows. Soon, sweat ran into both Vardon's eyes and Padruig's, yet despite previously battling four other men, Padruig displayed no fatigue, his expression totally absorbed in the fight. In spite of his hatred for the man, Vardon found himself reluctantly impressed.

Stubborn bastard, he thought as he evaded another of Padruig's blows. As Vardon twisted around, he saw an opening. Padruig had left his right side entirely exposed.

Time stopped. *One thrust*, he screamed to himself. *One and the whoreson is dead!* He raised his sword, his lust for revenge overtaking him.

And met Aimili's gaze.

The sight halted him in his tracks, and he put down his sword. She stared at him as if she knew him, knew exactly what had gone through his mind, but no, that was impossible. She was naught more than an innocent young girl.

There was a strange aura about her, though, almost as if she . . . *No*. Vardon discarded the thought that the girl could be more than she appeared. He forced an open smile to his face, and nodded to her.

"You fight well," Padruig said as he swiped sweat from his brow.

"Thank you, my laird. 'Tis good practice for me to go up against one as skilled as yourself."

"Hmph. Methinks you belittle your abilities."

You have no idea, Vardon wanted to tell him, but held his tongue and pasted a mild expression on his face. "I see that your lady has come to watch."

Padruig's head snapped around so fast that Vardon's eyes widened. So, the laird was not so indifferent to the lass as everyone said. No, he thought as he studied Padruig. Not in the least. He put the information away for further consideration, pleased that he'd not given in to the temptation to "accidentally" slay the laird.

He watched Padruig walk over to Aimili, watched the stiff way Padruig held his body, his slow steps. Oh, yes, there was more to be done here before he finished off Padruig MacCoinneach.

Much more.

"Aimili," Padruig said. "Do you need something?"

"I thought to maintain my skills with a blade." Nothing in her eyes or her tone suggested that she mocked him, but Padruig knew it all the same. She wore her usual attire, a green tunic and braies, with sturdy-looking brown boots. Her hair was plaited in one long braid down her back, and she wore a belted scabbard around her waist. In one hand, she held a battered, triangular-shaped shield.

"Oh?"

"Aye. As you so . . . forcefully reminded me, now that we are wed, I could be a target for your enemies. I must be able to protect myself."

If a lass could appear more guileless, Padruig had never seen it. Nor did he believe it for a moment. Not in this case. "That is why you are not to go outside the castle walls without a guard. Or two. Or more."

Aimili sighed. "Surely you agree that 'twould be a good idea for me to be able to defend myself, as well." She fixed him with a wide-eyed look. "What if my guard is overcome?"

"You are an excellent rider. I've no doubt you can outrun any pursuer."

"Hmm. While I appreciate your confidence in my ability to get away, I would prefer to keep my skills up." She gazed around at the ten or so men who lingered, listening to every word their laird and his bride exchanged.

"My lady, I would be happy—"

Padruig cut off the overly enthusiastic boy, Artan, with a hard glance. He smiled at Aimili. "If the lady wishes to . . . practice with her wee sword, it is her husband's duty to oblige her." He squelched a chuckle at the flush of anger his choice of words provoked.

"As you wish," she said, unsheathing a sword.

Padruig frowned at her. "Where did you get that?"

One of the guards snickered.

Aimili lifted her chin. "Our smithy made it for me. 'Tis called Judgment."

"You put a name to that . . . that sword?"

A few more guards snickered.

"Are you going to fight or just stand there?" she asked.

At the moment, Padruig truly wasn't sure. "Have you any training? At all?"

In answer, she sprang forward and attacked.

Padruig stumbled back, instinctively raising his shield. Behind him, he heard some of the guards making a wager and, by the saints, the curs were actually favoring his wife!

"Pay attention, Padruig," she ordered.

He idly blocked her sword. *Best to finish this quickly,* he decided. *The sooner the better the lass realizes she needs a man to protect her.* He twisted and brought his sword down hard onto her shield.

A flash of pain crossed Aimili's face as she dropped the shield onto the dirt.

"Do you yield?" he asked.

He was pretty sure he heard her say, "Go to hell," but he refused to believe it. She ran at him, and he swung his sword low, intending to stop her forward movement. Instead, she leapt over the sword as if the very air carried her. Before he could do more than stare in astonishment, she had the very sharp edge of her blade against his exposed throat.

The guards burst into raucous laughter.

Aimili rocked back on her heels and sheathed her sword. "Mayhap, next time you will provide me more sport," she said and sauntered from the field.

Padruig realized his mouth still hung open when Magnus walked up and pushed it closed.

"Good to see you are making progress with your bride," Magnus commented.

"What did I do to deserve this?" Padruig murmured.

Magnus laughed. "You would prefer a helpless lass who spent the day in her solar working and reworking the trim on your tunic?"

"'Twould be easier."

"And hopelessly dull."

The other men filed off the field, sending Padruig grins and nods of approval. "Good show by your lady,

Laird," one of them called.

"What am I to do with her, Magnus?"

His friend shrugged. "You have not been eager to accept my advice."

Make Aimili his wife in truth, Magnus meant. Padruig swallowed, wishing the idea was not so appealing. Oh, to be sure, he'd had his share of plump, full-breasted women, and enjoyed every one. Lately, however, his taste had changed to a woman with a lithe, strong body, one with skin touched by sunlight. He felt beads of sweat form on his forehead. "What was her father thinking? Why did he not find a strong, young man to take her in hand?"

"Perhaps none of those lads thought themselves able to, as you say, 'take her in hand.'"

"I am no sure any man could."

"Maybe you should simply take her as she is."

"I cannot. Not in the way you mean."

"How long will you do penance, Padruig?"

"It could never be long enough."

"I have been looking into the matter of Brona's death."

Hearing Magnus say Padruig's sister's name brought it all to the front of his mind. *You killed her!* his mother's voice shouted. *This is your fault!*

"I spoke with Brona's maid's sister, who yet lives in the village."

"Magnus, cease. We all know what happened."

"Padruig, I—"

"Cease! 'Tis bad enough that each day here reminds me of Brona's absence. Bad enough that every time I look at my wife I see Brona's passion for life, her innocence of the wickedness of men." He realized he was shouting, and clenched his jaw.

"Aimili is not Brona, Padruig."

"She is the very same age Brona was when she died. Died because I failed to see the madness in Symund. Died because I forced her to sneak off with Malcolm. She grew up within the protection of her clan, just as Aimili did. Brona knew nothing of what dangers the world held, either."

"You are afraid," Magnus said, his eyes widening.

"Nay."

"Aimili appears capable of protecting herself."

"She is like a child who jumps off the cliff without looking down for a safe place to land. Today, she got lucky."

Magnus shook his head. "She is your wife, Padruig."

"Aye. And I will keep her safe. From everything."

"Even yourself?"

"Especially myself."

"What if Brona's murder was not your fault, Padruig?" Magnus asked in a soft voice. "What then?"

"I thank you for your faith, my friend, but I know

the truth. If not for me, my sister would yet live. That is my truth. That is all there is."

Chapter Nine

Aimili nearly skipped as she made her way across the bailey. *Take that, you overbearing knave,* she thought. By the saints, the expression on Padruig's face had been beyond price. She giggled, wishing she could share her victory with the old guard at de Grantham Castle who'd taught her that trick.

Still basking in satisfaction, she pulled up short when a maid stepped into her path. "My lady, Lady Freya sent me to find you. She asks that you attend her and Lady Efrika in Lady Efrika's solar."

"Oh." Aimili cast about in her mind for an excuse. Surely she had something to do besides endure another discussion about how many joints of beef should be prepared for dinner. "I—"

"I will take you there." The maid was at least a head taller than Aimili, and her expression, though sunny and friendly, was determined. Clearly, Efrika and Freya had warned her of Aimili's likely reluctance.

"I suppose I can spare a short time," Aimili said,

ignoring the flash of humor in the maid's gaze. She followed the girl to a round, squat tower and up two flights of stone steps. The landing at the top opened into a large airy chamber, its three windows open to let in the light.

Freya jumped up from her stool. "Aimili, there you are!" She beamed a smile.

Aimili blinked in shock. Each time she'd seen Freya, the girl had been dressed in a soft bliaut and undertunic, her copper-colored hair always carefully arranged to curl around her face. Today, she wore garments almost identical to Aimili's, but of a dark blue instead of green. Her hair hung down her back in a single plait just as Aimili's own did.

Efrika sat on a nearby stool with a pile of fabric spread across her lap. She and Freya exchanged a look.

"I am ready," Freya announced.

"For—"

"Riding lessons. What think you of my attire?" She turned in a circle, laughing. "'Tis a very free feeling. I can see why you like to dress this way."

Efrika coughed.

"Oh, but look, Aimili," Freya said, pulling up a bundle of fabric from a basket in front of her. She shook it out and Aimili realized it was a bliaut of forest green wool, with pale blue vines embroidered around the neck and wide bottoms of the sleeves. "I shortened the hem and have not had time to embroider it yet."

"'Tis lovely," Aimili said politely.

"I am so glad you like it."

Aimili narrowed her eyes in puzzlement. Why did Freya care what Aimili thought of her gowns?

"'Tis for you to wear to supper."

"For me?"

"Aye." She draped the material over Aimili's shoulder. "'Twill look much better on you than me, do you not think so?"

"I, uh—"

"I am sure Padruig will think so, too." Freya flashed a wide grin.

"I doubt he will notice," Aimili muttered. "Particularly after I just beat him in a sword fight."

Freya's eyes grew as round as a bannock. "You did?" She clapped and turned to Efrika. "Did you hear that? Aimili bested Padruig!"

Efrika's mouth quirked in a smile. "What did Padruig say?"

Aimili couldn't help but grin. "Nothing. He was in too much shock."

"So," Freya said, laying her hand on Aimili's arm, "I will try to learn to ride if you will wear this gown to supper. And," she said slowly, gesturing toward Efrika.

Efrika held up a length of deep purple silk. "This is for you. Padruig had Freya purchase it from a traveling merchant."

Her words gave Aimili pause, and the beginnings of

a warm feeling in her chest. She would not have guessed that Padruig gave her more than a passing thought. "He did?"

"Aye." Efrika tilted her head. "I have begun sewing the gown, but, well, if you would prefer to do it yourself that is fine." She clearly assumed that Aimili lacked the skill.

"I can sew, actually, but I do not generally take the time for it. Perhaps," she paused and gulped, taking in the cozy atmosphere of the chamber, the surprising kindness and acceptance by Freya and Efrika, "I could help embroider the trim when 'tis time."

"Perfect."

Moments later, Aimili followed Freya down the steps and back out into the bailey. As the two crossed the sparsely grassed area, Aimili said, "Tell me about the fall you had."

Freya wrinkled her nose. "We were riding back from Ruthenshire. They hold a fair there each May Day." Freya took Aimili's hand. "We shall go. 'Tis filled with merchants from everywhere!"

"You shall have to ride," Aimili reminded her, more affected by the way Freya so easily took her hand than she wanted to admit.

"Aye. Well, 'twas a lovely day. The sun was warm, our stomachs were full from meat pies, fresh cheese, and wine, and my saddlebag held the most beautiful hair ribbons I had ever seen." She sighed.

"Were you riding astride?"

"Aye. The truth is, I have never felt very balanced atop a horse. I so envy people like you who make it look so very easy."

"You shall learn. Not everyone starts off just knowing how to sit a horse."

"Good. Anyway, we were not in a hurry, so we were just walking along the road. There were woods to one side and open land on the other. All of the sudden, for no reason at all, the horrible beast I was riding went completely mad."

Freya's tone was so piqued that Aimili had to suppress a smile. "What do you mean?"

"He jumped in the air, landed to the side of the road, and galloped off as if his life depended upon escape. Somewhere along the way, he swerved to the right. I went left. When I woke up, Padruig was carrying me into the hall."

Unfortunately, Freya's story was not all that uncommon, but still . . . why put her on a horse so easily frightened? "Who chose your mount?"

"I dinnae remember. A groom had him ready for me."

"When did this happen?" Aimili asked as they walked into the stable.

"Before Padruig left. Mayhap a year and a half ago."

"Ye should not have been on a horse who would react so."

210

Freya frowned. "I never thought of it that way."

Mist stuck her nose over the door to her stall and nickered in welcome.

Freya halted and eyed her.

"This is Mist," Aimili said, tugging Freya along. "She is my riding horse, and very sweet."

The girl is afraid?

Aye. Be verra gentle.

Hmph. I always am.

She was thrown badly by a horse that panicked, apparently at nothing.

Not nothing.

No, but 'tis unclear what happened. Freya didn't notice anything.

"Mist shall take very good care of you," Aimili told Freya as she led the horse from her stall. "I promise."

"She is rather big."

Aimili handed Freya a brush and spotted D'Ary leaning against a stall watching them. He unfolded his length and approached. "May I be of assistance?"

Freya peeked over Mist's back and squeaked in surprise. "Who are you?"

D'Ary flashed her a smile. "I am new in the stables. My name is D'Ary, my fair lady."

Freya giggled, and Aimili gave D'Ary a warning look, to which he responded by winking at her.

Aimili narrowed her gaze. Far too forward to be a mere stable hand, she thought once again, wondering about D'Ary's true background. "I have promised to give the Lady Freya instruction. She is not as comfortable riding as she would like to be."

"What she means is that I am a terrible rider, and a feartie-cat, as well."

"You suffered a bad fall," Aimili reminded her. "'Tis understandable to be fearful." She turned to D'Ary. "Lady Freya's horse took a sudden fright and bolted off with her."

"What frightened the horse?"

"Nothing," Freya told him. "At least naught that anyone could see. The damned beast, excuse my language, just took off."

D'Ary frowned. "A palfrey?"

"Aye. Hugo had to put it down. By the time it returned to the stables, it had broken its leg."

D'Ary looked at Aimili and she saw that he had the same thought she did. A well-trained ladies' palfrey, chosen to carry a young, fairly unskilled rider, should not have behaved in such a way.

"You will have no trouble with Mist," Aimili assured her as she saddled the mare. By the time they walked into the outdoor pen, Freya was biting her lip and slowing her steps. D'Ary stopped outside and leaned on the rail.

"I am no sure about this after all, Aimili."

"When have you last ridden?" Freya didn't answer. "Not since your fall?"

Freya shook he head, her cheeks flushed. "Nay. I

told you I was a coward."

"From this day forward, you may not say such things. If you name yourself a coward, then that is what you will be. Today, you are a brave woman who can ride and ride well. Now"—Aimili gestured to the stirrup—"up you go. I have her."

Though her reluctance was palpable, Freya swung onto Mist's back and took up the reins. She held herself as if an iron staff was permanently attached to her backbone, and her knees gripped Mist's sides.

"Freya."

"Aye?"

"Breathe. Mist is no going to run off."

Freya blew out a breath, and her body relaxed slightly.

"Go ahead and walk," Aimili told her. "I shall be right next to you. Focus on taking deep breaths and just moving with her."

"Very well." Freya squeezed Mist forward into a walk, but after a few steps pulled back on the reins. "She is going too fast."

Aimili put a hand on Mist's neck and looked up at Freya. "'Tis just her usual walk, no more. Breathe and move with her." Aimili cast about for ideas. "Imagine that you are a partially cooked custard."

"Custard?" Freya actually smiled at that.

"Aye. Soft, rather sticky, but not solid."

Freya started off again.

She is digging her knees into my sides, Mist told Aimili.

I can see that. Be patient, my friend. She is fearful.

"Relax, Freya. Be the custard."

When Freya giggled again, her body loosened.

"Try not to grip with your knees. It throws your body off balance."

"Truly?" Freya gazed down at Aimili with a puzzled expression. "I thought it would help me stay on."

"Nay." Aimili halted Mist and took one of Freya's legs out of the stirrup. "'Tis better to stretch this down and around Mist's belly. If you grip your knees, the rest of your body will stiffen, too."

"Oh. I guess I forgot."

"Who taught you to ride?"

Freya started Mist walking again. "Padruig, and sometimes Magnus." She smiled. "We had such merriment together. Both of them were very tolerant of me following them about."

"Merriment?"

"Oh, yes. But that was before Padruig took over for Father and, well, before . . ."

"Before?"

"Before poor Brona died. Padruig . . . well, you ken the story."

"Not really."

Freya sighed. "That bastard MacVegan murdered her because he couldn't have her. She loved Malcolm. Padruig was too late to save her." She pulled Mist to a stop and gazed down at Aimili. "He blames himself for everything, you know. 'Tis why he left."

"Why did he come back?"

"I dinnae ken. I am only grateful he did in time to save me from having to marry Angus Ransolm."

Aimili's mouth turned down. "I have never met the man, but he whipped Loki mercilessly."

"I am no surprised. He has a reputation for cruelty." Freya shivered and crossed herself. "If not for Padruig's return, I would be dead."

"And my father's aid," Aimili said before she could stop herself.

Freya stared at her for a moment. "True enough. I hope you will be happy here, Aimili. We are pleased to have you."

Aimili blinked back the sudden burn of tears. "Thank you."

"Padruig . . . he, well, he is changed." Freya bit her lip. "He does not trust himself anymore. And Mother . . ."

"I encountered your mother in the chapel. She called Padruig a murderer."

"Aye." Freya shook her head. "She hates him, and though he acts as if it is no matter, I know it pains him. They were once close."

"He did not kill your sister."

"Nay, but he feels as if he did. I fear he will never forgive himself. It is as if he sees himself too flawed, too stained to do so."

Aimili slowly began to understand, though the

knowledge brought naught but the heavy weight of hopelessness in her heart.

"Padruig used to be so different. He would tell me stories, and always tell me all about what happened during his travels with Father."

"I met him once at de Grantham Castle."

Freya gazed down at her. "Then you know what I mean." As she circled the ring, she shook her head. "'Tis a sad thing. I fear Padruig will never allow anyone to be truly close to him again."

"Nay. Why would he?"

"I am sorry, Aimili."

Aimili just stared at her. "So am I," she finally managed to say.

I am in hell, Padruig thought, watching Aimili walk into the hall accompanied by a grinning Freya. The boyish young girl he'd taken to wife was gone this eve. *Damn Freya and her meddling,* he swore to himself.

"A child, hmm?" Magnus murmured next to him.

"Shut up."

Magnus chuckled and leaned back on his seat.

Aimili wore a deep green bliaut with blue embroidery around the neck. Beneath the bliaut peeked an undertunic of a lighter green, and around her narrow waist she wore a girdle of silver. Someone, probably Freya, had laced the bliaut tight enough that the fabric outlined breasts Padrúig knew were plump and firm. Aimili's hair cascaded around her face and down her back. The candlelight picked up the copper strands in her hair.

She stared at him through big, dark eyes framed by sooty lashes.

Padruig shot back a drink of wine and frowned. By the saints, now he was thinking like some blasted poet.

"Do not scowl so," Magnus told him. "You shall upset your bride." Laughter underlay his words.

"I doubt that. Aimili is no frightened hare."

"Nay."

Padruig stood as Aimili and Freya approached. Efrika came in behind them with Alasdair. "Good eve," he said politely, before retaking his seat. He took a deep breath as Aimili settled in next him and had to grab hold of his chair to stop himself from leaning closer. What in heaven had she put on her skin? She smelled like flowers and something earthy, the combination making him want to bury his nose against her neck. He refilled his cup.

"Would you care for wine?" he asked, not looking at her.

When she didn't immediately answer, he glanced at her.

"Yes. Thank you."

How had this happened? Padruig wondered with

more than a hint of desperation. *You have been too long without a woman,* he told himself. *'Tis that simple.* He poured wine in Aimili's cup.

She took a sip, licking her lower lip when a drop of wine strayed.

She might as well have licked his rod for the effect it had on Padruig. He shifted on his seat, then looked up to find Efrika watching him with a knowing look. "I understand you and our Aimili had an interesting encounter on the field today," she said.

Alasdair guffawed.

"We did, indeed," Padruig said.

Aimili coolly popped a piece of cheese in her mouth. "'Twas not much of a contest."

"You took me by surprise. I was endeavoring not to harm you."

She leveled him with a look, one brow raised. "I told you I can take care of myself."

Padruig signaled the servants to begin serving the meal. "Still, you will take a guard when you venture out of the castle."

"D'Ary has offered to accompany me." She cut a piece of bread.

"D'Ary."

"Aye. He is also going to help me with my horses."

"I see."

"Padruig, Aimili is helping me ride again!" Freya said, as usual completely missing the undertones of the conversation. "It was fun."

Padruig's heart softened at the enthusiasm in his sister's voice. "I am glad, Freya. 'Tis past time you rode again."

"I know. I am a coward."

Aimili coughed and shot Freya a look.

Freya smiled. "Och, no, I cannae say that, can I? I am courageous and I will succeed!"

"Much better," Aimili told her. She turned to Padruig, her expression serious. "You were there the day Freya fell?"

"Aye." Thankful for a safe topic of conversation, he said, "We were lucky Freya did not suffer a worse injury. The horse was uncontrollable."

"Did you notice aught that caused the horse to bolt?"

"Nay. 'Twas the strangest thing. None of the other mounts reacted at all, but Freya's horse behaved as if death rode his flanks."

"Had the horse ever done anything like that?"

"I do not know." Padruig wrinkled his brow. "Actually, I do not recall much about the horse at all, other than the fact that Hugo had to put him down."

Aimili slowly chewed a bite of roasted mutton.

"You are not suggesting that someone deliberately tried to harm Freya?" Padruig asked in a low voice.

"I am no sure. Something about the event bothers me. I do know horses, Padruig."

"I ken. I heard you are having better luck with Loki."

"Aye."

"I hope you are wrong about Freya, though. I cannot imagine why anyone would want to hurt her. The clan has always doted on her."

A strange look passed over Aimili's face, then was gone. She shrugged. "Accidents do happen. And even the best behaved mount can take a fright."

"True enough. Thank you for taking the time to aid Freya."

"'Tis my pleasure." She delicately wiped her mouth with a square of linen.

Padruig found the sight so arousing that he decided the only way to survive the meal was to ignore her. He engaged Magnus in a lengthy discussion about the market at Inverness and somehow managed to get though supper without making an utter fool of himself.

Just as he was congratulating himself, he felt a hand on his arm. "Padruig?"

Suppressing a groan, he turned to his wife. "If you do not mind, I believe I shall retire," she said. "It has been a long day."

"Of course." Relief spilled through him, and he managed a smile. "Sleep well."

"Do you . . . do you wish to accompany me?" she asked softly.

Hell, yes! he wanted to shout. His mouth was so dry

he could barely swallow. "I have matters yet to discuss with Magnus," he said ignoring the snort behind him.

Aimili nodded, then turned to speak to the others seated on the dais before walking out.

Padruig forced himself not to watch her.

"Coward," Magnus whispered.

"Cease," Padruig whispered back, filling his cup once again.

"Ye are being foolish. 'Tis clear the lass wants you."

Padruig closed his eyes and fought for calm. Images spilled through his mind too fast for him to control, and the ache in his rod was insistent. "She does not know what she wants."

"Your lady is no as sheltered as you pretend." Magnus leaned close and said in Padruig's ear, "She breeds horses, remember. She watches while her stallions cover her mares. By the saints, man, she supervises the act herself no doubt."

"Shut. Up."

"The lass knows what mating looks like."

"Horses, Magnus. Not people."

"Is it so different?"

Padruig felt a drop of sweat trickle down his face. "She is an innocent lass to be treated with honor, with care."

"Mayhap, but I think your lady has a wildness in her soul." Magnus sat back and grinned.

"Do you not have somewhere to go for your trading ventures? Perth perhaps?"

"Nay. I am quite content here for the time. 'Tis proving to be very entertaining."

"Magnus, I—" Padruig broke off at the sound of a scream. He drew his sword and ran toward the doors to the great hall, his heart near to pumping out of his chest. Footsteps pounded behind him, but he didn't pause to glance back.

He burst out into the evening, flying down the steps into the deserted bailey. "Aimili!" he bellowed.

Magnus rushed to his side, holding a torch high. The flames flickered over the trodden ground, but there was neither sight nor sound of Aimili.

"Ivarr," Padruig called out. A guard peered down from the wall walk atop the curtain wall. "Have you seen Lady Aimili?"

"Nay."

"Did you hear a scream?"

"I did hear somethin', but I thought it was just an animal."

Padruig wasn't sure how he knew, but he knew to his bones that the scream had been Aimili. "Call an alarm."

The guard whistled three times in succession, and a troop of men streamed out of the gatehouse.

Padruig stalked across the ground toward the south tower holding their chamber. Magnus followed him. "Spread out and search the entire castle," he yelled at Randulf, one of the senior guards. "Lady Aimili is missing."

"She cannae be far," Magnus said as they hurried along. "'Twas only a matter of moments."

"Long enough to come to harm. I should have escorted her." Padruig's belly twisted in guilty knots. If anything had happened to Aimili . . . He couldn't even bear to finish the thought, a sick lump of dread and guilt spreading through his chest. Brona's still, white face flashed in his mind, but he shoved it away.

"Aimili!" he shouted instead.

The deafening sound of silence answered him.

He and Magnus arrived at the base of the south tower. "Wait here," Padruig told Magnus. "I shall check our chamber." He ran up the steps and through the doorway to the chamber. Cai raised his head from a spot in front of the lit fire. "Aimili?" he asked, quickly glancing around the chamber.

Cai jumped up and bumped Padruig's leg with his nose. "Aye, boy, we need to find her. Come." He ran back down the steps and shook his head at Magnus.

Magnus pointed at Cai. "Can the wolf track her?"

"Mayhap." Padruig looked down at Cai. "Find Aimili."

Cai tilted his head one way and then the other, before padding off into the expanding darkness.

Padruig chased after him, struck by the similarity to a time not so long ago when he'd followed Cai to find Giselle out in the woods, covered in blood and hysterical after being kidnapped by a monster. He gritted his teeth and sent up a prayer for Aimili.

Lights bobbed in the darkness, and voices called over and over for Aimili. It seemed like hours before Cai let out a woof and loped toward the back corner of the stables.

"There she is," Magnus said, his voice grim.

Aimili lay crumpled on the ground, her dark bliaut and hair blending in so well with the shadows that but for Cai they might not have spotted her. Padruig dropped to the ground and put his fingers against her throat, unable to breathe while he waited to feel a heartbeat.

She groaned and tried to put her hand up to block the torchlight. "Aimili," Padruig said. "'Tis all right now." He picked her up in his arms, and felt a bump on the back of her head.

"I . . . I am fine," she choked out.

"Magnus, tell the others I found her," Padruig said, ignoring Aimili's obvious lie. "Then, fetch Efrika. I am taking Aimili to our chamber."

"Aye, Laird." With a last worried glance, Magnus rushed off.

Padruig fought to rein in his temper. How dare anyone attack his wife within the walls of the castle? And what had she been doing over by the stables? D'Ary's face jumped into his mind, but he refused to give reign to his suspicions. With Cai bounding along beside him, he remained focused on getting Aimili up into their chamber, where he laid her gently atop the bed.

She blinked at him, and scooted to a sitting position, gingerly feeling the back of her head.

Padruig sat on the edge of the bed. "What happened?"

"I . . . I am no exactly sure. I was walking toward our chamber. I felt like someone was watching me, but I didn't see anyone."

"Why were you by the stables?"

She frowned. "Was I? I . . . I don't know."

"Did you see D'Ary?"

"D'Ary? No, I don't think so. I didn't see anyone, but suddenly something smashed into the back of my head. 'Tis the last I remember until you found me." She flushed. "Thank you."

"I heard you scream."

"You did? I dinnae remember doing so."

Efrika burst into the room carrying a basket. Freya followed close behind, and, lastly, Magnus. "My poor dear, are you all right?" Efrika asked.

"Aye, but my head hurts a bit."

"Who did this?"

Aimili started to shrug, then winced. "I never saw him. 'Twas too dark, and he came out of nowhere."

"This is terrible," Freya cried as she plopped on the bed to take Aimili's hand. "Are we not safe anywhere?" Though she held Aimili's hand, Padruig noticed that she gazed at Magnus.

"Magnus, have Randulf question the men," Padruig

told him. "Surely, someone saw *something*."

"Aye." With a last glance toward Freya, Magnus left.

Efrika felt the back of Aimili's head and tsked her disgust. "Cowardly, to attack a woman from behind. Padruig, you must find this foul miscreant at once."

Padruig held Aimili's gaze. "I plan to."

After pouring a cup of wine, Efrika heated it over the fire, then added ingredients from her basket, muttering all the while. When Cai inched closer to sniff, her gaze flashed up as if she were seeing him for the first time, though unsurprisingly, Efrika was not afraid. "These are not for you," she scolded.

"Cai found me," Aimili said slowly. "I felt his nose nuzzle my face."

"Aye," Padruig said.

"Well, he is indeed due for a treat, but not from my cache of herbs," Efrika said as she handed Aimili the cup. "Drink up. 'Twill help the headache."

"Thank you." Aimili took a sip and shuddered.

"I know, the taste is terrible, but it works."

Aimili gamely took another sip.

"Come, Freya," Efrika said. "Aimili needs to rest. Padruig shall take care of her."

"Are you sure? Aimili, is there anything else we can do?"

"Nay." Aimili squeezed the younger girl's hand. "I shall be fine."

"Where is Magnus?" Freya asked as she stood. "We

need for him to see us to the Ladies' Tower."

"Alasdair is waiting below," Efrika told her, "though I would not be surprised to see Magnus, as well." Over the top of Freya's head, Efrika sent Padruig a look that told him she suspected Magnus's feelings for Freya were not altogether brotherly.

For the first time that eve, Padruig smiled.

After the women filed out, Aimili asked, "What was that about?"

"I fear Magnus has developed a fondness for my sister."

Aimili's eyes widened. "And Freya?"

"I am no sure. Mayhap you could discover how she feels." He studied Aimili as she continued to drink Efrika's brew, clearly forcing herself to each sip. *She looks different*, he thought, and it struck him what it was. He had never seen his bride appear so vulnerable. Her hair was in disarray, and her bliaut was stained with dirt, but that was not the real change. The difference was in her eyes. A discomfiting mix of weariness, puzzlement, and fear clouded her usually clear gaze.

He took her free hand. "I shall discover what happened this eve, Aimili."

"Ah, yes, 'tis part of your *duty*, is it not?"

Duty seemed very far away at the moment. He stroked a fingertip over her jaw, where a bruise was beginning to form. Her skin was every bit as soft as he'd imagined and, by the saints, he'd imagined such more than he wished to admit.

Aimili's gaze darkened and he felt her breath hitch.

By God, a man could only take so much, he thought as he bent his head and kissed her, intending to press a light kiss of reassurance to her mouth. He knew at once he'd made a serious error in judgment. Her lips were soft and full, yielding to his and drawing him in for more.

One touch was all it took for his body to rouse into a fierce wanting. Padruig gripped Aimili's shoulders and deepened the kiss, delving into her mouth, tasting the wine sweetened with honey and herbs from Efrika. More, he needed more of her. He stroked his hands up her shoulders and slipped them behind her head to hold her in place.

She moaned. It wasn't a moan of desire.

Padruig reeled back, appalled at his behavior. Dear Lord, he'd been so caught up in the magic of plundering his bride that he'd forgotten all about her injury.

She gazed at him through wide eyes, her lips parted.

"Aimili, damn, I'm sorry." Padruig stood and paced across the room.

"What exactly are you sorry about?" Her voice was barely above a whisper.

He waved a hand. "I lost control. It will not happen again."

"Padruig, you are my husband."

"Aye. Which is why I should be protecting you, seeing to your welfare, not attacking you like some sort of beast." He splashed wine into a cup and shot it down.

"I would hardly call a kiss an attack."

He cautioned a look at her. Aimili sat on the bed still cradling her cup, a faint smile on her face. "You should rest," he told her as he headed for the door.

"Where are you going?"

He paused at the doorway. "To find the whoreson who hurt you." And to remove my sorry arse from temptation, he silently added. What in heaven had come over him?

Fool, his inner voice jeered as Padruig walked down the steps. *Lust came over you. Lust for your beautiful wife.* He stopped at the bottom of the steps, closed his eyes and fisted a hand. *I am a stronger man than that,* he told himself. *I am not governed by my body's desires. I will not be so ruled.*

If only he'd not heard Aimili's last words. *I'd rather you stayed with me,* she'd said.

She has no idea what she is asking, he reminded himself as he strode across the bailey toward the gatehouse. *Though she may not look like a child, inside she is. Innocent. Sheltered.* He had no doubt Aimili had never felt the touch of a man. If the kiss told him naught else, it told him that.

He groaned under his breath. Somehow her inexperience didn't have the dampening effect he'd expected, but the opposite.

No. He would protect her. He would safeguard her welfare. She was part of the clan now, and a very important part at that. He would not let himself loose on her person, no matter how hard it was. And it, or rather he, was indeed as hard as stone.

Aimili deserved better than that. Better than *him*. He traced the deepest scar on his face. Though there was no way to be sure, he'd always believed it came from the first slash by Connor MacVegan, Laird of the MacVegan clan.

He had only to touch the scar to remind himself that it was a brand of his arrogant stupidity, a permanent mark to let everyone know of his failure.

He knew in his heart and his mind that he did not deserve a lass like Aimili. She was like the blue center of a flame: reckless, beautiful, and pure.

And he, well, he was none of those things.

Sebilla stood in the antechamber of the archives, and fought the unqueenlike urge to stamp her feet in impatience. "Tell me you have found *something*, Arailt."

Arailt stood in the shadows cast by the tall, fluted columns set at ten-foot intervals on either side of the antechamber. Behind him, the immense gold-plated door to Paroseea's archives stood wide open. A warm breeze lifted the edge of his deep blue robe, the color traditionally worn by Paroseea's scholars.

"Sebilla, my queen, I am sorry. As of yet, I have failed to find a solution."

The touch of breeze did nothing to cool the heat rising in Sebilla's face. "How can that be? There must be something. At the very least, there should be a record of how our forbearers were able to imprison Vardon in the first place."

"We are still looking, your majesty."

She frowned and waved a hand. "Please dispense with the titles, Arailt. This matter is far too serious to waste time on such formality."

"As you wish, my, uh, Sebilla. As I said, we are still searching. The oldest records are difficult to sort through."

"After this is over, perhaps you should undertake organizing those records," Sebilla remarked.

"Aye, but for now—"

"Father!" Arailt's daughter, Vanasia, burst out of the doorway clutching a scroll in her hand. She stopped abruptly when she saw Sebilla, and curtsied, her face flaming red. "My apologies. I did not know you were here, your majesty."

Sebilla had to force her mouth into a polite smile. She knew Vardon's escape was not really Vanasia's fault, but the girl did bear some responsibility. If she had not snuck around with Vardon's guard, Paroseea would not now be faced with exposure and possibly worse.

"What is it, Vanasia?" Arailt asked, putting out a

hand to steady his daughter.

"I . . . I might have found something." She cast a timid glance at Sebilla.

Well, spit it out! Sebilla wanted to shout, but she forcibly reminded herself that queens did not lose their tempers upon timid young girls. "Pray, tell us, Vanasia," she said instead.

"I had forgotten all about it as it's been so long since I saw the scroll. It tells of how we defeated Vardon."

Sebilla held out her hand, excitement and hope rising in her. "Let me see this scroll."

Vanasia handed it to her, and Sebilla began to read. Immediately, disappointment crushed her earlier hopes. The scroll did, indeed, tell of Vardon's capture, but more as a story of Paroseea's triumph than exactly how it was done. She rerolled the scroll and tapped it against her palm. "'Tis not specific enough."

"Aye, I know, but . . . I thought it was a start."

"There must be other records, Vanasia. We need the spell of enchantment used to contain Vardon."

"Assuming it was written down," Arailt said with a frown.

"Oh, I am sure it was," Sebilla countered, never moving her gaze from Vanasia. "Somewhere."

The girl flushed again and ducked her head. Though Sebilla had been restrained in placing too much blame upon Vanasia, she had still let the girl know of her mistake. The secrets of the archives were to remain exactly that, not idle postfornication talk with a lover.

Worse, the girl could neither remember the location nor the information she'd imparted to Ulf. Vardon's doing, no doubt, Sebilla thought with an inward curse of frustration.

"Of course, your majesty," Vanasia said. "If you will excuse me, I shall return to our search."

Sebilla nodded, and the girl scampered back through the doorway.

Arailt looked at her with an odd expression. "Sebilla, is there aught else wrong?"

For a moment, Sebilla considered confiding in him, then rejected it. It was better Arailt stay solely focused on searching the archives, not worrying about his daughter's indiscretion or his queen's strange visions. "Nay, 'tis just difficult waiting. I want the matter of Vardon resolved."

"As do we all." Arailt sighed. "If there is an answer in the archives, we shall find it. That, I promise."

"Make haste, Arailt. I fear for the MacCoinneach clan."

He bowed and followed after his daughter. Sebilla stood for a moment in the large antechamber, absorbing the absolute quiet. The archives, the historical library of Paroseea's knowledge, were located at the very end of the central roadway, a place few ventured. Even if they did, access was severely limited to protect the irreplaceable scrolls and other documents.

She doubted if most of her people even gave the archives a thought. *Perhaps we have created too soft a life here,* she thought, turning to walk out of the wide, stone building. *We are ill prepared to take on one such as Vardon.*

A group of young children went skipping across the marble paved road, their laughter filling the air, and Sebilla paused to watch them with a smile. Why should they live in fear? Always on guard? No, that was the beauty of Paroseea, a beauty that she would die to protect.

The prospect of death did not worry her overmuch. She'd lived a long time, led a full life. At the last thought, her inner voice mocked her. *A full life?* Devoted to her people, to her duties, true.

Her thoughts strayed to D'Ary, the way he'd looked emerging from her pool, all golden muscle and gleaming amber eyes. What would it be like to lie with a man like that? A man who did not even make the pretense of deferring to her? She shivered.

It would be absolutely wondrous and absolutely foolhardy.

Chapter Ten

V ardon was having more fun than he'd had in three hundred years. By the gods, the expression on Padruig's face when he'd found unfortunate little Aimili's body on the ground had been something to savor. That one moment confirmed Vardon's suspicions.

He hadn't planned any of it, but he hadn't expected her to appear so close to his hiding place. It wouldn't do to have anyone discover the things he'd hidden. Not yet, anyway. Ah, how he loved an unexpected opportunity.

Chuckling inside, Vardon lay on his pallet and contemplated his next move. It was far too soon to finish off Padruig. Perhaps he should pick off his family members one by one, Padruig's pain and guilt increasing with each one. Oh, now that was tempting. The pitiful mother would have to be first. Silly woman, slinking about the castle like some sort of shadow. Oh, poor me. She was weak in character, and that was something he despised.

A flash of a long-ago face sifted through his mind, a woman beautiful and ethereal, her pale blond hair framing a soft face, blue eyes warm with tenderness. She'd been weak, too, weak and dismayed to find her only child capable of such strength of will, determined to improve his state in life.

She'd been content to labor for one of the "high" families of Paroseea. A bloated man and his vapid wife, surrounded by luxury yet undeserving of any of it.

Before she'd died, he'd taken over the lavish dwelling, but even then she'd refused to live there, somehow suspecting that Vardon had a hand in her former employer's timely demise.

So, Padruig's mother first? He wasn't sure she was even worth his effort. And surely Padruig cared little for her at this point. She'd made no secret of her rancor for her only son. Ah, sweet vengeance, indeed.

No, there was better prey to be had. His thoughts kept returning to Aimili. She had no idea how alluring her strength could be. This was no shapeless pillow of a lass, soft and yielding from countless hours of tedious women's work with little more in her head than which color of embroidery thread was her favorite.

No, Aimili was a different kind of woman, or nearly a woman. Strong in body from working with the horses, and from what he'd seen, strong in will. She'd certainly wasted no time dispatching dear Ciara.

For a moment, Vardon regretted Ciara's death, then inwardly shrugged. He'd thought of making her his whore after Grigor's imprisonment. Between Grigor's loose talk and what Vardon had witnessed himself, the woman had certain talents. Still, she'd nearly ruined his plans, and that could not be tolerated.

He decided the matter required more thought. He'd waited for too long for his revenge to make a misstep. Each step must be exactly right.

First, the MacCoinneachs.

Second, Paroseea.

Third, well, his course was only limited by his imagination, which was considerable, indeed.

He fell asleep with a smile on his face.

The next morn, Efrika stomped into Padruig's solar and shut the door with a firm click. She put her hands on her hips and stared at him.

"Good morn, Efrika," he said mildly, setting aside an account of foodstuffs in the storerooms compiled by Alasdair.

"Hmph." She sat on the window seat to the side of his worktable.

"Did you know that we have fifty barrels of pickled cabbage in the cellar?"

"I dinnae care for pickled cabbage."

"Obviously, you are no alone in your taste." He

looked over the piece of parchment. "What of pickled onions? How do you feel about that?"

"Padruig. I do not give a cow's teat about pickled onions. I am no here to talk about that."

Padruig sighed and put down the parchment. "Alasdair is doing a fine job as my seneschal."

Efrika waved a hand. "Of course, he is. Alasdair is a very skilled man."

"Ah, yes, skilled." Padruig grinned at her.

"You'll not distract me. I am no here to talk about me."

"I am doing all I can to shore up our stores for the winter, Efrika. Magnus is set to take men to Inverness to acquire what he can with the coin I found, and I have sent to an ally for aid, as well."

"What ally?"

"A friend. Lady Giselle is her name."

"A woman friend."

Padruig lifted a brow. "Obviously."

Efrika looked out the window. "I was beginning to wonder about you," she muttered.

Oh, no, Padruig thought. The very last topic he wished to discuss with Efrika, who had always lacked a sense of boundaries in her discourse, was his relationships with women.

"Who is this woman?"

"As I said, a friend."

"A former lover?"

"Nay. The lady is well wed, and has most likely borne her first bairn by now."

Efrika narrowed her gaze. "I am worried about Aimili."

Padruig started to rise. "Is she ill?"

"Nay." Efrika waved him back to his seat. "'Tis not that. Strong constitution, your lady has."

"Aye."

"Did you find out anything about who attacked her?"

Padruig scowled. "Nothing. None of the guards saw anything amiss, and, of course, Aimili did not see her attacker."

"Strange."

"I am putting patrols on the ground at night."

"Good." She smiled at him. "You are doing a fine job as laird, Padruig, as I knew you would."

He felt as if he was caught in a river's rapids, dodging rocks in the water, but it would not do to confess such to Efrika. "Thank you."

"But not such a great job as husband," she continued, eying him sternly.

"Efrika, 'tis—"

"Not my affair you are going to say, but I think it is. Who else is going to discuss this with you? Mairi?" Her mouth turned down. "God bless her, your mother's mind is no longer sound."

"She blames me for Brona's death. 'Tis hardly a sign

of madness. I doubt she is alone in her beliefs."

"Well, she is wrong."

Padruig blinked at the rush of emotion her emphatic words evoked.

"Have you bedded the girl?"

Padruig blinked again. "Efrika, I am taking the best care I can of Aimili. Do not fear."

"'Tis not what I asked."

"'Tis my answer."

"You have not." Efrika stood and began to pace. "Aimili told me you didn't want her, but I assumed she was simply overset with all that had happened in her life."

Want? Padruig wanted to laugh aloud. *Hardly a matter of not wanting*, he thought. "Aimili is very young."

Efrika whirled and frowned at him. "Aimili is seventeen years of age. Old enough to be wedded and bedded. Why do you reject the girl?"

He put his palms on the table. "Efrika, you know I had no choice but to wed Aimili. She had no choice, either."

"'Tis not unusual. I never even saw my Humfrey before the day of our wedding."

"Not everyone falls in love at first sight."

"You are saying you care nothing for the girl? 'Tis a lie, Padruig. I have seen the way you look at her, the way you behaved last eve when she was hurt."

"I didn't say I didn't care for the girl. Leave it be, Efrika."

"She is no happy, Padruig. I can see it in her eyes."

"And you think my lying with her will make her happy?" He barked out a laugh. "I doubt that."

For a long moment, Efrika tilted her head and studied him. "Do not squander your chance at happiness, Padruig. Leave the past where it belongs."

Padruig blanked his expression. "I have work to do."

"Aye, you do, indeed."

Before Padruig could refute her message, Efrika sailed out of the room. Padruig gripped the quill so tightly in his hand that it snapped in two.

When Aimili awoke the morning after her attack, she expected Padruig to be in their chamber. He was gone. She then expected him to check on her, to let her know if he'd made any progress in determining the identity of her attacker, but as the morning stretched on without any sign of him, she'd gradually come to understand that he was avoiding her.

It was the kiss. There could be no other explanation. Had she so repelled him? It hadn't seemed that way at the time. In fact, it had seemed very much like he was finally giving in to a desire he'd suppressed.

Obviously, she'd been mistaken. With a long, dejected sigh, she got out of bed, and caught hold of the bedpost as a wave of dizziness washed through her. She gritted her teeth and took small steps over to a basin of cold water.

After soaking the cloth, she cautiously pressed it against the back of her head. The bump had receded some, but was still tender to the touch. Shuffling over to the window seat, she kept the cloth in place, shivering as the cool water dripped down her back.

A knock on the door preceded Efrika's entrance, armed with her healing basket. She stopped abruptly. "Oh. Oh, my."

Aimili wrinkled her nose. "Do I look that bad?"

"Of course not, dear," Efrika said as she walked to the window seat and set down her basket.

"You are a liar."

Efrika laughed. "True. How do you feel?"

"A tiny bit dizzy, but I shall be fine. Thank you for your aid. I slept well."

"Headache?"

"Not too much. I can handle it."

"I've no doubt you can." Efrika glanced around the chamber and frowned. "Has no one come in with food and drink this morn?"

Aimili shook her head, immediately wishing she hadn't. "Mayhap they had orders to let me rest."

"Hmm. Excuse me for just a moment, child. I will summon—"

Freya poked her head around the door, her eyes bright. "Oh, good, you are awake." She tripped into the chamber. "Your horses have arrived!"

Aimili couldn't believe she'd forgotten that today was the day. She started to rise, but Efrika pushed her back down with a surprisingly firm grip. "Freya, can you find someone to bring wine and food? I need to mix something for Aimili's headache."

"Aye." Freya walked to the door, then turned. "Aimili, I saw the most beautiful mare!"

"What did she look like?"

"White, with the prettiest face, and one blue eye."

"Zara. She is an Arab, about four years old."

"Can I ride her?"

Freya's expression was so excited that Aimili hesitated. She didn't want to discourage Freya, but Zara was not usually a calm, placid mount. Still . . . she'd never done anything mean-spirited. "Perhaps. Work with Mist first. She is easier to handle."

"You must see her, Efrika. She is beautiful," Freya said as she bustled out of the chamber.

Efrika looked at Aimili and quirked a brow. "Can she ride the horse?"

"Not yet. Zara can be very energetic."

"Mayhap this is a good thing. It will give Freya a goal."

Aimili nodded. "Aye. And Zara has never really bonded with me. She is very independent."

Efrika stood and swept Aimili's hair to the side. "Let me see your head."

Aimili removed the cloth and felt the light touch of Efrika's fingers. "The bump is almost gone," Efrika said.

"I have a hard head. 'Tis a fortunate attribute given how many times I've been thrown by a horse."

"You have no idea at all who struck you?"

"None. And I dinnae understand why someone would. It makes no sense. I have no enemies here." As she said the words, Aimili remembered the sense of danger she'd long felt, the same feeling shared by Mist, the same voiced by the mysterious Queen Sebilla.

She turned the problem over and over in her mind while Efrika concocted another drink to ease her headache. Freya returned and chattered on about her new love, Zara. Thankfully, neither expected her to participate much in the conversation.

Over Efrika's protest, Aimili dressed in her usual attire and headed out for the stables with Freya. She tried to keep from looking over at the training field, but in the end couldn't help herself.

Padruig was indeed there, taking on two men at once, and from the expression on his face, having a wonderful time doing it.

"He was most worried about you last eve," Freya

said. "I have never seen my brother display such fear. Or such anger."

"No doubt he considered the attack to be an affront to his rule, a message that the laird was too weak to protect his people." Aimili knew she sounded more than a little petulant, but she was past caring. How could he kiss her like that, and then bolt like a panicked horse?

"Oh, nay." Freya took her arm. "You did not see his face. 'Twas concern for you."

Aimili refused to believe it. She had only to recall the way he'd abruptly pulled away from her, as if he'd suddenly discovered he'd gone mad. Rather than dispute the point with Freya, she just walked into the stables.

"Good morn, my lady," Hugo called out. "We've just about got 'em settled."

Welcome home, my friends.

A chorus of responses flooded her mind, and Aimili put her hand over her mouth to hide her smile.

Topaz, a mare ever anxious to fill her already expansive belly. *Could you please tell that man that I am near to starved?*

Ruby, another mare, who, no matter how many times Aimili reassured her, was always convinced she would be turned out or sold to some horrible place. *Th . . . thank you, my lady. Oh, thank you. I can tell that this place will be very fine.*

She paused at Argante's stall. Across the walkway, Loki stared unblinkingly at the mare, who ignored him completely. *Argante, how do you fare?*

I am fine, but for that . . . beast who will not stop eyeing me as if I am naught but a bowl full of honey and oats.

He is most anxious to become better acquainted.

Hmph. I know exactly what he wants, but he's going to have to wait a few more days.

Loki let out a long sigh and dipped his head.

Aimili gave Argante a pat and moved down to halt at Zara's stall. Freya leaned against the wood and clucked. "Come, girl."

Ever regal, Zara turned and eyed them.

You have a new friend, Aimili told her.

Zara walked over and stuck her nose out for a treat.

Freya stroked her head. "What a pretty girl you are."

The girl has a good eye, Zara told Aimili.

Aye, but she is not a skilled rider yet.

Freya giggled. "She licked my hand!"

"She likes you."

"Where did you get her, Aimili?"

"From an acquaintance of Father's. He knew I was looking for an Arabian mare to add to my breeding program. Zara is from the Outremer, though I know not exactly where."

"So far away."

"Aye." Aimili rubbed Zara's nose. "I have only had her just over a year."

"Have you bred her?"

"Not successfully yet."

Freya sighed. "Her baby would look like a wee angel."

"Why don't you give her a brush? I need to make sure the rest of them have safely arrived and have been put in their new stalls." *Be nice, Zara.*

Why would I not? The girl is sweet, and I need to rid my coat of the dust of travel.

Aimili smiled. Perhaps Freya and Zara were a good match, she thought. Certainly, they were both beautiful, knew it, and indulged in more than a bit of vanity, though each was good-natured enough that one didn't mind. Aimili wandered down the stable walkway, trying to listen to the horses but finding her thoughts returning again and again to her enigmatic and increasingly infuriating husband.

Freya was clearly mistaken. She wanted to think of her brother as he once was, wanted to think of him as embracing the marriage, but it was all a lie. Aimili made herself take a deep breath and push back the pain. There was nothing to do but make the best of it.

She ended up standing in front of Tor's stall. He lifted his head and pushed his nose into her hand. Tor was a young, bay stallion for whom she had high hopes. Even at two years, he showed promise to be a powerful combination of strength, speed, and intelligence. *How is my handsome boy?*

Hungry.

You are always hungry. I hope you will be happy here.

'Tis a nice stable, and Hugo seems a good sort, but . . .

But?

Can you not sense it, my lady? 'Tis in the very air. Something is not right here.

It always surprised Aimili how perceptive horses could be. Of all of them, with perhaps the exception of Mist, Tor was the most sensitive. *Aye, there is darkness here, but I have not discovered the source.* She fingered the hilt of the dagger she now wore hidden beneath her tunic.

We will help as we can.

My thanks. Once again, Aimili wished she could confide in Padruig, but he would dismiss her feelings as nerves or something equally frivolous. It seemed to be her fate to have no one to confide in save her animals. Thank God for them at least.

"Aimili?" Freya called.

"Aye?"

"I am finished. I am going to help Efrika work on your gown. We shall be in the Ladies' Solar."

Aimili smiled. "Please give Efrika my thanks."

"'Tis not necessary. You are family now." Freya breezed out, after giving Zara a last pat.

Family. Aimili just stood in the walkway, overcome by Freya's airy announcement. What would Freya say if Aimili told *her* the truth, told her Zara thought Freya sweet? What of Efrika? Would they accept her, or turn away in fear, making a sign against evil?

She couldn't take the chance. Other than Morainn, only one person had ever discovered her talent. Aimili could still see Una's expression as she backed away, horrified to find that her good friend could communicate with a beast. Never mind that because of Aimili's ability to do so, they had avoided being attacked by one very menacing, very hungry wild boar. Una had run back to the village as if Aimili had transformed into some wicked creature more frightening than the boar. Within a fortnight the family moved to another estate held by Aimili's father, and Aimili had never seen her friend again.

Nay, not a friend, not in truth. Surely a truehearted friend would be shocked, maybe uneasy at first, but ultimately accept that Aimili was simply different. Wouldn't she?

My lady, what is amiss?

She'd forgotten that she still stood next to Tor's stall. *I would never give up the chance to talk to you, but sometimes it is a burden, as well. Most other humans are fearful of what they do not understand.*

Other humans? But you are not fully human.

What? Aimili whirled to stare at Tor, who snuffled in a pail for some leftover oats. *What are you talking about? Of course I am fully human. I simply have an . . . unusual talent.*

Are you sure?

Yes!

My mistake. I assumed you must have inherited your ability from someone . . . special.

Aimili chewed on her lip. She'd never really thought about the source of her ability. It had just always been there, and for a long time, she thought it was perfectly normal, though none of her siblings exhibited the same gift. The very thought of Wautier finding himself being addressed by his horse and actually understanding him brought a smile to her face. Her pompous brother would probably faint dead away.

Had her mother such an ability? Try as she might to remember, Aimili could not. She'd been but three years of age when her mother died, her memories barely a kiss of affection in her mind.

Aye, you are mistaken. 'Tis a gift from God. At least, that's the way Aimili had always thought of it, though she knew others, like Una, would attribute the source as something evil.

"Aimili!" a voice shouted. "Come quickly!"

She ran out of the stables to find Pythia, one of her mares with foal, in a full-out panic. Hugo had hold of her reins, but the mare was rearing and trying to run backward. Her eyes were wild, the whites showing, her nostrils flared, and her ears were pinned back flat to her head.

As Aimili neared them, Pythia kicked out with her left leg and caught Hugo in the stomach. With a grunt of pain, he stumbled back and dropped the reins.

Pythia bolted back, but there was nowhere to go. Her rump slammed against the rail and she let out a high scream.

Aimili crept forward. "Easy, girl."

"Be careful, my lady," Hugo shouted.

Pythia snorted and shook her head. D'Ary stepped

up next to Aimili. "She's hurt," he said.

Easy, girl. Everything is all right. You are safe. Very slowly, Aimili picked up the reins.

The mare was so agitated she didn't respond. She jerked her head up and nearly tore the reins out of Aimili's hands.

Aimili tightened her hold and braced her body. "Easy now, Pythia." Out of the corner of her eye she spotted Padruig approach.

"What happened?" she asked anyone.

Hugo answered her. "Didn't want to go into the stable. Fought me somethin' fierce, and ended up hitting the rail so hard it split and cut her. Made it worse."

Let me go, my lady. Please.

It is all right, Pythia. I promise.

No! Danger.

Aimili was so startled she nearly dropped the reins herself. She tilted her head around to view the mare's rump and saw a stream of blood. "Come on, girl. We will take care of you." She gave a little pull on the reins, but it was like trying to haul a large, living boulder that had dug its heels into the ground.

"Why not put her loose in the ring for a bit?" D'Ary suggested. "Let her calm down."

Though she hated to give in, Aimili could see the wisdom in his idea. The last thing Aimili wanted was for Pythia or her foal to be hurt because Pythia did something stupid out of fright. "Come, girl." She started walking away from the entrance to the stables. *You can go in the ring for now, but I need to see to that cut.*

Send me back.

I cannot do that. This is my home now.

I don't like it.

Zeus is already in a stall.

Pythia let out a sigh and followed Aimili, though with obvious reluctance. Aimili knew the mare had a soft spot for Zeus. When they were out in the pasture, they stood with their heads close together like an old married couple. Or at least how Aimili imagined an old married couple might behave.

She glanced toward Padruig, who stood watching her with his usual guarded expression. The child in her resisted the urge to stick out her tongue. "Good girl," she told the mare as she led her into the ring and removed her bridle.

"I shall fetch some water and ointment," D'Ary said.

"Thank you." As Aimili slung the bridle over the rail, she searched for Hugo. He sat on an overturned barrel with one hand to his chest, the other holding a cup.

"Are you all right, Hugo?" she called.

He nodded. "I'll be fine, my lady. Mare caught me in a rib, but 'tis not broken. Not the first time."

Aimili spared him a smile.

"Not sure what set the mare off, though," he said.

"'Tis a new place. She is likely more fretful with

being in foal."

Carrying the foal has nothing to do with it.

Aimili concealed a smile at the disgust in Pythia's tone. *You must trust me. I know there is a darkness that hangs over this place, a threat. I will find out who he is.*

I am afraid.

Aimili rubbed the mare's withers. *I understand.*

You are afraid, too.

No. The image of Queen Sebilla arising from the depths of the loch sprang into Aimili's mind. *Maybe a little*, she corrected.

Pythia's skin shuddered beneath Aimili's fingertips, as if a chill slithered down her spine.

D'Ary appeared with a pail of water, and a crock. He murmured to the horse and stroked her before putting a wet cloth on her flank and wringing the water into her wound. "Silly girl," he said.

"She is more settled now. 'Twas a good idea you had, D'Ary."

He looked up and grinned, a flash of merriment in his gaze as if he knew she suspected him of knowing very little of horses. "Thank you, my lady. I am pleased to be of service."

Aimili rolled her eyes at the subservient tone of his voice. "Save the servant routine, D'Ary. It doesn't suit you."

He only laughed and smoothed ointment onto Pythia's cut.

From outside the ring, Padruig stood and watched

Aimili gentle the horse. His conjecture about the woman herself outweighed his suspicions about her relationship with his new stable hand, and that was saying something. Damn the man and his familiarity.

The image of Aimili and the wolf in the woods burned in his mind. He'd told himself that she couldn't possibly be communicating with the beast. Such a thing was impossible.

He'd told himself the same thing when he'd spied her with Cai one afternoon, the wolf bounding and yipping about her heels, with Aimili laughing as though Cai had made a jest. Probably at his expense.

But now, well, he could tell himself he was imagining things all day long but it didn't make it true. That horse looked at Aimili as if it understood her perfectly, even when Aimili was not speaking aloud.

Had her father known? Was that why he was so eager to foist her onto a man like Padruig, a man who would be hesitant to cause more turmoil in his clan by setting his wife aside?

It made a strange sort of sense, he decided as he watched Aimili and D'Ary walk out of the ring, looking very much like a well-matched team. It explained the rare quality of her stock, her reputation for breeding and training top-quality animals. It also explained her affinity for the forest, and her lack of fear. Why be fearful when you can call on the animals to aid you?

Padruig wasn't sure if he should applaud her or run.

She stopped when she neared him.

"Is the horse all right?" he asked.

"Aye. Just a bit nervous." Her voice could have carved through solid ice.

"Good. The others?"

"Fine." She turned to go and Padruig suppressed a groan.

"Aimili."

She paused.

"How do you feel?"

"Much better."

By the saints, if she were any more formal he would imagine himself at the English court of that weakling, John Lackland. "Be careful. I dinnae want you going about alone."

Aimili frowned and started to speak, but D'Ary came up beside her. He smiled at Padruig. "Worry not, Laird. I am honored to guard your lady."

"Surely you have duties in the stables," Padruig said through a clenched jaw.

"Lady Aimili's safety is more important. Do you not agree, Hugo?" D'Ary asked the stable master.

"Of course."

"And," D'Ary added with a shrug, "as Lady Aimili is most often in the stables, I shall be able to perform much of my work anyway."

"How convenient."

"Aye." D'Ary seemed not to notice at all the fact that

by now Padruig was glaring at him. Or maybe he did.

"See to it, then." Before he could make an utter fool of himself and challenge the man for no clear reason, Padruig stalked off.

"A fiercesome man, your husband," D'Ary remarked to Aimili. "I believe he is jealous."

Jealous? Aimili laughed before she could stop herself. "Nay."

"Hmm. I would be if I were wed to such a beautiful woman."

"Did you suffer a blow to the head earlier that I missed?"

"I am simply stating the truth. Do you not see yourself as beautiful?"

"Morainn has always been the beautiful one."

"Morainn?"

"My younger sister."

"Ah, yes, I have heard mention of her."

"Oh?"

"'Tis said she is a comely lass, indeed. Does she enjoy embroidery?"

"Excessively."

"Supervise the kitchen in preparation of delicious fare?"

"In detail."

"Ensure the hall is cleanly swept of refuse?"

"Every day."

"Clothe herself in fine silk bliauts to set off her

delicate coloring?"

"With superb taste and refinement."

"Perfection, then."

"So everyone tells me."

D'Ary put his hand on her shoulder, and Aimili felt that odd tingling again. "I am sure that your sister is a fine woman, but all of that sounds rather boring to me. I prefer a woman who differs from what is expected."

Aimili narrowed her eyes. "Are you flirting with me?"

"I could if it would make you feel better, but nay. I am simply pointing out that there are different concepts of perfection."

"Morainn is not much of a horsewoman."

"Know how to use a dagger?"

"For eating only."

"Not a sword, surely."

"Oh, heavens, no. 'Twould get caught in her skirts." Aimili felt the beginnings of a smile curve her lips.

"Och, 'tis a shame. The lady is not perfection after all."

Aimili turned to look at D'Ary, her heart lighter than it had been in a long time. "Why do you aid me?"

He leaned close and winked. "I like you, my lady. I can assure you such a tender emotion does not often strike me."

"'Tis my good fortune, then."

"Aye. More than you know."

Chapter Eleven

After the incident with Pythia, Aimili was forced to admit, if only to herself, that between her injury and Padruig's bewildering behavior, she had had enough. She made her way back to her chamber, feeling weighted down, her steps slow and careful. By the saints, how weak she'd become, she thought in disgust.

The back of her head throbbed with a constant, though minor ache, but most of all she simply felt exhausted. She climbed up the steps to her chamber, bracing against the cool stone walls as she ascended.

When she entered her chamber, it was empty. Though Cai invariably found his way back before nightfall, he spent most of his days out prowling the countryside or trying to filch food from the kitchen. Aimili smiled as she thought of the big wolf and Cook playing their game of Cai trying to be sneaky and Cook pretending that she was horrified at having him underfoot. Aimili had seen Cai more than once happily sprawled out under Cook's worktable, patiently waiting for scraps of food to fall and Cook slipping him some when she thought no one was looking.

Castle MacCoinneach was probably the only castle with a resident wolf.

Aimili cracked the window shutters open to let in some air, then sat on the edge of the bed and drew off her clothes. They fell in a pile at her feet. For a moment, she stared at a folded chemise, but decided that the trunk was simply too far for the effort.

She snuggled under the soft linen sheets, tucked a blanket over top, and closed her eyes.

Padruig came in from the training field just in time for supper. By the saints, it had felt good to spend the afternoon honing his skills. There was not a man at Castle MacCoinneach who could beat him, but more than a few were skilled enough to provide a wee bit of challenge. With a grunt of satisfaction, he took his seat and poured a cup of wine.

A pointed cough interrupted the passage of wine from the cup to his throat. He glanced over to find Efrika eyeing him. To her side sat Alasdair and Freya, each with identical expressions of rebuke on their faces.

"What?" Padruig looked down and smoothed his tunic. To be sure, he had not taken time for a bath, but that was hardly unusual. He swept a hand over his face and it came away with no more than a smudge of dirt. Ignoring them, he took a long drink of wine.

"Where is Aimili?" Efrika asked.

"How should I know?"

The looks of chastisement darkened.

"I am a busy man," Padruig announced. "I cannot spend all of my time following her about."

Freya rolled her eyes.

"Asides, it appears that you two have taken the girl in hand."

"Along with D'Ary," Freya said, her mouth curved in a teasing smile. "He is most helpful."

Padruig refused to rise to the bait, despite his own qualms about the man. "No doubt."

Efrika pulled the jug of wine out of Padruig's reach. "One would think after last night you would display more concern."

Padruig sighed. Clearly, his family would not be content to wait for Aimili to finish whatever task she undoubtedly had in the stable to come for supper. Probably busy discussing her horses with D'Ary, he thought.

"She was tired, Padruig. Perhaps you should check your chamber," Freya told him. "Make sure she is all right."

He turned to signal for a maid, only to be caught short once again by Efrika's cough.

"Very well," he grumbled. "I shall check myself. Have supper served, Alasdair. I shall return anon."

Alasdair just grinned and gestured to the servers to begin.

Padruig tromped to his chamber, sure he was

wasting his time, but at the same time the tiniest bit concerned about his bride. She was not one to loll about in the usual course of things, but last eve had been anything but normal.

He pushed open the doorway to their chamber and stopped short, paralyzed by the scene before his eyes. The milky light of dusk drifted into the chamber through the partly open shutters. Aimili lay sprawled across the bed, the sheets twisted and mussed as if she'd been tossing and turning. Her hair had loosened from its plait, and was a swath of auburn silk against the pale sheet. The blanket lay crumpled in a heap at the bottom of the bed.

And his bride, the bride he'd told himself again and again and again was but an innocent child, was fully, amazingly, gorgeously naked from her soft shoulders to her shapely calves.

He found he could not draw a breath.

He sure as hell could not look away.

She looked like a statue, he thought. Even in sleep, her muscles were evident, her arms firm, her thighs toned, her belly . . . He gulped, his gaze drawn to the dark curls concealing her sex.

Dear Lord, aid me, he silently prayed, for everything male in him wanted to leap upon the woman in his bed and plunder that body until they were both too boneless to move. He fisted his hands and made himself take deep breaths, forcing images of battle into his mind. Bloody, vicious, lengthy battles.

Eventually, he recovered enough to steal forward and drape the blanket over her, praying all the while that she did not awake.

What would he say? *I apologize for ogling you like a starving man viewing a side of beef? Or perhaps, would you mind if I joined you?*

Sweat dripped down his back as he slowly backed away.

Aimili would be mortified to know he'd seen her thus, he had no doubt. The poor thing must have been so fatigued she forgot to don her usual chemise. He straightened, once more in control of his emotions. Aye, clearly she was in need of his care and protection. The incident last eve had been too much for her womanly nature.

He left the chamber, reassured of his role.

Now, if only his body would accept it.

Aimili fluttered her eyes open as Padruig fled their chamber. Obviously, he'd thought her deep in slumber, but in truth she'd awakened when the door swung open. Too embarrassed to admit that, she'd peered at Padruig from beneath her lashes.

She slowly smiled. Innocent she might be, but the expression of shock and sheer lust on her husband's face had been unmistakable.

Well, one thing was clear. She would be sleeping naked from this moment on.

For the next sennight, Padruig lived in abject fear of entering the chamber he shared with Aimili. He knew it was impossible, but it almost seemed as if his bride taunted him apurpose. Rather than return to her formerly modest ways, Aimili had apparently embraced the idea of sleeping without a single stitch of clothing.

Every evening, no matter how long he waited to return to their chamber, he was sure to be treated to an exposed shoulder, the sleek curve of a hip, or the smooth roundness of a breast. She had also apparently developed a distaste for the dark as there were always at least three candles lit, along with a fire, providing ample light for Padruig to torment himself.

Sleep soon became naught but a memory. Whether his eyes were open or closed, he saw the same thing—Aimili's body, calling him like one of the legendary sirens. If he wasn't so sure she had no idea what she was doing, he would confront her, but he knew to do so would just embarrass them both.

At least then she would draw on a chemise at night, he grumbled to himself as he arranged his pallet on the floor one night. Cai, his traitorous companion, lay happily on the bed snoring as if he didn't have a care in the world, which, truth to be told, he didn't.

Padruig gritted his teeth and took a pull of wine. Tonight, thankfully Aimili lay on her stomach. The sight of her taut buttocks was tempting, but he'd come to rank which exposed body parts were harder on his shredded control, and buttocks were relatively low on the list.

He blew out all the candles but one and sat back on the floor, propped up against the wall. He'd come to think of this temptation as a test from God, a way to regain some of the lost purity of his soul. To rise above desires of the flesh was surely an admirable undertaking. Wasn't it?

After a few more drinks of wine, he wasn't quite sure.

And then it happened. Slowly, sinuously, Aimili stretched, turned over onto her back, and parted her legs.

Holy God in heaven.

Sweat beaded Padruig's brow as he drank in the sight. Even in the dim light, he could see the tender flesh between her thighs. He swallowed and with a shaking hand lifted the flagon to his dry mouth. Perhaps he should send Magnus to fetch more of that brew he had obtained from Balcharn Abbey. At least if he passed out, he would no longer think about the unbearable coil he found himself in.

You are no better than an untried boy, he shouted to himself. *Be a man, and stop leering at her while she is sleeping and unaware.*

He couldn't have turned away if his very life depended on it.

His skin itched, verily itched to touch her, to cover her nakedness with his own. And his rod, by the saints, was close to splitting his braies. His blood pounded in his veins, clamped him in a rush of raw lust.

I cannot take this anymore, he thought. *I am weak.* Before he could stop himself, he groaned and closed his eyes. *Dear Lord, give me strength*, he silently prayed. *I am no beast, to give into my base desires.*

My duty is to protect. Even if I must protect from my own self.

The next eve at supper, a guard rushed into the hall. "Laird," he said as he barreled to a stop before the dais.

Padruig set down his eating knife. "What is it, Randulf?"

"Laird Ransolm seeks entry."

Freya gave a high cry.

"How many men accompany him?"

"No more than ten."

Padruig exchanged a glance with Magnus, who looked grim. "Escort them to the hall. We shall offer hospitality. To start. Make sure their weapons stay under guard in the gatehouse."

Randulf nodded and hurried from the hall.

"Why is he here?" Freya asked, her voice breaking.

"I am sure he will tell us," Padruig answered. "Dinnae fash yourself. I promise you that you have nothing to fear from Angus Ransolm."

The hall doors burst open and a man flanked by a troop of others strode into the hall. As he walked toward the dais, Padruig studied the man he assumed was Angus Ransolm. Not surprisingly, his years of debauchery showed on his face.

Once, he supposed Angus might have been considered a fair-looking man. No more. Matted gray hair hung around a heavy face, marked by flat brown eyes and a cruel set to his jaw.

He tossed a bag onto the table, where it landed with a clunk.

Padruig leaned back in his chair and took a sip of wine. "Laird Ransolm, welcome to Castle MacCoinneach."

The older man sneered. "I came for the girl." His gaze slid along the dais and lit upon Freya, whose face was a pale as the tablecloth. Angus smirked, and looked pointedly at her breasts.

Padruig caught Magnus's arm before he could rise. "Hold your temper," he whispered. In a louder voice, Padruig gestured to a seat at the end of the table farthest from Freya. "Would you care for food and drink?"

"Oh, I'll take your food and drink. For me and my men," Angus added with an arrogant nod toward the men standing behind him. "*After* we settle the matter of the girl."

"Did you not receive my message, Laird? Circumstances have changed. My sister will not be wedding you."

"I had an agreement with the laird of the clan."

"Grigor is dead. I am laird."

"Have you no honor? 'Twas a firm bargain." He pointed to the sacks of coins. "For which I paid handsomely."

"I returned your coin."

"'Tis not enough."

"It will have to be," Padruig answered calmly. "I have decided that my sister would be better served with a different match."

"Ye cannot just sit there and act as if this means naught. I had an agreement with the Laird of the Mac-Coinneach clan. A betrothal!" he shouted.

"I apologize for your inconvenience, Laird, but as I explained in my message, Freya will not be wedded to you."

"Why not?"

"Because I would never wed with you! I would die first," Freya swore.

For a moment, Ransolm's face reddened, but then he narrowed his gaze and licked his lips. "Grigor gave no hint of the lass's spirit," he said. He tossed another sack of coin onto the table. "I'll take her tonight."

"Nay," Magnus growled, his hand going to his sword.

"Ah, so the wee lass has a defender," Ransolm sneered. "How touching."

Padruig saw Freya's gaze flash to Magnus in surprise. He stood and braced his hands atop the table. "I assure you that my sister does not lack defenders. The betrothal is no more. You shall have to find another bride."

"Think well before you deny me. I ken how much your clan needs my coin. 'Twill serve you well over the winter."

Padruig gritted his teeth, hating that the man knew of the clan's sorry state. "My clan shall be taken care of."

"I'd heard you took a de Grantham lass to wife," Ransolm said, eyeing Aimili. "Surely you do not want to see her starve."

"I would rather starve than take anything from you," Aimili spat.

"Ah, another wench with spirit, though once again misplaced."

"A man who treats a horse as you have does not deserve any woman."

"A horse?" Ransolm laughed. "What are you blathering about?"

Aimili stood beside Padruig, her fists clenched. "Loki."

"Ah, yes, I remember. Worthless beast. Surely you cannot be upset about that animal." He shook his head and exchanged a chuckle with one of his men. "Horse

268

isn't worth the cost of feed."

"He is to my wife," Padruig announced.

"'Tis one more mouth to feed." He pointed to the sack of coin. "Your problem is simply solved. Give me the girl."

"Freya is not for sale."

Ransolm studied Padruig, then shrugged and retrieved his coin. "I believe I shall avail myself of your food and drink, after all." He sauntered over to an empty stool and sat, motioning his men to find their own seats below. "Though you make a poor decision for your clan, young laird."

"I do not think so." Padruig signaled a server and retook his seat.

"The man is a reptile," Magnus said in a low voice.

"I ken."

"This is the best fare you have to offer?" Ransolm shouted at a servant. He speared a chunk of mutton and eyed it with clear disgust, before fixing his gaze on Freya. "At Ransolm Castle, you would dine each day on the most succulent cuts of meat, the sweetest custards, soft breads, and fine wine."

Freya made a choking sound and fled the table.

"Overcome by the notion of a decent meal, no doubt," Ransolm said, smacking his lips as he watched Freya exit the hall.

Padruig expected Efrika to try to smooth over Ransolm's coarse behavior, but apparently he was too much for her, as well. With an audible sniff, she rose and followed Freya.

"Filthy bastard," Magnus swore under his breath.

"Find Ivarr. Tell him to double the guards tonight, and to keep a special eye on Laird Ransolm," Padruig said quietly to Magnus, then took a small sip of wine, bracing himself to listen to Angus Ransolm without giving in to the urge to separate his head from his shoulders.

When Ransolm muttered, "Even the cheese is moldy," Padruig had his sword partially unsheathed before Alasdair stopped him.

"He is a-trying to provoke you."

"He is doing a damn good job."

"I cannot tolerate this anymore, Padruig," Aimili said, frowning. "Pray excuse me."

"I wish I could accompany you."

For a moment, their gazes met, and a feeling far different from annoyance spread through Padruig's veins. *Damn*, he thought.

"As do I," Aimili said softly.

After a lengthy tirade of complaints by Angus Ransolm, in between ingesting vast quantities of food he deemed inferior even as he shoveled it into his mouth, he finally belched and turned to Padruig. "I wish to retire. Can you offer a chamber not ridden with fleas and a place for my men?"

"I imagine we can come up with something," Padruig replied, though he really wished to deny the boor any hospitability. "Alasdair will see you to a chamber. Your men can bed down in the gatehouse." In a low voice, he said to Alasdair, "See him to the small chamber in the east tower."

Alasdair stood. "As you wish, Laird."

Ransolm stood and grabbed up a flagon of wine. "Tastes like piss, but I suppose it is the best you can do," he said, his expression contemptuous.

"Good eve, Laird Ransolm," Padruig said coldly.

"Good eve."

Padruig let out a sigh of relief as the man marched out behind Alasdair.

Freya could not stop shaking, sick with disgust over Angus Ransolm's behavior. When he'd talked about serving her the most succulent cuts of meat, she'd known he'd been referring to her, not food. That was how he saw her—the best portion of beef, carefully prepared to satisfy his appetite.

She shuddered as she made her way to the stables. Thank the Lord Magnus and Padruig had stood up for her. She'd thought Magnus would attack Ransolm when he'd offered more coin. Unfortunately, the clan could, indeed, use Angus Ransolm's coin.

The thought of submitting to that man made her want to retch. She could not make such a sacrifice. Surely, Padruig would find another way to feed the clan.

As she entered the stable, she let out a long breath. The sounds of horses snuffling and munching on hay filtered through the stable, with an occasional sigh of contentment. It was dusk and quiet, the hands having gone to find their own suppers.

She leaned against Zara's stall, and the horse put her head over the wall to brush against Freya. "What a sweet girl you are," she said as she stroked the mare's velvety nose. "I wish I'd thought to bring you a treat, but I was too upset over that horrible man."

Zara flapped her lips on the edge of Freya's bliaut.

"Nay, I have nothing. I am sorry. Tomorrow, I shall find you a ripe apple."

Another horse stuck its head out to eye Freya, which she recognized as Loki. "You know what I mean, don't you, boy? You once belonged to that monster."

Loki blew out a breath, and just looked at her.

"I suppose I should go to my chamber," Freya told them, but she was reluctant to close herself in with only her thoughts and fears. It wasn't as if she'd never had a man look at her with interest. Men had been doing that since she was ten years of age. Angus Ransolm, however, had looked at her with the kind of lust that made her skin crawl, made her feel soiled.

She found a brush and slipped into Zara's stall. As

she ran the brush over Zara's smooth coat, Freya felt a little of her tension lighten. On the morrow, Angus Ransolm would be gone. She would never have to see him again.

Suddenly, Loki let out a neigh and kicked the door of his stall. "What is it, boy?" Freya asked. She left Zara's stall and latched it, peering down the dim walkway.

Loki kicked again.

"Easy, boy," she said, stepping forward.

Before she could reach Loki, a hand caught her hair and hauled her against a barrel-chested body. Laughter sounded in her ear, and her blood ran cold.

She twisted around, ignoring the pain. "Let me go."

Very slowly and deliberately, Angus Ransolm flexed his thick fingers and let go of her plait. He raised a whip and gently laid it against her throat. "I do not like to be denied."

Freya pressed back against Zara's stall. "My brother—"

"Your brother is a fool. He will be the ruin of the clan with his weak sentiment."

"Leave me alone." She glanced up and down the walkway and spied a man standing at the end of the stable. "You there!" she called.

"My man," Ransolm told her with a smirk as he drew the end of his whip down her chest.

"If you hurt me, my brother will kill you," Freya hissed and tried to get around him.

He easily caught her back, this time wrapping his

beefy arms around her and roughly palming her breasts. "I dinnae intend to hurt you, lass. Well, mayhap 'twill hurt a bit."

By the saints, he intended to rape her right here in the stable, Freya realized with dawning terror. She struggled against his grip, and stomped on his foot.

He grunted, loosening his hold. Freya tried to run, but he grabbed her arm and threw her against a vacant stall. "'Twill go better for you if you cooperate."

"Cooperate? Are you mad? You sicken me."

"Bitch." He casually ripped her bliaut down the front, and tore open her chemise.

Mortified, Freya tried to cover her breasts, but his greedy fingers were there first, kneading and pulling at her flesh. "Stop!" she shouted.

His gaze grew feverish and his breath became audible, like an animal finding its prey. "Nay, lass. I bargained for you and I intend to take my due."

She slapped him, but he just laughed. Then he slapped her back, and her head struck the wall so hard her vision blurred. *No,* she thought. *Help me. Someone, help me.* She stumbled and went down onto one knee.

"That's right, wench. Down onto the ground. Spread those soft young thighs for me. You'll be thanking me in a few minutes."

Freya crawled a few paces, but he dragged her back by her ankle, laughing at her struggles. "No!" she cried. "Ye cannae do this."

"I can do whatever I want." He gripped her chin in his hand. "Little bitch, thinking you are too good for me. You'll be learning a lesson this night."

He shoved up her skirts, baring her thighs. Freya tried to buck him off, but he was too heavy. "No!" she yelled.

"Yes," he said, his lips drawn back in a feral smile.

Freya heard Loki scream, followed by a thunderous crash.

Ransolm's head snapped up and his eyes widened. "Demon horse," he swore and leapt up, raising his whip.

Freya scooted up against the stall, tucked herself into as small a ball as possible, and prayed. Loki stamped his foot and let out a sound very close to a growl.

"Get out of here," Ransolm snarled, taking the whip and laying it on Loki's shoulder.

Loki backed up, snorting.

Ransolm hit him again. "Be gone, ye worthless piece of horseflesh."

Freya whimpered, silently praying for Loki to do something, anything to aid her.

Loki's gaze caught hers, and Freya sucked in a breath. His eyes were hard, the whites visible. *He hates Angus Ransolm every bit as much as I do*, she thought.

What happened next was a flurry of motion. Loki charged, hooves flailing, and Ransolm landed hard on the ground.

"Help me!" he shouted, raising his whip.

When Ransolm's man ran up behind Loki, Loki

kicked him so hard he went flying back.

Ransolm flayed the whip against Loki's legs, but it was as if the horse didn't even feel it. Freya watched, half-relieved and half-horrified as Loki reared up and came down on Angus Ransolm again and again until his shouts were no more.

A profound silence settled over the stable, as if every horse understood what Loki had done and why.

"Loki," Freya croaked.

The horse turned and walked over to her, lowering his head to nuzzle her shoulder as if to reassure her. Freya wrapped her arms around Loki's head and struggled to her feet. She didn't even have time to pull together the edges of her torn gown before a throng of men rushed into the stables carrying torches.

"My lady!" Ivarr shouted. He turned to another guard. "Fetch the laird."

Freya swayed and held tight to Loki. She could taste blood from where Ransolm had struck her lip, but none of it seemed real. Ivarr bent down and gave Ransolm a shove with his foot. "Dead," he announced.

A hand touched Freya's shoulder, and she flinched. "'Tis only me," Magnus said softly.

With his touch, Freya's numbness shattered and she collapsed against him, sobbing and holding on to his tunic. He caught her up in his arms, turning her into his shoulder so that she would not be exposed to the men streaming into the stable. Freya shut her eyes and let him carry her away.

Padruig wasn't sure if he was angrier with Ivarr for failing to keep careful watch over Angus Ransolm or himself for failing to protect Freya. *I promise you that you have nothing to fear from Angus Ransolm*, he'd told her just that evening. A promise he'd broken within hours.

"Take your master and leave," he told Ransolm's man. "At once."

The man stepped forward, his arms crossed and his expression defiant. "Someone must pay for this. Our laird is dead."

"Your laird abused my hospitality by attempting to rape my sister," Padruig shouted, within a breath of wrapping his hand around the man's throat.

"So you say." The man nodded at another, who stood supported by yet another of Ransolm's men. "Donn tells a different story."

"I dinnae care what fable the man spins."

"The wench offered herself to the laird," the injured man insisted. "Said she'd made a mistake in refusing him, that you forced her to do it."

"Is that why her gown is ripped? Did she do *that* herself?"

Donn shrugged. "Mayhap she sought to display her tits."

Padruig growled and drew his sword. "Lying bastard. You are as dishonorable as your laird. My sister would never act thus, and all knew of her distaste for Angus."

He sensed Aimili come up beside him. Her face was pale, her mouth set into a grim line.

"Your laird got exactly what he deserved," she said.

"What of the horse?" Ransolm's man asked.

Padruig put a hand on Aimili's shoulder. "The horse will get what he deserves, as well."

He smiled. "An extra measure of oats at the least."

Ransolm's man cursed. "We shall not forget this."

"Nor shall I." Padruig glared at the man. "Count yourselves fortunate that I do not throw the lot of you in my pit. Had I known of Angus's treachery, I would have slain him myself. Now, begone!"

Grumbling, the men retrieved Angus's body and tied it to his horse, before mounting themselves. They rode out of the bailey and disappeared.

Padruig turned to find Aimili stroking Loki's nose. "What a brave boy you were," she told him. She bent to spread some kind of ointment into the cuts on his legs.

While Padruig was mighty glad the horse had saved Freya, the method still troubled him. "What think you of this?" he asked Aimili.

"What do you mean?"

He gestured toward Loki, who now appeared calm and content. "My own destrier is trained to attack, of course, but this was beyond that."

"He saved Freya."

"Aye, and I am thankful."

"But?"

"Is he dangerous, Aimili? Tell me true."

"Nay."

"Are you sure?"

"Aye. When Angus attacked Freya, it reminded him of the many times Angus Ransolm had beaten him. Indeed, Angus beat him again, as you see."

"And he killed him."

"He had to. 'Twas the only way to stop him."

"Did Loki tell you that?"

"Aye."

Padruig waited for Aimili to realize what she'd just admitted.

"Uh, I mean, 'tis obvious. I can see from his wounds that Angus whipped him. And we know he was intent on raping Freya."

"Ah, yes. Obvious."

Aimili peered at him over the stall door, her gaze wary. "Do ye mock me, my lord?"

"I am but concerned about the horse." He decided to let her secret remain so for the time being, though curiosity burned through him. Could she, indeed, communicate with the beasts? On the next breath, another question occurred to him—what else might she be capable of? And why?

"Loki was a hero this day. He fought back against that vile man."

"Aye. Do ye trust him, Aimili?"

"I do."

He nodded. "'Tis good enough, then. I am to see Freya."

Aimili lifted a brow. "I imagine Magnus is taking good care of her."

Padruig smiled. "I imagine so."

"He cares for her."

"I ken. I am no sure of Freya's feelings, though."

Aimili laughed and the sound spilled over Padruig like warm fingertips stroking his skin. By the saints, his traitorous body was at it again, he thought in disgust. *Cease*, he told himself.

"I dinnae think you need to wonder about that," Aimili said. "'Tis clear Freya adores him."

"As a brother, or perhaps a cousin, or—"

"As a man, Padruig. A lover."

"Ah. Well." Padruig wasn't sure what to say. Somewhere in what should have been a safe conversation, they'd veered into territory best left alone. "I'd best check on them still." He wheeled around and tromped out of the stable, pausing only to scowl at the place where Angus Ransolm's body had lain. The horse had done them all a favor. Had Padruig killed Angus, it would

have created even greater dissension between the clans.
Still, he wished he'd had the pleasure.

Chapter Twelve

Two days later, Aimili found herself being towed away from her duties to attend a local market with Freya. "I really do not need anything," she told the girl as they rode toward the village of Morisaig. Four men from the castle, including Magnus, rode with them. Since Freya's attack, Aimili noticed Magnus was seldom far from her side.

Freya grinned and wrinkled her nose. "*'Tis not about needing anything.* 'Tis about having fun and seeing what wares are there."

Aimili smiled back at her. Truth be told, she could not refuse Freya so soon after the horrible business with Angus Ransolm. Though on the surface Freya acted as if she'd fully recovered, her gaze held shadows it had not had before and she was easily startled. "Are you comfortable riding Mist?"

"I am." Freya patted the horse. "'Tis amazing, but I do not feel afraid. I cannot tell you what a wonderfully different feeling that is for me."

They crested a hill and Freya pointed. "See, we are nearly there."

Morisaig was a large village, set in a wide valley. As they came to the village outskirts, Aimili could see a cluster of buildings with cultivated fields spread out beyond. In a grassy field stood a number of wagons, horses, and tents, with people milling about.

Magnus halted them a short distance from the village, along the edge of a winding stream. "We shall leave the horses here. 'Twill be safer and they can graze." He appointed the guards in two alternating groups to watch their mounts.

They entered a warren of narrow streets lined with wattle-and-daub buildings. Children played in the open doorways, beyond which Aimili could see the smoke of cooking fires, and smell the earthy odor of animals and people living together in close quarters.

"This way," Magnus said, taking Freya's arm. Two of the guards walked along close behind Aimili. As they walked deeper into the village, the street widened until it ended at a large, central green.

"Aimili, look!" Freya said, pointing to the tents and stalls jammed into spaces around the green. She clutched Magnus's arm, her eyes bright. "Surely we shall find something special today."

"Is there something in particular you are looking for?" Aimili asked her, pausing to study a table piled with wooden bowls of various sizes.

"Nay, though Efrika bid me purchase some cowbane if we find it." She tugged Aimili over to a large tent.

Freya picked up a brooch fashioned of gold and set with rose-colored stones. "How pretty this is."

"'Twould look most lovely on you, my lady," the merchant offered. He named a price but Freya shook her head.

"'Tis too dear."

"I would be happy to buy it for you," Magnus told her. "The merchant is right."

"Nay." Freya looked so dejected that Aimili was tempted to buy the brooch herself. She had a cache of coins that her father had sent with her, more than enough to acquire the piece.

"Let us find something to eat and drink," Magnus suggested. He prodded them forward, but not before slipping some coins into one of the guard's hands and whispering to him.

Aimili grinned. "Fine idea."

After they bought pork and cheese pies and tankards of ale, they wandered through the market. Aimili was amazed at the variety of goods. There were stalls selling all kinds of fabrics, from rough wools to fine silks. Other stalls sold leather goods, cheese, eggs, pots and pans, various tools, and even some livestock.

"Here, Freya," Aimili said as she spied a purveyor of spices. The merchant eyed them carefully, before apparently adjudging them not up to stealing the valuable contents of the pots he had spread out on a table.

"How may I serve you, my lady?" he asked.

"My friend requires some cowbane," Aimili told him. "Have you any?"

"'Tis for my cousin," Freya said brightly. "She used the last of it on a filthy whoreson who sought to marry me to a man even worse."

The merchant's eyes widened, and Aimili laughed. "Ah, I see," he said.

"She did not use enough to kill him, of course."

"Of course. Uh, well, let me look."

Freya cut a glance at Aimili and giggled.

"Aye, I do have some cowbane." He poured a small amount into a pouch and held it up. "Is this sufficient?"

"I should think so."

Magnus paid the merchant, and they continued their exploration. Suddenly, Aimili saw a different type of stall at the edge of the village green. This one contained dogs, many dogs, yipping and barking their unhappiness at being penned in such tight confines. Aimili drifted over to the tent.

Freya sniffed and wrinkled her nose. "My, what a stench."

Aimili's heart broke at the condition of some of the dogs. Many had matted, dirty hair and looked as if they hadn't eaten well in a very long time. Their collective sadness battered her. A man stepped out of the tent. "Looking for a hunter? I've got some fine greyhounds here."

"Come away from here, Aimili," Freya said. "Let us visit the jeweler over there."

"Not just yet." Aimili studied the dogs. "I do not need a hunter," she told the merchant.

He scratched his head, his hair every bit as dirty as the dogs' fur. "I dinnae have any used for bear baiting, if that is what you seek."

She glared at him. "Of course not. 'Tis barbaric entertainment." She stepped forward, putting her hands on the smooth heads of the dogs. They rubbed against her, sensing her sympathy.

In the corner of the tent, she saw something that looked like a pile of yarn. She peered closer and saw two dull eyes staring out of the small mound of fur. "Is that a dog?" she asked, pointing.

"Supposed to be. I never seen anything like it before."

"What are you looking at, Aimili?" Freya asked, trying to see into the tent without getting too close to the other dogs. "Ugh," she said, holding her skirts back. "Aimili, I am going to look at those pretty pots. We shall not be far."

"I will be fine," Aimili replied without looking up. She crouched down and the little dog toddled over. She brushed her nose against Aimili's knuckles, and licked her hand.

Take me with you. Please.

Aimili looked into the dog's sorrowful eyes. "How much do you want for it?"

The man scratched his head again. "I dinnae know, my lady. That dog isn't worth much. She's ailing besides. You would be better to choose one of my hounds."

"This is the one I want." *Do not worry, little friend.* Aimili stood, took a silver pence from a pouch tied to her belt, and handed the coin to the merchant.

He smiled, revealing a mouth mostly devoid of teeth. "Thank you, my lady."

Aimili scooped up the dog and held her close. She nodded and exited the stall, anxious to escape the noxious place, wishing she could buy all of the dogs and take them home. The poor little dog trembled in her grasp.

Do not be afraid. You belong to me now.

I belong to you.

Aye.

With a sigh of contentment, the dog snuggled close.

Aimili looked down at the bundle of filthy, tangled fur in her arms and smiled. The merchant was right. There was nothing very useful about the dog save perhaps the most important, one she would not understand—a friend. Her smile widened when she considered what Padruig, a man who kept a wolf as a pet, would think of her purchase.

"He will just have to accept you," she told the dog, who was asleep. "As will Cai."

At the next stall, Aimili looked around for Freya and

the others, but didn't see a familiar face. *Freya probably saw another bauble she must examine,* Aimili thought. She slipped between the stalls, thinking to look among the ones in the next row.

A young woman blocked her path. Her hair was hidden beneath a mantle, but her eyes were brown and sharp as she met Aimili's gaze.

"Excuse me," Aimili said, and made to walk around her.

The woman didn't move. "You are the new wife of the Laird of the MacCoinneachs, Padruig?"

Something in the woman's softly worded question put Aimili's senses on alert. "Do I know you?"

The woman gave a bitter laugh. "Nay, my lady." She tilted her head, studying Aimili.

"My friends will be looking for me," Aimili said, once more attempting to brush by the woman. With one hand, she held the dog, but the other slipped inside the folds of her mantle to grasp the dagger.

"Please, my lady," the woman said, clutching Aimili's arm. "I pray you listen to me for just a moment."

Aimili stopped. "Who are you?"

"My name is Madeleine MacVegan."

Aimili's eyes widened and she pulled free of the woman's grip. "MacVegan!"

"Please, my lady. I mean no harm, I swear."

"What do you want of me?"

"I only wish to speak with you."

Aimili shifted the dog in her arm and drew the

dagger from beneath her mantle. "If this is a trick to hold me while your clansmen gather, be assured that I am not helpless. I have killed before and would do so again."

"Nay. 'Tis only me."

"Whatever you wish to say, be quick about it."

The woman glanced down at the dagger, then lifted her gaze. "I am . . . was sister to Symund MacVegan."

"Brona's murderer."

"No! That is what I must tell you. I thought that you being not of MacCoinneach blood might believe me. Symund and I were very close. He was my twin. I know that he loved Brona, loved her deeply. It grieved him true that she favored another, but Symund loved her."

"Loved her so much that he could not bear for another man to claim her heart."

Madeleine shook her head. "Symund would *never* have hurt Brona. I would swear this to you on my brother's grave." Her eyes filled with tears. "Padruig slew the wrong man."

"You cannot know this. According to the story, Padruig found Symund with the blade in his hand, yet wet with Brona's blood."

"I remember the day well. And the *story*. It was not Symund."

Aimili wanted to disbelieve her, but she was so earnest, so passionate in her plea that it gave Aimili pause. "It is hard to believe a relative, a sibling, could be capable of such an act, but—"

Madeleine stepped closer, a flush reddening her cheeks. "You do not understand. Symund was my *twin*, my best friend. Though I was not there, I *knew* the instant Symund found Brona dead. I felt his anguish rip through his soul as if it were mine own."

Aimili stared at her and knew in her heart the woman spoke true. On the heels of her realization came a sudden, crippling sense of danger. It wound around her chest and tightened in her throat. And Madeleine MacVegan was not the source.

"Aimili!" a man's voice shouted.

Alarm flashed in Madeleine's eyes. "I must go," she whispered, then ran, pulling the hood of her mantle close around her face.

"Aimili!" the voice shouted again.

"Here." She stepped out from between the stalls to find a clearly furious Padruig, followed closely by Magnus, Freya, and the other men. Each wore an identical expression of concern, but Padruig's was colored by anger.

Aimili quickly tucked away her dagger.

"Oh, Aimili, where have you been? We thought something had befallen you." Freya's face was pale, and she touched Aimili's arm as if to reassure herself. Aimili immediately felt guilty for bringing distress to Freya, already overset by the Angus Ransolm incident.

"I . . . I got turned around, 'tis all." She smiled at Freya. "'Tis very crowded."

Ignoring her husband's scowl, she asked, "What are you doing here, Padruig? I did not know you were joining us today."

She was pretty sure she heard him grind his teeth.

Instead of responding, he turned to one of the men behind Magnus. "Why were you not guarding my wife?"

The man's throat worked. Aimili started to excuse him, but Magnus stopped her with a shake of his head.

"I . . . we were but watching the monkey for a minute, Laird," the guard said, pointing to a small brown and white monkey drawing a piece of bread from behind a startled onlooker's ear. "When we turned back, the lady was gone."

Aimili frowned. She'd not seen the guards when she emerged from the dog seller's tent. Perhaps she'd simply missed them in the crush of people.

Before she could think on it further, Padruig turned, his disapproving gaze focused on her. "And *you*, my lady." He opened his mouth to continue, but at that moment caught sight of the dog. "What . . . is that?" he asked, pointing.

The dog chose that moment to awake and let out a yelp.

Freya giggled, choked it back, then burst into gales of laughter. "Oh, Padruig, if only you could see your face."

Aimili tried to maintain her composure, but in the

end gave up and joined Freya in laughter. When she could catch herself, she announced, "My new guard dog."

Even Magnus tittered at that.

Padruig looked up at the sky as if asking God for assistance. His shoulders began to shake and when he lowered his head, Aimili was stunned to see that her taciturn husband was actually laughing.

"Well," he said. "I can see I have nothing to worry about, then."

As soon as they returned to Castle MacCoinneach, Aimili bustled off to the kitchen with her new charge. Padruig headed for the sanctity of his solar, but Magnus intercepted him.

"Why did you come to Morisaig, Laird?" Magnus's gaze was patently suspicious.

"I am no sure."

"Missed your bride?"

"No. I, uh, decided I should likely inspect what might be available for purchase locally." By the saints, did his reason sound as feeble to Magnus as it did to him?

"Ah." Magnus's tone said it all.

Padruig glanced at his friend. "'Twas not because I

distrusted you to watch over Freya and Aimili."

Magnus gave him a wry smile. "Though that is exactly what happened."

"Aimili is not the easiest lass to keep track of. I fault the other men. They know better than to allow themselves to be distracted. A fortnight of supervising the gong farmers should remind them."

"I purchased this for Freya," Magnus said, pulling the brooch out of his pouch. "She admired it, but refused to buy it."

"Freya? My sister passed on the opportunity to buy a pretty trinket? She should have had enough coin."

"She did not wish to part with it. Her only purchase was some cowbane for Efrika."

"Cowbane?"

"Aye." Magnus chuckled. "I believe Efrika mixed up something special for Grigor afore your arrival."

"God bless the woman, though at times she scares me. Cowbane." Padruig shook his head.

"I think Freya feels guilty about the loss of coin from Angus Ransolm."

Padruig sighed. "'Tis not her fault. It was a bad bargain from the outset."

"Aye, but Ransolm was right about one thing—his coin would have greatly benefited the clan."

"At the cost of Freya's happiness and most likely her life." Padruig scowled as he pushed open the door to his solar. "I did not return to Castle MacCoinneach for that."

"Perhaps you should explain as much to Freya. 'Twill put her heart at ease."

"I shall."

Alasdair awaited them in the solar. He sat on a stool staring at a piece of parchment.

"Tell me you bear good tidings," Padruig said as he sat and stretched out his legs.

"I fear not, Laird." Alasdair's expression looked as if someone had died. "There is a problem with our stores of grain."

"A problem?"

"The oats have been destroyed by some kind of insect."

"All?"

"Nearly. Some of the wheat, as well."

"How did this happen? What kind of insect?"

"I am no sure. The grains are eaten up."

"What have we left?"

"Very little. 'Tis bad, Padruig. We can possibly last through Christmas, with very judicious use of our stores. 'Twill be, at best, a lean winter."

"Damn Grigor," Padruig cursed, standing to pace across the room. "Until I hear from Giselle, we hunt. Magnus, you know which of the men are the best hunters. We must do what we can to supplement our stores. The women and children can gather mushrooms and berries, and fish the loch. Everyone must join together in this."

"The Lady Giselle—"

"Will aid us, I am sure." Padruig scowled, hating that he could not solve the clan's dilemma himself. But he could not feed his people on will alone.

"Some of your lady's horses could be sold," Alasdair commented.

"Mayhap," Padruig told him, inwardly cringing at the idea of relying further on a de Grantham. *A Mac-Coinneach now*, he reminded himself. *At least in name.* "I shall explain our dilemma to the clan at supper."

Magnus clapped him on the shoulder. "We shall get though this, Laird."

"We have no choice." Not for the first time, Padruig found himself wondering if the travails of the clan were a sign from God of his disfavor. Had he been right to return? To be sure, Grigor was worse than useless, but would another man be more worthy to bear the title of laird? Was this more punishment meted out by God for Padruig's mistakes? He set his jaw. It was of no matter now. He was laird, the clan was in trouble, and it was his responsibility to see they survived.

Somehow.

Aimili sat curled on the window seat that eve waiting for Padruig. It had become a regular vigil, though this night she wore a chemise. *I wonder what Padruig would do if he walked in and found me sitting here naked?* She snorted. *Most likely take one look and flee.*

Though he was not completely immune to her. For too many nights, she'd lain in bed listening to him sitting in the darkness, her ears straining to hear the clink of a cup, a sigh, the uneven sounds of a man kept awake.

She looked down at Lyoness, as she'd christened her new dog. Once scrubbed and combed, she still resembled a tawny jumble of yarn, but just the occurrence of a bath and food had revived her.

Cai had yet to emerge from beneath the bed. *What is that thing?* he'd asked earlier. *A rat?*

When she'd told him Lyoness was a dog and her new companion, he'd snorted in obvious disgust. *Looks like no more than a biteful.*

Be nice, she'd told him.

Throughout their conversation, Lyoness had remained silent, her big brown eyes fixed on Cai's muzzle sticking out from under the bed.

Aimili sighed and leaned against the wall of the window seat. Lyoness jumped into her lap and settled in. "I cannot believe things are so bad, and Padruig did not tell me," she told the little dog, recalling Padruig's grave announcements at supper. She stroked Lyoness, who gave her hand a lick.

The thunk of boot against wood preceded Padruig's entrance. Aimili blinked and raised her head. She must have fallen asleep for a few moments, she thought. The fire had burned down and a brace of candles flickered in the draft from the doorway.

"Why are you not abed?" Padruig asked, poised in the open doorway.

Dear Lord, how tired she was of this, Aimili thought. Each night, seeking her bed and pretending to be asleep, knowing that her husband would delay coming to their chamber until he was sure he would not have to face her. She wasn't sure how long she could . . . would keep up the polite pretense. "I want to talk with you."

Padruig slowly shut the door and entered the chamber. "Is there something you require?"

Yes! she wanted to shout. *Your attention. Your affection. Your treating me like something other than an unwanted burden!* She said none of these things, gritting her teeth instead. "I did not know how bad things were."

He sat with a grunt and poured a cup of wine. "'Tis not your worry."

Aimili made herself count to ten. "I am your wife. I am a part of the clan now."

"You have no interest in the management of Castle MacCoinneach. You have told me so more than once."

His comments stung with truth. "Still, you should have told me, shared the problem with me."

"Why? 'Tis my responsibility to deal with."

"We are wed. We are supposed to share responsibilities."

"Aimili, why distress yourself? Aye, we are wed, but . . ." He sighed and shook his head. "You would be just as happy living in the stable. The horses are your only concern. I accept this."

I want more! she yearned to scream. *I need more!* She swallowed. "I . . . I feel that I should help."

"By doing what? You know naught of seeing to the castle's needs. This is a serious matter, Aimili, best left to those with knowledge of how to deal with it."

He spoke as if he chastised a child.

"There must be something I can do."

"Do you even know how many people I must see are fed and cared for? How many loaves of bread are required each day? How many barrels of ale? The number of cows we typically slaughter for use during the winter?" His voice rose and rose until he was shouting.

Aimili felt each question like the lash of a whip. She gripped Lyoness tight and stiffened her shoulders. "I told you afore we wed that I knew little of such things. You should have heeded my words and taken Morainn."

He stared at her, his gaze cold. "Morainn was not offered to me."

The blow would have been kinder had it been with his fist. "I am no a stupid woman. I can learn." Why she would wish to, she did not know, but pride demanded the words.

"Aye, but that would mean time away from the stables."

"I do know there are about four-score folk here at Castle MacCoinneach. I am not completely ignorant of affairs."

"Oh? And what do you suggest they eat?"

She glared at him. "This is not my fault, Padruig."

Her words seemed to deflate him, and he stared down at his cup. "Nay, it is not. I am sorry to be so harsh."

"I could send to my family for food."

"They have already rendered me a great service. Asides, I have sent to someone in England who will help."

"England? Who?"

"Lady Giselle of Kindlemere. She owes me a boon."

Aimili's stomach turned over. A woman. "I see. Is that where you lived when you were . . . gone?"

"No at Kindlemere, but in England, aye."

"Where you met Lady Giselle?"

"Aye. A good woman." His voice held the unmistakable warmth of true affection.

Aimili's throat burned. It appeared his cool indifference was reserved only for *her*. He clearly thought she could be of no help in solving the clan's food shortage, as much as accusing her of only caring about her horses.

With the thought, Aimili sat up straighter. Her horses. Of course. "Have Magnus take Thunder and Pearl with him to Inverness. Thunder particularly should fetch a good price. If no one there can offer for him, tell Magnus to go to the Laird of the Burdine Clan."

For a moment, Padruig appeared taken aback, obviously surprised she would make such an offer. What did he think of her? Did he believe her so selfish to hoard valuable animals rather than help the clan avoid starvation? "My thanks," he finally said.

"You do not need to stand alone, Padruig."

"I know no other way."

"Mayhap, but has that way proved so successful for you?" She regretted her words at once when shadows darkened his face. "Padruig, I am sorry. I did not mean—"

"Aye, you did. 'Tis no more than many of the clan think. 'Tis no more than I deserve."

Aimili debated telling him of her strange conversation with Madeleine MacVegan, but held back. He would be angry to discover she'd encountered a member of the MacVegan clan. Even if he believed Madeleine's words, it would only make things worse.

"I did not know how much Grigor had let conditions deteriorate," he said. "Perhaps you should return to de Grantham Castle for a time."

"You . . . you wish to send me away?"

He didn't look at her. "'Twould be safer. I promised

I would see you well taken care of, and I can no longer guaranty that."

"An excuse," she spat, anger mingled with hurt bubbling up inside her.

"You heard me at supper, Aimili. The situation is dire."

"I am no child to be coddled, sent away to safety."

"You will feel differently when your stomach cramps because it's empty and the clan begins to gaze upon your horses with hungry eyes."

"I will not leave."

He stood. "You shall if I decide 'tis best."

"You would force me—"

"Aye, if need be." He picked up his flagon of wine and strode out of the chamber. "I will not watch you starve to death."

Aimili stared at the doorway. "What difference would it make?" she asked the empty space behind him.

Sebilla was blissfully immersed in a warm bath when D'Ary suddenly appeared next to the tub. She shrieked and bent forward in the water, glaring at him. "How dare you?"

D'Ary looked every bit as astonished as Sebilla felt.

His mouth opened and closed, but nothing came out and he gripped the side of the tub as if to hold himself upright. "I . . ." His golden gaze dropped and his jaw snapped shut.

"Get out of here," she commanded in her most queenlike voice.

With a visible shake of his head, instead D'Ary looked up, caught her gaze, and gave her the most devastatingly seductive smile she'd ever seen. "I could wash your back," he offered. "Or your front."

"Get out." By the gods, her voice was shaking.

"Are you sure?"

"Yes. Go!"

When he stood, the bulge in his braies turned her mouth dry. She clenched her fists under the water.

Whistling, he thankfully left her bathing chamber.

Hastily, Sebilla sprang out of the tub and pulled on clothing. *Of all the times for me to decide to bathe without attendants*, she thought, pulling a comb through her loose hair. Her hands were shaking and her whole body tingled in embarrassment and . . . No.

After plaiting her hair, she took a deep breath and walked into the room where she received visitors, though that was a rare event.

D'Ary stood in the center of the octagonal chamber waiting for her.

Sebilla paused at one of the fluted columns encircling the room, and gave him a haughty look. "Do not ever intrude on my privacy again."

He shrugged. "'Twas not apurpose, my queen. I cannot seem to manage the portal well."

Surely he lied, Sebilla thought with a frown. "I thought you claimed to have powers."

"I do."

"Then use them to land *outside* my quarters, not within."

"You have a lovely body, Sebilla. I had thought so before, but now I am sure of it."

"You . . . you should not have looked."

He laughed and put his hands out to the sides. "I am a man. How am I supposed to come upon a beautiful, naked woman and not look?"

"A woman who is your queen."

"But still a woman," he said softly.

Sebilla looked away, unexpectedly caught by the burn of tears. No one had ever seen her as more than queen, or before that, as one destined to rule. Not one person, male or female, had ever looked upon her simply as a woman. Forcefully, she gathered the frayed threads of her composure. "I refuse to continue this discussion. Have you discovered Vardon's identity yet?"

He frowned. "Not yet, but I sense his hand of revenge at work."

"How so?"

"He has brought the MacCoinneach clan to the brink of starvation. 'Tis as if the land itself is tainted. Many of the animals have sickened and died, and the grain harvest, already poor, has been partially destroyed."

"Can they survive?"

"Not without aid."

"Then we must aid them. Wait here." She wound through a labyrinth of corridors, finally coming to a locked door. After opening the door with a key she always wore on a chain around her neck, she lit a candle and studied the contents.

Within a few minutes, she gathered a pouch of valuables and returned to the chamber where D'Ary waited. She handed him the pouch. "See that Padruig MacCoinneach gets this."

He poured the contents onto a low table. Gold flashed and stones of red, green, and blue caught the light. "'Tis a fortune in his world."

"Castle MacCoinneach is a place of many hidden secrets. Perhaps an ancestor hid this cache away from enemies who would seize it."

D'Ary scooped up the stones and coins and returned them to the pouch. "I could claim I got lost and—"

"No. Hide the pouch by the pool.

"'Tis more complicated."

"Aye."

"Why?"

"It shall be as my queen wishes."

Sebilla gave a very unqueenlike snort. "Methinks you do as your queen wishes when it suits you."

He walked closer to her. "You have enough fawning subjects surrounding you."

"My advisors are good and wise men and women."

"I did not say they were not."

When had he moved so close? Sebilla wondered.

"Have you ever been with a man, Sebilla?"

She froze. "Wh-what?"

He leaned forward, his breath mingling with hers, and she found herself unable to move, barely able to breathe.

And that was before he kissed her.

Oh, goddess, help me, Sebilla thought as his lips closed over hers. It was not more than a brief touch, yet the force of it shot through her body like a tempest.

"I am thinking that one day soon, you will."

She could do nothing more than watch him leave, finally bringing her fingertips up to touch her lips. Had D'Ary just kissed her?

Aye, he did, her inner voice shouted. And promised more than that.

Chapter Thirteen

By the time Aimili woke up the next morn, the jumble of emotions her last conversation with Padruig fomented had distilled into a deep sense of resentment. She'd not *asked* to become the wife of a laird. *He* had brought it all to pass when he decided to reclaim his birthright and seek her father's aid to do so. If not for Padruig MacCoinneach, she would still be at de Grantham Castle living as she'd always done.

Riding and training her horses. Watching precious new foals being born.

Leaving tasks such as managing an estate to her father, brother, and sister. Oblivious to concerns over crops and livestock.

And still holding on to the dream of Padruig MacCoinneach.

In the face of Padruig's censure, she'd realized something else. Her family, save perhaps Morainn, had never really approved of her, yet their attitude was generally of benevolent tolerance. A roll of the eyes. A shake of the head.

Of course, she'd minded, had longed to hear her father do more than grunt when one of her horses brought seventy pounds into the de Grantham coffers.

Still, it was nothing next to Padruig's disproval, his complete dismissal of her value.

She would flee if not for the horses.

Clenching her jaw, she rose, washed her face, and pulled on her usual attire. Not surprisingly, her husband was gone from his fur pallet, if indeed he'd ever come back. Telling herself not to care, she grabbed her mantle, gathered Lyoness under her arm, and trudged out.

By the saints, she would not cry, she vowed to herself as she rushed to the stable.

Today, we shall run, she told Loki as she quickly saddled him. Thankfully, the stable was empty. As she walked into the bailey, she looked around, considering whether she should seek out D'Ary.

No, she needed no protector. After all, she had Lyoness now. *And the dagger*, her inner voice reminded her.

She mounted Loki and eyed the path out of the castle.

What are you doing?

Escaping. She tucked the dog down the front of her tunic so that only her face protruded.

Must we take that thing?

Aimili giggled. *My guard dog.*

Loki sighed.

As they passed beneath the gatehouse, Aimili pasted

a sunny smile upon her face.

"My lady, where is your guard?" a guardsman called down from atop the wallwalk.

"Oh, they are just ahead. Did you not see them?"

"Nay, but I have just come on duty."

Aimili's smile never shifted though she knew very well that the guards had rotated watch only moments ago. "We are visiting the village, 'tis all," she assured him as she rode outside the castle walls.

Run?

Not yet. Wait until we are out of sight.

What guards do you speak of?

The ones my husband and jailer has ordered me to take.

They are not waiting.

Nay.

They rode a ways until they passed over a hill. Aimili twisted around and looked back toward the castle, but the hill blocked her view, as it would the castle guards. She blew out a breath. *Now, we can run,* she told Loki, squeezing him.

He took off and Aimili laughed. Lyoness whimpered and buried her head inside Aimili's tunic.

Over the grass they flew, the early morning sunlight warm on Aimili's cheeks. She closed her eyes, breathing in the verdant scent of grass, earth, and heather.

Must we go so fast? Lyoness sounded terrified.

Aimili sat back. "Easy, Loki."

He settled into a rocking canter. Stride by stride,

the hard lump inside Aimili's chest softened. Eventually, her body relaxed and she simply let Loki carry her along. *Would that I could ride on forever*, she thought. *Fly into the very heavens.*

The sun was high in the sky by the time Aimili slowed Loki to a walk. She stroked his withers. *Did you enjoy that?*

Aye, my lady. 'Tis a fine feeling to run on such a day.

The dog poked her head out. *Are we going to stop?*

Have you not enjoyed the ride? Aimili asked her.

I have, actually, but I would like to be on the ground for a bit and, well, you know.

They stopped in a grove of rowan trees, with a small stream skirting the edge. After they all had a drink, Aimili wrapped Loki's reins around a low branch and sat back against a tree trunk. Loki contentedly grazed while Lyoness ran around, clearly happy to be back on solid ground.

Aimili closed her eyes, letting the combined sounds of Loki shifting back and forth, Lyoness scuffling in the grass, and the trill of birds lull her.

Guards, she thought with an inward sneer. She never felt safer than outside, never found such a feeling of peace elsewhere.

Finally tiring, Lyoness climbed into Aimili's lap and plopped down for a nap. Aimili put one hand on the dog and the other on the soft grass.

Loki's scream woke her.

She blinked her eyes open to find a man standing before her. At first, she thought the guard at Castle Mac-Coinneach had sent someone after her, but slowly she realized the man had a length of fabric wrapped around his face concealing his features. All she could see was a small slice of skin and his eyes. Black, empty eyes.

Danger, Loki shouted.

Aimili pressed tight against the hard bark of the tree. "What do you want? I've no coin with me."

The man drew his sword. "I care naught for your coin."

Was his voice familiar? Aimili frowned, staring hard at him. "Who are you?"

"A good question, but I fear you could never understand the answer."

Was it her fate to be judged witless and foolish by every man she met? "You might be surprised."

"Perhaps, but I doubt it."

Aimili set Lyoness aside, and rose. She slipped her hand around to her back, where she'd tucked the dagger. "You conceal yourself. I ask again, who are you?"

His low laugh skittered down her spine. "Death." He lunged toward her, his sword raised.

With a squeak, the dog raced off.

Aimili pulled the dagger free, knowing it was little defense against a sword. Still, if she were to die today, she would not go without inflicting as much damage as she could.

At the sight of the dagger, her attacker froze, halting his sword in midswing. "Where did you get that?"

Aimili was so terrified she could scarcely draw a breath. "From the Queen of Paroseea," she spat, expecting him to laugh.

Instead, the part of his face that she could see reddened in rage. "Give it to me."

"Go to hell." Aimili held the dagger in front of her. Her attacker howled and raised his sword.

It was as if an invisible shield surrounded Aimili, a radiant nimbus of silver flecked with green. When the blade struck, it glanced off with a chime as if metal met metal.

Aimili managed to swipe the man's chest, but instead of jumping back, he wrapped his hand around hers. "I believe the question is—who are *you,* my lady?"

He thrust her away from him and murmured words she couldn't understand, raising his sword once more. "I asked you a question, wench."

She gave him the same answer he'd given her. "Death," she snarled, leaping forward and plunging the dagger up into his shoulder.

Blood gushed out and the man sank to his knees. "You'll not defeat me so easily."

"It seems that I have." She pulled the dagger free with a sickening, sucking sound.

Soaked with blood, Aimili stumbled to Loki, barely noticing that Lyoness had been trying to chew his reins free. She swept up the dog and flung herself onto Loki's

back. *Take me home.*
Hold on.

"Laird, I would speak with you."

Padruig glanced at D'Ary, then held up his shield to halt his opponent's attack. Sweat stung his eyes, and he wiped it away with the sleeve of his tunic. "Aye?"

"I have failed you," the man announced.

Padruig narrowed his eyes, the beginnings of unease trickling into his gut. "What is amiss?"

"Loki is missing. As is your wife."

"What? Where is she?"

"That, I do not know. The guards report she left not long past sunrise."

Before Padruig could control himself, he had his sword at D'Ary's throat. "I thought you were to accompany her."

"I was." D'Ary did not flinch as the sharp steel cut a line into his neck.

Padruig was so furious it took a rigid exercise of control not to let the blade slice deeper. "You are telling me that not only did my wife disobey my orders to take a guard with her, but she rode that uncontrollable beast, as well?"

"Loki has been much improved of late," D'Ary offered.

"I will find her," Padruig snarled. All the way to the stable, across the bailey, beneath the gatehouse, and across the vast expanse of his land, Padruig cursed the girl who had fast become both his greatest irritation and his greatest temptation. *Damn it to hell.*

What was he to do with her?

A few hours later, Padruig stared around a blood-soaked grove and regretted every single unkind thought he'd ever had about Aimili. If not for the men accompanying him, he would just sink to his knees and howl to the heavens.

"This is my fault," he told Magnus.

Silently, Magnus handed him a bloody piece of green fabric. "We've not found a body."

"She is dead, Magnus. Look at the grass. There are clear signs of a fight. And the blood . . ."

Magnus's mouth turned down. "It does not look good, I grant you that."

"I have done it again. 'Tis just like Brona."

"Laird, you told Aimili not to leave the castle without a guard."

"Aye, but—" He broke off, shaking his head. "I drove her to this, Magnus." He could see her face clearly in his mind, the hurt he'd inflicted in his anger over the threat to the clan. Why would she not wish to escape Castle MacCoinneach? He had made it clear to her that she did not belong, that he did not want her. In his pathetic quest to protect Aimili, he'd instead driven her to her death.

Failure choked him and robbed him of breath. He should have done more to keep watch over her, particularly after she'd been attacked within the castle itself. Instead, he'd focused on the clan's needs and used that as an excuse to avoid her, leaving her care to others.

Randulf stopped in front of him, his gaze pitying. "There are signs of two horses, Laird. A trail of blood leads to one."

"Which direction did they go?"

"Toward the castle."

Padruig's belly clenched. "'Twas the same bastard who attacked her before."

"It would seem so."

"But, you have found no—"

"Nay," Randulf answered Magnus. "No body, but . . . I am sorry, Laird." Randulf bowed his head.

Padruig shook with the effort to maintain his composure. Aimili dead. He could not get his mind around the very idea, even though he knew he must. "Someone shall pay for the deed done today," he swore.

As they rode back to Castle MacCoinneach, the image of Aimili's face played over and over in his mind. No matter how many times he'd seen death, sometimes caused it, it never ceased to surprise him how life could be extinguished in the blink of an eye. Somehow, it had always seemed a desecration of God's will that his children be so fragile in the end.

Particularly one as vital as Aimili.

The men rode in silence, even Magnus grim and quiet for once.

It was not until they approached the gatehouse that Magnus spoke. "Clearly, this was aimed at you, Laird."

"Aye." Bile rose in the back of Padruig's throat. Aimili had been as much a sacrifice today as she'd been in marriage to him.

Magnus reached out and pulled Padruig's horse to a stop, motioning the other men forward. "I cannot fathom who would be doing this, Laird. I have talked to most of the clan, listened to others. I've heard none express the kind of animosity toward you that this deed indicates."

"Clearly the bastard is one of us. All signs point to it."

"I agree, but I still do not understand."

"Perhaps one of the stable hands saw someone take a horse."

"I shall question them myself."

"Thank you, Magnus."

Magnus clapped a hand on Padruig's shoulder. "These are dark days, Laird."

"Aye." Padruig squeezed his mount forward. "My fear is how much darker they will get."

Magnus had no answer.

Aimili was so upset she didn't realize for a while that Loki had veered from the path back to Castle MacCoinneach. By the time she regained her senses, they were across the loch from the castle.

Loki, you went the wrong way! By the saints, this was not what she needed. She fought the urge to break down and sob.

I am sorry, my lady. This day has been . . . strange.

'Tis not your fault. I should have been paying better attention. Aimili slid off the horse and stretched. She put Lyoness on the ground, where she promptly sat and just stared up at Aimili.

It has been quite a day, has it not?

Aye, Lyoness answered, her gaze unblinking. *I am sorry I could not be of more aid to you.*

At that, Aimili had to chuckle. Though she was nearly oblivious to everything but getting away from the grove, she did remember seeing the dog with a mouthful of rein. If determination could have freed Loki to help her, Aimili was sure her wee guard dog could have done it.

She looked down and grimaced at the sight of her torn and bloody tunic. Even her hands were streaked with reddish-brown marks.

You'll not defeat me so easily, the man had said. Could he be the one Queen Sebilla had warned her about? Aimili shivered. Well, surely he was dead now. No one could survive losing that much blood so quickly.

She waded into the shallow edge of the loch and splashed water onto her tunic until it ran clear, scrubbing her hands until the blood was gone. Finally, she splashed her face, sickened to find that water came away red, as well.

After draping the mantle she'd tied in a roll to Loki's saddle over her and Lyoness, she started back around the loch to Castle MacCoinneach. As she rode, the sun dimmed, then vanished behind an increasingly dark band of lowering clouds. She peered up at the sky, and squeezed Loki into a canter, hoping they could make it before the skies opened.

The sky grew darker and darker and a cold wind blew against Aimili's cheeks. She pulled up the hood of her mantle just as the rain began.

Perfect, Loki grumbled.

We do not have far to go. She was right, but a thick veil of rain obscured her vision and made the grass slick, forcing her to slow Loki. It seemed like days before they finally reached the gatehouse of Castle MacCoinneach, only to find the portcullis securely lowered against entry.

Aimili spied movement above, and yelled, "Open the portcullis!"

A guard looked down at her, but she could not make out his face. "Who are you?"

"Lady Aimili." She threw back her hood and blinked up at him while water ran down her face.

Thankfully, the portcullis immediately groaned open and Aimili rode straight for the stable.

"My lady!" a voice yelled, but Aimili ignored it, intent on seeing Loki settled and finding her chamber to dry off.

When she neared the stable, D'Ary ran out. Even through the rain, she could see the shock on his face. He reached Loki and took the reins. "Aimili, you are alive! Thank the gods."

Aimili gratefully slung off Loki's back. "Of course, I am alive."

D'Ary's throat worked and finally he grinned. "Of course. You had best go inform the laird of that fact."

"I need to see to Loki."

"I can do it. Aimili, my lady, the laird, well, we all believed you slain."

"What?" She took a step back.

"Your husband went out searching for you and found evidence of a fight. He presumed you dead."

Well, Aimili thought, wondering what Padruig was feeling now. Relief? No, surely he could not be that callous. He would likely be saddened, but blame her death on her own recklessness.

"Go, my lady. I shall take good care of Loki."

"Give him an extra measure of grain. He has worked hard this day."

"Aye." When Aimili turned to leave, he touched her shoulder. *"Are* you all right, Aimili? Truly?"

"Far better than the cur who attacked me."

"Please take me along the next time."

"I shall. I promise."

"Good luck with the laird."

She sighed and tromped through the mud toward her chamber. Everything would be better once she'd donned dry clothing and had a cup of wine in her hand.

Padruig sat in his chamber staring unseeing at the fire. The window shutters rattled with the ascending storm, and cool air trickled across his face.

To his surprise and dismay, he found his cheeks wet with tears. He'd thought himself beyond such tender emotions, but Aimili's loss cut him more deeply than he would have imagined.

He finally realized how badly he'd wanted to be the man she saw inside him, but now it was too late.

Her smell lingered in the chamber, and the bed-sheets were still rumpled from last night. *The night you insulted her, hurt her, and left*, he reminded himself.

By the saints, if only he could take a day back.

His lips twisted into a bitter smile. How many times had he thought exactly the same thing about Brona? Just one day, Lord, one day to do over, to make the right choices instead of the ones that brought pain and death.

Unfortunately, God did not see fit to grant him that boon.

He lifted his cup in a silent toast and downed the wine.

"God, I am sorry, Aimili," he whispered. "I failed you."

"Padruig," her voice said.

He put his head in his hands. "Och, lass, now *your* ghost haunts me, as well."

"I am no ghost, Padruig."

Slowly, he stood and turned. Blood rushed to his head, and he swayed before catching himself. "Aimili?" He took a step toward her, sure that he was seeing a vision, and that she would fade away just as Brona did.

Instead, she shut the door and pulled off her mantle. Water dripped a line on the floor as she hung it on a hook.

Could ghostly clothing drip water? Padruig wondered.

The dog popped its head out of the top of Aimili's tunic. Aimili put it on the floor and it scampered over to where Cai lay on the floor in front of the fire. His wolf raised his head, gave a sigh, and let the dog snuggle up next to him.

"How strange," Padruig said. "I've never seen a ghost dog."

Aimili's ghost frowned at him. Her hair was plastered to her head, and her clothing was wet. He peered closer. Was she shivering? Ghosts did not feel the cold. Did they? "Padruig, are you sotted?"

"I should be. God knows I have tried."

"What is wrong with you?"

Padruig opened his mouth to tell her it was his fault she died, when Aimili began stripping off her wet clothing and tossing it into a heap on the floor. With each garment, his jaw dropped lower and lower.

By the saints, even as a ghost she aroused him, he thought, wanting to protest when she wrapped a sheet around her body.

"I am freezing," she announced.

"Is that possible?"

She looked at him as if he were absolutely witless. Gradually, another expression spread over her face and she walked close to him. When she was no more than a handbreadth away, she dropped the sheet. "I am no ghost, Padruig."

He felt as if he were caught in a dream, reaching out to touch the curve of her neck. His fingertips brushed cool skin. Solid skin. "Dear God, you are not dead."

"Just cold. Very cold."

Surely it was someone else who said, "I can help with

that."

Aimili held her breath as Padruig's roughened fingers drifted across her skin. She was not sure what bit of bravery had prompted her to cast aside the sheet, but everywhere he touched grew warm and warmer yet.

This time, his kiss was desperate, marauding, claiming. Aimili clung to his broad shoulders and gave herself up to him. It was as she'd dreamt, only better. Far better. She tasted the wine on his tongue, but mostly she tasted his desire.

When he cupped her breasts, her moan mixed with his. "Dear God, how I've wanted to do this," he rasped, the words torn from him as he kissed her throat.

Aimili gasped, her body tingling as he brushed fingertips over her nipples. When his mouth closed on one, she jumped and cried out. Dear Lord, how glorious. She glanced down, and her knees buckled at the sight of him suckling her.

Within moments, he'd swept her onto the bed.

She watched him strip, greedily drinking in his hard body, the spread of his shoulders, the smooth planes of his belly, the silver glitter of his eyes. Her gaze dropped lower and she stared. Perhaps she should be embarrassed, but she was not. She surely was not afraid, anticipation coiling into a hard knot in her center.

He stretched out on the bed next to her and brought his mouth down to hers once more, plundering her lips, her tongue, everywhere, stroking, devouring her mouth like a man who'd not eaten in a sennight.

Dimly, Aimili realized that his hand stroked down her body, between her breasts, over her belly, and yet lower.

"Open for me," he whispered, his fingers splayed in the curls covering her sex.

Aimili swallowed, gazing into his eyes. When she relaxed her thighs, he let out a hiss. Never losing her gaze, he slid his fingers lower, stroking her body's opening, spreading the moisture he found there. Aimili's breath became more uneven and she pushed against his hand, at the same time shocked and thrilled at her body's instinctive response.

He watched her as his thumb found a place that shot her off the bed. She shook her head, suddenly frightened as tension gripped her body. It was as if some irresistible force had taken control of her. She moaned, unable to stop from bucking against him, desperately needing more.

"Let go, Aimili."

Everything within her built into a coil of feeling, then burst apart with such incredible pleasure that she cried out. Even as her body yet trembled, Padruig slid between her legs and pushed just inside her.

Aimili dug her fingers into his arms.

He kissed her, hot and openmouthed as he pushed deeper. Aimili trembled, but she tilted up to meet him, knowing somehow that this was what she'd waited for.

With a groan, he filled her.

Aimili caught her breath. Dear God, he was so deep, so big and hard inside her. Her legs fell open farther and she was filled with the wild need to be taken by this man.

The friction of him sliding back out made her whimper.

"Are you all right?"

She stared into his eyes. "Yes. God, yes."

With the kind of smile she'd thought reserved only for others, he began thrusting, rocking against her, gently yet firmly, relentlessly. She slid her hands down his chest, learning him, claiming him as her own.

When she traced the ridged skin of a scar, he paused. "Pray do not stop," she whispered.

He briefly closed his eyes and bent her legs, opening her more. Aimili gasped as he pounded into her, such a big, invasive presence that she panted with each thrust. He consumed her, hurled her into another place, where only the demands of her body mattered, only the heat of his body covering hers.

She was shattering into a million pieces and it felt so right she didn't care. Aimili threw her head back and rode a wave of pleasure so intense it engulfed her senses. She barely heard Padruig's shout, just before he collapsed against her.

Aimili fought to get her breath back. Her heart thundered in her ears and she never wanted to move.

Padruig rolled to the side and lay on his back, one hand flung over his brow. "By the saints, I am an animal," he cursed.

Aimili sat up. "Oh, no. You will not belittle me so."

He looked at her. "What are you talking about?"

She clenched a length of sheet in her fist. "I am your wife. You made love to me. There is naught wrong with that."

"I should have—"

"Done so before, I agree."

He blinked, then slowly smiled. "Think you?"

"Aye."

He leaned up and brushed hair from her face. "I am heartedly glad that you are no a ghost."

She blew out a breath. "As am I."

"What happened?"

Before answering, she rose, poured a cup of wine, and returned to the bed. For some reason, it felt entirely natural to be reclining without a bit of clothing and talking to Padruig. "Though it pains me to admit it, you were right. I should have taken D'Ary with me."

To her surprise, he managed not to appear either smug or chastising. "Next time you shall."

"Aye." She took a sip of wine. "I stopped to rest in a grove."

"We found it."

"I must have fallen asleep. When I awoke, a man stood there."

Padruig's gaze narrowed. "Who was he?"

"He was disguised. Something about him seemed

familiar, but I could not identify him."

"Did he speak?"

"Not much. He . . . intended to kill me, Padruig."

Padruig's body was still, but she felt his anger nonetheless. "Instead, I killed him." She retrieved the dagger and placed it in his hands. "With this."

"Where did you come by such a piece?" He turned it over in his hands. "'Tis most unusual."

"Aye." She gazed at him and thought, it is time. "A woman gave it to me."

His brow furrowed. "Who?"

"She claimed to be the Queen of Paroseea."

"Where? I have never heard of such a land."

"I do not understand it yet, but I think it is a land of . . . magic." When Padruig frowned, she raised a hand. "Listen to me. When I held out the dagger, 'twas as if the man's sword could not touch me. That is how I bested him. And he wanted it, Padruig. Badly."

"Where did you meet this . . . queen?"

"In the loch." She shook her head. "I know it sounds impossible, mad, but 'tis true."

"As impossible as a person being able to communicate with animals?"

Aimili gulped a drink of wine. "You—"

"Guessed, aye."

"Oh." Aimili waited for him to turn from her, waited for revulsion and fear to cloak his face, but he calmly gazed at her.

"What a wondrous ability that must be," he said.

"You . . . you do not mind?"

"Only that I cannot do the same." He looked over at Cai, now sleeping in a tangle with Lyoness. "Is he content here?"

Aimili laughed. "You do not need any special ability to decipher that. Look at him."

Padruig shook his head. "I never thought to see him curled up with a bit of fluff."

Aimili sobered. "Lyoness tried to aid me today. I had tethered Loki's reins to a branch. When that man . . ." Her throat closed and she forced herself to take a deep breath. "She tried to chew the reins free."

"Och, a wee hero." Padruig rose, pulled on braies, and fetched a cup of wine, all the while holding the dagger. "I have seen this design afore."

"It looks like a sea creature."

"Aye, a dolphin. I have seen such in my travels."

"But we are not near the sea."

"This design," he said, pointing to the pattern etched into the steel blade. "See, the dolphin is set within the circular lines. I have seen that symbol carved somewhere." He drummed his fingers against his cup.

"Here?"

"Aye, but I cannot recall exactly where." He glanced at her. "What did this . . . Queen of Paroseea say to you?"

"'Twas confusing. She said that there was danger

here from a man, that I would help defeat him."

"And so you have."

"Perhaps." *You shall not defeat me so easily.* "You did not find his body in the grove?"

"Nay. 'Twas empty. Most likely the man had a companion who carried his body off."

"I saw no one else." She tried but failed to stifle a yawn.

"Rest." He approached the bed, and suddenly his face turned to stone. "By the saints, I bruised you."

Aimili looked down to where his gaze was fixed. Already bruises formed from where his hands had spanned her waist. "'Tis of no matter. I bruise easily."

"No matter? It is to me." He grimaced, his obvious self-disgust a splash of icy water on the mood in the chamber.

"Padruig, I—"

"Rest now." His voice was back to cool and impersonal. "I will explore the castle to see if I can find this symbol."

The warmth that had so briefly seized her fled as she watched Padruig hastily throw on his clothes and exit their chamber.

He never even looked at her.

"Damn that bitch," Vardon muttered as he rode his horse slowly back to Castle MacCoinneach. "Both of them."

He'd barely escaped being found by Padruig Mac-Coinneach and his weak-willed followers, spelling himself and the horse with invisibility just in time. By far the only pleasure to be had in the whole affair was the tortured look on the laird's face when he believed his woman slain.

By the gods, she should have been.

What was the queen of nothing thinking to give that human the dagger of Artemis? He'd recognized the blade at once, of course. Long ago, he'd held the dagger in his own hand, felt the power burned into the steel.

His horse stumbled, and Vardon had to catch at its mane not to tumble off. Damned nag. It was a crime that he'd been reduced to riding a horse simply because it was easy to steal. For a moment, when the wench had plunged the dagger into his shoulder and his blood had run like a pulsing river, he'd thought she'd truly killed him, but as he'd hoped, the dagger was not enough to finish the deed. Still, blood oozed from him, and weakness wound through his limbs, pulling at his eyelids.

"Bitches!" he swore aloud.

He'd made a mistake in underestimating the laird's lady. There was more to her than a simple lass good with horses, but he could not detect what it was. The dagger guarded her though, and that meant something.

She hadn't expected it, he'd seen that in her frightened gaze. Though she might possess the blade for now, clearly Sebilla had failed to explain its power.

Foolish woman. When he possessed the dagger of Artemis, he would never let it out of his sight.

He took deep breaths, focusing on reaching the castle before someone noticed his lengthy absence. In between chanting spells of healing to hasten his recovery, he considered how best to deal with Aimili MacCoinneach.

In a way he enjoyed the fact that she would not be as easy as he'd expected. The gods knew no one at Castle MacCoinneach had proved to be any challenge at all thus far. Easily manipulated, easily harmed. In light of the latest scourge to the grain supplies, he'd heard more than one of the clan wonder aloud if the laird bore a curse.

He chuckled, wishing that were, indeed, the case, but that was a power he'd not been able to regain.

Aimili really had to die. Now, he knew how devastated Padruig would be. All he had to do was come upon her when she did not have the dagger. Perhaps when she was bathing, he thought, liking the idea more and more. After all, she owed him.

Aye, Aimili would die, he would take the dagger, and poor Padruig would be so overwhelmed with guilt that he would never recover.

Instead, he would die with the certain knowledge that he had failed. What perfect vengeance.

"Padruig," Freya shouted when he entered the hall. "Is it true?" She ran to his side, her face pinched and pale.

Silence gripped the hall as expectant faces turned toward him.

"Aye. Aimili is fine."

Freya swayed. Magnus, who stood just to her side, grabbed her around the waist.

"Our lady lives," Padruig announced to the folks gathered for supper.

A chorus of excited voices flowed through the hall as Padruig took a seat next to Alasdair and Efrika.

"Praise the Lord," Efrika said, her hand clutching Alasdair's. "What happened, Padruig?"

Well, it appears our wee Aimili found herself a magical dagger and defeated her attacker, Padruig thought. Instead, he said, "She rode out alone, despite my orders. A man did attack her, but she managed to defend herself."

"A brave lass you have, Padruig," Alasdair said.

"Aye. At least now she has learned her lesson."

"Where is she?" Efrika asked.

"Abed. She was exhausted from her travails."

Magnus slid in beside him. "I can imagine," he

commented, with a pointed look at Padruig's tunic.

Padruig glanced down and cringed. By the saints, he'd put the garment on inside out. He clenched his jaw and motioned for food to be served. "'Tis not every day a lass faces down an armed man."

Freya peered around Magnus. "Who attacked her? Is he dead?"

"She could not identify him. He concealed his face, but aye, he is dead." He smiled at his sister, whose face remained pale. "Do not worry, Freya. You are not one to take the kind of risks Aimili does. No one shall harm you."

"Ye cannot promise that, Padruig. If . . . Loki . . ."

"Shush," Magnus told her, taking her hand. "Angus Ransolm shall never hurt anyone again."

"I wish to learn how to defend myself," Freya announced. "Like Aimili."

Oh, no, Padruig thought. All he needed was for his sister to begin emulating his bride. He would have two irresponsible women to rein in. "No."

"'Tis a good idea, Padruig," Magnus said. "I shall see to her training."

Padruig looked at Freya's determined expression and knew he didn't stand a chance. "Very well. It cannot hurt to teach her a few tricks."

"Perhaps all of the women in the castle should learn some basic defense," Efrika commented.

Visions of Efrika and Freya leading a troop of

women all bearing swords danced through Padruig's mind. "Efrika, 'tis man's duty to protect the women of the clan."

"And we appreciate it." She beamed a smile at Alasdair. "Still—"

"Fine," Padruig said. "Do as you will. Just try not to hurt yourself or anyone else."

Efrika scowled at him.

Padruig ignored her and speared a chunk of cheese.

"You must be heartily relieved to find your wife unharmed," Magnus said, his tone suspiciously light.

"Of course. 'Tis a miracle."

"So relieved that you finally claimed her as a woman."

Padruig sighed. "Aye, but—" He halted himself and glared at Magnus, who grinned back at him. "'Twas a mistake."

Magnus cocked a brow.

"'Twill not happen again."

"Oh?" Magnus swigged down some wine. "Would you care to make a wager on that?"

"I would, but it would not be seemly."

Magnus burst out laughing. "You are a terrible liar, Laird."

Padruig looked away and found himself gazing into Efrika's knowing eyes. He put his attention to his food. Damn romantic fools, he thought. He was surrounded by them. Efrika and Alasdair looked at each other like lovesick puppies and he could tell Freya and Magnus were but days away from exhibiting the very same. Even his wolf was fast becoming attached to a knot of yarn with the ridiculous name of Lyoness.

God forbid that he fall prey to such soft emotions.

He gripped the stem of his goblet so tightly it snapped in two. Over laughter, Magnus sent for a new one. "You are in a sorry state, indeed, Laird."

"Did you find out if anyone else had taken a horse, or have you been too busy drooling over my sister?" Padruig tried to sound harsh and demanding but found he couldn't. Truth be told, he was pleased that a man such as Magnus found favor in Freya's eyes.

"None whose whereabouts I could not verify. 'Tis a puzzle. Could it have been a MacVegan, do you think?"

"Why hide his face? A MacVegan would *want* me to know who had killed my wife." The thought of it sent such fear into Padruig's mind that he wanted nothing more than to rush back to his chamber to make sure Aimili was, indeed, alive.

But you know that very well, he told himself, unable to keep his mind from drifting to the past hours. In the shock of believing her dead, and then finding her alive, he'd lost what few wits he'd managed to keep intact after Aimili de Grantham entered his life. He should have had more control than that, but instead he'd taken her hard and fast, without regard to her youth and innocence.

She didn't seem to mind, his inner voice mocked.

By the saints, what a tangle.

"I have tasks demanding my attention," he announced, unable to remain at supper a moment longer under the watchful and knowing eyes of his kin.

"As you say, Laird," Magnus replied, his eyes twinkling.

Padruig suppressed a groan and strode out of the hall.

Chapter Fourteen

Sebilla was conferring with Lucan when one of her attendants announced that Arailt and Vanasia sought to speak with her. "Send them in," she told the attendant, exchanging a hopeful glance with Lucan.

Arailt entered first, his countenance unusually grim. Sebilla's hopes dipped. He moved aside and Vanasia rushed forward, her head bowed. She sank to her knees clutching a sheaf of old vellum, her hands visibly shaking.

Sebilla looked from the girl to Arailt, then back again. "She told you," Sebilla said to Arailt.

Arailt gave a jerky nod, far from his typically courtly demeanor.

"There was no need," Sebilla told the girl.

Vanasia did not look up. "I . . . I remembered everything, your majesty. I felt I had no choice but to confess my shame."

"You remembered?"

"Aye, your majesty." The words came out on a sob.

"And Ulf?"

The girl's head hung lower. "Aye."

"How interesting," Lucan commented.

Sebilla looked at him, puzzled, as well. "Perhaps Vardon's power weakens?"

"'Twould be folly to assume such a thing, but it is a possible explanation."

"I shall, of course, immediately withdraw as your advisor and as master of the archives," Arailt said.

Sebilla rose and went to him. "You shall do no such thing, old friend. Now, come, both of you, and sit." She took Arailt's hands and pulled him to a chair.

Vanasia didn't move.

"Lucan?" Sebilla asked, gesturing to the girl.

Lucan murmured something to her, and eventually Vanasia sat beside her father.

"I found something," the girl whispered.

Sebilla's breath hitched. "Tell me."

Before speaking, Vanasia cast a glance at her father's stricken face. The barest flicker of emotion appeared in his eyes.

"I am close to the answer, your majesty." She slid the sheets of vellum toward Sebilla. "'Tis complicated, though."

"Tell me. Now."

Aimili woke up and slowly stretched, her eyes still closed. What wonderful dreams she'd had, she thought with a smile. Padruig had finally looked upon her as more than a child to be endlessly cosseted. Her husband had become one in truth, loving her with an intensity she never realized simmered beneath his controlled surface. She sighed, reveling in memories of his warm, hard body pressed to hers, the slide of skin, her unexpected burst of pleasure.

Her eyes flashed open. By the saints, it had not been a dream. She looked around the chamber, but Lyoness and Cai were the only other inhabitants, curled together at the bottom of the bed.

Where was Padruig?

It was then she remembered all of it. Yes, he'd loved her, joined with her so sweetly, so desperately that it had been all she'd ever imagined and more. They had actually *talked* without him passing judgment on her. He'd been so accepting Aimili had begun to think perhaps the Padruig of her dreams still existed.

And then he'd turned from her, appalled at what he'd done. He'd not even been able to look at her before he left.

She climbed out of bed, trying to tell herself that it was still a beginning of sorts. Wasn't it? She'd barely dressed when the door swung open and the object of her thoughts stood there.

"I found it," he said.

"Good morn to you, too," she replied, pulling on her boots.

"Aimili—"

"I am coming."

He eyed her as if he wasn't sure it was safe to be in her presence. "Are you . . . well?"

"Fine." She marched over and looked him in the eye. Thankfully, anger overrode her feelings of disappointment and hurt. "Let us go."

She followed Padruig's steady stride out of the tower and into the bailey. It was very early, dawn barely a hint of light gray in the sky. Aside from the occasional clump of a guard's footfall from the wallwalk, the bailey was quiet. Aimili remained silent as she followed Padruig.

Eventually, they came to a narrow door. It was cut into a big stone tower flanking the main tower. If Padruig had not led her straight to it, Aimili would have passed it by without a second glance, so cleverly cut into the wall it was.

Inside, a single candle split the inky blackness. Cold air drifted from someplace inside. Padruig lit a rushlight and glanced back at Aimili. "Stay close."

"What is this place?"

His voice echoed off the thick stone walls. "Over the years, it has been used for many things. Storage of supplies." He lifted the torch higher, illuminating a small alcove cut into the wall. Broken pieces of iron littered the earthen floor. "Prisoners."

Aimili's gaze fixed on a rust-colored stain on the stone.

The passageway curved, then led to steps leading down. The air grew close and heavy with the stale smell of disuse. Once they reached the bottom of the steps, Padruig paused. "These passageways are not known to the clan. Only to me." He gave her a meaningful look. "And now to you."

Aimili's heart thumped. "I will not tell anyone."

"I did not think you would." He pressed three stones in quick progression and an opening appeared. Padruig had to bend down to clear it, but Aimili had no problem.

They continued walking, and Aimili gradually realized that the walls reflected the rushlight in tiny flickers of silver. "Padruig, what is in the stone? I can see flashes of something shiny."

She sensed more than saw his shrug. "I dinnae ken."

It didn't take long for Aimili to become completely disoriented. They turned right, then left, climbed down steps, then up others. Several times Padruig stopped and found an opening in the wall that had not been there before. Aimili silently focused on keeping calm, repeatedly telling herself that Padruig knew where he was going and, more importantly, knew the way out.

"There," Padruig finally said, lifting the torch high.

She looked up and blinked in surprise. Carved into the stone was the very image etched into the dagger.

"'Tis the same."

"Aye."

"But . . . there is nothing else here."

"No."

"I do not . . . wait." She bent close to study the stone. "Look. 'Tis the shape of an opening of some kind."

Padruig brought the light close. The flames showed the faint outline. "I know of no way to open this."

Aimili put her hand against the stone and pushed. For a moment, nothing moved, then she felt the slightest shifting of stone. "Padruig, help me."

To her surprise, he put his hand over hers and pushed.

The stone opened so easily Aimili fell forward, landing on her knees. The light wavered behind her, and then Padruig apparently caught himself. Aimili looked around, sensing space, but unable to see beyond the pool of light.

Padruig touched the flame to candles mounted on the walls, and the chamber gradually came into view.

Aimili's breath caught when she spied the center of the large chamber. It was a circular pool, the water's surface as smooth as the loch on a windless day.

"By the saints, what is this?" Padruig asked. "My father never mentioned this chamber."

"Perhaps he did not know of it." Aimili stood and brushed off her braies. She walked to the edge of the pool. "Mayhap 'tis the gateway to Paroseea."

"Aimili, 'tis simply a pool. Most likely, at one time

the clan used it for a source of water immune from poisoning by its enemies."

The water rippled.

"I do not think so, Padruig."

Padruig tromped around the chamber, shining his light into the corners. "I hoped to find something of use in here, but 'tis empty."

The ripples widened and a soft mist formed on the water's surface.

"Not empty," Aimili said.

"Water is not what the clan needs."

The mist thickened.

"Perhaps this will help," a woman's voice said.

Padruig whipped around so fast, his rushlight dropped to the ground and sputtered out.

Queen Sebilla stood next to the pool. Her silver hair was elaborately braided into what looked like a crown. She wore a flowing bliaut of shimmering, pale blue silk and silver slippers adorned her small feet. Around her neck hung a pendant bearing the dolphin symbol. She held a dark blue velvet pouch in her hand.

"Good morn, Queen Sebilla," Aimili managed to say over a smile. The expression of amazement on Padruig's face was even better than when she'd bested him with her "wee sword."

"Greetings, Aimili," the queen said. "And you are Padruig, Laird of the MacCoinneachs, descendent of Aelfric."

It took Padruig a few attempts, but eventually he said, "Aye, my lady, uh, your majesty."

"Sebilla will do." She turned to Aimili. "I am very pleased to find you unharmed."

"The dagger saved me."

"Aye. I thought it might be of aid."

Aimili was surprised when Padruig moved up to stand beside her. "What do you know of the attack?" he demanded.

"'Twas Vardon, of course."

"Vardon? There is no man of that name at Castle MacCoinneach."

"He would not use his real name."

"Well, regardless of what he calls himself, he is dead by Aimili's hand."

Aimili peered up at him. Was that pride she heard in his voice?

"I fear not," Sebilla said.

"But I stabbed him," Aimili told her. "Blood was everywhere. No man could survive such a wound."

"I agree, but Vardon is not simply a man."

"I do not understand," Padruig said, his frustration evident.

"Nay, you could not. I ask you both to come with me. We must talk and I would prefer to do so in more comfortable surroundings."

"How?"

Sebilla smiled. "All you must do is step into the

pool." She walked close and put the pouch into Padruig's hand. "You may leave the pouch here. No one will find it."

He tugged the top open and peered inside, his eyes widening. "My thanks."

"'Tis in part my fault that your clan is in trouble."

"What do you mean?"

"Please. Come with me and I shall explain as best I can."

"Come with you where?"

"To Paroseea, of course." She walked into the center of the pool, gliding across the surface as if it were solid.

Without thinking, Aimili slipped her hand into Padruig's and held tight. She sensed no danger from Sebilla, but this was by far the strangest invitation she'd ever received. At the same time, she felt compelled to go.

As soon as she and Padruig stepped into the water, the chamber vanished.

"Welcome to Paroseea," a woman's voice announced.

Aimili had to blink a few times to clear her vision and recognize the voice as belonging to Sebilla. She and Padruig stood in a large chamber ringed with columns. The floor beneath them was of creamy white marble, the golden wood furnishings piled with brightly colored cushions. There were no walls and the air was warm and sweet smelling. The sounds of splashing water and birdsong broke the silence.

"Please, be comfortable," Sebilla said, gesturing to

a grouping of long wide benches covered by cushions. She clapped her hands and a young woman appeared. The woman had pale skin, long flaxen hair, and her pink bliaut was so light it wafted about her legs with each floating step she took.

Aimili noted her glance of surprise and fought the urge to grimace, aware she must look like a drab sparrow next to a delicate butterfly.

"Cinara, please see that refreshments are brought at once for my guests."

The woman nodded and glided from the room.

Aimili carefully sat on an emerald green pillow. Clearly ill at ease, Padruig posted himself by her side, but did not sit. "This is lovely," Aimili told Sebilla.

The queen's eyes twinkled. "Oh, you have seen but a tiny bit of the beauty of Paroseea."

Behind her appeared three men and three women. They were each dressed in fabrics finer than Aimili had ever seen and each carried himself or herself with an air of elegance.

"Laird MacCoinneach, Lady Aimili, may I present my advisors. Lucan, my chief advisor," she said waving her hand.

A handsome, dark-haired man clad in a deep blue tunic and matching braies bowed low.

One by one, they each made a sign of respect. Toward the end of the presentation, Aimili looked at Padruig in puzzlement. He just shook his head, clearly as bewildered as she.

Sebilla remained quiet while another troop of people delivered platters of food and colored-glass ewers of drink.

Aimili took a hesitant sip of wine from a blue glass goblet. It was unlike anything she'd ever tasted—light and golden with hints of fruit and honey. Padruig remained standing, his wine untouched.

"Where are we?" Padruig asked. "What is this place?"

"You are in the receiving chamber of my palace." Sebilla gave him a soft smile. "Paroseea is a special place, a magical realm, if you will."

"I know naught of magic."

"Mayhap not, but surely you have heard of places most people never see. The otherworld of the druids? The secret refuges of the Tuatha de Danann? The fabled island of Atlantis?"

"Legends. Stories told when the snowy winds howl down from the mountains and there is little to do."

"Paroseea is such a place. I will show you my kingdom and you will understand. For the moment, however, we must discuss the threat of Vardon."

"Who is he?" Aimili asked. "You said he was not simply a man."

Sebilla frowned. "No." She took a sip of wine. "This is difficult. I must ask that all of what I share with you will stay between us. Long ago, we realized that the only way to retain our way of life was to remain separate from your world."

"You speak as if you are something more, something different from us," Padruig said.

"We are. Most of us of Paroseea have some type of magical power in varying degrees. For example, some are healers, and others have the gift of fertility. Those of us with the purest bloodlines are born with a particular mark on our skin. We possess the most power."

"Vardon is one of you?"

"No. That is just it. He is of humble birth. Nevertheless, he manifested powers far beyond what he should have had. You must understand. We are a peaceful people. Paroseea is a place of bounty, of great beauty. We do not fight amongst ourselves. There is no need."

Sebilla rose and took a few steps, clasping her hands together. "Vardon was different. He lusted for power. He wished to rule Paroseea and tried to murder our rightful ruler." Her gaze grew cold. "We stopped him and imprisoned him."

"How did he escape?" Padruig asked.

"He learned enough of the magic used to imprison him to suspend it for a brief time."

Padruig frowned. "Why come to Castle MacCoinneach? We have naught to do with him or Paroseea."

"But you do. It was Aelfric, your ancestor, who once aided us in vanquishing Vardon. Vardon has not forgotten that, I am sure."

Aimili set aside her cup. "What can we do?"

"Our ancestors foresaw the possibility of Vardon's escape. It is written. This time, to thwart him, we need both of you to defeat Vardon. One," she nodded toward Aimili, "a woman of fey blood. Two," she turned to Padruig, "the true Laird of the MacCoinneach clan."

Aimili saw Padruig's start of surprise. "Nay," he said, his gaze darkening. "Aimili shall have nothing to do with this."

"She must. It is her destiny."

"You are mistaken, Queen Sebilla," Aimili told her. "I am not the woman of your prophecy."

"Aye, you are."

"But I am not of fey blood." A chill ran down Aimili's spine.

"Are you not?" Sebilla lifted a brow.

"The animals," Padruig said.

"Aye."

Aimili could not meet Padruig's gaze, afraid of what she might find there. "I am not . . . I just have an unusual ability with animals. My parents were normal."

Sebilla smiled. "I consider myself normal."

Aimili flushed. "I did not mean to insult you."

"I know this is a shock to you, but that does not make it any less true. You bear the mark."

Aimili felt the blood drain from her face. "No, 'tis just a tiny birthmark."

Sebilla walked close and slowly slipped her gown off

one shoulder. Her skin bore the small but unmistakable outline of a heart.

Just as Aimili's own did.

"My family, my sister and brothers, they—"

"Did not inherit your fey ancestry. Only you."

A strange kind of relief surged through Aimili. At last, she knew why she was different. She turned the news over in her mind. "You are saying that one of my ancestors was from Paroseea?"

"Yes. We are not sure who yet." Sebilla tilted her head toward a man who'd identified himself as Arailt. "Once we deal with Vardon, Arailt can search the archives if you like."

"I would like that, yes." She smiled at Arailt.

He inclined his head.

"This Vardon," Padruig said, frowning. "How long ago did he escape?"

"Over a year."

Padruig's frown deepened. "And you do not know by what name he calls himself?"

"No. Not yet."

"How are we to defeat the man if we do not even know who he is?"

"We are working on it. You must be alert, as well. You know your clan."

"Can he appear as another?"

"I am not sure. 'Tis possible. His powers have grown. Even I do not know the extent of them now."

"You are queen of this place. Do your powers not exceed one rebel's?"

For the first time, Aimili saw fear in Sebilla's eyes. "I am not sure."

"Yet you would put *Aimili* at risk to help you? No."

"I have no choice. It is destined."

"Can you promise me her safety?"

"I can promise you nothing but that we must find a way to defeat Vardon, else both our worlds are in peril."

"And how do we do so?"

"I am not sure yet. There is a way, I feel certain."

"Find a way that does not involve Aimili."

"That I cannot do." Sebilla put her hand on Padruig's shoulder. "Laird, I am heartily sorry that we allowed this creature to escape to your world. I have already lost one good friend to Vardon. I would not lose one person more, nor would I put either you or Aimili in danger if I had any other choice."

Padruig's gaze was hard. "Aimili is not a warrior."

"Aimili can speak for herself," Aimili said, irked by Padruig's paternalistic attitude.

Padruig cut her a look, which Aimili ignored. "We shall *both* help," she told Sebilla.

With that, the advisors excused themselves, leaving only the queen, Padruig, and Aimili. "Let me show you something of my home," Sebilla said.

"I would prefer to return," Padruig said. "I have

much to do."

"Of course." Her smile faded. "Another time, perhaps. You are both welcome to visit."

"I would like that," Aimili said.

"When we discover the means to defeat Vardon, I shall come to you," Sebilla told them. "Until then, be very careful."

"I ken he means the clan harm," Padruig said.

"He means to see you both dead. The rest of the clan is merely a diversion for him."

Upon their return, Aimili stalked off in the direction of the stable. Padruig followed her and caught her arm.

"Aimili, wait a moment."

"Why? So that you can tell me once again what a helpless child I am?"

He clenched his jaw. "We both know you are no child." *Not anymore*, he thought, picturing again the bruises marring her skin.

"I need to check on Pythia." She pulled her arm free.

"Aimili, I am no sure what to think of this Sebilla. There is magic afoot, no doubt, but too much I do not understand."

"You do not believe her?"

"I am no sure what to believe. A hidden kingdom? A fey race with magical powers? An escaped creature with malice toward the clan? 'Tis a lot to take in." By the saints, in the span of one day his whole world had been torn asunder. He wasn't sure he knew anything anymore.

"It makes sense."

"Does it? Why would this Vardon attack you? Why not me, if I am the one descended from his enemy?"

Aimili frowned. "Perhaps he simply took advantage of a chance opportunity."

Or the bastard sensed more of Padruig's feelings than he was willing to admit. "If you wish to ride outside the castle, I will accompany you. You shall not give him another opening."

"Fine." She glared at him, and Padruig fought the sudden urge to smile. "I shall have the dagger in the event that we encounter Vardon," she added smoothly.

"I can protect myself, Aimili. And you."

"Ah, yes, that is your duty, is it not?"

"There is nothing wrong with duty."

"There can be, when it leads one to poor decisions."

"Poor decisions?" He did not like the sound of that at all.

"I am your wife, Padruig, not your *child*. There is a difference."

By the saints, he knew *that* all too well. "I still have a duty to protect you, just as I do every member of the clan. 'Tis why I do not want you involved in Queen

Sebilla's plans."

"I have a feeling 'tis too late for that."

"The whole idea is beyond my ken. Surely a sword can kill this Vardon as well as any man."

"Apparently not."

"All the more reason for you to stay out of it. You do not know what kind of danger this man presents."

"Nor do you."

"But I have trained for years to fight. I am skilled at it."

"I am not without skill."

"Aimili, you have lived your life shielded by the protection of your family. You have no idea what kind of dangers exist out in the world. I shall not see you fall afoul of what you cannot possibly be prepared to face. Not you, too."

"Too?" She narrowed her eyes. "You are speaking of Brona."

"Aye. I failed to protect her. I shall not make the same mistake again."

"I am not your sister, God rest her soul."

"Ah, but that is just it. You are much like her." Far too much for his peace of mind.

"You still blame yourself for her death."

He cracked out a bitter laugh at her tone of surprise. "Of course. 'Tis my fault."

"You did not slay her."

"Not with mine own hand, true, but I drove her to

peril and failed to stop Symund from exacting his vengeance."

A strange look passed over Aimili's face. "Are you sure he killed Brona?"

"I found him with a dagger in his hand, Aimili. A blade covered in blood."

"Who else was there?"

Padruig frowned. "Several of my men accompanied me. 'Tis of no matter. Brona is dead. Though I killed Symund, it was too little too late for Brona. I shall not see you endure the same fate."

"I am not going to die."

"No. I will take care of this Vardon. 'Tis my responsibility. I did not return to see my clan destroyed by some power-mad outcast with a grievance against my family."

Aimili stuck out her chin. "*Your* clan, Padruig? *Your* family? What am I?"

"You are my wife. What do you want of me?"

For a moment, Padruig thought he saw pain shimmer in the depths of her eyes, but then her gaze turned challenging. "You are right. I am your wife in truth now. Have you so easily forgotten that?"

"Hardly." Padruig took a step back, hating himself for his weakness but unable to stop it.

She followed. "Was it so horrible, Padruig?"

Horrible? His mouth opened but no words emerged. *Wonderful*? *Amazing*? *World-altering*? All of those, certainly, but *horrible*? If only that were the case, he would be safe. "You are far too delicate for such rough treatment. My only excuse was that I was overwrought by finding the grove and assuming you had perished."

"Dear God, how well you play the martyr."

"I simply speak the truth."

She gave him a look of utter disgust. "You are a liar, Laird. I am surprised you have the energy to do anything at all after expending so much effort building those protective walls around yourself."

This time when she turned to go, Padruig let her.

Aimili stomped into the stable to find D'Ary apparently aiding Freya in saddling Zara.

"Ah, my lady, there you are," D'Ary said. "I was just about to seek you out."

Freya bounced over and gave Aimili a tight hug. "I am so happy you are all right. What a horrible thing. 'Tis fortunate you know how to wield a blade. I told Padruig that I am going to learn. So is Efrika and perhaps others. Magnus agreed to teach me."

"Oh." Aimili felt a bit as if she'd been buffeted by a strong wind.

"You are well, are you not? All of the sudden, you

look a bit pale."

And just like that, Aimili felt like crying. A part of her wanted to just curl up somewhere and cry until she ran out of tears. Why did life have to be so complicated? "I am fine." Aimili forced herself to smile. She walked over and gave Zara a pat. "What are you doing?" she asked Freya.

Freya bit her lip and exchanged a look with D'Ary. It was obvious they'd been planning before Aimili's arrival. "I want to ride Zara."

"She is not Mist."

"I know, but I have improved. And she is so beautiful and sweet I am sure she will do naught to harm me."

Zara?

I like the girl.

She is not a skilled rider. You cannot just decide to speed up unless she asks you to.

I understand.

"Aimili? Please say that I can ride her." Freya reached out and rubbed Zara's nose. The horse let out a long sigh.

"Very well." Aimili followed them all out to the ring.

"We shall be fine," Freya called out. "You shall see."

"Just be careful. And remember, she needs clear direction from you."

With a bright smile, Freya nodded. D'Ary held Zara's reins while Freya mounted, then returned to stand with Aimili outside the rail.

"She is not afraid anymore, thanks to you."

Freya squeezed Zara into a smooth trot and sailed by, clearly enjoying the ride. "I think she was always a better rider than she thought she was. Her fall was—"

"Likely Vardon's doing," D'Ary commented.

Aimili's head snapped around so quickly she felt a twinge of pain in her neck. "What did you say?"

"I imagine you had the same thought. No one noticed anything to startle the horse, yet a mount that should have been calm and gentle turned uncontrollable."

"You . . ." Aimili gulped. "You are not from a village called Parth, I think."

He chuckled. "Nay."

"Look, Aimili!" Freya shouted.

Aimili made herself look over, praying she didn't appear as stunned as she felt at D'Ary's calm revelation. She clapped. "Well done."

"They belong together," D'Ary said.

"Aye." She gripped the wood railing, suddenly needing to anchor herself to something solid. Had it been only yesterday she set out on Loki? Too much had happened for her to take in. She'd fought off an attacker who intended to kill her; made love with her husband who now, once again, wanted no part of her; traveled to a magical kingdom; discovered she was linked to them; and now found her stable hand was far from just that. "Why are you here?"

"Sebilla initially sent my brother to retrieve Vardon. He killed him." D'Ary's expression was stark, his eyes hard.

"Oh, no. I am sorry, D'Ary."

"I volunteered to come to Castle MacCoinneach to find the bastard. He is here. I can smell the stench of his evil, but I have not found him."

Aimili didn't know what to say. So many questions tumbled through her mind. "Sebilla, Queen Sebilla seems to think Padruig and I are meant to be a part of this."

"Then you are. Sebilla is seldom wrong."

Something in his voice made Aimili turn and look at him. "You . . . you like her."

"It appears so."

He sounded so disgruntled that Aimili's mood lifted. "She is very beautiful."

"Aye."

Freya eased Zara to a stop in front of them. She looked happier than she had since the Angus Ransolm incident, her green eyes without shadow, her features relaxed.

"You do very well together," Aimili told her.

Freya stroked the horse's withers. "Thank you for letting me ride her." She looked wistful.

"Is something wrong?"

"I wish I could buy her from you, but I have little coin. I am sure she is a valuable horse."

"Freya, we are family now." *Despite what your brother might think*, she added silently. "I would still like to breed her, but other than that she is yours."

Freya's eyes filled with tears. "Truly?"

"Truly. I have always believed that oftentimes a horse claims its rightful owner. For Zara, that is you."

"Thank you, my sister."

Aimili just nodded, unable to speak past the lump in her throat.

Chapter Fifteen

Padruig fetched the largest jug of wine he could find
from the buttery and closed himself in his solar. On
his worktable, he set the ewer and the pouch Queen
Sebilla had given him. By the saints, what a strange morn.

Who would have suspected the castle held such an
extraordinary secret? He knew he'd been rude to Queen
Sebilla, but the lavish chamber, the host of people he'd
encountered, and the dangerous story of Vardon were a bit
much for one man to absorb in the span of a few hours. If
Aimili hadn't been with him, he would have been tempted to dismiss the whole thing as some kind of delirium
brought on by excessive worry and tainted food.

But she *had* been with him. If he'd known that
Queen Sebilla would pronounce Aimili a vital part of the
battle against Vardon, he'd have left her safely in their
chamber, blessedly ignorant of Paroseea and her connection to it. He'd seen the expression of doubt in the
queen's eyes when he'd questioned her. Though she'd
expressed confidence, it was apparent that she wasn't sure

in the end they could best Vardon, that he had not become too powerful.

How could he possibly allow Aimili to become a target in the center of a battle they might lose?

She is already a target, his inner voice reminded him. *Vardon, or whatever the hell he calls himself, has already tried to kill her once, and from everything the queen said, will undoubtedly try again.*

Still, it went against everything he was, every bit of honor bred into him, to put a woman at such risk.

He took a swig of wine and poured the contents of the pouch out on the scarred wood surface. "Dear Lord in heaven," he said softly, reaching out to palm a vivid green emerald. Even in the slivers of light barely dispelling the shadows he could see that spread across the table was a veritable fortune.

Gold coins. Sapphires. Rubies. Emeralds. Other stones he wasn't knowledgeable enough to identify.

It was more than enough to save them.

He stood and paced across the chamber, wishing he did not feel beholden to Queen Sebilla for the gift. *I owe her nothing*, he tried to tell himself. *It is her fault that the clan is on the brink of starvation. She admitted as much,* though he did not understand. *This is nothing more than an effort to make recompense for allowing the evil of her world spill into his.*

It didn't work. Even if she'd not given him anything, he would still feel bound to lend aid, if nothing else to protect his clan.

Life was a hell of a lot simpler in his former stone cottage where he had only himself and Cai to care about.

Magnus flung the door open and stepped in. "Padruig, we have visitors." His eyes gleamed and he looked as if he were on the verge of laughter.

"Who?"

"A most interesting man who claims he knows you. Gifford is his name."

Padruig smiled. "Ah, yes."

"He brings three wagons piled high—" Magnus broke off and stared at the table. "What . . ." he said, pointing.

Well, how was he to explain this? Padruig wondered.

"My God, this is incredible," Magnus said, walking over to look more closely at the jumble of coins and gems. "Where did these come from?"

Queen Sebilla's words rang through Padruig's mind. *I must ask that all of what I share with you will stay between us.* "I . . . I found it completely by accident. I was in one of the lower storerooms and tripped against the wall. A stone loosened and I found the pouch."

Magnus tore his gaze from the table long enough to give Padruig a look that said he didn't believe a word of Padruig's explanation. "How fortuitous," he remarked.

"Aye." He returned the treasure to the pouch and tucked it inside his tunic once more. "Let us see what

Gifford brings."

Aimili followed shouts into the bailey. A man with white hair sticking up from his head, wearing a mail hauberk clearly made for a much larger man, and possessing the most engaging green eyes she'd ever seen, stood waving his arms and shouting directions to a band of castle folk clustered around three large wagons.

"Who is that?" Freya asked her.

"I have no idea."

"Aimili, look," Freya said, pointing to a man unloading a large bolt of cloth. Before Aimili had time to answer, Freya was off, like a hawk spotting prey.

"You there," the man called to a guard. "Tell the laird I've come from Lady Giselle."

At the mention of the woman's name, Aimili halted in midstep, taking time to look over the man's companions. No women accompanied him, much to Aimili's relief. When she neared him, he halted his instructions and fixed her with an engaging grin.

"Ah, I should have known that Scots devil would have a beautiful woman about," he said.

Aimili blinked and glanced toward Freya, who now clutched the cloth to her chest like long-lost treasure.

The man followed her gaze.

"I am corrected. Two beautiful women." He took her hand. "I am Gifford."

"Aimili."

Freya came to stand beside her. "Aimili is our lady."

Gifford's eyes widened. "Padruig wed?"

"Aye."

"Hah! Good for him, the lucky bastard. And who might you be, my lady?" he asked, smiling at Freya.

"I am Freya, Padruig's sister."

"Well, well. And where is that boy?"

"Welcome, Gifford," Padruig said, as he approached and clapped the other man on the shoulder.

"Padruig." Gifford waved a hand toward the wagons. "I've brought provisions, as well as Giselle and Piers's good wishes."

"My thanks. How do they fare?"

"Quite well. Giselle, bless her ever-patient soul, delivered to my nephew the sweetest little girl you have ever seen."

Relief, and a fair bit of envy, spilled though Aimili. So, the Lady Giselle was wed. Well, that was something at least.

"That is good tidings, indeed," Padruig said. His gaze flickered to Aimili. "This is—"

"Your lovely wife, aye. We have already met. Now, let us adjourn to the hall. I badly erred and ran out of ale hours ago." He said the last as if it were nothing short of a travesty.

Aimili laughed and took his arm. "Come with me, my lord. Freya and I shall see to your comfort."

"Bless you, my lady," Gifford said, patting her hand with his. "You are a woman not only of beauty, but also rare grace."

"I shall join you after I see to the wagons," Padruig said.

"Worry not, Padruig. I shall entertain your ladies," Gifford said. He marched toward the hall with Aimili and Freya in tow.

After they'd settled on stools before the fire and a helpful boy had extricated Gifford from his hauberk, Gifford drank his second cup of ale and fixed Aimili with a curious look. "So, Aimili, tell me how you came to be the Lady of Castle MacCoinneach?"

"Padruig needed my father's aid to oust the former Laird of the MacCoinneachs. I was the price."

"A fine bargain for Padruig."

She managed to give him a thin smile.

"You know, when Padruig was at Falcon's Craig, he was a most intriguing puzzle. No one knew from whence he hailed, nor why he lived without kin."

"How did he come to visit Falcon's Craig?"

Gifford's eyes brightened. "Ah, now there is a story. I have two nephews. Cain, the Earl of Hawksdown, and Piers, his younger brother. Both of them stubborn simpkins when it came to women. Fortunately for them, they had me to guide them."

Freya giggled.

"Cain managed to snare his bride first, with no small amount of effort on my part. Then, one day Giselle appeared." He filled his cup, shaking his head. "Fresh from the nunnery she was, and Piers just as fresh from a woman's bed."

Aimili blinked.

"It did not seem a good match in the beginning, but I always knew there was more to Giselle than initially appeared. Piers, of course, failed to sense this." Gifford took a deep drink. "I did mention he was a simpkin when it came to women?"

"Aye."

He nodded. "Well, 'tis a long story, but along their path to wedded bliss, Giselle ran away from Falcon's Craig."

"Alone?"

"Aye. Foolish, but there you were. The poor girl knew nothing of the world. I immediately set off to find her."

"What of Piers?"

"Oh, he came along. In any event, it turned out that Giselle was most fortunate. When a group of ruffians came upon her, Padruig stepped into the fray and saved our Giselle. We all owe him a great debt, which we are happy now to partially repay."

"And we thank you."

"My pleasure. We knew something momentous was

to befall Padruig though." He beamed a smile at Aimili. "Giselle will be most pleased to learn Padruig has taken a bride."

Aimili's heart lifted a bit.

"I suppose becoming laird once again and wedding a beautiful lass was what that," Gifford put down his cup and looked carefully around the hall, "ghost meant."

"Ghost?" Freya squeaked.

"Aye. I take it you have not seen her?"

Freya looked at Aimili, who shook her head. "Uh, no."

"Good. Cannot abide them myself." He filled his cup once again, and Aimili wondered how he managed to drink so much without exhibiting any effects at all. "Ah, Padruig, there you are," Gifford said, raising his cup. "Join us."

"Thank you for delivering the provisions, Gifford," Padruig said as he pulled a stool over. Magnus slid in next to Freya.

"Wouldn't have missed the adventure. Asides, I will stop to see my grand-niece at Tunvegan."

"Where is Saraid?"

Gifford sighed. "Wanted to stay with Amice, who is set to give birth any time. My wife," he said to Aimili. "And my heart."

Aimili sipped wine, averting her gaze from Padruig.

"The ladies tell me your ghost is gone," Gifford said.

To Aimili's shock, Padruig stiffened. Obviously, he

knew exactly what Gifford was talking about. When he exchanged a look with Magnus, she realized that he knew of the spirit, as well. "Who is she?" Aimili asked.

Before Padruig spoke, Aimili could see from his expression that he was not going to be truthful. "I dinnae ken. She only appeared to me once at Falcon's Craig."

Magnus looked down at the floor.

"Odd," Gifford said. "I have not known them to be so quickly obliging."

"Have you much experience with . . . ghosts?" Surely the day could not become more bizarre, Aimili thought.

"More than I would like. 'Tis another story, I fear. Now, I would hear tell of affairs here."

Padruig shrugged. "As you know, another man ruled as laird after I left. His mismanagement and a host of misfortunes left the clan very short of stores. I had no choice but to send to Giselle."

"And she is pleased that you did." Gifford's gaze narrowed and he looked from Padruig to Aimili and back again.

He knows, Aimili thought. *He sees that Padruig would hardly describe me as "his heart."*

"I would rest afore supper if you have a place to spare," Gifford told Padruig.

"Of course."

Aimili stood. "I shall see him to the northeast tower chamber."

Gifford grabbed up the jug of ale and gave her a bow.

"Lead on, my lady."

She left the hall without looking at Padruig.

As soon as they were outside, Gifford said, "Another simpkin, 'eh?"

"Aye."

"'Tis a good thing I am here." Gifford puffed out his chest and took Aimili's arm. "I cannot understand what is amiss with men these days. When I found my beloved Saraid, I did not hesitate to tell her of my feelings."

"Padruig is a complicated man."

Gifford snorted. "Love is not complicated unless one makes it so."

Truthfully, Aimili had never thought so before, either, but now, well, now *everything* seemed complicated, not the least of which was her own mixed feelings for her husband.

"Padruig was always a secretive man. Even Giselle, who knew him best, did not know he was really a laird, though a fallen one apparently."

"There was a tragedy," Aimili told him as they entered a side tower. "Padruig's sister died and he blames himself for it."

"Ah. Guilt. 'Tis a terrible burden to carry."

"Here you are," she said, motioning into a chamber. "I will have someone bring a brazier to warm the room."

"Thank you." He took her hands and gazed intently into her eyes. "I can tell that you are a special lady, and I have great respect for Padruig. 'Twill all work out, you shall see."

Aimili tried to smile but failed.

He winked. "But perhaps now that I am here, I can help things along a bit."

Her lips quirked. "Perhaps you can." Something about Gifford was so direct, so confident, that Aimili allowed herself the tiniest kernel of hope.

The more Aimili thought about the circumstances of Brona's death, the more she became convinced that the story was flawed. For one, she believed Madeleine MacVegan. If Symund MacVegan had not killed Brona, the question was, who had? Her love, Malcolm? That made no sense, either. Brona had made it clear he was her choice.

Knowing Padruig would not discuss the matter, she decided to seek out Magnus. After over an hour of searching for him, she found Magnus and Alasdair huddled in close conversation with an old man Aimili did not recognize.

When the men spotted her, they fell silent. Magnus pressed a hand to the old man's shoulder and handed him a basket of food. "Thank you, Art."

The old man nodded and with a brief glance at Aimili, shuffled away.

"I want to talk to you about the day Brona was killed," Aimili said.

Alasdair's brows rose nearly to his hair.

"Why would you wish to think of such a bloody, dark day, my lady?" Magnus asked. "'Tis not a matter to concern a new bride."

"Do not patronize me," she snapped. "I get enough of that from your laird."

For a moment, Magnus looked stunned, then he smiled. "My apologies, my lady. Clearly, some of Padruig's loutish behavior has infected me."

"I do not believe it happened as people have said."

Magnus and Alasdair glanced at each other.

"Neither do you," she guessed.

"My lady—"

"No," Alasdair said, cutting off Magnus. "We have too many unanswered questions."

"That day . . . Padruig cannot forgive himself."

"Please sit," Magnus said, gesturing to a bench just inside the garden. He sat beside her. "Unfortunately, I agree. Padruig will not allow himself to live with the weight of Brona's death hanging over him."

"'Tis why Magnus and I have begun looking into the matter," Alasdair told her.

"Symund did not kill Brona."

"Why would you say that, my lady?"

"Call me Aimili, please." She looked between the two men, considering how much to tell them. "I met

Madeleine MacVegan. Symund's sister."

Magnus's eyes flared with concern. "You encountered a MacVegan? Where?"

"At the market. That is why you could not find me."

"My lady, Aimili, I am beginning to understand why Padruig despairs of keeping you safe."

She rolled her eyes. "I was in no danger. Madeleine simply wished to speak with me."

"And?"

"She did and quite convincingly. Madeleine swore Symund would never have deliberately hurt Brona."

"Well, of course, she would say that. Nevertheless, we found Symund holding a dagger dripping with Brona's blood. 'Twas a horrible sight for all of us, but particularly for Padruig."

"Who reacted as any loving brother would. Still, what if the dagger did not belong to Symund?"

"She has a point, Magnus," Alasdair said. "In the aftermath of the battle, we never recovered the dagger."

"I do not know. The look on Symund's face . . ."

Aimili shook her head. "Could it have simply been pain? Madeleine and Symund were twins, best friends. She said that she felt his anguish upon finding Brona dead. I was skeptical at first, too, but in the end I believed her."

Magnus stood and paced a few steps. "I do not like this."

"No." Alasdair frowned. "'Tis becoming clearer

that someone was behind the events that day."

"Who was the man I saw you speaking to?" Aimili asked.

"Art, from the village. He remembers seeing a rider racing toward the MacVegan holdings that day."

"Who?"

"He could not say."

Could Vardon have been behind this? Aimili wondered, remembering her suspicions about Freya's fall. Fear took root in her belly, the kind of fear that was paralyzing in its intensity. Until this moment, she'd not really understood how far Vardon would go, how scheming he could be. Freya could have been killed by her fall. Brona, her lover, and Symund MacVegan had died, along with numerous members of the MacCoinneach and MacVegan clans. And Padruig had been left a haunted shell of himself, tortured by guilt and failure.

"We think whoever caused this tragedy is still here," Alasdair said softly. "Perhaps he is even the man who attacked you."

"You must be very watchful, my lady," Magnus added.

Aimili fought down hysteria. They truly had no idea what, or who they faced, and she could not enlighten them without betraying Queen Sebilla's trust. "Who could it be?"

"We are no sure yet. We are compiling a list of men there that day."

"If what we suspect is true, this person's ire is ultimately aimed at Padruig," she said slowly.

"Aye. That is our fear, as well."

"We must stop him, Aimili said."

"First, we must determine who he is."

Aimili thought over the many clan members she'd met since arriving at Castle MacCoinneach. No one stood out as particularly discontented or unusually resentful of Padruig or of her arrival. She frowned. Vardon was obviously a master of disguise. She sensed his dangerous presence, as did some of the horses. D'Ary said he felt his stench, but none of them had any idea of the mask behind which Vardon hid his evil.

"We shall find him out," Magnus tried to reassure her. "He is a traitor to the clan and shall be dealt with as such."

"He tried to kill me once," Aimili reminded them, stamping down the terror of that day. Vardon had not only wanted her dead, but he'd also wanted the dagger she now kept with her constantly. "He thinks to strike at Padruig through me." Even though Padruig didn't want her as his wife, Aimili knew her murder would be a terrible blow to his honor, be viewed as another failure.

"He may try again. 'Tis why I pray you be more prudent in your actions," Magnus said.

Perhaps it was the effect of too many shocks in one day, but a strange sort of calm settled over Aimili. "Why not give him the chance?"

"No," Magnus said. "Are you mad? Padruig would . . . by the saints, I cannot even imagine the depth of his rage should we do such a foolish thing!"

Aimili stood and put her hand on his arm. "Listen to me, Magnus. Someone's hand of malice threatens us all. As long as we do not know who, I am not the only one in peril. What of Freya?"

Magnus paled.

"Let us set a trap for that bastard," she said. *I fought him off once. I can do so again, she told herself. And with Magnus and Alasdair's aid, tear off his mask.*

Alasdair blew out a breath, clearly torn. "My lady, I cannot decide if you are incredibly brave or incredibly reckless."

"A bit of both I think."

Padruig stood at Brona's grave, his mind filled with memories of his sister. Brona had approached each day with an almost childlike anticipation. Unfailingly kind, endlessly trusting, Brona had never expected anything but the best from people.

Images assailed him. Sparkling blue eyes, the joyful sound of her laugh, the air of confidence and enthusiasm she'd brought to every task.

Other images invaded, pushing out the happy ones. Her sightless eyes, her favorite violet bliaut stained red, and perhaps the most heartbreaking of all, her delicate hand even in death reaching for Malcolm.

God, what an arrogant idiot he'd been.

The only time he'd sought to exert any control over Brona had been on the subject of her marriage. He should have known she would defy him and go her own way. It was her nature.

Just as it was Aimili's.

Before he could stop it, the images of Brona shifted, took on Aimili's visage. Instead of blank blue eyes, he saw brown. Instead of a bloody bliaut, he saw a worn, once green tunic.

And she reached for no one. Why would she?

He sensed movement behind him and whirled, drawing his sword. His mother's contemptuous gaze bored into his. "So, guilt drives you even now to her grave," she spat.

Padruig realized that until this moment, he'd not seen his mother outside her chamber, though he'd heard of her confrontation with Aimili in the chapel. He turned back to look upon Brona's grave, wondering what his mother would say if he told her he'd seen and spoken to Brona's ghost many times. Probably fault him for that, too.

"She would have been nineteen years of age in three days."

There was nothing for him to say.

"Would that Symund MacVegan had taken his ire out upon you instead of my poor Brona."

"Why would he have borne me ire? I supported his suit." He told himself to ignore the fact that his own mother would have preferred him dead.

"So easily fooled. How does it feel, Padruig, to know you were such a fool?"

"I made a mistake in favoring Symund, Mother. I have never denied that."

"Yet still you remain a fool," she said, her voice taking on a sly tone. "I have seen your new bride." She laughed. "'Tis fond she is of that handsome stable hand. But you probably do not see that, either, telling yourself you are such a man that she would never betray you."

"You do not know me at all if you believe that." He turned to look at her, struck anew by her appearance. Though her eyes flamed with hatred, the rest of her was a faded husk of the woman she'd once been.

"I know you do not deserve to be laird any more than you are worthy to stand at the grave of my daughter."

"And my sister."

His mother's lips curled. "You remember that now, when 'tis too late."

"I always remember. What of you? I understand your hatred of me, but what about Freya? She has done nothing wrong."

"She is alive," his mother said dully. "She is alive

while my Brona is dead."

It was then Padruig understood his mother's grip on sanity had snapped. In a strange way, it took some of the sting out of her words, yet in another it compounded his guilt. "I shall leave you to your prayers," he told her and turned to go.

As he walked down from the hilltop graveyard, he heard his mother's prayer.

"Dear God, please see that Padruig receives the punishment he has so richly earned. Banish him to hell where he belongs."

She really doesn't know me at all, he thought. *For I am already there.*

The next morn, Aimili was attempting to teach Tor a sideways movement when he stopped, dropped his head, and let out what could only be termed a long-suffering sigh.

Aimili clucked at him and tried to push him over with her leg, but he craned his head around and just looked at her.

From his position outside the ring, D'Ary started laughing. "I dinnae think that is working."

"Nay." Aimili leaned back and briefly closed her eyes. "I should have known better than to try to teach him today. My thoughts are too jumbled."

Are we finished? I am hungry, Tor told her.

She patted him. *You are always hungry, my friend, but aye, we are done. I am too distracted today.*

Are you all right?

Yes, but there are many difficult issues in my life at the moment.

The laird.

And others.

Danger.

Yes. I need to discover the source.

Would that I could help you, but it is as if a blanket conceals danger's true face.

"Aimili," D'Ary called over. "I have an idea."

She lifted a brow.

"Come closer. I'd not announce this to others."

Dismounting, she led Tor over to D'Ary.

"Did you have a chance to see much of Paroseea yesterday?"

"No." She frowned. "Padruig was anxious to return."

"Let us go, then. It is a wondrous place."

"Is this an excuse for you to see Queen Sebilla?"

He grinned. "I shall never admit to such."

"Och, no, of course not." She tilted her head, studying him. "Who are you, D'Ary? Really? Sebilla told us something of your culture."

"I am of old blood, my lady."

What a curious way to put it, Aimili thought. "Do you have . . . powers, as well?"

D'Ary threw back his shoulders, spread his legs, and gave her a haughty look. "Oh, yes, my lady," he said in a gravelly voice. "I surely do."

She giggled.

"We must let your laird know, or he shall go into a panic if he finds you gone."

"I suppose." Aimili wrinkled her nose, reluctant to seek Padruig out.

"You should probably inform him without me by your side. He is already jealous."

Aimili rolled her eyes as she led Tor back into the stable. "Shall I meet you . . ." She paused and looked carefully around them. "Inside the tower?"

"'Tis not necessary." He leaned close and winked. "One of my powers."

Despite Aimili's concern that Padruig would prove difficult, he just absently nodded in response to her announcement, his gaze never even leaving the sheet of parchment in his hand. Aimili sternly admonished herself to be grateful and almost managed to stamp down her hurt at his indifference.

"You will let me know if Queen Sebilla has made any further discoveries," he said.

"Aye." She waited for him to look at her, but when he didn't, she slipped out. As she walked back across the bailey, she realized she'd not told him D'Ary was to accompany her. In fact, she'd not told him D'Ary was from Paroseea.

Padruig would not be pleased about it, either, but it was his own fault. Why should she bother to discuss anything with a man who wouldn't bother to look at her?

After Aimili left, Padruig slowly looked up from the parchment he'd been pretending to read. He set the sheet aside before he gave in to temptation and crumpled Alasdair's carefully written inventory in his fist.

At least the clan's fortunes had improved. Between the provisions Giselle sent and the valuables from Sebilla, he could protect the clan from starvation. Assuming Vardon did not find a way to further sabotage them. He scowled and rose to look out the partially open window shutters. It was a typically dreary Highland day—cool and damp with the promise of rain in the air.

The same kind of day upon which Brona had died. His thoughts returned to that day, as they so often did. Why had she and Malcolm gone so far from the castle? Had she been cold? Had she watched Malcolm die, or had Symund killed her first? Had she felt much pain, or had death claimed her quickly as he hoped? Had she cursed Padruig with her last breaths, blaming him for giving Symund the belief she belonged to him?

Perhaps one day he would ask her, if her ghost ever made a reappearance.

As rain began to drip from the skies and tendrils of mist formed over the loch, he thought of Paroseea. It seemed made of sun and warmth, and he'd not even seen most of it.

Such a place was not for him. He belonged to the rugged landscape of the Highlands, to steep, rocky crags; crystalline streams; and slate-colored skies.

At a sudden noise, he turned.

Gifford burst into his solar. "Ah, Padruig," he said, careening to a stop. "I am in search of your lady fair. Where might she be?"

Something told Padruig that Gifford would accept the existence of a place like Paroseea far better than Padruig did, but it was not his secret to reveal. "I dinnae know. The stable, most likely."

"Already checked there." Gifford perched on a window seat and tossed back a drink. Padruig had never seen the man without a jug of ale in his grasp. "Have to introduce your wife to Piers. Both of them crazy for horses, though of course, now that Piers pulled his head out of his arse and realized what a treasure he had in Giselle, he focuses on his wife." Gifford beamed a smile at Padruig.

"Piers is a lucky man to have a special woman like Giselle."

"Aye, even with that business of her having the 'sight.'" He sighed, shaking his head. "What a family I have. Not boring at least." Gifford tipped back more ale and peered at Padruig over the top of the his jug. "You dinnae look surprised to hear about Giselle."

"Nay. She confided in me the first time I found her in the forest."

"Lucky, that. You will always have the deepest gratitude of the Veuxfort family."

"The supplies you brought are more than sufficient thanks."

"Weel, I feel there might be a bit more good I can do whilst I am here."

Oh, no, Padruig thought. He had just enough experience with Gifford to know that the man was, at best, unpredictable and meddling.

"What are you doing, Padruig?"

Padruig pretended not to understand. "I am very busy being Laird of the MacCoinneachs. After my departure things fell into disarray. There is much to be done."

"By the saints, you sound like the old Cain. Always prattling on about the state of the fields, the health of the cattle, and such." Gifford drank more ale and pulled himself up straight, fixing Padruig with an intent stare. "I am speaking, of course, of your *bride.*"

"What of her?"

Gifford slammed a palm against his forehead. "I

was *right*."

Padruig had the sinking feeling he could not dismiss Gifford as easily as he did Magnus.

"She is not happy, Padruig. What are you going to do about that?"

"Gifford, I appreciate your concern, but you have newly arrived. Aimili and I are but weeks into a marriage neither of us expected. 'Twill take her time to settle into her new life."

"What a load of horse dung. Any fool can see that you are in love with her and she with you, though to be brutally honest, I am beginning to wonder why."

Padruig's mouth dropped open. "You . . . you have misread the situation. Aimili is very young. She is also, as you noted, interested solely in her horses."

"Have you bedded her?"

"I am not going to answer that question. 'Tis none of your affair."

Gifford snorted. "You have." He eyed Padruig with amusement. "Probably shook you so badly you ran like a hunted rabbit."

Padruig stuck his head out the door and bellowed for someone to bring him wine. *Dear Lord, how had Gifford read him so easily?* He returned and gave Gifford a solemn look. "Aimili is nearly a child."

"Reminds you of your sister, doesn't she? The one who died, I mean. Aye, I heard the story. Terrible thing, that."

"It was."

Gifford leaned forward. "Do ye think ye are the only one to make mistakes?"

"Of course not."

"Hmm. Just the only one who is not permitted to."

Where is that wine? Padruig went to the door, relieved beyond measure to spot a servant rushing toward him with an ewer and two cups. He seized them from the man's hands and shut the door.

"Your sister made the decision to leave the castle with no protection. She defied you to be with her lover."

Padruig splashed wine into a cup and took a long drink. "She did not understand the danger."

"Oh? I understood she was a woman grown."

"I failed her, Gifford. 'Twas my responsibility to protect her and I *failed*."

"What of this Malcolm?"

"He did not possess the skill. 'Twas but one of my objections to him as a husband to Brona."

"Yet she chose him."

"I was and am laird. Brona was my innocent sister. It was my duty to see to her welfare, just as it is my duty to see to Aimili's welfare."

"By the saints, you really do love her."

Padruig gulped down half a cup of wine. "Nay."

"My brother is a terrible liar," a woman's voice said.

Gifford teetered, nearly dropped his jug, then recovered himself. "Brona, I presume," he said politely.

Padruig tilted his head back and groaned.

"Aye," Brona said as she floated over and settled next to Gifford.

To the man's credit, he didn't even flinch. "A pleasure to meet you, my lady. I am heartily sorry it could not be in the flesh."

Brona shrugged. "One becomes used to it."

At that, Gifford shivered slightly. "'Tis good you are here, my lady. We have much work ahead of us with your brother."

"He is terribly stubborn."

"He is also sitting right here listening to you both," Padruig said with a frown.

"Not well enough, obviously," Gifford retorted. He crossed his legs and turned toward Brona. "I am most disheartened by the attitude of these young men. My nephews were much the same as your Padruig."

"Determined to complicate something as fundamental and uncontrollable as love."

"Exactly." Gifford reached out to pat Brona on the arm, then apparently realized she lacked substance and brought his hand back. "I vow I do not understand it. Was your Malcolm like that?"

Brona smiled. "Oh, no, not at all. 'Tis one of the reasons I loved him."

"Well, at least you had that, though for too short a time."

"Aye. I wish the same happiness for Padruig."

They both turned and stared at Padruig as if he'd done something wrong. "What?" he asked.

Gifford sighed. "Brona, now that you are here, I have an important question for you."

"Gifford—"

The older man cut him a glance made of steel. "Shush. Now, Brona, do you blame Padruig for your early demise?"

Her form faded a bit. "Nay. None of what happened was his fault."

Gifford looked at him in obvious triumph.

"Brona," Padruig said, his heart sinking as she faded farther. "What do you mean? Tell me!"

She disappeared.

Gifford frowned and tipped back some ale. "Hate it when they do that. Just when you think you'll get some real answers, these ghosts up and vanish. Death apparently steals them of manners."

Padruig hadn't a thing to say in response to Gifford's calm pronouncement.

"Seems to me you've been given a second chance, Padruig," Gifford said as he stood. "You are laird again and you've a beautiful, kind young bride. Make something of it!"

"I intend to."

Gifford rolled his eyes. "Duty is all well and good, Padruig, but there is more in life. Much more. Dinnae hide behind duty, else you will miss the best parts."

Within moments after taking D'Ary's hand, Aimili found herself standing on a beach made of soft, powdery pink sand and stretching as far as she could see. The water was a clear turquoise blue, gently lapping against the shore.

"We call this the Crystal Sea," D'Ary said. "It surrounds Paroseea."

"'Tis beautiful."

"Aye."

Aimili turned and shielded her eyes from the bright pinkish gold sun. Beyond the silken beach, deep green bushes awash in yellow flowers led to stands of odd-looking trees, with smooth bark and wide canopies of big green leaves. A marble-paved path led through the trees, and beyond Aimili could see the rise of a mountain in the center of the land.

The air was warm and soft, the salty tang of the sea blending with an exotic floral scent. She bent down and picked up a handful of sand. It felt as powdery as it looked, slipping through her fingers like water.

Suddenly, a series of screeches split the air.

D'Ary laughed. "You have a visitor, Aimili."

She looked up to see a dolphin skittering across the

water on its back fin. A real dolphin! "I have never seen such a creature. And it is pink! I did not know they were pink."

"Not all of them are. In your world, I believe they are a grayish color. On Paroseea," he stopped and pointed, "they are different colors."

Aimili's mouth dropped open as she stared at the water. Two other dolphins had joined the first. One was a sparkling blue color, the other a rich violet. They jumped and splashed in the water.

"Can you communicate with them?"

"Oh. I do not—"

Come and swim!

Yes, come swim with us.

"I suppose I can," Aimili finished.

"Can you swim?"

"Aye. I often swam in the loch as a child, much to the dismay of my father."

The violet dolphin came close, rolled over onto its back, and slapped the water with its tail fin.

"I do not speak dolphin, but I think that is an invitation."

Aimili pulled off her boots, regretting that she'd not brought different garments with her. It was so warm she could have easily swum clad in nothing at all, but not in an unknown land with D'Ary present.

"I am sure Sebilla will lend you dry garments," D'Ary said, clearly guessing the reason for her hesitation.

"Think you?"

"I am sure of it."

Aimili grinned and dove into the water. It was every bit as soft and warm as it appeared, gliding over her skin as she swam out into deeper water. She heard a splash behind her and turned. D'Ary swam toward her, his wide shoulders bare, and a wide smile on his face. "'Tis too fine a day to stay on the beach."

The three dolphins encircled them.

Take hold of my fin, the blue one said.

No, mine, the pink one insisted. *I saw her first.*

But I am the prettiest, the violet one said.

Aimili giggled. *You are all beautiful.* She reached out and stroked the nearest one, who happened to be pink. "This is incredible," she told D'Ary.

"What do they say to you?"

"They want me to grab hold of a fin."

"Then, let us do it." He wrapped a hand around the top fin of the blue dolphin. "Come on, Aimili. I have done this before."

She took hold of the pink dolphin's top fin and shrieked when the dolphin rose slightly off the water's surface, then sped across the water. *By the saints, what an amazing feeling*, she thought. She could feel the dolphin's powerful body flex back and forth as they sliced through the water. It was almost as good as riding Mist across the moors.

The sun lit the water to silvery blue, and Aimili

tasted the salt of the sea, felt the rush of water against her legs. *Thank you*, she told the dolphin.

My pleasure.

Aimili let go and slowed, turning onto her back to simply float. The violet dolphin came up beside her and tilted its head to the side, gently touching her body, almost as if it just wanted to idly float with her and soak up the perfect weather. "Is it always like this?" she asked D'Ary, who floated nearby.

"Aye."

She sighed. "I could grow accustomed to this very quickly."

"You would be welcome."

Something in his voice made her lift her head.

He cocked a brow. "There would be a place at Paroseea for you if you wished it."

"D'Ary, I cannot imagine leaving the Highlands."

"Dinnae make up your mind until you see the rest of Paroseea."

Aimili spent the next hours doing just that. As promised, D'Ary sought out Sebilla, who graciously agreed to provide Aimili with dry clothing. Aimili felt like some kind of fairy princess. The chemise and bliaut she wore were a soft, light sea green and jeweled slippers covered her feet. One of Sebilla's attendants plaited Aimili's hair with silver and pale green ribbons.

Before setting off to explore Paroseea, they'd dined on creamy cheese wedges, fluffy white bread, savory slivers of fish, and honeyed wine. Once they began walking the central roadway, Aimili was astounded at the lavishness of the stone dwellings, the rich fragrance of the gardens, and the idyllic feel of the place. Everyone they encountered had a ready smile and an air of contentment.

It struck Aimili that she felt accepted here, felt that she had found friends in both Sebilla and D'Ary. Friends, who viewed her ability to communicate with animals as perfectly normal, even desirable. She could never remember feeling so at ease, so unfettered, not even when she raced Mist into the wind.

"I can see why you would go to great effort to protect this," Aimili told Sebilla. "'Tis paradise."

"Aye." She slid a glance at D'Ary, who walked beside them.

Aimili hid a smile. It was apparent that Sebilla was every bit as interested in D'Ary as he was in her, but wouldn't reveal it. "How do you choose your ruler?" Aimili asked.

"It has always been a woman of my lineage," Sebilla said. "If there is more than one woman eligible at once, all of the Paroseeans have a vote."

"Do you have a designated successor?"

"Nay. We live for many years. My hope is that one day I shall have a child to follow me."

Aimili cut a look toward D'Ary, who was trying very hard to appear only mildly interested in the subject of their conversation. "Then I suppose you must wed."

"That would be best, yes." Sebilla sounded rather forlorn over the prospect.

"Have you a man in mind?" Aimili watched D'Ary's head snap up.

"I . . . I have not given it much thought. The problem of Vardon has occupied my thoughts."

D'Ary let out a snort.

"Did you say something, D'Ary?" Aimili asked him.

He looked at Sebilla. "You will have to let a man close, first."

Aimili dropped back a step. Neither Sebilla nor D'Ary noticed. "You say that as if I am incapable of doing so," Sebilla snapped.

D'Ary shrugged. "Are you?"

"You . . . you are without exception the most . . ." Sebilla finished with a groan of frustration.

"Intriguing man you know?"

Aimili giggled.

"I know many interesting men. Educated, thoughtful men."

"Men to fawn over you."

"I *am* queen."

D'Ary glanced back at Aimili and winked. He cradled Sebilla's chin with his hand and leaned close. "Have we not had this conversation before? Your majesty?"

"I cannot possibly recall every conversation I have."

He laughed. "I shall be happy to remind you."

This time, Sebilla's gaze found Aimili, her eyes pleading for aid.

Aimili just smiled.

"You are a woman, Sebilla. And not a woman who needs a weak-willed man who places her on a pedestal to worship from a respectful distance."

"You scarcely know me." She tried to twist out of D'Ary's grasp, but he easily held her.

"I know you. Soon, I shall know you even better."

"A promise or a threat, D'Ary?"

"Mayhap a bit of both." He smiled and released her. "For now, 'tis time for Aimili and I to return."

They had already discussed the progress, or lack thereof, on eliminating Vardon. Sebilla was convinced they had all but a few lines of the spell needed, but it was not yet enough to take on Vardon, whomever he was pretending to be. Aimili lightly touched Sebilla's arm. "Thank you for sharing Paroseea with me."

Sebilla's face relaxed. "I am pleased that you like it. It is, after all, a part of your heritage." She straightened and gave D'Ary a cool look.

"It was a pleasure to see you, your majesty," he said. "I hope that you have a most pleasurable evening and dreams that satisfy your every desire."

He took Aimili's hand. The last thing she saw was Sebilla's face, eyes open wide, cheeks a deep pink, and an expression somewhere between outrage and keen interest.

One moment, Padruig was grooming his destrier, Thor, and in the next his wife appeared. He blinked, his hand resting on Thor's withers, more for support than anything else. "Aimili?"

She slowly turned to where he stood in Thor's stall.

Padruig sucked in a breath. He had never seen her look so beautiful, but there was something more in her eyes, in the way she held herself. She wore a pale green gown that floated around her ankles, her hair was arranged in an elegant array of braids and ribbons, and her dark eyes seemed fathomless.

Behind her stood D'Ary, sporting the kind of light smile that made Padruig want to cleave the man in two.

He blinked again as realization sank in.

"You," he said, pointing at D'Ary. "You will attend me in my solar."

"As you wish, Laird."

Padruig put aside the brush and closed Thor's stall. Aimili had yet to say a word. Suspicion and anger pooled into a hard lump in his belly. He stopped before her. "I trust you enjoyed your visit?"

She flinched at his mocking tone, but held his gaze. "Very much."

"You neglected to tell me you were taking a companion." He was surprised he could speak, his jaw was so tense.

D'Ary stepped forward. "I see it as part of my duties to accompany Aimili when she ventures outside the castle."

"My solar. Now."

"You have no right to be angry," Aimili said, lifting her chin.

"Oh?" He closed the space between them.

"Nay."

"I will speak with you after I finish with your"—he glared at D'Ary—"guardian."

Aimili rolled her eyes. "Addlepated fool," she muttered. "I am going to find Gifford. At least he displays some *sense.*"

Sense? Padruig wanted to shout. Nothing made sense anymore. He was receiving advice from an ale-sotted man he barely knew *and* his sister's ghost, his wife had just popped into view like some sort of woodland fairy, and his newest stable hand was obviously much more than that.

To top it off, he still had no idea who Vardon might be.

He glanced at D'Ary, whose expression remained faintly mocking, and stalked off toward his solar, with the other man following.

By the time they reached his solar, Padruig found his fingertips repeatedly brushing the pommel of his sword. He walked in and poured a cup of wine from the ewer left there.

The door shut.

"There is naught between Aimili and me but friendship, Laird," D'Ary said. "My interest lies elsewhere."

Padruig took a sip of wine and looked at the other man. D'Ary stood in the center of the solar, his arms crossed, with an accusatory gleam in his eyes that Padruig chose to ignore. "You are of Paroseea," Padruig said.

"Aye."

"Why are you here in the guise of a simple stable hand?"

"You are thinking that perhaps I am Vardon?" He shook his head, his expression turning hard. "The whoreson slew my only brother."

"You are here for revenge."

"Justice."

Padruig smiled at that. "'Tis often the same."

"Words. I want the bastard dead. That is all I know."

"Do you know of Sebilla's pronouncement? That I must aid her in defeating Vardon?"

"Yes. Along with Aimili."

"I have not agreed to that."

"You may not have any choice."

"There is always a choice. The question is whether a man makes the right one."

"Just so."

Padruig's eyes narrowed as he studied D'Ary. He

supposed that to a woman, the man would be appealing. He was nearly as big as Padruig, clearly strong, and without a single visible scar. Perhaps the people of Paroseea do not scar, he thought, disgusted at the envy such an idea provoked. "You have been spending much time with my wife."

D'Ary cocked a brow. "I have come to consider Aimili a friend. She is an interesting woman."

"She is an innocent."

"Is she?"

Fury ripped through Padruig and before he thought about it, he drew his dagger. "What do you say?"

"I have not touched her."

"Why should I believe anything you say? You have lied from the moment you arrived at Castle MacCoinneach."

"It would not be good for Vardon to learn of my presence."

"Who is he?"

"I do not know yet."

Padruig lips curled in a derisive snarl. "I see. You people of Paroseea are quick to give dire warnings, make impossible demands, but slow to provide any real information."

"Impossible demands?" D'Ary cocked his head. "Ah, we are back to Aimili."

"We have never been far from her."

"You say she is innocent. I think you tell yourself

that to keep the lady at a safe distance."

Well, hell, Padruig thought as he stared at D'Ary. *Were these Paroseeans mind readers, too?* "I will not let her sacrifice herself for anyone."

"Nor will I. As I said, Aimili is my friend."

"Your friend."

"Aye." D'Ary's gaze challenged him.

Slowly, Padruig replaced his dagger. "You said your interest lies elsewhere. With whom?"

Padruig watched with no small amount of astonishment as D'Ary's stony expression turned soft. By the saints, 'tis another one, he thought, wondering if there was something in the air to create one lovesick casualty after another.

"A woman in Parosea," D'Ary bit out. "'Tis no concern of yours."

By God, this was the most enjoyment Padruig had had all day. "Hmm. Does the lady know of your intentions?"

"She is . . . stubborn."

"Sebilla."

D'Ary's face turned from red to white in an instant. "Nay, I—"

Padruig waved a hand and laughed. "Good luck with that one."

"I shall need it," D'Ary muttered as he left the solar.

Padruig laughed again.

The first thing Aimili removed was her belt with the dagger attached. She set it on a blanket next to Loch Moradeea, even going so far as to look around, as if she sought to reassure herself no one was nearby.

Please, let Vardon be watching, she silently chanted. She'd decided that she alone may not be sufficient bait for him to risk an attack so close to Castle MacCoinneach. He wanted the dagger though. Badly.

Hidden behind a thick bushy growth Magnus and Alasdair stood watch.

She removed her slippers and stuck a toe into the cool water, mentally comparing it to the Crystal Sea. Had it only been that morn that she'd basked in the warmth and sun of Paroseea? Within moments of her return, she'd faced a clearly annoyed Padruig, who had yet to seek her out at all. Perhaps that was just as well. What could she say to him? Yes, she had enjoyed her time in Paroseea, far more than she'd expected. She peered up at the leaden sky. Though it was just past noon, the sun was well cloaked by clouds and a cool breeze blew across the loch.

Not the best day for a swim, but with luck she wouldn't be in the water all that long. Fighting the urge to glance toward Magnus and Alasdair's hiding place, she sat on the blanket, wrapped another around her shoulders, and gazed out over the loch as if she were deep in thought.

Come on, you whoreson, she thought. *Show your evil face. Here I am, all alone. Easy prey.*

A low bank of clouds swept across the sky, and the breeze died down. Aimili focused on taking deep, even breaths, and bent her head as if in prayer.

After a time, she stood and dropped the blanket. Aimili slowly removed her beautiful silk bliaut and set it with her pile. She felt a little discomfited at Magnus and Alasdair seeing her clad in only her chemise, but she wanted to appear as vulnerable as possible.

Glancing at the dagger, she took a last look around her before wading into the water. Though she knew it was cool, she felt warm as she floated away from shore.

Before Vardon appeared, she sensed him, the hint of malice in the air, the feeling of a threat nearby. She stayed in the water, but idly moved closer to shore.

By the time he came into view, she was only a few feet from the edge of the loch.

Hatred poured from him so strongly Aimili was surprised she didn't see it shimmering in the air.

"Bitch," he snarled, snapping up the dagger.

She forced a mocking smile to her lips as her feet found purchase in the muddy bottom of the loch. "I thought you dead."

"'Twill take more than a puny lass to end my life." He laughed. "Particularly since I have the dagger of Artemis."

Aimili inched closer. As before, the man's features were concealed. The eyes, she thought. I know those eyes.

Magnus and Alasdair stepped out from the bushes, swords drawn. "You have more than a lass to face this time," Magnus snarled.

Vardon turned. "Only two of you? It hardly seems worth the effort."

"Did you kill Brona?" Magnus demanded.

"Of course not. Everyone knows 'twas Symund MacVegan."

"Show yourself," Alasdair said, taking a step forward. "Only a coward hides his face."

Instead, Vardon drew his sword and lunged.

Aimili sprang out of the water, drawing the real dagger of Artemis from its sheath tied to her leg. She looked for an opening to attack Vardon, but he was surrounded by Magnus and Alasdair.

They tried to force Vardon back, but he held his own, twisting and slashing his sword. The thwack of blade against shield filled the air, the grunts and shouts of the men intensifying as they continued to fight.

And then Alasdair stumbled.

Vardon smiled and leapt toward him, his sword raised for a killing blow.

"No!" Aimili shouted, and charged into the fray. She held the dagger tight, the blade warm and vibrating in her palm. Before Vardon could bring his sword down, she ducked under his arm. She drew back to plunge the blade into his chest, but he danced away and she only managed to slash across his chest.

"Aimili, no!" Magnus shouted.

She watched in horror as Vardon whirled, his sword still poised to strike. Distracted, Magnus failed to raise his shield in time. Aimili felt as if she were trapped in a slow-moving whirlpool. Red bloomed on Magnus's chest. He met her gaze and slowly crumpled to the ground.

Over her daze, she heard Alasdair shouting at her, but couldn't make out the words. Then, she heard a bellow of pure rage and the pounding of hooves. She looked up to see Padruig bearing down on them, his sword drawn. "Get back, Aimili," he yelled. "Alasdair!"

Vardon looked at her and smiled in triumph.

Aimili fought Alasdair's arms pulling her away. The dagger burned in her hand. "Let me go! I can help." Helplessly, she watched Padruig close in, terrified that he could not match Vardon.

But instead of engaging Padruig, Vardon bolted for the loch. He plunged beneath the water and disappeared.

Padruig reined in, jumped from his mount, and raced toward the loch. There was not even a ripple to mark Vardon's passage.

Aimili saw Padruig's shoulders stiffen and dreaded the moment he turned around. She pulled away from

Alasdair and dropped to Magnus's side, touching his neck in desperate hope of finding a heartbeat, dropping her head in relief when she did. "Magnus."

"I am sorry, my lady. I failed you," he whispered.

"Nay." She started to say more, but her words halted when strong hands hauled her up from the ground and thrust her aside.

Padruig put Magnus up on Thor and mounted behind him. He glared down at her.

"Padruig, I—"

"Do. Not. Say. One. Word. Alasdair, please see that she returns to the castle."

"Aye, Laird."

Padruig kicked Thor and they ran for the castle.

Alasdair gently put a blanket over her. "My lady, let us go."

For a moment, Aimili just stared out over the loch. "Cowardly bastard," she spat.

"Would that we had seen his face."

Aimili slid on her slippers and followed Alasdair to the castle. By the time they reached the great hall, the castle was in an uproar. Men streamed over the high wall walk, clearly looking for signs of Magnus's attacker. Alasdair took her arm and led her silently into the great hall.

Magnus lay on the long table, his gambeson heaped on the floor. Freya stood beside him, tears washing down her face while Efrika put her hand on his chest. Her lips were pinched, and her face pale.

Alasdair left Aimili and went to Efrika's side. "How can I help?" he asked.

Aimili stood to the side, wrapped in her blanket. She shivered, though not from the cold but from the bitter shame of failure.

A heavy hand landed on her shoulder. She looked up at Padruig and braced herself not to pull away. His eyes were a piercing silvery blue, and the scars on his face stood out in white lines against his taut skin.

She swallowed. "Magnus?"

"Was fortunate. The angle of the strike sliced flesh, but did not puncture anything vital as best we can tell. Still, he will not be fighting any time soon."

"Oh."

"Come."

"Mayhap I should stay and help—"

"Efrika will tend to him." He took a firm hold on her arm and steered her out of the hall. With every step it seemed as if his temper grew. Once they reached the bailey, he began walking so quickly that Aimili could not keep up. "I . . . slow down," she said, trying to yank free of his grasp.

He simply picked her up, tossed her over his shoulder, and carried her to their chamber. By the time he sat her down, none too gently, Aimili was light-headed.

"What were you doing?" he bit out, just before he slammed the door.

"We thought . . . I thought that we could unmask

Vardon."

"What do Magnus and Alasdair know of this?"

"They suspect, as I do, that someone else was behind Brona's murder. I think it might have been Vardon."

"What?" Padruig shouted. "You have been meeting behind my back? Discussing my sister?"

He was so furious, Aimili could barely find her tongue. "Aye."

"You . . . you could have been killed!" He stalked to her and gripped the fabric of her chemise in both hands. "How can you be so reckless? Do you give no thought at all to your own safety? To the safety of others?"

"I—"

"Damn you, Aimili," he swore, right before he kissed her.

No, Aimili thought with what few wits she managed to hold onto under the deluge of his exploding passion. Not a kiss. More than that. She felt the rage swirling within him, tasted the violence in his kiss. She leaned into him, pressed close, beset by the need to crawl inside his strength, trusting him even as she understood most of his fury was directed toward her.

He broke the kiss, fisted one hand in the neckline of her chemise and ripped it in two.

Aimili was so shocked she could only stare at him. His gaze crawled over her body like a predator deciding which part of its prey looked the tastiest. Aimili's breath shortened, then stuttered when he yanked the torn garment away completely, leaving her naked and exposed.

"Padruig, I—"

"Dinnae talk," he rasped, cupping her breasts in his calloused hands. His fingertips caressed the tips into points as he nuzzled her neck. When he moved lower and took her nipple in his mouth, Aimili gasped, arching instinctively closer, each pull of his mouth drawing heat into her center.

He wasn't being gentle, his touch, his mouth just short of painful, but all the more arousing for that.

She wound her arms around his wide shoulders and cradled him close.

He stopped only long enough to draw off his tunic and undershirt, then seized her lips in a bruising kiss. Dear God, how she loved his mouth, Aimili thought. It was addictive, like a mysterious, intoxicating drink she could not get enough of.

His hands spanned her waist, then moved to her buttocks. His fingers spread and gripped her close, rocking her against him, hard and hot. When his hand slipped between her legs, she caught his lips and nipped, panting for breath.

He just held her gaze and stroked, his fingers sliding easily over her damp body, slipping into her. She clenched down, her body needing that, needing more.

"You want to be reckless, my lady," he growled. "I can give you that."

Aimili was so scorched with pleasure that she barely heard him, barely realized he was moving her across the floor until she felt cool stone against her back.

With one fluid movement, Padruig lifted her and plunged inside her.

"Aahh," Aimili moaned, writhing to take him in, her gaze locked with his. She hadn't even known he'd untied his braies.

His eyes turned smoky blue as he invaded her body, in and out, slowly yet relentlessly, holding her in place when she would have arched into him, taking control completely. Her body burned and ached yet he came on, his powerful thighs wedged beneath hers, holding her open for him.

She started shaking. Dear God, it was too much, too strong.

She realized she'd spoken the words aloud, when Padruig's mouth curled into a half smile, his eyes gleaming. He knows, she thought, buffeted by spirals of heated pleasure.

There was nothing she could do but hang on and ride the storm. Nothing she wanted to do.

Not when his fingers dug into her thighs and opened her even farther.

Not when he thrust inside her even deeper, filling and stretching her.

Not when his thrusts came faster, his powerful body bucking and pounding into hers. Faster and yet faster until she was keening, moaning, tears running down her face, her body screaming for release.

Not even when he roared and thrust one last time, his fingertips skating over her in that perfect touch that set her body into an abyss of pleasure that seemed to go on forever.

And particularly not when he stayed buried in her as he carried her to their bed to begin all over again.

Afterward, Aimili fell into a boneless half sleep, her body deliciously spent, her emotions wrung out, churned and muddled by Padruig's raw hunger. He lay beside her, one arm flung across his forehead.

"By the saints, I am a beast," he cursed.

Aimili's heart sank.

He turned his head, his eyes once so filled with passion now regretful. "I am sorry, Aimili. I vow I do not know what came over me." He rolled off the bed and stood, searching for his braies.

Aimili stared at his muscled back, his taut buttocks, his heavy thighs, and memories of that powerful body joining with hers sent a shiver of longing through her. "Why do you do this?"

After pulling on his braies, he turned. "I have been unable to fully control myself." He frowned. "I am deeply sorry for using you such."

"Surely you jest." Aimili wrapped a sheet around her nakedness and swung her legs over the side of the bed.

Padruig lifted a brow. "I do not take your meaning."

"Do I look so very fragile, Padruig?"

His lips thinned. "Aimili, I took you against the wall, for God's sake, like one of the guards might take a willing maid."

"Oh, yes, how terrible. I have heard those maids shrieking in protest."

"'Tis not the same. By the saints, you are my wife, not some lowborn wench to give herself so. And I am the laird, not a simple guardsman to couple in any convenient spot."

"I did not ask to be put on a pedestal." She stood and couldn't catch herself without wincing at the sudden pain in her thighs.

"Look at you. Now you understand why I did not wish to wed with you. You are a young, innocent lass, deserving of a gentle man with a comely face and mild desires."

"Padruig?"

"Aye?"

"You are a fool."

His face darkened. "I ken I behaved badly."

"I am not talking about that!" she shouted.

"You are justified in your anger." He drew on a tunic. "I shall fetch Efrika to bring you something calming."

Aimili briefly closed her eyes, praying for strength and patience. "Did you not enjoy making love to me, Padruig?"

His jaw clenched so tight she wouldn't have been

surprised to hear a tooth crack. "Aimili, I—"

"Answer me, damn you. Did. You. Enjoy. It?"

"I am a man."

"What the hell does that mean?" She stomped over to him. "'Tis a simple question, Padruig. Did you enjoy it?"

"It is not that simple."

Love is only complicated if one makes it so. Gifford's words jumped into her mind. She put her face close to Padruig's. "I did."

She might as well have flung a burning brand into his face. First, he flushed, then he took a step back. "'Tis because you were understandably overwrought by Vardon's attack." He glared at her. "Which you invited."

"Do not change the subject. This is not about Vardon. This is about you and me."

"These are dire, dangerous times. Neither of us is ourselves."

"Who are we?"

"Dinnae mock me. You know what I mean."

"Nay, I am afraid I do not."

"You have never been in battle before. The risks, the threat, makes one do things, want things that should not be."

"Oh, for heaven's sake. Surely, you do not expect me to believe that the only reason you just made love to me until I screamed in pleasure was because of Vardon."

"Aimili, I cannot fully explain my actions, other to

convey my apologies for treating you so roughly."

"You sanctimonious son of a bitch."

His eyes popped wide open.

"Don't you dare hide behind some ridiculous idea of nobility you've pounded into your deluded brain! You wanted me, Padruig. Your wife. And in case you are too stupid to grasp even this, I wanted you, too! There is nothing complicated about that."

"You are wrong. You are simply too young, too inexperienced to understand." He turned away, picked up his boots, and left, shutting the door behind him with a decisive thwap.

She picked up a cup and threw it against the door.

It hit her then—he was never going to change. No matter how wildly or sweetly he loved her, in the end he would always view it as a shameful loss of control, would always look at her with sorrow and regret in his eyes. He wouldn't accept anything else.

She tried to blink back tears but they fell anyway. How *weak and pathetic I am*, she thought, clenching the sheet tight. *I am the real fool.*

She'd thought she'd been able to put away her dreams of the man she'd thought Padruig was, her dreams of a happy, loving life filled with warmth and caring. God, how wrong she'd been.

Her dreams had been the product of a young girl's infatuation, a bright memory.

Perhaps it was one of her weaknesses—to care for

wounded creatures. She could save a horse, a dog, but Padruig was right. A man was too complicated.

The very worst part of it all was that somewhere along the way of watching Padruig care for his people, stand for Freya, yet do nothing for himself, she'd fallen in love with Padruig all over again.

He would never allow himself to feel the same even if by some miracle it grew in his hardened heart.

She realized that until this moment, she'd believed that somehow in the end it would work out between her and Padruig, that Gifford's blunt wisdom would have an impact, that Padruig would care enough for her to change, to let himself live life again. She knew now that she'd been deluding herself, clinging to hope where there was none.

In a daze, she slowly drew on a new chemise and her green bliaut. She pulled the ribbons from her hair and put it in one unadorned plait. She felt like someone else in her skin, her thoughts somehow clearer, sharper, though the knodledge cut through her like the finest honed blade.

She hunted down Magnus, who was resting, not surprisingly, in the Ladies' Solar. Freya hovered over him and Magnus gazed at her as if he'd been granted the best gift in the world. It made Aimili's chest tighten with envy and sadness.

"Aimili," Magnus said, thankfully his voice much stronger than it had been earlier. "Are you all right?"

"Aye." She grimaced. "I am sorry, Magnus. I am so relieved you were not hurt even worse."

"I should have been more prepared."

Aimili blew out a breath. "I distracted you. 'Twas not your fault."

"What happened after I fell?"

"I am no sure exactly. When Padruig arrived, the man dove into the loch. We could not find a sign of him."

"How odd."

"Aye," Aimili agreed. Inwardly, she was troubled. Where had he gone? Water made her think of Paroseea. Could he have returned, have kept a hiding place there?

"You need to rest," Freya told Magnus, patting his hand.

"I should be helping Padruig."

"My brother can ferret out one man, and he has others to aid him, even if they are not as brave or skilled as you."

Aimili rolled her eyes, and Magnus chuckled, clearly enjoying Freya's attention.

"I will rest if you will remain and talk with me."

Freya pulled out a basket of sewing, and pulled a stool close to the pallet where Magnus lay. "'Tis a bargain."

"I shall leave you both," Aimili said.

They were so occupied looking at each other that they never even noticed her departure.

Aimili resolved not to question it, but somehow she knew how to navigate her way through the labyrinth of passageways she'd previously traveled with Padruig. Quickly, she sped around one bend after another, opening doorways with her touch until she got to the final portal.

She flattened both hands against the stone and pushed.

With a soft hiss, the stone swung open.

Holding her rushlight high, she easily spotted the pool. Just as before the surface was so smooth it almost seemed like as shiny rock. She didn't hesitate, but set the light down and jumped into the water.

This time, when she arrived in Paroseea, she landed on thick, emerald-colored grass. In front of her, a group of children stood pressed against a white-railed ring within which three snowy white horses walked around, each carrying another child.

She must have made a sound, for as a group, the children turned to gaze at her with bald curiosity.

"Hello," Aimili said, smiling.

The children just continued to stare at her.

"Please forgive the children," a woman's voice said.

Aimili stood and fought to keep her mouth from dropping open. A tiny woman approached, not much taller then the children themselves. She had huge lavender eyes; raven black, curly hair; and a bright, welcoming smile. Aimili half-expected delicate wings to sprout from her back.

What was perhaps most strange, she wore long purple braies and a matching tunic, with a thick silver bracelet on one wrist.

"They are surprised to see you," the woman continued.

"I . . . I am Aimili."

"Of course you are. I am called Shirlei. Welcome." She turned to the children, many of whom stood with mouths gaping open. "Greet our visitor, children."

A chorus of welcomes followed.

"If you will excuse me for a moment, I must see to my students," Shirlei said. She vaulted over the rail and floated into the ring, clapping her hands.

Curious, Aimili found an empty spot at the rail and leaned against the wood, folding her hands beneath her chin.

"Mayven, pay attention, please. You look like a sack of wheat up there."

Aimili smiled. Shirlei was right—the little girl did look exceedingly stiff and uncomfortable. When the horse stumbled, she shrieked and grabbed the horse's mane, nearly tumbling off the side in the process.

Shirlei shook her head, and looked over at Aimili. "'Tis a challenging job I have at times."

Aimili shifted on her feet and ran into a leg. She glanced over and saw a young boy with a mop of red hair staring at her. Slowly, she looked around and realized the children had moved close.

A small hand tugged on her sleeve. "Can you ride, my lady?"

Aimili looked down and blinked. Another fairy, she thought. This one had pale blue eyes, golden hair, and pink cheeks. "Aye, I do."

"My name is Sinana. I am only six, but I am learning." She beamed a smile at Aimili. "Can you help me?"

Aimili gestured toward the ring where Shirlei was talking earnestly to another child. "You have an instructor."

The girl's mouth turned down. "She is soooooo busy."

"I see."

"I have my very own horse," Sinana announced. "Come." She took Aimili's hand. "I will show you."

Why not? Aimili thought. She let the child pull her along, smiling when the rest of the children followed. On one side of the ring, partially hidden by a thick copse of trees, stood a huge, white stable. Horses stuck their heads out of openings cut into the outer walls, a few neighing greetings as they approached.

The interior was even more amazing, clean and filled with light, each stall front clearly decorated by its owner. Hearts and flowers dominated, but several had dolphins drawn on them, as well.

And the horses. Aimili wasn't sure which one to look at first. They were beautiful, magnificent animals every one, horses the wealthiest laird would be proud to own.

Sinana halted before a stall and reached up to rub a bay horse's nose. "This is Princess. Is she not the most beautiful horse ever?"

"That she is." Before Aimili was quite sure what had happened, she found herself spending a good part of the day teaching the children how to ride, joined by Shirlei, who was more than happy for the aid.

At last, they finished. Aimili looked down at her fine gown and grimaced at the dirt stains.

"Thank you, Aimili," Shirlei said. "The children are all so excited to ride, but I can only handle so many at one time."

"'Twas my pleasure." And it was, she realized. She'd enjoyed the children's attention, their determination, their thanks. It had helped to soothe away the hurts from earlier and lift her spirits. At the same time, it left a hollow, empty feeling in her chest, knowing that she would never have a child of her own. Never have her own precious little fairy, she thought, thinking of wee Sinana.

Something of her sadness must have shown on her face, because Shirlei patted her shoulder. "You must come again. I am sure the children will be asking about you, particularly Sinana."

"She is a sweet girl."

"Aye. A shame about her parents. She lives with

her grandfather, but spends most of her time with her horse."

"What happened to her parents?"

Shirlei shook her head. "'Twas a terrible accident. Her parents fashioned the most beautiful jewelry." She held out her arm, displaying the silver and amethyst bracelet. "They made this. One day, something in their workshop caught fire and exploded. They were both killed at once."

"How horrible."

"Aye. And Sinana's grandfather is quite old, even for one of us."

"There is no other family?"

"No. Someone will take her in, though, when needed."

Someone like me, Aimili thought, then inwardly chided herself for such an impossible notion. "I should go, but I shall return one day soon."

"We shall look for you."

Aimili smiled and walked away. She *should* return to Castle MacCoinneach, she knew that, but . . . She paused and looked around her. Surrounded by grassy fields, stone cottages in the near distance, the sun changing from pink to violet, she found herself wishing she was simply walking back to her home, a snug, warm cottage close to the sparkling blue sea.

D'Ary had been right. He'd known Paroseea would draw her.

Paroseea and the image of an orphaned fairy child

by the name of Sinana.

Padruig leaned against the rail and watched two of Aimili's mares play. One trotted over to Padruig, batting his arm with her head, then rubbing against him. The other horse joined them to see what was going on.

"Argante likes you," D'Ary said as he walked up.

Padruig chuckled as the horse continued to rub on him. "She has an itch."

"She likes to do that, but I have only seen her do it with Aimili."

"Aimili has a way with the horses."

"I suppose that is one way of describing her talent."

Padruig blew out a breath and gazed out across the bailey. "Where is she?"

"Paroseea."

"Why did you not go with her?"

"'Tis not necessary. She is in no danger there. Asides, she needs to find her own way."

And he definitely did not want her sanctimonious son-of-a-bitch husband to be with her, Padruig thought, wincing inside. He wondered if she would even come back.

She would, but not for him. She would return for the horses. They were the ones who held her devotion.

And why not? They did not take advantage of her innocence, fail to protect her, force her into marriage with a man she could never love.

"Laird!" a voice shouted.

Padruig looked to see Ivarr running toward him, his gaze dark and angry. "Something is wrong," Padruig told D'Ary, walking toward Ivarr.

"Laird, 'tis the MacVegans," Ivarr spat.

"What has happened?"

"A group of the bastards attacked the sheep. Killed Diarmad's son."

Padruig clenched his jaw. By the saints, Diarmad's son was but ten and two. "How many sheep did they steal?"

"None."

"What?"

"They slaughtered six and left them lying in the field."

"I thought the whole point of these raiding parties was to steal food," D'Ary said.

"It is," Padruig told him. "This is odd." He turned back to Ivarr. "Gather a score of your men."

Ivarr rushed off.

"Can you use a sword, or are you mostly for decoration?" he asked D'Ary.

The other man grinned. "I can wield a sword. Many in Paroseea consider me the best, in fact."

"Hmm. Well, let us see you display some of that

skill upon the MacVegans this day."

Within a short time, Padruig led his men to the spot where the MacVegans had attacked. Padruig dismounted and walked between the bloody sheep carcasses to where three men and a woman stood. Beyond them, a boy watched the remaining sheep.

One of the men had his arm around the woman, clearly holding her up. Padruig could see the boy's body on the ground.

"Diarmad," Padruig said "I am sorry."

Diarmad's gaze glittered with rancor. "Damn Mac-Vegans. Why kill a boy? Hate, 'tis all it is." *Because of you*, Diarmad's eyes said, though he did not voice the accusation aloud. His wife keened, and crumpled to her knees.

Padruig shoved down the familiar feeling of shame. This was a day for revenge. "Who else was here?"

Diarmad gestured to the boy across the field. "Taogh. He came to fetch us." Diarmad's expression dared Padruig to rebuke the boy for abandoning the herd.

Padruig ignored it and walked over to the boy. As he got closer, he saw the boy's shoulders shaking. His eyes were bright with tears. Padruig pretended not to notice.

"What did you see?"

"The bastards just rode up and k-killed Gilles. Didn't even say nothin'. One of them pulled a sword and just ran poor Gilles through. Then, they laughed." Tears leaked down the boy's cheeks.

"Did you hear any names?"

Taogh shook his head. "I ran, Laird." His voice was almost inaudible.

Padruig put a hand on the boy's shoulder. "Taogh, you did the right thing. There was nothing you could do to help Gilles. You were unarmed."

"I should have been able to do *something*."

"Your task is to take care of the sheep, not fight off armed enemies of the clan. That is my responsibility."

"You will find them, Laird?"

"We ride now. And from now on, you shall have at least one guardsman out here with you."

Taogh visibly slumped with relief.

"Do you know why they slaughtered the sheep?"

"No. Don't make no sense. Mayhap they just wanted to kill somethin' else. Gilles weren't enough for the bastards."

"Alasdair will be here shortly to collect the sheep. We shall not let them go to waste. He will give you a portion for your family."

"Thank you, Laird."

Padruig wished he possessed some magical words to comfort the boy, but there was nothing more to say. Diarmad was right. The MacVegans hated each and every member of the MacCoinneach clan and lived for the chance to rid the world of one, though attacking unarmed boys tending to the sheep was low, even for them.

He nodded to Taogh, marched back to his men, and mounted Thor. "Randulf, have you tracked their direction?"

"Aye."

"Lead on, then."

Though Randulf was a skilled tracker, anyone could have followed. The MacVegans had made no effort to conceal their trail. By late afternoon, they'd come to the edge of MacVegan lands, but there was no sign of the men.

"What think you?" Padruig asked Randulf.

"I think there is a village not far from here."

"They would be fools to stop there, so close to our land."

"They were fools to slay an unarmed boy and a handful of sheep."

"Aye. Let us ride on, then."

Padruig held up a hand to halt the men on a rise overlooking the village. It was a sizeable one, with a large stone tower in the center, presumably to provide the villagers with some refuge. They looked down on fields of wheat, empty now but for broken pieces of stalks.

"They are there," D'Ary said.

Magic, Padruig thought. "Ye cannot know that."

D'Ary pointed. "The hoofprints lead right there."

"They probably stopped to refresh themselves, then continued on."

"Mayhap."

"We shall find out." Padruig drew his sword and directed Thor toward the village.

At the sight of him and his men riding down a path

into the village, people scurried inside, grabbing children and running for doorways.

"Stop," Padruig told a woman, driving Thor to block her flight.

She clasped her hands as if in prayer. "Please, do not kill me. I have children; I—"

"I do not slay innocent women," Padruig bit out. "Even if they are MacVegans."

The woman's face lost all color as she realized just who she faced.

"We are looking for a group of men who attacked my holdings, killed a child. Are they here?"

"Kill . . . killed a child?"

"Aye. Just a boy tending the sheep."

The woman crossed herself. "They are here," she said, her voice hard. Pointing down the dirt path, she said, "In the center of the village, next to the green is a tavern. They are there, drinking and whoring while they wait."

"Wait? For what?"

"I, uh, please, Laird, I can say no more." She darted under Thor's neck and disappeared into a wattle-and-daub house.

Padruig exchanged a glance with Randulf. "What do you think she meant?"

Randulf shrugged. "I think we'd best see to this business and return to our own lands."

"Agreed." Padruig spurred Thor forward. Just as the

woman had said, the road led to a large green. On one side sat the stone tower, and on the other, a squat timber building with tables set up outside. Four men sprawled on benches, cups and jugs in front of them.

One of them spotted Padruig and let out a shout.

Within moments it was over. The villagers had been wise enough to stay out of the fight, and the MacVegan guardsmen were too sotted to adequately wield a sword. Padruig took two, D'Ary one, and the other was no challenge at all to the other MacCoinneach guards.

The tavern owner emerged from the building, his eyes wide.

Padruig dismounted. "We mean you no harm," he said. "We do not war on the innocent."

The man's throat worked, and then he turned and yelled something into the building. A boy rushed out. "Fetch a wagon," the tavern owner told him.

The boy cut a frightened glance toward Padruig and ran.

"Oh, my God!" a woman's voice screamed. Padruig whirled about to see a young woman. Her gown was splattered with blood, her dark hair in disarray around her face. She took one look at Padruig and bolted.

He chased her down, easily capturing her arms. She kicked back into his shins. "Let me go!" she shouted.

Instead, he dragged her back to his men, who had found seats and were in the process of helping themselves to ale.

"Do you need aid, Laird?" D'Ary called.

"Nay." He winced as the woman's boot tramped down on his foot.

She tried to yank her arm free. "Leave me be."

He shoved her onto a bench and crossed his arms. This was no simple villager, he thought. Even splattered with blood, he could see her bliaut was a finely woven wool. "Are you hurt?"

"No. I was assisting with a babe." She tried to rise, but he pushed her back down.

"Who are you?"

She cut a glance to the bodies of the men and said nothing.

"They were waiting for *you*," D'Ary said.

"No."

"You are a MacVegan," Padruig said.

"Obviously."

Something in the woman's eyes, her voice was familiar. "What is your name?"

Before she answered, a man ran to the tavern owner and whispered something in his ear. The owner briefly closed his eyes and nodded.

"You must leave," he told Padruig. "Men from the castle approach. I want no more battles in my village. If you must kill each other, do it elsewhere."

The woman made to run, but D'Ary wrapped a hand around her wrist. "I suppose we will have to take her with us."

Padruig nodded.

"Nay!" the woman shouted. "You cannot!"

"Actually we can. Your men came onto our lands today. Killed an unarmed boy."

She paled. "Nay. They were to stay here."

"They became bored, my lady," the tavern owner explained, spitting on the ground. He shook his head. "Go now, all of you. We want no more trouble."

D'Ary flung the girl onto his horse and mounted behind her.

Padruig tossed the tavern owner a coin and pressed Thor into a gallop.

On arriving back at Castle MacCoinneach, Aimili headed directly to the stable. Spending the day instructing the children on Paroseea had made her realize she'd been neglecting her own horses of late. *Too caught up in the tangled mess of your life*, she thought in disgust.

She stepped into the stable and halted, allowing the familiar sounds and smells to wash over her. A low nicker, a sigh of contentment, the flapping of hungry lips searching the ground for a missed piece of hay, the earthy scent of horses.

A stable had always seemed like another world to

her, whether it was a sturdy, plain structure or the lavish quarters she'd just seen on Paroseea. Either way, a stable had long been her special place, her refuge from demands she could not or would not satisfy. The horses had their own unique way of life, a much simpler view of things. Most importantly, they accepted her without censure and without lies.

Mist poked her head out and gave a nicker of greeting. *How do you fare, my lady?*

Well enough. Aimili stopped to stroke Mist's velvety neck.

What is that smell? Mist pulled her lips back over her teeth and stuck her head out.

Paroseea.

Who?

What, actually, and a long story, my friend. Do you feel like a ride?

Aye, but I suggest you take out Loki. Run some energy out of him. He is in a lather over Argante and she wants nothing to do with him.

Aimili chuckled. *She will in a few days.*

You'd best keep a close eye when that happens. He is about to jump straight out of his stall.

I will. Aimili moved down the row of stalls, stopped at Loki's, and burst out in laughter. *What in the heavens are you doing?*

What does it look like?

Oscar came up beside Aimili and peered into Loki's

stall. His young face turned pink and she saw his lips quirk as if he was trying to hold in his mirth.

Loki ignored them and continued with his task. His erection stuck out from his lower body and he was trying without success to rub it against the side of his stall.

You are going to injure yourself, Aimili told him. *Or get a splinter. I am not digging it out, either.*

He snorted and lifted his back leg, then stretched it behind him.

"Do ye think he'll fall down, my lady?" Oscar asked.

"I doubt it, but I also doubt he will succeed in his endeavor."

Naysayer, Loki cursed. He tilted more to the left, and tried again, almost managing to reach the wall. *Just a little farther,* he said. He leaned farther over.

I know what you are doing, Argante shouted.

Loki jerked and landed on the straw with a grunt.

At that, Aimili was laughing so hard tears trickled from her eyes. Oscar gave up his attempt to be mature about the whole thing and snickered. *Be patient, Loki.*

Easy for you to say.

When she didn't respond, Loki heaved himself to his feet and gazed at her. *Oh. I am sorry.*

'Tis not your fault my husband does not want me.

Fool. Loki shook himself all over, like a dog emerging from the loch and throwing off the water.

Ready for a ride?

Might as well. I am surely not gaining anything by standing in my stall staring at that obstinate wench across the way.

Aimili glanced over and saw that Argante was standing as far back in her stall as she could get, her gaze carefully averted. *Soon, my friend.*

Loki just sighed.

"Are you goin' to take 'em out, my lady?"

"Aye. He needs to run, do you not agree?"

Oscar grinned. "At the very least. You'd best stay within the castle walls though."

Aimili looked around the empty stable. "Where is D'Ary?"

"Rode off with the laird and a band of guards, my lady. Those damned MacVegans attacked. 'Tis said they killed one of the lads watching the sheep as well as some of the animals."

"A boy and some sheep?"

"Aye. Filthy whoresons they are, pardon my language."

Aimili shivered. Even though she knew the MacVegans had been feuding with the MacCoinneachs since the day Padruig killed Symund MacVegan, she'd not really understood the danger. For the first time, she gave some credit to Padruig's insistence that she not ride out alone. "My husband went after them?"

"Aye." Oscar pumped out his chest. "Dinnae worry, my lady. The laird will see that those bastards get what they deserve."

"Of that, I am sure."

With Oscar's aid and Loki's cooperation, it didn't take long before Aimili was mounted and steering Loki toward a long grassy area close to where the men trained.

Where are we going?

I thought you might benefit from work on a straight line.

They passed a group of men training, their swords clanging, curses ringing equally in the air. Aimili squeezed Loki into a trot. *Come on boy, carry yourself and me.* She pulsed the outside rein slightly back, then released it. *Think about where your feet are.*

On the ground.

Ah, a jest. You must be feeling good.

"Good" is not the word I would use. He sounded so frustrated Aimili had to smile. *Think lift, and by the saints, pick up that hind end. You act as if you are dragging your rear along on the ground. That will not impress the mares.*

Loki came up under her. *Yes. That is it. Step up.*

It does not feel right.

It is. You are not used to it.

I can do this?

Yes. She pushed him into a canter. *Just try to stay straight.*

Again, he came through. It was such a different

feeling, Aimili felt like cheering.

Suddenly, from the training field she heard shouting. Angry shouting. "You bastard!" one the men yelled. "That was a low trick."

"Only because I bested you."

Aimili turned Loki in a big circle and brought him down to a trot. The first man, whose name she didn't know, delivered a punch into the face of Huwe, another guard. Huwe tackled him, and the two men rolled across the ground, pounding and cursing each other.

Loki stumbled, nearly pitching Aimili off his neck. *Loki, are you all right?*

Beneath her, she felt Loki tremble, actually tremble. *What is it, boy?*

He shied sideways and started to bolt, but Aimili held him back. *Easy, boy.*

It is him.

Aimili gazed out over the training field. The two men still fought, and a score of others watched. *Him?*

Hang on. This time when Loki took off, she let him, clinging to the saddle and giving him his head. He thundered into the stable, and Aimili slid from his back.

Danger, Loki said. *That man is danger. He is the one we have felt.*

Who? Which one is it?

Loki pushed past her and rushed into his stall. The other horses neighed and stamped their feet, feeling Loki's agitation.

He is the one called Huwe.

Hours later, when dusk was fast approaching, Padruig led his men through Castle MacCoinneach's gatehouse. He was tired, dusty, and starving, not necessarily in that order.

He also wanted to see his wife, wanted to try to explain, well, he wasn't sure what exactly, but he felt he needed to try to make peace with her. It seemed as if all he did was hurt her.

Surprisingly, the MacVegan lass hadn't made a sound during their journey, though he could feel the intensity of her gaze upon him nearly the whole way. It felt like much more than the usual enmity of a Mac Vegan. From time to time, he was tempted to turn and demand she tell him why, but he'd decided to wait to confront her until they had her within the confines of Castle MacCoinneach.

He halted Thor near the stable and whistled before dismounting. Oscar ran out, a hunk of cheese still in his grasp. When he saw Padruig and the men, his face brightened. "Did ye hunt down those murderin' MacVegan bastards?"

Before Padruig could answer, D'Ary moved forward. Padruig could tell the moment Oscar spotted the MacVegan wench by the lad's look of astonishment. He pointed at her. "Who is that?"

"A MacVegan, though beyond that I dinnae ken." Padruig glanced back at her. "Yet."

Oscar's eyes widened even farther. He grabbed Thor's reins, moving his hand just in time to save his cheese. "I'll take care of your horse, Laird."

"My thanks." Padruig walked over to D'Ary and the woman. "Come," he told her.

"So that you can throw me in a pit somewhere?"

"I am no like your clansmen."

D'Ary lifted her down and she landed on her feet with a wince.

"Are you hurt?"

"Nay. A bit stiff, 'tis all." She looked at him as if he were some kind of apparition, her gaze slowly traveling over the scars on his face, though to her credit, she did not so much as flinch.

He took her arm in a firm grip and pulled her toward the great hall.

"Why are you doing this?" she asked, her voice remarkably calm.

"Who are you?" he asked instead.

She pressed her lips together.

By the saints, he had no time for this, Padruig thought as he drew her into the hall. Would that he could deposit the lass somewhere until he'd dealt with other more pressing troubles.

But she was a mystery, and that fact, combined with

her guards being responsible for today's savage attack, was more than enough to warrant a close look at the woman.

The hum of voices quieted at the sight of Padruig leading a strange woman through the hall. He grimaced, wishing he'd had the woman stop to rinse the blood from her bliaut, then decided to ignore the suspicious stares from some of his people. If he had meant the woman harm, she would surely not be walking along, head high.

One by one, those seated on the dais turned toward them. Freya and Efrika's eyes bulged with patent curiosity. Alasdair simply crossed his arms and stared. Gifford, of course, was off his seat in an instant, ever the noble champion of the fair sex.

And finally, Aimili, who gazed at them in utter shock, her face leached of color, her eyes deep and dark.

He realized the woman with him had stopped when he kept moving forward and encountered resistance. Thinking she was nervous at the prospect of sitting with members of the hated MacCoinneach family, he turned and scowled at her, tightening his grasp.

It was then he saw she was paying him no heed whatsoever, but was staring at his wife.

"Madeleine?" Aimili said. "What . . ?" She turned to Padruig.

For a moment, he knew such fury he felt as if it ripped asunder his very soul. Aimili knew this woman? This MacVegan? "I had no idea you were acquainted with my wife," he growled at the woman in his grasp.

Madeleine MacVegan bit her lip, but did not look at him. In fact, she said nothing. Gradually, it dawned on him that she was waiting for Aimili to speak.

"You know this woman?" he asked Aimili, fighting but failing to keep accusation from his tone.

She visibly hesitated, then slowly nodded.

"My solar." He turned and started towing his "guest" back out of the hall when he felt a hand on his arm.

"Padruig, is the lass injured?" Gifford asked, his expression unusually somber.

"Not at my hand. She says nay."

"I shall escort the lady. You will no doubt wish to see to your wife."

Afore Padruig could mouth a protest, Gifford smoothly transferred the woman's hand to his arm and sailed down the hall.

"Gifford," Padruig called.

Gifford paused and looked back. "Aye, Laird?"

"Do not venture far ahead of me. She is no friend of the MacCoinneachs." He stalked to the high table, grabbed up an ewer of wine, and motioned to one of the servers. "Ask Cook to please see that food and drink are delivered to my solar."

"Aye, Laird." The young man scurried off.

"Padruig, who is that woman?" Freya whispered.

He fixed his gaze upon Aimili. "Apparently, she is called Madeleine."

"I have not heard of a woman with that name."

He kept his gaze on his wife. "Madeleine MacVegan."

Freya sucked in a breath.

Aimili simply stood and followed him out of the hall.

Padruig couldn't bring himself to speak to her at all until they were closed within his solar. "Explain this to me." He drank straight from the ewer.

"Padruig, at least let me seek out food and drink," Gifford said, clutching his own jug of ale. "The poor girl looks to dropping."

"I am fine," she said.

Gifford patted her on the shoulder.

"I have already requested the same, Gifford," Padruig told him. "'Tis not my intention to mistreat the lass."

"Madeleine, you must tell him," Aimili said.

"Clearly, you have not told him. If you did not think he would believe you, why should I even bother?"

"I have told others." Aimili gave Padruig a wary glance.

"One of you shall tell me what is going on," Padruig said. "Now."

Madeleine MacVegan drew herself up straight, though Padruig could see her face was drawn with fatigue. "You have no learned patience in your time away from the Highlands," she said. "Nor learned to stop and think."

"You know nothing of me. I have neither time nor tolerance for secrets."

"I am Symund's sister," she announced.

Had they searched the wench for weapons? Padruig wondered. Surely D'Ary had checked. He drew his sword. "Gifford, back away from her."

Gifford looked between them. "Why?"

"Do it. Now," Padruig barked.

Gifford retreated to a window seat and settled down with a huff of annoyance. "Really, Padruig, ye cannot think the girl a threat."

"'Tis in the blood. Her own brother was a murderer." Now he knew why the woman seemed so familiar. She looked exactly like a female version of Symund MacVegan.

"Nay." Madeleine shouted, standing and walking toward Padruig. She stopped with his blade at her throat. "He did not murder your sister."

"Padruig, please listen to her," Aimili urged.

"Sit down," he told Madeleine.

She did. He sheathed his sword and stared at Aimili. "How do you know this woman?"

"We met in Morisaig, at the market."

"'Twas the first time?"

"Aye. The only time afore today."

Padruig's rigid shoulders relaxed, and it struck Aimili that he had actually suspected her of complicity with the MacVegans.

Aimili looked at Madeleine and saw the woman had picked up on it, too. "Now you understand," Aimili told her.

"I am sorry, Aimili. I did not realize, well, I did not

mean to put you into this kind of difficulty."

"What are you talking about?" Padruig demanded.

"'Tis obvious you do not trust your wife," Gifford commented before swilling back some ale. "Simpkin," he added, with a pointed look toward Aimili.

Bolstered by Gifford's support, Aimili resisted the temptation to give her husband a good smack across the face. Somehow, she'd gone from foolish child to scheming plotter in one huge leap.

"I . . . I am sorry, Aimili," Padruig said. "You must understand, I—"

"Should be quiet and listen," Aimili snapped. "Madeleine?"

A banging on the door preceded a trio of servants bearing ewers of ale and wine and platters of food. Gifford's eyes lit up at the sight and he bounded from his seat. After seeing that Aimili and Madeleine had cups of wine, he splashed ale into a cup and sat next to Madeleine. "Please explain, my lady," he said to her. "I am guessing there is far more to this story than we know."

"As I told Aimili, I know that Symund did not kill Brona."

Padruig shook his head. "We all saw—"

"What someone wanted you to see," Aimili interrupted. "What better way to spawn a killing feud between the clans?"

"Symund wanted Brona. I know that." Padruig paced across the floor. "By the saints, I approved of him for the match."

"He loved her," Madeleine told him.

"Of course he did." Padruig threw up his hands. "That changes nothing. When he found her with Malcolm, he went wild with jealousy. He killed them both. And then, well, I killed him for the deed."

Tears ran down Madeleine's cheeks and she just shook her head.

"Padruig," Gifford began, then cast a look about the solar. "Do you not remember what *she* said?"

"She?" Aimili asked.

"Aye." Gifford tossed back more ale. "Brona's ghost. Quite a pleasant spirit, but damned cryptic as they all seem to be. Said her death wasn't Padruig's fault. Stands to reason she meant it wasn't this Symund's fault, either."

Madeleine rocked back and forth, gripping her cup in one hand and her skirt in the other. "I would have known if he'd killed her. I was his twin. We shared thoughts, feelings. I would have known, I swear it."

Padruig frowned.

"Do not dismiss this, Padruig," Aimili told him, ignoring Gifford's amazing comment. Ghosts? Most likely a product of too much ale. "You must look more closely at what happened."

"I was there." He did not sound as convinced as before.

"Alasdair and Magnus agree with me. They have been looking into the events of that day. We believe someone else was behind everything."

"But who? Who would . . ." Padruig's words trailed off and he met Aimili's gaze, clearly beginning to think what Aimili had already accepted as truth.

"One of the villagers saw a rider heading for the MacVegan holdings that day."

"I remember that," Madeleine said. "A rider came to warn the laird that Symund was in trouble. I was not privy to the conversation. The laird believed the messenger because he said he'd been sent by a friend of Symund's."

"What? A MacCoinneach?" Padruig asked.

"Aye. His name was . . ."

"Huwe," Madeleine and Aimili said together.

"No," Padruig said, his voice breaking.

"Aye," Aimili said, her gaze telling Padruig what she could not say in front of Madeleine and Gifford.

"That whoreson is dead." Padruig turned to march out, but Aimili caught his arm.

"No, Padruig. Not yet."

"You are saying he killed my sister!"

"And more."

Padruig's eyes were wild.

"Ye must wait," she told him, her voice low. "You know this."

Padruig visibly fought for control. Finally he nodded. "I will, but I will also tell Sebilla that the time has come to end this."

"We will tell her together."

Padruig looked back at Madeleine. "I believe you. Would that I could live that day over, but I cannot."

"We were all fooled, weren't we?"

"Aye."

"But, why?"

Aimili realized she would have to come up with an explanation without mentioning Paroseea. "We think that Huwe, whoever he really is, bears a powerful hatred for the MacCoinneach clan, particularly Padruig. All of what happened was to cause trouble for Padruig and the clan."

"Why does he hate you?" Madeleine asked Padruig.

"I am no sure," he answered slowly. "The best I can guess is that he hates me because I am the laird, not because of anything I have done."

"Poor Symund was just a sacrifice."

"And Brona and Malcolm and many others," Aimili added.

"Of course. 'Tis just that Symund . . ." Madeleine paused and took a sip of wine. "He was very dear to me." She looked up at Padruig. "What will you do?"

"Kill him."

Padruig gazed upon the man who called himself Huwe. Though Padruig knew he must conceal his true thoughts, it was quite possibly the hardest thing he'd ever done. How could he have missed this? How could none of them have seen the traitorous serpent in their midst? Even Freya liked the man.

"I need a man I can trust," Padruig said, marveling that he didn't choke over the words, but knowing they would appeal to Vardon's arrogant nature. "Normally, I would press Magnus into service, but after that foolish business by the loch he is still recovering." Padruig grunted, as if he considered Magnus weak to be still healing from such a paltry wound.

"I am pleased to assist you, Laird."

Assist me to my death, Padruig wanted to say, but he forced himself to nod. "I found something in the vaults that intrigues me. It appears to be a doorway of sorts, but I cannot open the stone by myself."

"A hidden doorway?"

"Aye," Padruig said, wondering how the bastard could appear so nonchalant when he knew Vardon had to be both surprised and very interested. Padruig leaned over his worktable and dropped his voice as if to share a confidence. "You know we lack enough stores to see us through even with what Gifford brought. I am hoping there is something of value beyond this door."

"Ah. A treasure perhaps?"

"'Twould be most welcome."

"Aye. A terrible thing what has happened to us, between the animals dying and the crops being destroyed."

Vardon shook his head. "Bad luck, to be sure."

"In the form of Grigor's poor leadership."

"Of course." This time Vardon did not meet Padruig's gaze, which was just as well. Padruig was finding it more and more difficult to hide his rage.

"Come, Huwe. Let us find this treasure, if one is to be had." He must have done a passable job of hiding his true feelings because Vardon followed him easily. When they reached the final passage, Padruig pointed up at the dolphin symbol carved into the stone overhead. "What think you of that, Huwe?"

If he had not been watching the man closely, he would have missed the instant of shock on Vardon's face. "An odd symbol," he answered.

"My thought, as well. Help me push this open."

They bent to the task, and the doorway swung open. Padruig walked in and lit a candle mounted on the wall. "I do not see anything in here. Huwe, check the other side. Or," Padruig continued in a mild tone, "should I call you Vardon?"

Vardon whirled around. "Who?"

"Please. You may drop the pretense."

"How did you know?"

Padruig smiled. "You are not as clever as you think."

Behind them, the water in the pool began to froth and splash. Vardon whirled around at the noise and drew his sword.

Queen Sebilla rose up out of the water and hovered on the surface. "'Tis time for you to return to where you belong, Vardon."

"Never." He stepped toward the pool.

She stretched out her arms, and the silver flecks in the stone walls began to glow. As two worlds join together, a power arises that is invincible, Sebilla chanted. "One woman, of us but no longer with us. One fallen laird, descended of Aelfric's honor and strength."

Vardon laughed. "One of the things that has always annoyed me most about you exalted ones is your devotion to gibberish that means nothing. 'Tis a mark of how truly pathetic and weak you are."

Sebilla's blue gaze narrowed. "You have always resented your birth."

"No," he sneered. "I resent being treated as a lesser being because of it."

"Your father—"

"Was obviously of your ilk. No doubt took advantage of my mother. After all, she was little more than a servant, not worth any showing of respect, but only valued for her use to her betters. A whore would have received more."

Padruig glanced back and saw that Aimili had crept into the chamber. Not surprisingly, Gifford snuck in behind her, his eyes bulging with curiosity.

Sebilla glared at Vardon. "You know nothing. Your father was Llyr, one of the greatest scholars Paroseea has ever known."

Vardon stumbled back a step. "You lie!" he shouted.

"No. 'Tis hard to believe," she said with a contemptuous look. "I discovered your parentage only recently. 'Twas in a lost cache of Llyr's papers."

"It does not matter now."

"Does it not? surely you have long wondered. Now you know. You know the lineage you honer."

Padruig glanced at Aimili, who now stood next to him. "What does this mean?" she whispered."

"I have no idea," he answered, his voice just as low.

"You betray your father with your abuse of power just as you betray Paroseea, Sebilla stated, her voice rich with condemnation."

"*I* betray *him*? He did *nothing* for me, nothing for my mother. Never acknowledged me in any way."

"That is not an excuse to turn to darkness."

Vardon gave a bitter laugh filled with so much pain and loathing that Padruig again exchanged a glance of concern with Aimili. "By the gods, how righteous you sound. An easy thing to do when you have had everything handed to you. When the people have always worshiped and adored you."

"There is great responsibility attached to such treatment."

"Oh? Well, naturally I would not know. Niece," he snarled. "For I had nothing I did not seize for myself, an outcast from my birth. Even when I began to display powers, I was treated with disdain, an unnatural freak of

Paroseea's perfectly ordered hierarchy."

"Niece?" Padruig and Aimili asked together.

"You were evil!" Sebilla shouted. "From your birth you revealed the evil in your soul. That is why your father pretended you did not exist. Everyone knew if you developed any powers you would use them for personal gain without regard for anyone or anything."

She stood in front of Vardon. "Surrender to me."

"Fuck you."

Sebilla again raised her hands to the side. A nimbus of glowing, multicolored mist swirled about her body. "I commend you to live in darkness, just as you were born of darkness."

Vardon roared in fury and swung his sword, but it glanced off the circle surrounding Sebilla.

"As Queen of Paroseea, I denounce you."

"No!" Vardon shouted. "Not this time." From the tip of his sword spewed a black cloud that grew and enveloped Sebilla. She crumpled to the ground with a high scream.

"Bastard," Padruig swore and rushed him. His sword arced through the air, striking Vardon's sword so hard it went flying, landing at the base of a wall.

Vardon simply smiled and held out a hand. Padruig went crashing aside as if he were as light as air. He tried to rise, but an invisible force held him down.

Across the chamber, Aimili heard Sebilla continuing to chant though her voice was weak. Her pain-filled gaze caught Aimili's. "Daughter of my blood," she said. "Finish this."

Aimili gripped the dagger in both hands. When she turned back to Vardon, he was standing over Padruig, a look of pure satisfaction on his face. Though Padruig was clearly fighting to get free, he was no match for Vardon's power. Sweat poured down Padruig's face, and his mouth twisted in agony.

"No!" she shouted. The dagger thrummed in her hands, spreading a tingling feeling through her body. "Move away from him," Aimili ordered, striving to keep her voice even.

"Or what?" Vardon didn't even look at her. "Ye cannot best me."

"Oh, yes, I can," she swore. In her hands the dagger shimmered and glowed, widening and lengthening until it became a blinding sword.

Vardon turned, his eyes blazing hate. "You can watch your beloved husband die first."

No, she thought, rushing forward. As she neared Vardon, Aimili realized all around her shimmered silver. A hum of sheer power crackled through her veins.

She swung the sword with all her strength. For an instant, Vardon's eyes widened in disbelief.

The blade sliced through his neck almost effortlessly.

Vardon's head thumped to the floor, followed by his body.

Drawing in a breath, Aimili stared at Padruig. Between them, blood spread over the stone.

D'Ary burst into the chamber, utter panic etched into his features. "Sebilla!" he shouted.

Padruig stood alone on the battlements, looking out over the empty expanse of MacCoinneach land.

It had been three days since the battle against Vardon.

Three days since his wife had transformed into a powerful sorceress who had chopped off Vardon's head with a magical dagger-turned-sword.

Three days since he'd lain on the ground trapped by Vardon's magic, completely dependent on Aimili to save them all.

Three days since the castle had begun to awaken, as if emerging from a deep, dark sleep.

Three days since Aimili had followed D'Ary and a wounded Sebilla to Paroseea.

She was not coming back.

He knew it in his heart. He couldn't even pretend surprise, let alone put any blame on her.

To questions, he just shrugged and told people Aimili was away for a time. Eventually when it became apparent to everyone that she was not simply off visiting someone, he would have to bring a few into his confidence, come up with a believable story to explain to the clan why their lady was gone. An illness perhaps, one that forced her to live in a warmer clime?

Aye, that would be best. Just let her go. Let her be happy

Aimili sat on the soft pink sand, gazing out over the water. Bright sunlight turned the surface into a glittering blue. Far out in the sea, a pod of dolphins splashed and played, and a tiny white bird hopped along the sand just above the waterline. Some kind of sweet flower scented the air.

It was hard to imagine that such a place of beauty could spawn the likes of Vardon. She shivered despite the warmth of the day. Many times, she had gone over the fight in her mind, and she still wasn't exactly sure what had happened or how. When she closed her eyes, she could clearly see her sword, now a dagger again, slice through Vardon's neck, the surprise in his eyes.

Horrific as it was, she felt no regret. Vardon would have happily killed them all, had come perilously close with Sebilla. She was still weak, though Aimili suspected part of the reason for here slowly recovery was that D'Ary had not left her side, plying her with food and drink, even telling her stories to alleviate her boredom.

Idly, she drew patterns in the sand with her fingertips. She'd been afforded a hero's reception here in Paroseea. She'd lost count of the number of people who'd thanked her, the ones who pointed at her, telling others, "She is the one who saved us."

Sebilla had expressed her gratitude by gifting Aimili with her stone cottage by the sea. She'd offered Aimili far grander homes, but Aimili knew what she wanted and it was perfect.

All in all it was very tempting to stay.

"Lady Aimili?" a child's voice asked.

Aimili turned her head to find Sinana standing a few feet away. She held a pale blue silk pouch in one of her small hands. "Sinana." Aimili smiled. "How do you fare?"

"Well, my lady." She sat on the sand next to Aimili, tucking her legs beneath her. "What are you doing?"

"Not a thing except looking at this beautiful sea."

"Do you not have a sea out there?"

"Out where?"

"Where you are from. Scot Land."

"Ah. Yes, we do have seas and many lochs in Scotland. None look like this, though."

"What is it like, your home?"

For a moment, Aimili didn't speak, struck by the thought that she was no longer sure where "home" was. "Scotland is much cooler than here and very green. It is quite beautiful in its own way."

Sinana bit her lip and gazed up at Aimili. "Were you

452

very afraid?"

"Of Vardon, you mean?"

The child nodded.

"Aye, I was, indeed. He was a bad man, and very powerful."

"But you slew him," Sinana said proudly.

"I . . . I had to. It was much more than anything I had ever done before, even imagined I could do."

"You did it to save your husband."

The image of Padruig down on the stone floor flowed through Aimili's mind, anger and frustration burning in his gaze. How he must have hated being rendered helpless, she thought. *How he must resent me.*

"You must love him very much." Sinana sighed.

Aimili's throat burned. "I have always loved him."

"Here," Sinana said, handing her the silk pouch. "I brought you something."

Touched, Aimili gave the girl a hug. "You did not need to give me anything."

"I want you to have it."

Aimili poured the contents of the pouch into her palm. It was a pendant, Paroseea's symbol worked in silver with pale blue stones for the dolphin's eyes. "This is lovely, Sinana."

"My parents made it."

"Oh." Aimili squeezed her hand. "I do appreciate the gift, but surely you wish to keep it."

"No. It is in thanks for your bravery."

"Well, then, I accept your gift."

"It shall remind you of Paroseea."

"I need no reminders, but thank you."

"Do you think you shall stay in Paroseea sometimes?"

"I am not sure what I am going to do. I now have a wonderful cottage, thanks to Queen Sebilla."

"Do you have children?"

"I, no, I do not." The lump in Aimili's throat grew.

Sinana stared at her unblinking, and Aimili understood. She put her arm around Sinana's thin shoulders and pulled her close. "I am no sure what I am going to do in my life right now. I love Paroseea, but my home has always been the Highlands, which I love, as well."

"What of your husband?"

Aimili stared out over the sea, trying to find the words to explain the complicated story of Padruig MacCoinneach to a child. In the end, she just shrugged. "He does not share my feelings."

"He does not love you?"

"Nay. He does not."

"Then perhaps you should stay here. With me."

"Perhaps I shall."

Padruig was in his solar working his way through

yet another ewer of wine when the invasion occurred.

The leader, not surprisingly, was Gifford. What was somewhat surprising was that he had apparently enlisted quite the group to join him. Efrika, Alasdair, Freya, and even Magnus filed in behind Gifford.

They each gazed at Padruig as if he'd completely lost his wits.

"I am busy," he said.

"You are a stubborn, prideful fool," Gifford said with a snort.

Nods of agreement followed his pronouncement.

"I suppose Gifford told you all everything?"

Efrika bustled forward and slapped a hand on his worktable. "Aye, thankfully he did. I cannot imagine what you were thinking to keep such a secret from us."

"He was thinking that he and only he had the ability to fix the problem," Alasdair commented. He crossed his arms and gave Padruig a stern look that reminded him of his father.

"'Tis my responsibility."

"By the saints, you are near as mule-headed as Cain," Gifford said, rolling his eyes. "No, mayhap more. Brona, are you about? We could use aid."

"Gifford, ye cannae just call a ghost," Padruig told him, taking another slug of wine and wishing they would all just go away and leave him to his misery.

"Actually, he can," Brona said, her form slowly taking shape next to Gifford.

Freya squeaked and fainted. Luckily, Magnus was close enough to catch her with his good arm. He gently lowered her to the floor.

Efrika and Alasdair just stared at Brona's ghost openmouthed.

"Padruig, go to her," Brona said.

"And say what?"

"The truth," Gifford said, scowling at him

"I do not—"

"Oh, for heavens sake," Efrika interrupted. "Ye cannae be *that* thickheaded. 'Tis obvious that you love the girl. Tell her! 'Tis no such a painful thing to say."

Alasdair put his arm around her and smiled.

"I . . ." Padruig tried to deny it, but the words just wouldn't come.

"Ye know now that you were not responsible for my death," Brona reminded him. "'Twas Vardon who did everything. Once the MacVegan woman explains the truth to her clan, you can come to a peace. You are free," she finished in a soft voice.

"I fear 'tis too late," Padruig said, trying but utterly failing to quash the surge of pain the thought evoked.

Brona smiled and shook her head. "'Tis never too late, Padruig. Not for love."

Gifford beamed a smile at her. "Well said, my lady."

Padruig stood, more afraid than he'd ever been in his life. "I shall try, but Paroseea holds a powerful pull for her."

"*Nothing* is more powerful than love."

He stared at Brona, a spark of hope taking hold in his heart. Could they be right? Could it be that he'd not squandered his chances with Aimili, hadn't managed to kill off any feeling's she'd once had for him?

You have never been a man to run from a challenge, he told himself. *When you are facing the greatest one of your life, it is not the time to start.*

He strode from the room.

Aimili was watching some of the children ride when Sinana tugged on her tunic. "Who is that?" she whispered.

Before Aimili looked, she knew it was Padruig. She drew in a deep breath and slowly turned. He strode across the thick, green grass, the afternoon sunlight turning his hair to gold. His gaze found hers, tender and determined all at once. It was so like her dreams, her heart turned over.

"Is that the laird?" Sinana asked.

"Aye."

"Oh." She slid behind Aimili. "He looks very fierce."

"He can be." She wrapped the pieces of her heart in a protective mantle, taking strength from the other children flanking her.

He stopped just short of them. "Come home."

Aimili clenched her jaw. "That is it? The great laird arrives and delivers a command?"

"Please." He edged closer, and Aimili pressed as far as she could against the rail with Sinana stuck behind her.

"Why?"

Astounded, she watched a myriad of emotions cross his face. Pain. Sorrow. Regret. And doubt. "You are my wife," he said.

A broken piece of her heart escaped her protection and shattered into dust. "Sebilla gave me a lovely cottage here. I am thinking to stay."

"You belong at Castle MacCoinneach."

"Do I? I am no sure anymore." Sadness swamped her so strongly that she could barely breathe. How pathetic she was to expect more of him.

"Aimili, I ken I have made a mess of things. I did not expect"—he paused and gestured around them—"any of this. I did not expect you."

"You have made that abundantly clear."

"You do not understand."

"Aye, I think I do. Finally."

Aimili heard a big sigh from behind her. She felt movement and Sinana stuck her head out. "Tell her you love her, ye great simpkin!" the child shouted.

For a moment, Padruig looked as if he'd been struck by the blunt edge of a sword. He looked at Aimili, then Sinana, then back again. "I do love you," he said.

Aimili was sure she'd misheard. "Padruig, you need

not—"

"Damn it, I love you! I did not want to. By the saints, I have fought it as hard as I could. You are beauty and innocence. Look at me, Aimili. I am a hulking, scarred man who failed his clan."

Aimili started to smile. "But now you know 'twas not your fault."

He scowled. "Aye."

"'Tis hard to let go of being a martyr, I suppose."

He took her arms in a gentle hold. His gaze turned soft, his mouth curving in a sheepish smile. "I am willing to try if you will give me another chance."

"I used to dream of you, you know," she said haltingly. "You were the man I wanted."

"I dinnae know. I wish I would have. Or mayhap not." He sighed. "In truth I am not the same Padruig you met as a child."

"Nay. I have come to realize that."

"I do love you, though. I want you to share my life. Be my partner."

Aimili's smile widened, and her heart swelled.

"And this I vow," he said, dropping to his knees and taking her hands. "From this day forward, I shall devote my every waking moment to being the man of your dreams."

"Och, well, that is all a woman can ask."

Padruig stood and lifted her high, laughing and swinging her in his arms.

The children started cheering.

A Lost Touch of Paradise
Amy Tolnitch

For the first time in his life, Lugh MacKeir, Laird of Tunvegan, finds himself in a battle he cannot win. His precious daughter is dying of the same illness that claimed his wife.

The Isle of Parraba is a whispered legend, a place rumored to be ruled by a sorceress, an isle no one can reach. Yet, legend speaks of a powerful healer as well. Lugh MacKeir, desperate, determines to find Parraba and face its mysterious ruler.

Iosobal is the Lady of Parraba, mystical and magical, a woman apart from the world around her. Drawn to something familiar in Lugh's child, however, she reluctantly agrees to help her in exchange for Lugh clearing the blocked entrance to a very special cave.

But the child's illness defies Iosobal's skill, and Lugh's task proves more of a challenge than he anticipated. In the end, the secret to saving Lugh's daughter lies in Iosobal's ability to open her heart to a brash warrior who has invaded her tranquil sanctuary. She must find the courage to end her isolation, and the wise innocence of a child must lead them all to . . .

A LOST TOUCH OF PARADISE.
ISBN#9781932815665
Jewel Imprint: Amethyst
US $6.99 / CDN $9.99
Available Now
www.amytolnitch.com

A Lost Touch of Innocence

I am a part of you now.

The words haunt Piers Veuxfort, and he has only his own recklessness to blame. By touching a magic crystal, he freed the essence of a decidedly wicked Fin Man, who now resides within Piers. If that isn't bad enough, a surprise for Piers arrives at Falcon's Craig Castle. A bride. A bride, moreover, who was raised to be a nun, and views him as something just short of the devil. What can he do but send her back?

You are a wicked abomination.

With that condemnation of her "sight", Giselle St. Germain's future is irrevocably altered. Her life in the secluded nunnery is over, and she is thrown into the world, a world that includes betrothal to a man who is unrepentantly devoted to his pleasures, and who increasingly displays a dark, troubling side. What's a girl to do but cling more tightly to what she knows?

The rules have changed. For both of them. And Piers and Giselle are about to discover that sometimes fate delivers a destiny beyond your imaginings. That destiny is theirs to win. Or lose. It will take all the courage that lies within their deepest hearts to seize it, and to find . . .

A LOST TOUCH OF INNOCENCE
ISBN#9781933836096
Jewel Imprint: Amethyst
US $7.99 / CDN $9.99
Available Now
www.amytolnitch.com

For more information
about other great titles from
Medallion Press, visit

www.medallionpress.com